D0506368

THE MUTINY RUN

By the same author

FIFTY THOUSAND OVERCOATS
THE BARBARY RUN
WAITING FOR ALEC

THE
MUTINY RUN

Frank Eccles

MICHAEL O'MARA BOOKS LIMITED

479797

MORAY DISTRICT COUNCIL
DEPARTMENT OF
LEISURE AND LIBRARIES
F

First published in Great Britain in by
Michael O'Mara Books Limited
9 Lion Yard
Tremadoc Road
London SW4 7NQ

Copyright © 1994 by Frank Eccles

All rights reserved. No part of this publication may be reproduced, stored
in a retrieval system, or transmitted, in any form or by any means,
without the prior permission in writing of the publisher, nor be otherwise
circulated in any form of binding or cover other than that in which it is
published and without a similar condition including this condition being
imposed on the subsequent purchaser.

A CIP catalogue record for this book is available from the British Library

ISBN 1-85479-966-5

Typeset by Servis Filmsetting Limited

Printed and bound by Clays Ltd, St Ives plc

In Memory of my dear brother Dennis, who
served aboard a latterday H.M.S. *Adamant*

CHAPTER ONE

Midshipman John Lawson rubbed at the raindrops on his face, blew into his hands and tucked them under his armpits. Nearby, sheltering in the lee of the ship's launch, a man coughed. Lawson peered at the dark shape.

'Is that you, Mr Hampson?'

'It is, sir,' the captain's elderly coxswain replied.

'What an awful night! Are there many rivers as miserable as the Mersey?'

'I think they're all much the same at this time o' year, sir,' Hampson replied in the avuncular manner he adopted with the young gentlemen. 'But it *is* nasty weather.'

'And you've got a bad cough, by the sound of it. Why don't you keep under cover out of this drizzle, Mr Hampson? I'll send for you when the captain makes his signal.'

'No thank you, sir. I'll be reet. It can't be far off midnight, sir, and he'll 'appen be getting ready to come aboard.'

Lawson sighed in exasperation. He had a soft spot for old Hampson. His homely Yorkshire accent and lined face always reminded him of his grandfather, a stubborn, hard-working man, who had spent a lifetime fishing out of Whitby.

'I'll bet the captain's warm enough,' another voice muttered sulkily in the darkness.

1

'Perhaps you'd like to talk to him about it in the morning, Parker?' Lawson said sharply.

'Not I, sir.'

'Then keep your observations to yourself. Aren't you supposed to be on anchor watch?'

'Just been relieved, sir.'

'So you should be looking across the river. Get your eyes on that tavern door and report every time it opens.'

Lawson felt angry with himself for having lost his temper. He knew that Parker was testing him. The man would never have dared to make such a remark if any of the senior warrant officers had been near.

The rain stopped, and the sky began to clear. The cold northerly breeze carried the acrid smoke from the Liverpool chimneys, and also the occasional sounds of revelry from an ale house on the waterfront. Warmth and comfort, drink and women would be found there, but Britain was at war with France and Holland, so the Navy took precautions against losing its men to the lure of the land. Apart from the guard-boat, which was rowed around any king's ship anchored within swimming distance of the shore, ordinary fishermen kept a sharp lookout for swimmers. The reward for capturing a naval deserter in 1797 was more than they would earn from a week's fishing.

'I should think that the captain'll come now that it's dried up,' Hampson said, looking at the fleeting clouds.

Lawson nodded, but his attention was taken by a light that had appeared in front of the wheel. His men were interested too. The end of the watch was near, and the duty petty officer had just opened the binnacle. Droplets from his tar-coated felt hat sizzled on the cowl of the lamp as he stooped to examine the hour glass. When the last grains of sand ran out, he would sound eight bells, and they could all go to their beds. The middle watch would then have to row across the river for the captain. Hampson, who would be in command of the launch whichever watch rowed it, continued to look across the water.

'The inn door's just opened, and there's a feller coming out wi' a light, sir,' he warned.

'Yes, I see him,' Lawson replied.

It had been agreed by the midshipmen that the men who were actually on duty when the captain made his signal would row ashore for him.

'Ring that bloody bell,' a voice whispered urgently.

They watched breathlessly as the distant light advanced towards the jetty. Now, it began to swing, three from side to side followed by three hoists, repeated. That was the signal. Someone cursed quietly. Lawson turned to the men in the shadows.

'Look alive, my lads. Captain's waiting. Let's have that launch over the side.'

No sooner had he spoken, than the ship's bell rang its four double beats announcing the end of the watch.

'Can't our relief take it, sir? It's just on midnight,' a man whined plaintively.

'You know the rule, Jenkins. Get your hands on that rope and heave,' Lawson said tolerantly.

'Quite right too,' a cultured voice commented half a yard behind him.

Midshipman Heward had arrived to take over the watch. Lawson was too busy to speak to him. Apart from supervising the hoisting of the boat over the side without thumping it against the timbers of the ship, he was concerned about old Hampson. The captain's coxswain looked about done. Now, he would have to steer the launch over to the jetty and perhaps wait half an hour or more for the captain to emerge from the tavern.

'Get below, Mr Hampson,' Lawson said on impulse. 'I'll go for the captain. That's an order now, so don't argue.'

'Well, I do declare we have an angel in our midst,' Midshipman Heward drawled when Hampson had gone. 'Saint John, they'll call you. There's a pot of cocoa waiting for you below. Wish I'd drunk it myself now.'

Lawson turned from his supervision of the boat and tilted Heward's hat over his nose.

'Wind's north by west. We've one and a half hours' ebb, and we're swinging between wind and tide on two bow anchors. The ship's all yours, Sunshine. Look after her.'

Having made his formal report, he nodded and swung himself over the side onto the scrambling net. There he paused, his head just above the level of the bulwark.

'*Do* keep those masthead lights burning. I don't want to spend half the night finding my way back, especially with the captain breathing down my neck.'

Heward waved a cheerful acknowledgement and Lawson descended. He could have allowed himself the luxury of leaving the ship by way of the entry port and stepping genteelly into the launch at the foot of the gangway, like royalty. He would have enjoyed the novelty, but he felt that he had to do the same as his men this night. Jenkins was a simpleton and could therefore be forgiven for questioning orders, but he had been prompted by a whisper before he spoke. Lawson had no doubt that Parker was responsible.

John Lawson was tall and broad in the shoulder for his eighteen years, but he was agile with it. He landed lightly by the stern thwart whilst two of the oarsmen were still struggling to get into the bucking craft. He gripped the tiller in both hands.

'Let her go,' he commanded.

Parker, in the bows with a boathook, and the two oarsmen on the side nearer to the ship, prodded the launch away from her uneasy mooring. Oars thumped against the tholes and they turned their bows towards the land, taking a light spray as cold as ice as they fought against the wind and the ebb.

As Lawson had expected, Captain Brewster was not waiting on the quayside for their arrival, nor was there any sign of life as they approached the jetty. He steered to the down-river side for protection against the force of the tide, noted the turbulence around the stone steps and decided it would be safer and drier to go ashore by way of the vertical wooden ladder secured to the quay beyond. He gripped the rungs above his head and hoisted himself clear of the oily surge.

'Wait here,' he ordered. 'You will be in charge, Parker. If the captain decides to use the stone steps yonder to get into the boat, see to it that you keep clear of the corners, or you'll stove a plank in for sure.'

He heaved himself up the remaining rungs, stepped on to the quay and made his way over the uneven cobble stones to the tavern. There, a creaking sign above the door bore the name Saracen's Head.

It was a low-ceilinged place, reeking of stale tobacco smoke. Despite the lateness of the hour, there were two men before the fire and a group playing cards at a table. Lawson removed his hat and looked around for the captain. A bleary-eyed fellow in his late forties lurched to his feet and stood before him.

'Ye'll 'ave come for the captain, sir?' He touched the peak of his greasy cap. ''Twas I that made the signal on 'is 'ighness's orders, and it were made in a seamanlike manner, as ye'll have noticed.'

'Where is he?'

'Sitting in the parlour, talking to the widder. At least, 'e wuz talking when I seed 'im last.'

He winked lewdly. Lawson stepped round him, but he was detained by a clutching hand on his sleeve.

'Served all me life with the Fleet, sir. Now I'm on the beach, as they say. I 'aven't even the price of a drink.'

'That makes two of us.' Lawson replied drily, detaching his arm.

He strode across the room, attracting no more than a cursory glance from the customers, but the serving girl was interested. She smiled and smoothed her long black hair as he approached.

'Good evenin' to you, sir,' she said with a saucy bob. 'You look half starved wi' the cold. Will you have somethin' to warm you? T'kettle's on the hob and it'll not take more'n a minute to mix you a hot toddy.'

'I've come for Captain Brewster,' Lawson said.

He had found of late that most women were very pleasant towards him, but he was shy in the presence of young ones. Heward and Saunders were forever ribbing him about it in the midshipmen's mess.

'Captain Brewster will take no harm. I dare say he's comfortable enough,' she observed, reaching for the bottle.

'No thank you, miss. I must get the captain away. I have men waiting out there on the water. Perhaps you'll

5

be kind enough to tell him that I'm here.'

She curtsied extravagantly with a mischievous twinkle in her eyes. The door to the private rooms was set between shelves loaded with bottles of all kinds. She tapped twice, listened, then opened it. Lawson could see his captain sprawling in a cushioned chair with his broad back towards him.

'The boat has arrived for the captain, ma'am,' she said.

Captain Brewster waved a hand in acknowledgement, not even turning his head, but now the woman came into Lawson's line of vision. She carefully but firmly took the glass from the captain's hand, set it down, and coaxed him to his feet. She was not small but he towered over her. She wrapped a scarf around his neck, reaching up on her toes and standing very close. He looked down at her and placed his huge hands on her shoulders.

'Very well, my dear. I'll go to my bed, if you insist.'

The door was closed at this stage, so whatever happened thereafter, Lawson could only guess. Judging by the giggles, which could be heard clearly, the widow was enjoying it. So was the serving girl, but it was the handsome midshipman's unworldly embarrassment that delighted her. Lawson was unable to meet her eyes.

'Oh it's you, is it?' Captain Brewster grumbled a few minutes later. 'Where the devil's Hampson?'

He tripped over his feet and fell to his knees. Lawson struggled to get him up, now assisted by the old seaman who had asked for the price of a drink. Together, they steered him through the door, and supported him as he stumbled over the cobbled quayside. There would be no chance of getting the captain down the vertical ladder in safety, it seemed.

'Take the boat around to the stone steps,' Lawson shouted to Parker. 'I shall want two of you ashore to help. Look alive now.'

'Capital woman that,' Brewster said to no one in particular. 'Fine place she's got too.'

Lawson made no comment. The watery moonlight revealed slimy steps leading to the river, with the swell breaking and frothing over the lower reaches. The ship's launch was leaping wildly up and down, being held clear, with difficulty, by Parker's boathook and the oars of two men. A sober man in daylight might find it difficult to get aboard.

'We'll never get him away dry,' the older man panted from under the captain's left armpit. 'He's a very heavy man. Me back's about broke now.'

'Is there a hoist on the quayside?' Lawson asked.

'A hoist! What the devil do you want with a hoist?' Captain Brewster roared indignantly, thrusting his two supporters aside.

He drew himself to his full six feet two inches, jerked his rumpled coat straight and pulled his tricorn hat firmly about his ears. He advanced to the top of the steps, gripped the handrail set in the wall and descended with drunken dignity. Lawson kept close, ready to grab him if he slipped. Captain Brewster had always treated him in a kindly manner, and Lawson had a great affection for him.

The captain required no assistance. He clawed his way past a section of moss-covered wall that had lost its handrail, and caught at the chain that replaced it at a lower level. The water surged up over his shoes, but he didn't pause. Lawson hovered anxiously.

'Stay in the boat, you men,' Brewster shouted, seeing that two of them were about to jump for the steps.

Lawson was impressed. Captain Brewster had been in difficulties walking across the floor of the tavern but now, after a good sniff of the sea, he was managing as well as a midshipman twenty-five years his junior. Even when an unexpected heavy swell crowded into the confines of the stairway and rose to his thighs, setting his coat-tails afloat, he remained steady, waiting for the right moment to cross the step and reach the pitching gunwales of the launch.

Parker was at the nearer end, apparently straining with his boathook to keep the planking clear of the corners of the stone steps, when the captain lurched across. He might have deliberately pushed harder at the critical moment, or it could have been an unexpected surge of the water. The gap suddenly widened and the captain's outstretched hands missed.

'Christ! He's fallen in,' someone shouted.

'Hold that lantern up. Feel around, all of you,' Lawson ordered urgently, now up to his waist in water.

A huge hand clamped onto the transom of the boat, and the captain's balding head appeared. The other hand emerged clutching a tricorn hat, spewing water as he jammed it on.

'Get me aboard, blast you,' he said peevishly.

Lawson grinned his relief and leapt across the gap into the launch.

It was cold on the after part of the main gun-deck where the midshipmen took their morning navigation lessons, but none of them ever suggested closing the gun-ports. Apart from the need to keep at least two of them open to let in the light, there was also the fact that Mr Atherton, the elderly ship's master, was a fresh-air enthusiast, and no one ever won an argument with Mr Atherton. The five midshipmen shrank deeper into their collars, shivered and tried to concentrate upon the mathematical problems associated with astro-navigation.

'Well, Mr Clayton, we are all awaiting your answer,' Atherton said irritably, peering over his iron-rimmed spectacles.

Midshipman Clayton who, at thirty-two, was twice the age of the youngest in the class and bigger than anyone, shuffled his bottom uneasily on the bench and rubbed at his chin with a massive hand.

'Will it be –?'

'Not, "Will it be", Mr Clayton. State your ship's position as ye find it.'

Looking far from happy, Clayton read from the paper in his hand. 'Fifty-five degrees and seventeen minutes north by thirty-one degrees east, sir.'

Heward's handkerchief slid across his face to hide the grin. The other midshipmen were embarrassed, except for Atkins, the youngest. He was bubbling over to give the right answer until a dig in the ribs from Lawson made him think better of it.

The master's wizened face grew even longer and he sighed in despair.

'When will ye lairn, Mr Clayton? When will ye lairn?' He shook his head. 'Your ship's time is two hours *behind* Greenwich. That places ye thirrty-one degrees tae the west, not the east. Look at the chart, mon. The position ye have given is somewhere in the land of oor ally Russia.'

He jerked his head to the left. Heward cut short his snort of amusement and made a great show of blowing his nose.

'Oh dear!' Atherton said in mock concern. 'Oor colleague seems tae have caught a wee cold. Not enough o' God's fresh air, Mr Heward. That'll be your trouble. Ye'll spend the afternoon watch inspecting the standing rigging on the foremast top. That should gi' ye a guid blow tae clear oot your lungs.

Heward looked sick. The master began to gather the charts from the tables, pausing to examine each midshipman's calculations.

'Mr Clayton, ye will ha' tae study chapter three of your navigation book which deals wi' the rotation of the earth. Mr Lawson will report tae the captain immediately. I believe he has a small matter tae discuss wi' ye.'

There was the suspicion of a twinkle in his eye as, clutching the charts to his chest, he shuffled away in his slippers. The class visibly relaxed. Heward's gloomy face jerked into a grin.

'Discussion with the captain! He'll keelhaul you after dropping him in the river last night. What do you think, Saunders?'

Saunders, a slimly built, intelligent-looking young man, smiled at Lawson sympathetically and patted him on the shoulder.

'Be more useful if the old man put him on watch and watch about. That way, we'd all get more sleep.'

They all grinned except Clayton. He looked drained and grey. He gathered his papers and books and walked away without a word. Lawson's eyes followed him, obviously troubled, and the hilarity died.

'Can't we do anything to help old Clayton?' Lawson asked when the senior midshipman was out of earshot. 'You're the best, Saunders. You could explain things to him more clearly. Mr Atherton is a good navigator but a bloody awful teacher: too impatient by half.'

'I've suggested that we do some work together,' Saunders shrugged. 'He feels his seniority too much. No, that's not fair. He just seems –' the young man gestured his inability to express himself adequately – 'He was at sea before I was born, and he's been a bo'sun for umpteen years. It's difficult for him. He's too full of the fact that he came up through the hawsepipe and he can't mix with the likes of us. I suppose that family . . .'

He broke off embarrassed. Atkins took up the theme.

'Of course, family has everything to do with it,' he said loftily. 'It's always the same when they push common sailors into the officer class. They can never fit in.'

'Your captain served before the mast,' Lawson reminded him coldly.

'I am painfully aware of that, Mr Lawson. That is, no doubt, why he has hands like spades and why he eats nothing other than salt pork and cabbage. It would be pleasant to serve under a civilized captain for a change. Next time he condescends to invite me to dinner, I think I shall decline.'

'Then we shall have the pleasure of seeing the gunner tan your arse. Should he fail to do so, I will kick it,' Lawson told him with an angry gleam in his eyes.

'What I should like to know,' Heward intervened airily after a brief silence, 'is what the captain means when he says that he wants to see a midshipman immediately?'

Lawson glared at Atkins and hurried away. Heward walked languidly over and examined his plump, pasty-faced junior with undisguised distaste.

'You know, Atkins, for a young fellow who is not yet seventeen, you have rather a lot to say for yourself. Probably your boldness arises from having a few admirals in the family and a father who moves in government circles. Reflect, my lad, upon your present situation. You are the most junior midshipman aboard a mere fifty-four-gun ship, a common workhorse, not an exalted first-rate man-o'-war. Furthermore, we are detached from the Fleet, so no matter how influential your kinsmen may be, they are remote. Mr Lawson's boot is not.'

'Lawson!' Atkins scorned. 'His manners and speech

remind me of my father's head gardener.'

'Then he'll be a Yorkshireman, this head gardener of yours, and anyone born north of the Humber is a barbarian, no doubt?'

'Their language is crude enough.'

'Ah language!' Heward said in mock rapture. 'The niceties of speech! How can anyone succeed if he lacks the manners of the Court?' He prodded Atkins with his forefinger. 'Did you ever hear of the great Captain Cook? I believe he was as Yorkshire as they come and, like Captain Brewster, he started his career in the lowliest capacity.'

'An admirable seaman, according to my Uncle Oliver, who served under him at one stage, but not', Atkins sniggered, 'the sort of person with whom a gentleman would care to associate – outside the strict line of duty.'

He shrugged lightly and turned away, gathering his books. Heward's lips smiled but his eyes were hard.

'I pray that you will be persuaded to follow your father into politics at the first opportunity. That's where your talents lie, I do believe. I have a feeling there will be deep trouble for you, and others, if this ship ever leaves the Mersey.'

CHAPTER TWO

Midshipman Lawson jerked the wrinkles out of his coat, removed his hat and smoothed down his hair outside the captain's quarters, well aware that the armed marine sentry on duty was having difficulty in keeping his face straight. The whole ship knew about the captain's midnight swim, and bets were being taken on the lower decks as to the outcome. He tapped on the oak panel, listened for a reply and entered, holding his hat under his arm.

The captain was seated at his desk scowling over a bunch of papers. To his right stood the acting second-in-command, Lieutenant Trevelyan, looking harassed, mopping at his balding head with a handkerchief. In the background, making a long job of replacing the charts that had been used by the midshipmen, was Mr Atherton, looking more cheerful than he had during his lesson. Obviously he was either enjoying Trevelyan's discomfiture, or looking forward to Lawson's interview.

Captain Brewster abruptly gathered the papers and thrust them at Trevelyan.

'Not enough water on board, Mr Trevelyan,' he grumbled.

'They suggested ashore that we should take fresh water just before we sail, sir. That was why I –'

'Is this ship to be dictated to by dockyard maties?' Brewster interrupted irritably. 'Surely you know the score, Mr Trevelyan? The French are likely to land in Ireland. That's why we're here. "Fifty thousand caps of freedom" they're promising to plant. Now, if one of our frigates comes in with news of a French fleet similar to that which anchored in Bantry Bay last Christmas, I shall want to put to sea immediately. We'd look bloody silly if we had to wait for water to be taken on board. I'll have three months' supply maintained at all times. Please see to it without delay.'

'Yes, sir. Will that be all?'

'No. Wait, Mr Trevelyan.'

The captain turned an expressionless face to Lawson.

'You will recall the details of last night, Mr Lawson?'

'Yes, sir.'

'I lost my purse and my watch.'

'When you went over the side, sir?'

Brewster sighed irritably.

'Mr Lawson, I see that you are wearing a lanyard attached to your belt. What's it for?'

'In case I drop my knife, sir. It's fastened to the lanyard.'

'Well now, I've been at sea for nigh on thirty years, boy and man, long before you were born. Do you think I wouldn't have learned to secure my possessions? The watch was lashed onto my waistcoat and couldn't come adrift on its own. The purse was battened down inside my breeches pocket, three buttons no less. I felt for my watch and purse whilst I was still in the water. The purse was there but the watch was not.'

'So you lost the purse in the boat, sir?'

'I did and I've got it back. Jenkins is in irons waiting for punishment.'

'Jenkins, sir!' Lawson exclaimed in dismay.

'Aye. He and Webb dragged me into the boat, if you recall. I missed the purse as soon as I got back here, so I took the master-at-arms and searched the pair of them before they had the chance to hide it. We found it in the pocket of Jenkins' jacket.'

'I'm very surprised, sir.'

'Are you? Well, you've a lot to learn.'

'Surprised it was Jenkins, I mean, sir. He's not – not

altogether – er – not very clever, sir.'

'You think it might have been the other fellow, eh? So did I, but we must work on the evidence and it'll be Jenkins who will come up for punishment. Now, as to the watch, the pawnbroker wouldn't give you more than two pounds for it, but it's of sentimental value. There was yourself and that fellow from the tavern; he does odd jobs about the place: Green, I think they call him.'

'I know nothing about your watch, sir,' Lawson protested.

'Didn't think you would, Mr Lawson, but you'll know this man Green if you see him again.'

'Yes, sir.'

'So you'll go ashore this afternoon with Mr Trevelyan's party and find him. Take your two messmates, Mr Heward and Mr Saunders to assist you.'

'Mr Heward has a wee task tae perform, sir,' Atherton said drily from the shadows behind the chart rack. 'He has orrders tae inspect the foremast standing rigging this afternoon.'

'Oh in that case,' Brewster said, with the suspicion of a smile, 'you'll go without Heward.'

He jerked his head in dismissal. Lawson bowed hurriedly, hardly able to believe his good fortune, and left the cabin. Brewster turned to his lieutenant.

'Mr Trevelyan, do you understand your orders with regard to the new people?'

'Would you care for me to repeat them, sir?' Trevelyan asked with an air of boredom.

'I would,' Brewster growled.

Trevelyan raised his notebook and tilted it to the light of the window. He was a man of medium height, about forty years old and elegantly dressed, so far as naval regulations would allow, but the cut of his expensive jacket could not hide the fact that he was getting fat.

'I am to take three midshipmen, now amended to two,' he began, ostentatiously making an alteration with his pencil, 'with my party, which will consist of the master-at-arms and twenty men. Once ashore, the midshipmen are to go about your business. I am to go to the prison to select suitable men from the criminals on offer, and see if

14

we can pick up any likely seamen on the way.'

'Two arms, two legs and under fifty, provided they're not obviously consumptive or poxed up,' Brewster specified. 'Oh, and watch out for gaol fever. You know the signs.'

Trevelyan's pencil scribbled busily. Brewster sighed in exasperation at the delay.

'There's no need to take down everything I say.'

'It has always been my practice to make notes, sir. However, if it displeases you . . .' He placed the notebook and pencil in his pocket, buttoned the flap, then regarded the captain coolly. 'If the midshipmen manage to catch this fellow who is *thought* to have stolen your watch, do we hand him over to the constable or bring him aboard, sir?'

'Not the Law. It's a capital offence to steal anything above the value of fifteen shillings. I'll not have a man hanged for my watch. Find a stinking sewer and dunk him in it a couple of times, after he's shown you where he pawned it. Then you can let him go.'

He took out his purse and selected two sovereigns. 'Mr Lawson will need money for the pawnbroker,' he said, handing the coins to Trevelyan. 'Tell him to search Green to see if he has any money left.'

'Very good, sir. Will that be all?'

'Yes. You and the two midshipmen can join me in the Saracen's Head later, if you have a mind to.'

Trevelyan bowed, a supercilious smile on his face. 'Thank you, sir. That is most kind, but I have a lot to do on board receiving the fresh water supplies. If you will excuse me, I should prefer to return with the shore party.'

'Suit yourself,' Brewster said abruptly, 'but be sure to pass on my invitation to the midshipmen.'

'You seem to be in high favour with the captain,' Lieutenant Trevelyan observed, after they had climbed ashore from the launch.

'I was not aware of it, sir,' Lawson replied guardedly.

Trevelyan, as first lieutenant, could make life hell for a midshipman if he were so minded, and it was generally known that he detested Captain Brewster. On several occasions he had tried to make trouble for Mr Atherton, who was obviously Brewster's friend, but the canny old Scot was more than a match for him. Lawson could be easily broken.

'Not many midshipmen would have escaped so lightly if they had dropped the captain in the sea,' Trevelyan observed. 'You come from the same part of Yorkshire, I understand. No doubt you have connections?'

'No, sir. I did not know Captain Brewster before I joined *Adamant*. His home town is Malton. I am from further north. As to the accident, sir, the boat was pitching about and –'

'And the captain was drunk,' Trevelyan added contemptuously.

They walked in silence to the entrance of the Saracen's Head where Lawson and Saunders were to begin their search. Behind them they could hear the voice of the master-at-arms, getting his party into two ranks ready to march.

A light coach approached, drawn by two horses. A naval officer leaned out of the window and shouted to the driver, who pulled at the reins. Struggling against the bit, the horses clattered and skidded to a halt on the cobbles, half slewing the coach across the road.

'I say there, Lieutenant, I'm looking for *Adamant*. Do you know where she is lying?'

Trevelyan walked over to the coach. 'I am from *Adamant*, presently second-in-command. Can I be of service?'

'You'll be Mr Trevelyan then,' the officer said, his eyes taking in the impeccable cravat, well-cut jacket and tailored trousers. 'My name is Prendergast. I am pleased to make your acquaintance.'

He climbed down from the coach and shook Trevelyan's hand. They eyed each other speculatively. Trevelyan knew that they were expecting another lieutenant on board. Was this the man? If so, was he senior to him? Certainly, Prendergast looked younger.

'I have dispatches from London. Can you get me out to *Adamant*, Mr Trevelyan?'

'Certainly, Mr Prendergast. We have a boat standing

by. However, the captain is not aboard. He has – business ashore.'

'No matter. I shall await his return.'

Trevelyan turned to face the master-at-arms, now approaching at the head of twenty seamen marching two abreast.

'Halt your men.'

The master-at-arms, a tall, powerful man in his late twenties, called a halt, then came across and saluted.

'Detach two men to take this gentleman's baggage and have him rowed across to *Adamant*,' Trevelyan ordered.

He waited while Prendergast supervised the unloading of his baggage, noting his dishevelled and dusty clothes and, in particular, the dispatch case embossed with a gold crown. Was he, in fact, merely a messenger?

'Must be something important to bring you all the way from London.' Trevelyan observed with a nod towards the dispatch case. 'Damnable journey too, I should imagine.'

'Yes. The roads are in an atrocious state.'

'The French have not invaded, I suppose?' Trevelyan said with a half-laugh, shrewdly eyeing the messenger.

Prendergast gave instructions to the seamen who had been ordered to carry his luggage, then he took Trevelyan by the arm and led him away from the coach and the openly listening driver.

'There is serious trouble in the Channel Fleet,' he said quietly. 'Petitions have been received by Lord Howe since February, but no action has been taken. Now government agents have reported a planned mutiny to take place at Spithead on the sixteenth of April, ten days from now.' He indicated the seamen lined up at the side of the road. 'I should not have anticipated your captain in passing on this information were it not for the fact that you have men ashore. Mutiny breeds like the plague.'

'Are you suggesting that I should send these men back to the ship?' Trevelyan asked, with raised eyebrows.

'I suggest nothing. I merely give you the facts,' Prendergast replied coolly.

'And I thank you for them. The launch awaits your pleasure. Good day to you, sir.'

Trevelyan bowed, turned away and walked briskly over to the midshipmen.

'Your captain's watch will have to wait. You will both accompany this party to the bridewell, one on each side of the column. If any man speaks to a passer-by, I shall hold you responsible.'

A few ragged children called after them as they marched through the streets to the prison, and two women waved, but the sailors had been ordered to speak to no one and Trevelyan was known as a vindictive officer, so they confined themselves to winks and lewd gestures. In fact, there were remarkably few people on the streets and no young men to be seen at all, except for an idiot cripple who hobbled behind them waving a flag. This was the press gang, and the warning would be going on ahead of them, clearing the taverns and bawdy houses. Few wanted to serve in the Royal Navy.

At the bridewell, the head turnkey, a villainous-looking fellow, lined up fifteen prisoners, stinking vilely, for inspection. Trevelyan chose eleven, then changed his mind and settled for nine. He did not ask what their crimes were. They fitted the captain's specifications and it mattered not if they were maniacs with homicidal tendencies so far as he was concerned. A good dousing on the open deck, fresh clothing from the purser's store, and they would be no different from at least a third of HMS *Adamant*'s company, since they too had been recruited from the magistrates' courts and prisons throughout Lancashire and as far north as Whitehaven.

'I don't want to go to sea,' one of the chosen prisoners, a scrawny, pathetic creature shouted suddenly.

Trevelyan smiled thinly as he turned to the man. 'Don't you though?' His eyes hardened. 'We don't particularly want to have you, but the King needs every man he can get his hands on, even trash like you, so we're obliged to take you. Secure his arms. We'll take no chances of him running.'

The petty officer passed a cord about the man's chest, caught his upper arms in two hitches and braced them back expertly, forcing his shoulderblades together. He then passed the cord twice around the man's neck and

18

finally secured it at the wrists. He would now have no chance of outpacing his escort.

'Take me in his place, sir,' one of the rejected prisoners pleaded on impulse. 'He's a married man with a sickly wife and two bairns, and he's due out next month anyway.'

'A philanthropist in gaol, be damned,' Trevelyan drawled. 'What's your name, fellow, and what are you in for?'

'Adams, sir, and I was sent to prison for poaching. We was caught together, both of us, sir. Six months we got for one little rabbit.'

'Then, Adams, you'll most likely be due for release next month also.

'Yes, sir, but I'm not married, and Jeff 'ere, Mr Morgan, is me sister's 'usband, and they've – they've got two bairns. Please take me, sir, and let 'im go.'

'I've already decided not to take you. I don't like the colour of you underneath all that filth. You have the look of a consumptive.'

'I'm – I'm 'ealthy, sir, and – and I'd be more use to you than me brother-in-law. 'E's got no trade.'

'And you have?' Trevelyan asked, suddenly interested.

'Just out of me time when I were arrested. I used ter work for Mr Greenwood and 'e'll speak for me, I know. 'Is workshop's over by t'rope-walk at the end of Orange Lane. I'm a carpenter.'

'Ah!' Trevelyan exclaimed, his eyes gleaming in triumph. 'A carpenter indeed! We can always find employment for the likes of you, even if you are a consumptive and a thief.'

The wretched man's thin face twitched nervously under Trevelyan's scrutiny but, as the lieutenant turned away, he smiled encouragingly at his brother-in-law, a fleeting, pale-lipped smile that did not extend to his troubled eyes. Then he began to cough quietly, clutching his collars closer about his chest with one hand and striving to muffle the sound in a swab of cotton waste.

Trevelyan had beckoned the head gaoler over.

'I've changed my mind. I'll take ten instead of nine. Include this fellow on your list.'

'What – what about Jeff, sir?' Adams faltered.

'Don't worry about him. He's now going to learn a trade. Then he'll be able to support his wife and children without having to steal other people's property. March them off.'

Surprisingly, Adams began to cry. Midshipman Lawson, embarrassed, looked away, then turned determinedly to speak to Trevelyan. His friend Saunders shook his head vigorously and mouthed the word 'No' behind the lieutenant's back. He was right, of course, Lawson realized. Nothing would be gained by appealing to the man's better nature. He was a thorough swine.

'What is it, Mr Lawson?'

'Do you want us to continue with the escort, or are we to go about the captain's business, sir?' Lawson asked woodenly, hating himself.

'Nothing has happened to change my orders, Mr Lawson. You and Mr Saunders will stay with the party until all are safely in the boat. Then you will both watch from the quayside lest any of these men should try to swim for it before we can get them aboard *Adamant*. Thereafter, you may search for the captain's treasured watch. He'll not want to lose anything valued at two pounds,' he added sarcastically.

The journey back was as uneventful as the one to the bridewell, except for a gaunt, hollow-eyed woman with a child in her arms and another clinging to her, who walked silently along, keeping pace with Morgan. She remained standing on the quayside in the cold breeze long after the two midshipmen had gone about their other business. Her eyes, listless and defeated, stared unseeingly at HMS *Adamant* lying out in the river, whilst her older child wailed fretfully and pulled at her skirt.

CHAPTER THREE

The two midshipmen searched until late afternoon for the man who was thought to have stolen the captain's watch. Then they went along to the Saracen's Head, as instructed. They found Captain Brewster and Mr Atherton comfortably seated at a round table before the fire, smoking long clay pipes. The widow was just lighting one of the lamps with a spill. Lawson advanced apologetically.

'So you haven't found him?' Brewster said affably. 'Didn't think you would. Sit down and try this Madeira. Pass the bottle, Mr Athcrton.'

The usually dour Scotsman smiled encouragingly at the two diffident midshipmen as he poured generous measures into their glasses.

'To the confusion of all thieves,' Brewster toasted.

Atherton went the rounds with the bottle again, finishing it off. The captain immediately ordered two more, then turned to the midshipmen.

'That watch has cost me plenty over the years in repairs, but it was my father's and made in my home town of Malton. That's Yorkshire, Mr Saunders. A long way from your part of the world. You're a Kentish man or a man of Kent, aren't you? I never understood the difference. Now Mr Lawson will know Malton, I'm sure. Your home is not far away. Whitby, isn't it?'

'Yes, sir. I'm sorry about the watch. We searched all the taverns.'

'I suppose ye looked in at Tom Thumb's place?' Atherton said from the blazing hearth, where he was scraping out his pipe.

'I haven't seen a local tavern of that name, sir,' Lawson said.

'It's no' a tavern, mon,' Atherton said scathingly. 'Thought every sailor who had spent any time in Liverpool would ken aboot Tom Thumb's. It's always guid for a few prime seamen when the port is busy, especially if ye cover the boltholes at the back o' the building. Took nine one night. Made those who could still walk carry the ones who had smoked too much.'

'Opium, sir?' Saunders asked.

'Aye, an opium pipe is what the maist of 'em go for,' Atherton said drily. 'There's also rot-gut liquor and,' he lowered his voice for the benefit of the widow who was setting a table at the far end of the room, ''tis a brothel of sorts: little girls, twelve years and younger, children who are not old enough to work the streets.'

'Would you like us to search there for this man, sir?' Lawson asked.

'I think you might get more than you bargained for in a place like that,' Brewster said with a grin. 'How far is it, Mr Atherton?'

'Five minutes' walk or thereaboots, sir.'

Brewster rose energetically, setting his pipe on the mantelpiece. 'Let's go. Nothing like a bit of education for young midshipmen, Mr Atherton. We'll be back by the time the food's ready,' he called to the widow.

They left their wine and followed the captain out of the Saracen's Head. Atherton took the lead. He swung left down the first back alley, where a prostitute tried to interest them, and into the dingy street beyond. Now there were prostitutes in plenty, but the captain's purposeful stride and the two midshipmen at his heels suggested a patrol rather than a group of sailors out for pleasure. They held back. There were faceless men too who watched from the shadows, but the captain and the master wore swords and the midshipmen had dirks. The watchers withdrew into the darkness to wait for the solitary drunks.

'Here we are,' Atherton said, as he halted at the end of a row of dilapidated buildings. 'Tom Thumb's fairyland is doon in the basement here. Make sure that your purses are oot o' the reach of thieving hands. You're aboot tae see how the sweepings o' humanity spend their money.'

Captain Brewster led the way down the stone steps. The door was bolted. He thumped on it with his fist. A face appeared briefly at a window. Excited voices were heard but the door remained shut. Brewster took a step back, then charged at it with his shoulder and burst it open. A huge, bald-headed man wearing brass earrings, moved swiftly towards them with an iron bar poised ready in his hands.

'No need for that,' Atherton said sharply. 'I ken your master weel. Tell him Mr Atherton's come tae see him.'

The man's eyes darted from the captain to the midshipmen.

'Go,' he snarled, raising the bar threateningly.

Captain Brewster hit him hard in the guts, followed it with a knee at the crutch, wrenched the bar from his hands and brought it down on the back of his neck. The big man sprawled unconscious at his feet. A short, thick-set man appeared, struggling with a pistol snagged in his waistband. He stopped short when the point of Atherton's sword pricked his throat.

'Leave it alone, Tom. An auld shipmate like you should know better,' Atherton remonstrated.

'Mr almighty bloody Atherton!' the man snarled.

'Aye, it is.'

'And you'll have your gang out there, I suppose?'

'Twenty guid men, front and back, armed wi' cutlasses and clubs,' the master lied cheerfully. 'But we've no' come tae press any o' your customers this time, Tom. Just one man we're wanting, so if ye'll be kind enough tae let me have your pistol the noo, we'll start looking.'

He seized the pistol butt as he spoke and yanked it clear. Then, he lowered the sword blade. Tom Thumb felt at his neck. There was blood on his fingers and murder in his eyes.

'Take that lanthorn, Mr Lawson. We'll maybe need a bit o' light,' Captain Brewster ordered.

'The press gangs will be the ruin of my business.'

'If it were no' for the fact that this stinking hole is useful tae His Majesty's Impressment Service, ye'd have been closed doon years ago,' Atherton told him. 'Noo lead on. Show us the delights o' the place.'

The basement had evidently been a warehouse. Now it was partitioned off into sections of varying sizes. On the right were open, stable-like stalls, each with its own table and benches. To the left was a timber wall lined with bunks such as might have been found in a large fishing boat, or the midshipmen's mess on *Adamant*. Beyond the bunks were doors obviously leading to small rooms. At the far end was a candle-lit alcove lined with bottles, presided over by a busty, painted woman who, arrested in the act of placing a bottle and glasses on a tray, held by a small girl, examined the approaching group suspiciously.

Suddenly she dismissed the serving girl with a jerk of her head, but the wide-eyed child missed the gesture and had her ear cuffed for her inattention. She went off with her tray, blubbering.

It was evidently not a busy time of day. Only one of the stalls was occupied, and that by two derelicts who sat opposite each other with a bottle between them. They looked on with stupid, uncomprehending faces whilst Lawson and Saunders checked the few occupants of the bunks in the light of the lantern. Everywhere was the pungent stink of opium and tobacco smoke.

'He's not here, sir,' Lawson said, letting the head of the last drugged sleeper fall back onto the pillow.

'Try the bedrooms,' Brewster ordered.

The first was occupied by a great fat man, smothered in tattoos, and a girl who could hardly have reached up to touch his shoulders. Both were naked.

'Piss off,' the man snarled, starting from the bed.

Lawson closed the door and moved on to the next. There was the fellow they were seeking, sprawled unconscious. An opium pipe lay neglected on the floor.

'Here he is, sir.'

'Fetch him out,' Brewster ordered.

Saunders and Lawson each seized an ankle. They

dragged him unceremoniously off the low couch and trailed him into the open space outside the room.

'Yes, that's Green all right,' the captain said. He turned to the brothel-keeper and his face hardened. 'This man paid for his pipe with my watch.'

'I know nowt about a watch. 'E gave me three shillings when 'e came in this morning.'

'What time?'

'Around 'alf nine. No, it was later, maybe ten.'

'Go through his pockets, Mr Saunders. He should have some money left,' Brewster said.

Saunders bent down and began to search, but the captain was watching Tom Thumb. The man was licking his lips nervously and his shifty eyes were darting about, looking for an escape.

'He won't find as much as a brass farthing, will he, Tom?' Brewster said quietly.

'I don't know. Maybe 'e give some to 'is missus,' the man shrugged.

'No money, sir,' Saunders reported.

Brewster's huge hand shot out, gripped the front of the brothel-keeper's jersey and jerked him closer. Fierce eyes shrivelled the bravado from the man's face. He was badly frightened.

'How much did you steal from him, Tom?' Brewster growled menacingly.

'Nothing, Captain. I swear I took nothing.'

'Mr Atherton,' Brewster said quietly, 'what was this man's trade when he went to sea?'

'Gunner's mate, sir.'

'Well now, he's not too old to take a ramrod in his hands again. We'll ship him aboard *Adamant* and sign him on. Bind his arms.'

He pushed the man towards the midshipmen. Saunders held him whilst Lawson deftly unbuckled the man's belt and, slipping it under his armpits, jerked it tight behind him, bracing his arms back. The prisoner's hands were free but he would need them to hold his trousers up.

'No, Captain, I can't go to sea,' he shrieked. 'My business will be ruined if I leave it. Christ! It was only fifteen shillings and sixpence, an' it was the girl what took it, the little bleeder. I'll pay it back. Look, I've got the money 'ere.'

He indicated with his eyes that his money was kept below his jersey.

'Release him,' Brewster ordered.

Lawson cast the belt loose. Tom Thumb rubbed his arms, then pulled at a steel chain about his neck and produced a thonged leather bag from under his jersey. With trembling fingers he felt inside, selected several coins and offered them. Brewster's right fist closed on them, then he hit the man with the back of his left hand, sending him tripping over the recumbent Green to crack his head against the solid wood of the door frame. He slid down, dazed, his leather bag spilling gold and silver over the floor.

'We'll have to take this drugged sot with us, it seems,' Brewster said calmly. 'Hoist him to his feet and slap his face until he comes to his senses.'

When they got back to the Saracen's Head, half carrying Green, they found a woman waiting for them. It was the same who had walked with the press gang, keeping pace with the wretched Morgan. Her children were still with her, cold and whimpering.

'In the name of Gawd, let me 'usband go, sir,' she pleaded. 'The childer will starve if you take 'im away.'

'This is your husband!' Brewster exclaimed incredulously, indicating the drooping figure supported by the midshipmen.

'Her husband and brother were taken to *Adamant* from the prison this afternoon, sir,' Lawson explained.

'From the prison!' Brewster shook his head. 'Then I can do nothing for him, woman. Here, take this for the children.'

The money he had received from Tom Thumb was still in his fist. He thrust it into the woman's hand and turned abruptly in through the door of the tavern, followed by the rest of his party. The woman looked at the coins and gasped. Three of them were gold pieces. Either the poor light in the brothel, or Tom Thumb's fright, had led to gold being mistaken for silver.

Midshipman Heward hurried to meet them as they entered the room.

'Gentleman to see you, sir,' he whispered.

Lieutenant Prendergast rose from a chimney seat and bowed. In his hand was the dispatch case with the embossed gold crown. Obviously Heward had been ordered to accompany this officer ashore to find the captain. Now he formally introduced Prendergast to Captain Brewster and Mr Atherton. As the three senior officers walked over to the fire, Heward winked at his two equals in rank.

'What is it? Have we orders for sailing?' Saunders hissed.

Heward placed one finger at the side of his nose, suggesting that he had news of great import, so Lawson dumped the stupidly smiling Green on a bench and moved closer. They waited expectantly. Heward leaned forward confidentially, then grinned.

'Don't know a thing,' he whispered. 'He hasn't confided in me.'

Lawson gave him a dig in the ribs and they all turned their attention to the captain. He had taken a lamp and was withdrawing to a table in the corner. Prendergast followed him and handed over a heavily sealed canvas package. Brewster turned it over in his hands and checked the seal. Then he sliced it through with his pocketknife and peeled back the canvas. Prendergast walked back to the fire where Atherton was warming himself with his back to the blaze. The three midshipmen remained in a group somewhat apart and waited. Green's head slumped forward and a few minutes later he began to snore. The captain looked up from his reading.

'Waken him up,' he said irritably. 'I'll want some information from him directly.'

The midshipmen yanked the man from the bench, rushed him outside and thrust his head under the pump in the yard. He struggled feebly, but relentless hands pushed him under again. Then he vomited over the cobbles and Heward's shoes, so Heward cuffed him indignantly and that seemed to bring him to his senses.

'Fer Chris's sake, what yer doing ter me?' he whined.

'The watch,' Lawson growled. 'Where did you pawn the watch you stole from Captain Brewster last night? Tell us and you can clear off.'

'I don't know what you're talking –'

They thrust him under the pump again and worked the handle furiously.

'All right, all right, I'll tell yer.'

They pulled him upright. He looked at them fearfully.

'Will yer really let me go when I tell yer?'

'You'll be as free as the wind, when we have recovered the watch and not before,' Lawson told him.

'Honest?'

'I'll kick your arse if you don't get on with it,' Lawson threatened.

'I took it to Willy Simmons. 'E only gi' me a pound for it.'

'Is that a pawn shop?'

'Naw, Willy's got no shop,' he replied scornfully. ''E lives just round t'corner: does business in a quiet way and 'e doesn't give no ticket neither.'

'A fence?' suggested Heward.

''E buys and sells,' Green compromised.

'Right. You are going to take us to see this Willy Simmons in a few minutes. First we'll talk to the captain,' Lawson said, and pushed him towards the door.

They met Brewster's eyes as they re-entered the room with the dripping man. He beckoned them over to the table.

'Did you get anywhere with him?'

'Yes, sir. We know where to reclaim the watch.'

'Good. What's the state of the tide?'

'Making, sir. High water will be at ten minutes past eleven,' Heward replied.

'The wind?'

'Southwest, sir.'

'Thank you, Mr Heward.'

'The watch is not far from here, sir.'

'I'm pleased about that, Mr Lawson,' Brewster said, but clearly he had other things on his mind.

'Shall we redeem it, sir?' Lawson persisted.

'Aye, I'd like that. The three of you had better go. If you can transact the business in one hour, you'll dine here. Failing that, make sure that you are aboard *Adamant* by ten at the latest. We sail on the ebb.'

The midshipmen turned away eagerly, seized Green and hustled him outside. Brewster turned to the lieutenant.

'So you are to join us, Mr Prendergast. Pleased to have you.' He shook him warmly by the hand. 'I have noted that you are senior to Mr Trevelyan, so you will be taking over as second-in-command.'

'Thank you, sir,' Prendergast said quietly. 'What are your orders?'

'Go aboard immediately. Inform Mr Trevelyan of your authority and prepare for sea. We are to join Admiral Duncan at Yarmouth – giving Spithead a wide berth on the way,' he added with a smile.

'Keep clear of Spithead, sir?'

'It seems that they have trouble there, Mr Atherton. Petitions were sent from four ships to Lord Howe, demanding pay increases similar to those recently awarded to the army and the militia. There were also demands for better victuals, improved conditions of service and the usual grumbles of Jack Tar. Now a mutiny is threatened, according to the informers.'

Atherton looked surprised. 'The French are assembling invasion barges. The Channel Fleet is threatenin' mutiny, and oor orders are tae join the North Sea Fleet at Yarmouth? It doesna make sense tae me.'

'You've not heard the full story, Mr Atherton,' Brewster said grimly. 'In addition to the threat from Brest, Le Havre, Boulogne and the rest, the Dutchmen are getting busy in the Texel. Now these are the lads I worry about. We've chased the French back into port many times, but Hollanders are a different kettle of fish, as you well know.'

'Guid seamen,' Atherton said grudgingly. 'Who's commanding them?'

'Admiral de Winter, so they say, and he has fourteen ships of the line and umpteen troop-carrying barges, just waiting for the right moment to cross the North Sea.'

'I'm going aboard now, sir,' Prendergast said. He took up his hat, bowed and left.

29

Atherton grinned. 'That'll no' suit oor Mr Trevelyan's vanity. I'd love tae be aroond when Prendergast gives him the news aboot his changed status.'

'You'd miss your supper. Order a couple of bottles to give us an appetite.'

CHAPTER FOUR

The three midshipmen soon traced Willy Simmons. He was drunk and singing a song about Polly Flinders in a low tavern swirling in tobacco smoke and crowded with men and women who were not taking the slightest notice of his song. They pushed Green into a corner, sat on both sides of him and ordered beer. Eventually, Willy finished and received a desultory hand-clap from a few patrons nearest to him. He bowed, almost fell off the low platform that served as a stage and staggered towards a seat between two women. Heward and Saunders moved quickly. They each took an arm and helped him to the corner table.

'Wha's all this?' he asked, looking from one to the other of the men about him. 'I don't know you.' He peered at Green. 'Oh I know you though. Sold me a watch that don't work.'

'That's the one we want to buy, Willy,' Heward said.

'Do you though?' He looked cunning. 'It's not cheap, you know. Got to 'ave a profit to keep in business, 'aven't I?'

'Have you got it with you?'

'Oh yes, I've got it. Valuable family heirloom, is it?' He pulled it from his pocket and laid it on the table, keeping a tight grip on the chain. 'Yer can 'ave it for three pounds.'

Heward's hand closed on the watch. Willy sneered at him.

'You might be 'igh and mighty naval orficers, but my friends is 'ere, so don't try no fancy tricks. Two pounds ten shillings.'

'I'll give you the pound you paid for it, since it doesn't work,' Lawson said.

Eventually, they settled for twenty-five shillings. Lawson paid and put the watch in his pocket. At that moment, there was a disturbance around the tables nearest to the door. A woman shrieked.

'Hello, what's going on?' Saunders asked.

Willy did not answer. He shot off with Green half a yard behind him. A few other customers were also departing hurriedly. The law had arrived. With the officers was the busty woman who had cuffed the girl in Tom Thumb's place. She pointed to the midshipmen and the whole party moved in their direction, watched with great interest by everyone in the tavern.

'What can I do for you?' Heward asked languidly, as the half-dozen men positioned themselves oppressively close.

A tall, thin man carrying a staff of office surmounted by a crown looked from one to the other of the midshipmen. His face was unsmiling.

'I am Mr Binns, the constable of this district. I am investigating a case of murder and robbery. Earlier today, Tom Banty, locally known as Tom Thumb, was struck on the head and robbed. He has since died. This woman, whose husband was also attacked and injured whilst carrying out his duties, claims that you gentlemen were present when the said incidents occurred.'

Fifteen minutes later the three midshipmen, escorted by the full majesty of the law and followed by an excited crowd of drunks, idlers and stray dogs, descended upon the Saracen's Head. Constable Binns posted his men to keep the crowd away from the door and entered with the woman who had identified the midshipmen.

Captain Brewster and Mr Atherton were sitting down to their meal when the midshipmen approached.

'You're just in time.' Brewster said.

'I'm sorry, sir,' Lawson began, but he was interrupted by Binns, who advanced to the table.

'Captain Brewster?'

'Who the devil are you?' Brewster demanded aggressively.

The man removed his hat and explained both himself and his business.

'But it was nothing more than a slap across the face,' Captain Brewster said.

'So you admit hitting him?'

'With the back of my hand.'

'And there was sufficient force behind the blow to send him backwards against the wall.'

'He tripped over the fellow on the floor, but he did fall and he came up against the wall.'

The constable pursed his lips and nodded his head. 'The injury which caused his death appears to be consistent with what you have told me, sir. He had a fractured skull which suggests that the back of his head came into violent contact with the solid beams in the wall.

Brewster threw his napkin onto the table and stood up. 'Let me see the body,' he said.

'In good time, sir. There is also the question of the assault on this woman's husband.'

Brewster's eyes took in the woman standing in the background. He looked puzzled.

'Her husband? Do you mean the fellow on the door?'

"Course I do. You 'it 'im with an iron bar,' she shrieked. 'Nearly killed 'im yer did.'

'Be quiet,' Binns commanded.

He turned back to Brewster questioningly. The captain shrugged and explained the circumstances, calling upon the others for corroboration. Binns seemed satisfied.

'That leaves the charge of robbery. This woman accuses you of taking the contents of Banty's purse – a sum she claims which might have been in the region of sixty pounds including,' he consulted his notebook, 'two Elizabethan sovereigns: one of which has lost some of its original value on account of having been clipped.'

'I took what he gave me and no more,' Brewster said abruptly. 'Fifteen shillings and sixpence, the money he

33

had stolen, and I passed it on to the wife of one of the men we signed on today.'

'Her name please?' the constable asked, with his pencil poised.

'I don't know. Who was she, Mr Lawson?'

'The wife of a man called Morgan, who we collected from the bridewell today, sir.'

'I know her,' Binns grunted, making a note in his book. 'Now we shall go along to see the body, if you wish it.'

The crowd followed them through the streets and there were a few catcalls. The Navy was not popular in this quarter of Liverpool where they were used to seeing civilians escorted by naval patrols. Now the situation was reversed and the crowd loved it. The captain was flanked by his midshipmen and Mr Atherton, and the whole group was surrounded by officers of the law. It was thought that they had been arrested, as their side arms were not easily visible, and the law men were enjoying their moment of glory too much to enlighten the mob as to the true position.

'They've brought 'em to the scene of the crime,' someone shouted when they halted at Tom Thumb's place.

''Ang the bloody lot of 'em,' a woman's shrill voice demanded.

'Why 'aven't yer got the darbies on 'em, Binns? You'd 'ave 'ad us fastened up tight enough,' a man on the fringe of the crowd called.

''Coz them's chentlemen, don't yer knaw?'

There was a roar of indignation from the excited crowd. Constable Binns thrust open Tom Thumb's front door and stood aside for the naval party to enter. He left his men outside to keep the mob clear of the entrance and closed the door on the street.

The body was several feet from where they had left it. Brewster took a lamp, set it down and lifted the dead man's head. The back of the skull was clotted with blood. He felt around the wound carefully, then wiped his hands on Tom Thumb's trousers before standing up. Binns looked at him expectantly.

'You're right, Mr Binns. Murder has been committed, but it was done after we left here. Feel behind the right ear. You'll find a bit of a bump. That could have been caused by his head hitting the wall. On the opposite side, the skull has been stove in like a broken egg. That's where someone has clouted him, probably with an iron bar.'

Binns knelt and examined the body carefully. Atherton, at a sign from the captain, joined in the examination. The midshipmen did the same.

'Are you all agreed as to the bruise?' Brewster asked.

They replied in the affirmative.

'Mr Atherton, Mr Saunders and Mr Lawson, you gentlemen were present when I hit this fellow. Where did he fall? What say you, Mr Atherton?'

'Just here, sir,' Atherton said, pointing to the door-frame of the room from which they had dragged Green.

'Do you agree, Mr Saunders?'

'Yes, sir.'

'Mr Lawson?'

'Yes, sir, and if you will look closely, you will see a thread of wool from his jersey where it was caught on this nail.'

Binns examined the nail and carefully removed the wool which he placed inside his notebook. He looked far from happy.

'Now then, Mr Binns, the blow which killed this man was from something rather harder than this timber,' Brewster said, beating the doorframe with his hand. 'A head injury such as you see would have caused the blood to spurt. Can you find any trace of blood near the door?'

Binns nodded his head thoughtfully, but he made no attempt to search.

'Have a good look,' Brewster insisted.

'I can see where the blood is, Captain, and I agree that there is none near the door,' he said irritably.

'Very well, Mr Binns. The witnesses present will confirm that the money I took away was given to me by the victim. They will also state positively that they saw gold and silver pieces lying on the floor when we all left this building.'

Binns sighed and nodded his head. 'I will report all I

35

have seen and heard to the magistrates in the morning. You will be available for any further questioning?'

Brewster bowed, clearly indicating his acknowledgement. Heward was obviously about to remind the captain that they were due to sail, then he thought better of it. Saunders' darting glance at Atherton brought no response from his impassive face.

'Perhaps you will allow us to leave from the back of the building to escape the crowd,' Brewster suggested.

When they had gone, Binns sat at one of the tables and stared despondently at the corpse. He had been a fool, he realized. On the strength of a statement by a painted old tart in a brothel he had considered himself to have a cast-iron case against a Royal Navy captain. In his eagerness to make an arrest, standard investigation procedures had been forgotten. Now the drunken or drugged customers, who had been carelessly dumped in the street on his orders and allowed to disperse to God knows where, would have to be traced and brought back for questioning. So too would all those who had worked in the place and Binns had no doubts that the doorkeeper would disappear when he learned that the captain had not been charged.

'The woman!' he exclaimed, starting to his feet.

He strode to the street door and opened it. His senior assistant was standing on the threshold facing the street. The rest of his men were grouped on the steps bandying words with the crowd.

'Come inside, all of you and bring the woman.'

They trooped in cheerfully, expecting a few drinks at the expense of Tom Thumb's establishment, shut the door behind them and looked around.

''Ave yer let the naval orficers go, Mr Binns?'

'Of course I've let them go. Where's that bloody woman?' Binns snarled.

They looked around.

'She were with us on t'steps a couple o' minutes ago,' one of them said aggrievedly. 'I were talking to 'er.'

'Get after her!' Binns shouted, his eyes popping with rage born of anxiety. 'You two, find her and bring her back here.'

The two men ran out. The rest waited in silence. Binns scowled from one to the other, then gave them orders that would keep them busy all night. For himself he reserved the task of finding and questioning Mrs Morgan about the money that Captain Brewster claimed to have given to her. It was not that he doubted the captain's word; he needed a statement to complete his report for the magistrates in the morning.

Meanwhile, Captain Brewster was paying his score at the Saracen's Head and taking his leave of the widow.

'I'll be back one day, depend upon it,' he promised.

'Aye, we'll see,' she said sceptically.

He handed her the letter he had just written. 'Give this to the constable in the morning, me dear. Say nothing tonight, should he return, for I want no trouble with the civilian authorities and trouble there would be if he brought his men out to *Adamant*. We dare not delay sailing. If the wind shifts nor'ard a point, we could be here for a week.'

She smiled up at him, too brightly, then busied herself with the buttons of his jacket and the straightening of his scarf.

'I've got used to having you around,' she whispered. 'Think of me once in a while, won't you? Goodbye.'

She kissed him, stretching on her toes to do so. Brewster stroked her hair, then turned abruptly and left the tavern. Atherton and the three midshipmen were waiting on the moonlit quay, watching the progress of the boat that had been sent across the river to collect them.

On board *Adamant* everything was in readiness. Gangs of men who would normally never be seen on deck, carpenters, cooks, ropemakers and other tradesmen, had been turned out to help with the less demanding tasks involved in getting a ship off to sea. The real seamen were aloft in the maze of rigging, lying across the yards, preparing to cast loose the canvas. Forward in the bows, one of the great anchor cables was already being stowed away. The other had been bent onto the capstan. Soon the milling crowd of men taking their places on the capstan bars, marines and landsmen for the most part, would be ordered to haul the great ship up to its anchor to break it loose from the bed of the river.

'It's just about slack water now, sir,' Prendergast said quietly after the ship's company had waited in silence for a quarter of an hour.

Captain Brewster grunted an acknowledgement, looked aloft at the barely discernible burgee flying from the masthead, then consulted the compass. Atherton did the same.

'The wind has shifted nor'ard a mite, sir.'

'Aye, it has, Mr Atherton. It'll be hard work keeping to the channel, but she'll make it, I think.'

They now needed to sail as close to the wind as would be possible with a square-rigged, three-masted ship like *Adamant*, but the ebb tide would help them to get clear, Brewster estimated. He looked towards the shore. Several lights had just appeared near the Saracen's Head and now they were bobbing along the quay: lanterns in a crowd. The muted sound of excited voices came to them over the water.

'Get her under way, Mr Prendergast,' the captain ordered.

The second-in-command raised his speaking trumpet. 'Haul in the anchor. Cast loose t'gallants.'

The pounding of a hundred pairs of feet around the capstan, the clanking of the pawls and the crackling of stiff sails unfolding above their heads cut off the shore sounds. Now orders were being shouted by petty officers to their sections, and men were moving purposefully about their tasks. The erstwhile still and quiet ship was a busy, teeming world of ordered activity.

'Anchor's aweigh.' Clayton's voice shouted from the bows.

'Starboard braces, heave! Put your backs in it,' Trevelyan ordered.

The groups of men along the starboard side came aft in a concerted rush, carrying with them the ropes attached to the three topgallant yards high above the deck. Each pivoted around its mast, and the sails, which were lashed upon them and had been flapping uselessly, were now moulded into rigid curves by the breeze.

Morgan and his brother-in-law, Adams, had been

manning the starboard braces. Now there was no work for them and they were looking wistfully over the water as the lights of Liverpool slipped slowly past. They could not see Morgan's wife standing on the quayside, but she was there, watching. At her side was the angry Constable Binns. The coins that Brewster had given to the woman were in his pocket, including the clipped sovereign which bore the head of Queen Elizabeth. These were evidence of robbery, he believed.

'What are you crying for, fellow? Have you never been away from home before?' a high-pitched voice demanded.

Adams rubbed his eyes and looked in wonder at the sixteen-year-old midshipman.

'Why, no, I 'aven't bin away before.'

'Say "sir" when you speak to me, you oaf,' Midshipman Atkins shouted, 'or I'll teach you manners. I've been watching you, you idle, good-for-nothing. Next time you are told to heave, you'll put your back into it or you'll feel the end of this.' He shook a knotted rope under Adams' nose.

'You've got to watch that bastard,' one of the carpenter's mates whispered to Adams after the midshipman had moved on. 'He likes to use that starter, and he's a vicious little swine.'

'Is 'e an officer?'

'Naw, he's a midshipman, learning to be an officer, but he's got the right to hit you with that rope's end. If you hits him back, Gawd 'elp you. You'd be up afore the captain, and that'd be a few dozen for sure.'

'A-a few dozen what?' Adams faltered.

'Lashes. They strip you to the waist and use a whip on your back. The captain's a decent cove: best I've served under in twenty years, but he's gotta support authority, even if it's only a young pup like Atkins.'

He spat disgustedly over the side then reached inside his jacket and produced a plug of tobacco. He sliced a lump off and pushed it into his mouth.

'What about the officer what brought us 'ere?' Morgan asked.

'Keep your voice down,' the carpenter's mate whispered urgently. He glanced nervously over his shoulder, then leaned closer. 'Didn't see you come aboard. What did he look like?'

'Little fat feller in 'is forties, getting bald on top. Wearing clothes fit for a lord, 'e was.'

'Oh that one,' he said bitterly. 'Trevelyan they calls him. He's the most hated pig on board. He'd be another "Bread Fruit Bligh" if he got half a chance, which thank Gawd he won't ever have, for he'll never make captain now.' He looked around him before continuing in a whisper, 'If ever this ship rose agen its officers, which I hopes will never happen while we've got Captain Brewster, the first to go over t'side would be Trevelyan – and that bastard Atkins would be a close second,' he added with relish.

CHAPTER FIVE

Since the breeze was well forward of *Adamant*'s beam, good seamanship was essential to get her clear of the Mersey. She needed her topgallant yards fully braced on a port tack and her headsails as taut as drumskins to give her steerage. In this manner she was borne by the ebbing tide beyond the land and along the buoyed deep-water channel. On one occasion her keel scraped the unseen bank to leeward. Those who knew what was happening looked grim. The wrecks of many vessels lay beneath the shoal water beyond. The ship shuddered free of the mud and continued on her way. It was a great relief to all when she finally won through to the open sea with room to tack.

Their peace of mind was short-lived. The wind contrarily backed during the night and the barometer fell, a combination of factors which heralded a storm. Before dawn, they were stripped down to topgallants again, being pounded by enormous waves over the port bow and losing miles to leeward. They approached the coast of Ireland in driving rain and mountainous seas. They had to go about onto a starboard tack and thrash their way back, making a landfall to the south of Anglesey on the following day: over two hundred miles of sea to gain less than forty miles along the course they had to follow.

So it went on, day after day, over to Ireland and back to Wales, in the teeth of a roaring southwesterly, with

Adamant burying her bows constantly and shipping tons of water. Noise and discomfort dominated their lives: the crash of the seas, the straining of the timbers, the howl of the rigging and, beneath it all, the sighing of the pumps, for *Adamant* was a wet ship and her people suffered cruelly.

Her decks had been caulked during the idle weeks at Liverpool but her timbers had sprung under the strain, and freshly tarred oakum hung like creepers from the deck boards above, continuously dripping onto the gundecks, where the men ate and slept. Bedding was mildewed, clothing was damp in the sea chests, the food was not cooked due to difficulties in the galley, and everyone was weary with temper frayed.

Midshipman Lawson had to stop a fight at four in the morning on his way down to his bunk in the bowels of the ship, after standing the middle watch with Clayton and Trevelyan. The men involved were from his own section. They were furious after spending four hours in the foul weather on the open deck to find that others below had slung their hammocks on the hooks reserved for them to avoid the leaks in their own area. Having used his authority to move the trespassers, Lawson went below to meet trouble in the midshipmen's berth.

'Wake up, you thoughtless little swine.'

Midshipman Clayton had arrived below a few minutes earlier. Now he was shaking Atkins into wakefulness.

'What is it?' Atkins grumbled.

'*This* – is your deck coat, I believe,' growled Clayton, thrusting the sodden garment under Atkins' nose.

'So what?' Atkins said peevishly.

'When you came off duty at midnight, you hung it near my bunk. Now my bedding is wet, damn you.'

'Oh – I'm sorry,' Atkins shrugged and turned over.

Clayton whipped the blankets off him, seized an arm and one leg, hoisted the youth out of the bunk and dumped him unceremoniously on the wet deck boards.

'Now you can sleep in my bunk and I'll take yours. That way I'll know that you really are sorry.'

Atkins got to his feet, incredulity giving way to indignation when Clayton climbed into his bed.

'That bedding is my private property, bought by my father. Get out at once. I shall not sleep in that – that – purser's doss-bag that you –'

Clayton hit him across the face with the flat of his hand, a blow which sent Atkins sprawling against the table top, dislodging it from the midshipmen's chests on which it rested. He scrambled upright, his nose streaming blood and hatred in his eyes.

'You are not fit to share a berth with gentlemen, you – you spawn of the gutter,' he said venomously.

Clayton leapt out of the bunk and went for Atkins. The youth, now badly frightened, pushed the loose table top across his path causing him to trip, and fled past Lawson who was standing by the open door. Clayton heaved the obstruction across the tiny compartment and went after him, but Lawson slammed the door to and stood before it.

'Steady, Mr Clayton,' he cried warningly.

'Get out of my way.'

He seized Lawson by the shoulders, attempting to push him away from the door. Lawson resisted and the next moment they were locked in combat: the older and stronger Clayton mad with rage and trying to use his fists whilst Lawson was struggling to contain him. There was no one to help.

'Calm down. Trevelyan's not far away.'

Clayton wrenched his hand free and punched Lawson in the stomach. It doubled him up. Clayton barged him to one side. Before he could reach the door, it was thrown open. Lieutenant Trevelyan was on the threshold. Immediately, the tension went out of Clayton. His great fists unclenched and he stood like a penitent schoolboy.

'Well?' Trevelyan demanded icily when neither of them spoke. 'What is the meaning of this?'

Clayton was tongue-tied. Lawson got up from the deck and attempted to smile. His right ear was streaming blood from violent contact with the bulkhead.

'Just a bit of horseplay, sir.'

'Do you take me for a fool, Mr Lawson?' Trevelyan said witheringly.

Neither of them spoke. Trevelyan looked from one to

the other, then walked around the tiny compartment looking into the bunks.

'Midshipmen Saunders and Heward will be on duty. Where is Atkins?'

Clayton looked up shamefacedly. It was obvious that he was about to tell the whole story. Lawson got in first.

'Probably gone to the heads, sir.'

Trevelyan's eyes bored into Lawson's. He removed his watch, walked over to the lamp and examined it.

'More'n likely you drove him from his bed with the noise of your quarrel. I make it twenty-five minutes past four o'clock. You will both be on report before the captain,' he said, snapping his watch shut.

'I'm sorry,' Clayton said when Trevelyan had gone.

'That's all right,' Lawson replied, dabbing at his ear.

Clayton sat gloomily on the edge of his own bunk. 'I should never have gone for midshipman,' he said, after a while. 'Ought to have stayed as bo'sun. You can't escape from your class and I came from nowt.' He sighed. 'My old man was a tiler, out of work most of the time.'

'So you've done bloody well: better than the Atkinses of this world with money and influence behind them to smooth the road. Captain Brewster has faith in you or he wouldn't have recommended your advancement, and he's as good a seaman as you'll find, from all accounts. The men think he's God Almighty.'

'Aye, he's a great captain, and he's treated me very kindly, but I feel I'm letting him down. I don't seem to be coping with the lessons very well and now there's this business.'

Lawson grinned. 'He invited me to dinner after I'd dropped him in the river. We'll get no more than a mastheading for fighting, you'll see. As for the other side of it, Saunders helps us all with the navigation, and he'll be pleased to help you if you will let him.'

Adamant fought her way southward for nine days in the most appalling weather, logging over twelve hundred miles before the unmistakable Islands of Scilly gradually materialized out of a greyness that was neither sea nor sky, to give them their first reliable position in four days.

Then the awesome power went out of the wind, and the enormous seas subsided into a heavy swell. No longer was it necessary to use hands as well as feet to move about the vessel. Men were able to look around for gear and personal belongings long abandoned to the chaos of the lower decks. The cooks could once again perform their duties in the confines of the brick-lined galley without hazarding the life of the ship with their fire, or themselves with the scalding contents of the vast cooking pots suspended above the flames. Extra rations of beef and vegetables were authorized. There was also double grog, so the men went to their hammocks content for the first time since leaving the Mersey.

The following morning saw them sailing eastward over a calm sea with Lizard Point fine on their port bow and the gulls wheeling overhead. Gun-ports were opened, bedding and clothing were brought out to dry and the ship steamed under the influence of the warm spring sunshine.

Nowhere is an improvement in the weather more appreciated than at sea. Apart from the bone-chilling, all-pervading dampness and the danger to life and limb in the working of the ship, there had also been the ever-present threat of foundering. Many of the men, particularly whose who had never been to sea before, had felt that every day was to be their last. Now they were cheerful as they went about their tasks of setting the ship to rights and getting their gear in order, and even the heartaches of those who had been torn from their homes by the press gangs were temporarily forgotten.

Captain Brewster's face was not cheerful. Before him on the desk was an accumulation of bad conduct reports, which had awaited a moderation in the weather before they could be dealt with. Outside in the passageway were seven men under escort and looking very sorry for themselves, including the wretched Jenkins, accused of stealing the captain's purse. Brewster scowled at Clayton and Lawson standing before him.

'I will not have fighting among midshipmen under my command. Either of you could depend for his life upon the other, and the welfare of this vessel could be hazarded by your private squabbles.'

This second consideration galvanized him into action. He thrust himself from his chair and strode across to them.

'Do you understand me, Mr Lawson?'

'Yes, sir.'

'And you, Mr Clayton?'

'Yes, sir.'

'Are your differences resolved?'

'Yes, sir,' they both replied.

'Very well.' He walked across the deck of his cabin with his hands thrust behind him and his face thoughtful. 'Wait outside, please. You too, Mr Jones,' he added to the clerk sitting in the background.

They went, leaving the captain with his two senior lieutenants, Prendergast and Trevelyan. Brewster turned to them.

'Gentlemen, we have all been under stress for some time, and conditions on this ship have been hard enough for any of us to bear. On the gun-decks and in the midshipmen's berth it must have been hell. We have all experienced the latter, and we have had to fight for our rights at one time or another.' He picked up the papers from his desk and riffled through them. 'Six of these reports are for fighting, or disturbances of a – a trivial nature. None of the men concerned is an habitual troublemaker. One of them, Morgan, has been with us only since we left Liverpool.'

'He is charged with dumb insolence as well as causing a disturbance, sir,' Trevelyan interrupted. 'The report was made out following a complaint by Midshipman Atkins.'

'Very well. With the exceptions of Morgan and this fellow Jenkins, I intend to let them go with a warning this time. What do you think of that, gentlemen?'

'You are most lenient – er – generous, sir,' Prendergast said.

Trevelyan looked furious, but he made no comment. The six reports had been his, and the captain's refusal to punish the men concerned must be seen as a criticism of his own actions.

'You have nothing to say, Mr Trevelyan?'

'The decision must be yours, sir, since you have responsibility for the consequences.'

'Aye, you're right, Mr Trevelyan,' he said drily, 'I do have the responsibility. Now, let's get on with it. We'll have the midshipmen in again.'

After Lawson and Clayton had been sent away, rejoicing in their good fortune, the men were brought in and severely reprimanded before being sent about their duties. Now it was Morgan's turn. He looked badly frightened – a thin scarecrow of a man between two big, robust members of the provost staff. Captain Brewster examined him keenly. This was the husband and father of the wretched trio who had awaited his return to the Saracen's Head.

'You are charged with causing a disturbance in the galley and, when cautioned by Midshipman Atkins, you did roll your eyes in an insolent manner.' Brewster looked up from the paper he had been reading. 'What have you to say for yourself?'

'I don't know what insolent means.'

'Say "sir" when you address an officer,' the master-at-arms growled sternly from his position by the door.

'Yes, sir. I'm sorry, sir.'

'Insolent means that you treated him as if he were of no account.' Brewster said patiently. 'Is that right?'

'Oh no, sir. 'E 'its yer with a rope if yer don't jump to it, sir.'

'What about the trouble in the galley?'

'I didn't want to cause no upset, sir. I just tried to get the cook's mate to give me a bowl of broth, sir. For Adams, sir. 'E can't eat the stuff they dish up, sir.'

'What's Adams to you, and why can't he eat the same food as other men?'

''E's me wife's brother, and –' his eyes filled with tears and his mouth trembled – 'and I think 'e's dying, sir.' He rubbed his hand across his wet cheeks.

Brewster looked at the man in astonishment. 'Whatever makes you think that?'

''E coughs blood every morning, sir, just like 'is brother did afore 'e died.'

'Has he seen the surgeon?'

'Yes, sir. The surgeon give 'im some medicine, but it don't seem to do no good, sir.'

Brewster turned incredulous eyes towards Trevelyan. 'Did you investigate this, Mr Trevelyan?'

'Er – no, sir.' He fumbled with his cravat.

Brewster glared at him then turned back to Morgan. 'If what you have told me is true, there will be nothing more said over this report. Release him, master-at-arms, and pass the word for the surgeon.'

'Aye, aye, sir. Will you see Jenkins now, or shall I bring him to you later?'

'Now. Let's get it over with.'

Jenkins had been placed in irons before they had left Liverpool and the unfortunate man had been secured in the bowels of the ship throughout the storm with only the rats for company, apart from the twice-daily visits of the provost staff. During that time, the likely results of his alleged theft must have preyed on his mind, and he had been a weak, eager-to-please simpleton before this trouble had descended upon him.

'I didn't do it, sir. I didn't do it,' he babbled before Captain Brewster read the charge.

'Didn't do what?' Brewster growled.

'Didn't steal your purse, sir. I swear I don't know nuffin' about it.' He began to cry. 'I don't know 'ow it gorrin me pocket.'

'Do you think Webb might have slipped it in?'

The man shook his head wildly. 'I just don't know nuffin', sir,' he sobbed. 'Please don't 'ave me flogged, sir. Please.'

'Get on your feet, man,' the master-at-arms barked. 'Escort pull him up.'

Jenkins had fallen to his knees, grovelling in his terror. The two escorts jerked him upright and he stood with his head bowed, sobbing like a child. Brewster's face softened.

'I don't suppose we'll ever get at the truth,' he sighed. 'Take him away. See that he is washed, given clean clothes and fed. Then release him to his duties.'

Behind the captain's back, Trevelyan looked at Prendergast and grimaced.

They led Jenkins away babbling his thanks, spittle running down his jaw, pitifully demented. As the door closed behind them, there was a knock and Lawson entered. He held a paper, which he offered to the captain.

A semaphore signal from Lizard Point, sir,' he reported.

Brewster scanned it.

'Change course for Falmouth, Mr Prendergast. A sloop is on its way out with dispatches. We are to meet it.'

Some time later, whilst they were watching a tiny sloop-of-war dancing towards them around the headland of St Keverna, the brooding Trevelyan joined the first lieutenant over on the leeward side.

'What are we to do for discipline, Mr Prendergast?' he asked bitterly. 'Seven up on report and every one got off without punishment. I've never known the like of it in twenty-five years at sea. If we carry on like this, the men will laugh at us when we give an order.'

Prendergast looked around the decks and up at the towering masts where men lined the yards, clawing in the mainsails. Certainly, they seemed far more cheerful than usual as they went about their work. He shrugged noncommittally, raised his telescope and focused it on the distant sloop.

'What do you make of her?' Brewster asked a few minutes later as he joined Prendergast.

The first lieutenant looked puzzled as he lowered his glass.

'Don't rightly know, sir. The flag she's flying is certainly not ours, but it's difficult to say what it is at this angle.'

'You have never served in the Baltic, Mr Prendergast.'

'No, sir.'

Brewster smiled reminiscently as he raised his big brass telescope and clapped it to his eye.

'Yes,' he rumbled as he twisted it into focus. 'The sloop belongs to the Navy of our northern ally. Rather than spend the winter ice-bound in the Baltic, they joined Admiral Duncan off Yarmouth and King George has victualled them.'

'Russian, sir?'

'Aye. The sloop will be one of Admiral Hanikof's fleet, though what it's doing so far off station, the Lord knows.'

CHAPTER SIX

The Russian sloop came dashing up alongside *Adamant*, easily keeping pace with the larger vessel, now reduced to topgallants, and closed expertly against the wicker fenders lowered for her. Lines were thrown, but the visitor, with his dispatches slung around his neck, was already transferred, having leapt from the pitching starboard bow of the sloop onto *Adamant*'s rope ladder. Now, as the sloop fell away to a safe distance, he climbed rapidly to the deck. He was a British lieutenant of no more than nineteen years, confident, proud and exuberant, curbing his breezy manner for a brief moment of solemnity as he saluted at the entry port.

'Liaison officer, I should think,' Heward commented. 'Probably speaks fluent Russian. I wonder what's in the dispatches he's brought with him?'

The young man was now speaking to Captain Brewster who, calling on Lieutenant Prendergast to join them, led the way aft to his day cabin. Trevelyan stared gloomily after them, then began to pace the windward side, his hands behind him, obviously not taking kindly to his reduced status on board.

Ten minutes later, the captain's clerk handed him a note. Trevelyan read it and turned to the midshipmen on the other side of the quarterdeck.

'Mr Clayton!' he called. 'The stairway is to be set up

51

over the port side. Please attend to it immediately.'

The stairway was one of a pair that linked the forecastle with the main gun-deck when they were at sea. Now it had to be unbolted, hoisted by the derrick and swung over the side. It was a lot of trouble and therefore rarely used, except in harbour. Consequently there was a great deal of interest when Clayton organized a party to set it in position.

'Probably the sloop commander is too drunk to use the ladder,' Heward grinned, 'or maybe Admiral Hanikof's aboard.'

In the large cabin overlooking the stern of the ship, Captain Brewster pushed back the chair from his desk and gave the dispatches he had been reading to his second-in-command.

'Read them, Mr Prendergast. There's mutiny in the Channel Fleet. Our orders have been changed. We're to sail for France. I've marked the important passages.'

He joined the visitor by the stern window and examined the sloop, now in full view behind them, cutting across *Adamant*'s wake to take station on her starboard quarter. Brewster indicated the ornate gold lettering on her port bow as she sailed by.

'So the weird jumble of letters there spells *Catherine*?'

'Named after the late Empress herself, sir,' the liaison officer confirmed.

'I hope she's fast, Mr Grayson.'

'Very good, sir, especially in light winds, when she will out-pace most vessels. Was to have been a royal yacht: built at Stettin where the Empress was born and spent her childhood. Every nail driven home with loving care, so they say, sir,' he said with a smile. 'But she didn't want it for herself. It was a present for Grigori Aleksandrovich Potemkin.'

'For keeping her warm in bed?'

Prendergast's eyes jerked up from the dispatches he was reading. He looked shocked. The liaison officer grinned.

'He did that as well, sir, and it's general knowledge, but officially the gift was a reward for having gained the Crimea for Russia. The sloop was based at Sevastopol and

Potemkin used to race it every summer. When he died six years ago, the Navy took it over and converted it.'

'And now Admiral Hanikof is using it as a private yacht for his own family!' Brewster exclaimed. 'Why the devil can't he leave his women folk ashore like everybody else, or, if he must take them to sea, why doesn't he keep them on his flagship instead of sending them off on a cruising holiday in a sloop? Have these Russian aristocrats no discipline?'

'Admiral Hanikof appears to be a law unto himself, sir.'

Brewster's severity relaxed. He even looked amused. 'I'd like to be present when he hears that not only has his sloop been commandeered, but his wife and daughters too. You say they refuse to be set ashore, Mr Grayson?'

'That is correct, sir,' the liaison officer replied. 'Neither Commander Baratovski nor I can persuade Madame Hanikof to travel overland to Yarmouth to rejoin her husband. Nor will she take lodgings in Falmouth and wait until we get back. It is almost as if she wanted to participate in a sortie or two with the French before she returns to St Petersburg.'

'How does this Commander Bara— whatshisname view the commandeering of his vessel and the prospects of action?'

'Bara-tov-ski, sir. I think he's delighted, but he pretends to be angry when Madame Hanikof is about.'

'Good!' Brewster exclaimed. 'Report back to him now and ask him to set a course for Brest immediately. Then I shall be pleased if you and he will escort the ladies on board here for dinner in two hours' time.'

'Wear ship, Mr Prendergast,' Brewster ordered as soon as Lieutenant Grayson had returned to the Russian sloop. 'Bring her as close to sou'ward as the wind will allow. When we are fairly on our new course, I'll speak to the officers and explain the situation – No, damn it! I'll see to the ship. You make dinner arrangements. You'll have had more experience of fancy parties than me. Let's show these Russians that the British Navy can be genteel.'

After Brewster had brought the ship on its new course for France, and all on board, from Trevelyan down, were bursting with curiosity, the officers and midshipmen were assembled. Brewster looked around and smiled paternally upon them.

'Well, gentlemen, it has come to pass. The Channel Fleet has mutinied. The leaders will not allow ships to leave harbour. Every day those which should be on blockade duties at the French ports are joining the Fleet at Spithead.'

'Is it Jacobite inspired, sir?' asked the marine lieutenant, a severe young man with a large moustache.

'I don't know, Mr Pocklington, but I think not,' Brewster replied. Then continued, 'The mutineers have stated that they will immediately engage the enemy if they approach our shores, but ships anchored by Spithead cannot see what is happening at Brest. According to the dispatch I have received today, we have nothing between Brest and Ireland.'

'So there could be another Bantry Bay landing?'

'Yes indeed, Mr Trevelyan, but this time it would be in springtime, not mid-winter, as it was before. The man who arranged that little expedition was the Irish rebel –' He paused and thumbed through the dispatch in his hand.

'Wolfe Tone, sir,' Prendergast supplied.

'Thank you, Mr Prendergast. Perhaps I'd better read the Admiralty's account of the situation.' He held the dispatch to the light from the window. '*Theobald Wolfe Tone, a Dublin lawyer and alleged organizer of the illegal United Irishmen's Society is, without doubt, the person who initiated and planned the French attempt to invade Ireland from Bantry Bay last December. This traitor is now in Brest. Our agents there report that he has been seen on many occasions in the company of General Hoche and his staff. On the days from the thirtieth of March to the third of April, Wolfe Tone was present during embarking exercises, when infantry and artillery took up their allocated positions in the invasion barges moored between Brest and Quilbignon. General Hoche and Wolfe Tone were seen to be frequently in consultation during these exercises.*' Brewster lowered the paper and waited for the questions.

'How many men does General Hoche command, sir?'

'Sixty thousand, Mr Pocklington, and God alone

knows how many Irishmen would flock to his banner if he landed his army at Cork or some such place.'

'Why is he not taking advantage of the troubles at Spithead, sir? If his invasion fleet is ready, there's nothing to stop him embarking for Ireland, or England for that matter,' Trevelyan said.

Others looked as if they wished to offer their suggestions. Brewster waved them aside and continued.

'It is the opinion of the powers at Admiralty that the French Directorate is divided on the subject. Some of the enemy are for sailing immediately. Others wish to wait until the French naval ships in Brest are strengthened by their Mediterranean Fleet, which is at present at Toulon.'

'And that's where they're likely to stay if Admiral St Vincent has anything to do with it,' Atkins scoffed.

He smirked around him but found only disapproval. The captain's face was bleak. Atkins blushed and shrank back into his collar.

'Thank you, Mr Atkins. The French are divided because they are not fully informed about the extent of the mutiny. Has it removed all the ships that were taking part in the blockade? General Hoche suspects a trick to get him out on the open sea with sixty thousand men in clumsy barges, and only a small fleet to protect them. Each day that passes will add strength to this faction, which is demanding an immediate invasion of Ireland unless they see evidence of a British presence at sea.' He paused and looked around. 'That is the picture, gentlemen. The rest you can guess. Our orders are to keep a presence at Brest until we are relieved or, God forbid, until the Toulon Fleet manages to get past St Vincent at Gibraltar. Any questions?'

'Are we alone, sir?' Lieutenant Pocklington asked, looking fierce and twisting the end of his military moustache.

'Not entirely. The sloop which is keeping us company will be under my command.'

'She's armed with six-pounders, and I doubt if there are more than six of them,' Trevelyan grumbled. 'There'll not be much help from them, sir, particularly as the Russians do not have much of a reputation for gunnery from all accounts.'

'She's very fast, Mr Trevelyan, and that's more important for the task she'll have to perform. Have you the chart there, Mr Atherton?'

'That I have, sir.'

The master spread a roll of parchment over the table. Captain Brewster helped him to snap on the spring clips to hold it down, then pointed at the coast of Brittany.

'Brest Roads, gentlemen: a natural harbour big enough to accommodate the whole of the French Navy, and the Royal Navy as well for that matter. Brest lies to the north of the waterway, and the invasion barges are close to the town. They are protected by soldiers stationed ashore.' He looked around. 'We have to persuade the French to keep their barges there.' His thick finger prodded the chart again. 'There's le Goulet, the channel that leads into Brest Roads. It's narrow and the tidal stream can reach six knots. It shouldn't bother the Russian sloop, given a fair wind. The sloop's called *Catherine* by the way. She will enter every morning: just enough to be seen. Then she'll signal to *Adamant* and *Adamant* will pass on the signal to our nonexistent first-rates over the horizon. With luck, we'll fool the French for two weeks at least.'

'Do the Russians use Kempenfelt's signals, sir?' Prendergast asked surprised.

'I don't think they use any signals. Didn't in the old days, that's for sure. Anyway, I shall be sending a midshipman on board *Catherine*.'

There was a stir of interest among the midshipmen present. A spell on the sloop would be a welcome change from the routine of a fifty-gun man-of-war, and there would possibly be a chance for a midshipman to distinguish himself.

'Have any of you served on this coast?' Brewster asked.

'I have, sir,' Lawson said. 'I spent eighteen months with Lord Howe's fleet in ninety-three and ninety-four.'

'Yes, of course. You were serving on the frigate *Wakeful*, but you were only a child then.'

Heward looked at Saunders and rolled his eyes expressively. He had often voiced the opinion that

Captain Brewster had a special relationship with Lawson. 'I bet he doesn't know where I served before I joined *Adamant*,' he whispered.

'I was fifteen when I left the fleet, sir,' Lawson said, 'and most of the time *Wakeful* was doing much the same duty you have in mind for *Catherine*. We entered le Goulet on many occasions, sir.'

'Did you? Well, it looks as if you've got the job. You will join Commander Baratovski for dinner and be ready to move yourself and your gear immediately afterwards to the sloop. You will require a copy of the Numerary Code and the bunting to go with it.'

'Clean my shoes,' Lawson pleaded fifteen minutes later, as he lathered his face and took up the razor.

'Don't see why I should. You're too lucky by half,' Saunders said, taking up the blacking brush.

'Can I borrow that frilled shirt of yours, Heward?'

'I'll be glad to see the back of this fellow,' Heward grumbled as he rummaged in his sea chest.

Clayton was unable to enter into this bantering spirit but he was doing his best to get Lawson ready for his transfer to *Catherine*. He had his bedding neatly trussed and his heavy-weather, tarred clothing bundled in a seaman-like manner. Now he was polishing buttons.

'Well, you'll do, provided you don't eat too much,' Heward said as he examined the resplendent Lawson. 'Take an extra helping and those nankeen trousers will split for sure.'

'Damned coat's too tight,' Lawson grumbled, pulling at the armpits.

'You're growing too fast, that's your trouble,' Saunders told him. 'I'll buy that coat from you if you can get it off in one piece.'

Sometime later, the sloop, which was sailing five hundred yards to windward of *Adamant*, began to close and the captain's launch, manned by immaculate oarsmen, was sent across the intervening water to convey the guests to their dinner. Clayton was in charge. Midshipman Atkins was also aboard, but Clayton had not informed him that ladies were expected, so the youngest midshipman was taken completely by surprise when an attractive girl of his own age, to be followed by another, perhaps two or three years older, appeared on the deck of the sloop and descended the short stairway to the boat. Both had hair like spun copper.

'Hand the ladies aboard, Mr Atkins,' Clayton growled.

The younger girl's blue eyes smiled her thanks and Atkins was her slave. He hardly saw her sister as he helped her to her seat. Their mother clearly needed no assistance as she stepped lightly into the boat. She was a fine-looking woman in her late thirties, who accommodated herself to the pitching of the launch with the ease of an experienced sailor and sat on the other side of the tiller from Clayton. There she waved away the cushion hastily detached from the seat that she should have occupied further forward.

"So that's why the old man wanted the stairway over the side,' Heward mused, offering his telescope to Lawson. 'You'll have the company of ladies at dinner, you lucky dog, John.'

Lawson focused upon the launch. He noted the stocky figure of the Russian commander, Baratovski, with his short black beard, then he examined the ladies. The two girls and their mother were sitting bolt upright and looking to neither right nor left as the boat approached.

Watched by all the idle members of *Adamant*'s company, Madame Hanikof ascended the stairway and entered the vessel in a manner as regal as any of the crowned heads of Europe, with her daughters keeping pace behind her like ladies-in-waiting. Commander Baratovski followed unobtrusively, hovering on the fringe. Captain Brewster introduced himself and his officers, then led the way towards the palatial accommodation overlooking the stern of the vessel, with its curved window casement and balcony.

Lawson looked around him with interest. The place was greatly changed since Clayton and he had been summoned there earlier in the day. Some of the bulkheads had been removed. Now the captain's day cabin, the separate quarters of the first and second lieutenants and the office used by the captain's clerks, together with

58

the numerous small compartments, had become one, and the entire floor space was covered with new canvas. It was a transformation that never ceased to amaze the uninitiated, yet it was easily achieved.

The walls were held in place with wooden pins and iron bolts, tensioned by strategically driven wedges, as on every man-of-war. The carpenter's mates were drilled in the task of removing them and sending them below, together with the casement window and the furniture, whenever the ship cleared for action, leaving a completely open deck for the men to operate the guns. It was a poor crew that could not accomplish the work in less than thirty minutes.

'It is wonderful to be standing up with the straight back, Captain,' Madame Hanikof remarked some three glasses of wine later.

Brewster beckoned one of the blue-coated servants, took the lady's empty glass and passed over a full one from the tray.

'A bit more room than on the sloop, I should imagine,' he said with a smile. 'Perhaps it would be better if you and your daughters were to move over to *Adamant*.'

'I will think about this,' she said with a smile.

'We shall go in to dinner?' Brewster said.

She took his arm and he, self-consciously escorted her to where a table, set for eleven, gleaming with wine glasses and polished cutlery, had been placed. It was between two long guns, close by the vast window casement, with its numerous small panes of glass, affording a magnificent view of the sea. Through it they could see the sloop to the right of their wake, glowing redly in the rays of the April sun. It was riding easily over the swell, obviously under restraint to match the pace of *Adamant*: a thoroughbred in every detail.

'The sting in your tail?' Madame Hanikof said, indicating the guns.

'Yes, ma'am: twelve-pounders. Good for a mile or more at the right elevation when they're nicely warmed up. There are heavier guns on the deck directly below this one.'

She asked him a few technical questions. Obviously she

was well informed about warships and highly skilled in drawing out sailors unused to polite conversation. Brewster expanded visibly under her influence.

Mr Pocklington was placed between the two daughters. Lawson sat to the left of Annette, the older girl. Midshipman Atkins, who had been asked to attend at the last minute, was on the right of Victoria. On the other side of the table, between Lieutenant Prendergast and Mr Atherton, sat Commander Baratovski, a man of few words, it proved, and for those he was largely dependent upon the translations of Lieutenant Grayson, who occupied the opposite end of the table from Captain Brewster and Madame Hanikof.

Both girls spoke English almost as well as their mother and they were obviously enjoying this opportunity to exercise it. Victoria in particular, a vivacious, intelligent girl, found little time for eating as, in response to Pocklington's queries about St Petersburg, she described her life there among the families of the naval and army societies in a highly amusing manner. Even the dour Mr Atherton found himself smiling under the influence of her infectious laugh and her dancing blue eyes.

Atkins was captivated, but her glances were mostly for Lawson, who, whilst being monopolized by Annette on his right, was well aware that she seemed to consult Lieutenant Grayson more frequently than her linguistic needs warranted. Meanwhile, Madame Hanikof, seated at the head of the table and understanding all that was happening before her, was nevertheless able to charm Captain Brewster and match him, glass for glass, in whatever he chose to drink.

It was a delightful occasion for all present, particularly when it became apparent that Madame Hanikof and her daughters, far from being displeased by the turn of events, were looking forward keenly to the adventure and were happy to move into *Adamant*.

CHAPTER SEVEN

Mr Atherton brought the first handbill to the captain's cabin just as Brewster was getting into bed. It had been slipped into his pocket, probably as a friendly warning from a loyal sailor. It was printed on yellow paper and was identical to the sample copy received with the dispatches brought aboard by the liaison officer.

Shipmates! Fellow Seamen
Service in His Majesty's Ships is DEGRADING!
HARDSHIP! DANGER! DISEASE! POVERTY!
CONDITIONS so FOUL that our Officers FEAR to
Allow US the FREEDOM and PLEASURES of going ashore.
Lest WE should RUN from the ABOMINABLE lives we lead.
NOTHING is done to IMPROVE our SITUATION.
OUR PETITIONS ARE IGNORED
The Admiralty must learn to heed our JUST DEMANDS.
April 16th is the date, my lads.
The CHANNEL FLEET will REFUSE to put to sea.
Vessels at sea will sail to SPITHEAD and ANCHOR.
No violence should be offered to your officers:
UNLESS THEY RESIST!
GOD SAVE THE KING

'Same press, I think,' Brewster observed, comparing the two handbills. 'The Admiralty discovered that they

61

were printed in Portsmouth on the twelfth of April.'

'Which means that this didna' come aboard at Liverpool,' Atherton said, taking the paper from the desk and studying it. 'That leaves the sloop. Two officers, one o' them Russian, and three ladies joined us. There were also three servants who canna' speak a worrd of English.'

'None of those had anything to do with it. The liaison officer had a few British seamen with him. That's how it got here. One of 'em will have slipped this bit of paper and perhaps a few dozen more to someone among the crew of the launch. If we can find out who brought them aboard, we'll maybe discover how many handbills are circulating.'

'Do ye think it'll be guid thing tae scrat aboot, sir?' Atherton asked doubtfully.

'Obviously you don't.' Brewster grumbled, noting Atherton's wry face. 'And you're probably right,' he added after a pause. 'If we start making a fuss, they'll know that we're on to them, and that might be just the spark they need. We can take it that every man and boy on board will now have heard of the mutiny. Most of 'em will have discussed it over their grog but, as yet, they'll have no effective leaders. We must try to keep it that way as long as possible.'

'How do ye hope tae do that, sir?'

'First, we must identify them. If we pool our knowledge of the men in our sections, we'll soon come up with the likely ones. These will be the natural leaders. We can forget the trash. They'll lead no one that we need worry about. I can think of two now. There's Forster, captain of the foretop. Educated and intelligent, and the men listen to him. Another fellow is Bainbridge, purser's clerk: used to be a lay preacher, and he still likes an audience. I'll find something to keep them out of mischief, and any others we can think of.' He took out his watch. 'When do we reach le Goulet?'

'Dawn, if this wind holds.'

'So, we'll be seeing enemy territory. There's nothing like it for bringing out a rash of patriotism. God knows, these poor lads have little enough to be patriotic about. They've had no pay for nine months, no shore leave since they came aboard, and they have a bloody useless sawbones who don't know consumption from a common cold, and is likely to have us all infected. On top of that, they have an admiral who thinks he's God Almighty and can ignore a petition from twenty thousand men.'

He shook his head at the wonder of it, then noticed they were not alone.

'What is it, Mr Trevelyan?' he said sharply. 'I didn't hear you knock.'

'I'm sorry, sir. I thought I heard you bid me enter.'

'What do you want?'

'I've just handed over the watch, sir. I know it's gone midnight, but I saw the lamp burning in your quarters so I thought you would be interested to know that a shore light has been observed south by west. Could either be a fire or a beacon, sir.'

'It canna' be a shore light. Not if it's sou' by west,' Atherton said scathingly. 'Anyway, it'd need tae be a wunnerful big light tae see it at fifteen miles, and that's how far we are frae Ushant, which is due south from here – according tae *my* reckoning.'

Brewster reached for his trousers and pulled them on, stuffing his nightshirt inside. Atherton and Trevelyan left the cabin for the open deck, the lieutenant tense with anger after his humiliation, the master supremely confident and completely indifferent to Trevelyan's obvious hatred.

Fire at sea is always a compelling sight, particularly at night. This one persuaded many of the men below decks to leave their hammocks and crowd the starboard side of *Adamant*, where their excited comments penetrated the wooden walls of the Russian ladies' new quarters and brought them on deck.

Madame Hanikof appeared first, shortly followed by her daughters, all well wrapped up. Midshipman Atkins, who had the watch under Lieutenant Prendergast, hurried across the deck and offered his boatcloak to Victoria, but she laughed and waved her hand in a pretty gesture of refusal.

'Is it a ship on fire?' Madame Hanikof asked.

'A vessel of some kind, ma'am,' Brewster replied. 'I'm going to send the sloop to find out. Excuse me a moment.'

He walked over to the windward side, where *Catherine*, gleaming in the moonlight, was advancing in response to the signal light on *Adamant*'s poop. Now she was spilling air from her newly set topsails to reduce her speed to that of *Adamant* at a distance of less than thirty yards. Baratovski and his liaison officer could be clearly seen by the wheel.

'Go and investigate, please,' Brewster shouted and pointed in the direction of the fire.

The Russian commander waved an acknowledgement, not waiting for a translation, and shouted an order. Two men on the deck behind him heaved on a rope. The topsail filled into a smooth curve, and *Catherine* began to draw ahead.

'There is Mr Lawson!' Victoria exclaimed, pointing across the water.

She waved impulsively, much to the obvious annoyance of Atkins, who was still in attendance, but the distant Lawson, even if he had seen her, would not have dared to wave back whilst his captain was standing on *Adamant*'s quarterdeck within a few feet of the girl.

As it was, the sloop was occupying all Lawson's attention. She was a thoroughbred, a combination of elegance and strength: the work of a master builder. Judging by the orderliness of everything, from the jackyard atop the raked mast to the neatly stowed and covered guns on the open deck, Baratovski was a worthy commander. Certainly he knew how to get the best from her, Lawson realized, as the sloop pointed her steeply angled bowsprit towards the distant fire, sailing closer to the wind than ever *Adamant* could have done.

The sloop was still two miles away when the fire erupted into a blossoming incandescence, abruptly extinguished. They knew that whatever had been burning was blown up, even before the sound of the explosion reached them. Fortunately, the sloop's officers had the position plotted, so they were able to continue on a compass course until, in the light of the moon glowing just above the horizon, they approached a large area of wreckage: barrels, spars, ship's timbers and a shattered longboat. They searched for survivors.

As they cruised slowly around, Parker, who had been sent aboard with Midshipman Lawson to help operate the signal hoists, nudged his fellow signaller and pointed.

'What do you make of that?'

Lawson heard and looked in the direction indicated. The thing that had attracted Parker's attention appeared to be a ship's boat, but it seemed to have higher sides than usual. Suddenly, he realized why. It was full of men, all sitting still in silence. Obviously, they didn't want to be seen. Lawson informed Baratovski.

The Russian commander spoke softly to the helmsman, then went forward, giving a number of low-voiced commands to his men as the sloop turned towards the survivors. One of the Russian sailors was rigging a ladder over the bulwarks, but the rest were removing the covers from the twin bow guns. Behind Lawson, in the stern of the sloop, a swivel gun had been set up.

'I hope the man with the scatter-gun knows what he's doing. If he makes a mistake with that, he'll clear the lot of us off the deck,' Parker whispered.

The survivors were French. There were eighteen of them. They came aboard sullenly enough, as might have been expected. Their homeland was within a few miles, and they would have reached it easily if they had not been spotted. Now the prospect of dreary years as prisoners of war lay before them. A large man, wearing a coat which had been burned in places, approached Baratovski.

'I am Jean Duprez, first mate of the barque, *Ville de Dijon*,' he said in English. 'My captain is dead, I think.'

'Lieutenant Baratovski, Imperial Russian Navy,' the sloop's commander replied with a curt bow of his head.

'*Le Russe! Mon Dieu!*' the man exclaimed.

His obvious dismay was nothing compared with that of the French sailors close enough to have heard the exchange. Near panic was the reaction. '*Le Russe! Le Russe!*' passed quickly among them. They moved restively, looking for escape, clearly held in check only by the cutlasses which restricted them to the port side. Even so, one of them did attempt to leap over the bulwarks into the sea. He was roughly knocked back into the press. The officer recovered his poise.

'We are *marine marchande*, not *marine de guerre*. Our barque is wrecked by an unfortunate fire. It is customary to set shipwrecked mariners ashore.'

Baratovski spoke rapidly in Russian to the liaison officer at his side. Grayson nodded, then addressed the French mate in English. Lawson, who had drawn closer, looked at Baratovski with renewed admiration. The Russian commander was a wily bird, it seemed. He spoke French fluently and he could have questioned the mate in his own language had he chosen to do so.

'What was your cargo and where were you bound?' Grayson asked.

'Oil of the olive and hides, bound for Rouen.'

'What caused the explosion?'

The man shrugged and gestured expressively. 'All ships must have a gun – or pirates will snap you up very damn quick.' He snapped his fingers. 'There was a little gunpowder for them, perhaps two barrels. The fire reached them.

'It would take more than two barrels to blow the barque to bits and destroy your longboat in the water.' Grayson said.

'Perhaps there were a few barrels lying in the hold,' he replied with an extra shrug of his shoulders. 'One does not always remember to throw damp gunpowder over the side.'

The liaison officer began to translate into Russian, but Baratovski stopped him with an abrupt gesture. He had understood it all, in addition to the mutterings in French among the prisoners. Now he gave his orders.

'You are to be taken aboard the British warship HMS *Adamant* for questioning,' Grayson told them.

• They looked relieved as they waited in turn to be searched by the Russian sailors and sent below through the narrow hatchway set in the bows of the vessel. Obviously the possibility of being taken to England as prisoners was not as frightening as that of spending the rest of the war in Russia.

During the exchanges, Lawson had noted that one of the prisoners had been staring at him with a peculiar intensity. Now, as the Frenchmen were leaving the deck, this same man indicated with a widening of his eyes followed by a surreptitious half-wink that he wished to communicate secretly.

'Come here,' Lawson ordered sharply, pointing and indicating in no uncertain manner that he wanted the man out of the line.

He came forward with a great show of reluctance and Lawson began to search him, pulling open his jacket and running his hands around the man's chest and waist, coming into close proximity.

'Thought you'd never catch on,' the man whispered into Lawson's ear. 'Knock me about a bit until they're all out of sight.'

The accent was pure Dublin. Lawson pushed the man aft towards the mast, much to the surprise of Lieutenant Grayson who followed curiously, waiting for an explanation from a signal midshipman who had no business interfering with the prisoners. The Irishman's first words, after the French prisoners had been sent below, justified Lawson's action.

'My name's Maharg. Mr Atkinson at the Admiralty will want to know all about me. I'm his man, an agent of the Crown.'

'What were you doing on board the *Ville de Dijon?*' Grayson demanded.

'Setting fire to it, what else? If Mr Atkinson can't act on the information I sends him, on account of the Fleet being in a state of mutiny, then the agent must make shift to do what needs to be done.'

'I suppose she was not carrying olive oil and hides?' Grayson said.

'Gunpowder, muskets, rockets and ten cannon, to say nuthin' of the other hardware, all bound for the Republicans at Wexford. The great Wolfe Tone himself should ha' been aboard but, more's the pity, there was a wee change of plans at the last minute, and he couldn't leave Brest. Had he come, he'd have been blowed up with his military stores, and Ireland would have been saved a sea of tears, for he'll raise the standard of rebellion there one day and drench the land in blood.'

'It was a desperate business setting fire to a vessel full

of explosives,' Grayson said suspiciously. 'Your captain is lost as a result.'

'Mr Atkinson's work *is* a desperate business. One mistake and it's the big chop. They've got a wunnerful new guillotine in Brest. As to the captain –' he gestured the inevitability of his fate – 'he is dead because, unfortunately, I had to kill him.'

'You murd – killed your own captain!'

'Och! Don't apply the morals of one of His Majesty's naval officers to the work that has to be done in my trade. The captain caught me putting a match to his cargo, so he had to die. Aye, and don't be looking down your nose at me, for I've likely saved a thousand lives at Wexford. That might be more than you'll achieve throughout your career, even supposing you come to be an admiral.'

'We'll see what Captain Brewster has to say about it,' Grayson said angrily.

'Aye! Well, don't be sticking me down wi' that lot,' Maharg replied coolly. 'They suspect me and I don't want to be strangled yet. There's too much unfinished business in France. I'll need to be set back on French soil, ye understand.'

'Well, we'll not take any chances on you getting strangled while there's a possibility that the hangman might do it, so we'll keep you on deck until we rejoin *Adamant*. Tie him to the mast, Mr Lawson.'

'I don't think the feller likes me an awful lot,' Maharg said with a grin as Lawson secured him.

Lawson smiled at his infectious humour. 'Do they take you for a Frenchman?' he asked as he tied the final knots and tested the tension of the rope.

'Not a bit of it,' Maharg replied cheerfully. 'I've only a smattering o' the language. I'm supposed to be a member of Theodore Wolfe Tone's bloody United Irishmen. Sure, France is full of them.'

The French prisoners were taken from their cramped quarters on the sloop at dawn and rowed over to *Adamant*.

After reading Baratovski's report, the captain went

out to the sloop. He took with him Midshipmen Clayton and Heward and seventeen men from all departments of *Adamant*: men of many trades who appeared to have little in common. Each man had been chosen because he was thought to be the natural leader in his own group. All were sent to the whaler after breakfast, without warning. Now they were worried, thoughtfully looking at each other and casting quizzical glances at the captain.

Brewster waited until they were all safely on board the sloop before he satisfied their curiosity. He addressed them on the open deck with his coat-tails dancing, and clutching his hat to his head.

'Beyond that headland', he began, pointing at the misty outline of the Brittany coast, 'is Brest harbour. In there are assembled troop-carrying barges, ready to transport sixty thousand French soldiers across to our homeland. We don't know where they will be set ashore. It could be in your home town. Our womenfolk could be ravaged.' His voice had risen half an octave. '*We* – the men of *Adamant* and our allies in the sloop – must stop them.'

'Should have been on the stage, or stood for parliament,' Heward breathed into Lawson's ear. 'Just look at them lapping it up, and these are intelligent men.'

Brewster's eyes flickered in Heward's direction, causing that young man some alarm.

'We are only a small force but fate has been kind to us. We have a British agent with us who knows the exact location of the invasion barges. He will lead us directly to them. We also have the ideal vessel to enter Brest Roads – and get out again: a royal racing yacht; as fast as anything afloat. What about the men?' He looked around. 'You have been chosen as the most responsible of *Adamant*'s company. There will be forty marines sent ashore to delay the enemy, but *you* will be the ones who will perform the vital task of burning the barges and saving your womenfolk back home.'

There was a stir of interest and some apprehensive faces but most seemed to be enthusiastic. At a sign from the captain, Parker held up a blackboard with a roughly drawn chart upon it. Brewster pointed to the channel.

'This is le Goulet, the gut in English. You'll pass through tonight under cover of darkness. The sloop will anchor as near to the barges as is sensible, then you will be set on board these barges by *Adamant*'s cutter at three different points. Any questions so far?'

'Are these barges all together, sir?' Forster, the top-man, asked.

'Let's ask Mr Maharg for details,' the captain said, turning to the Irishman who had been looking on but saying nothing.

'Sure, they're all together like a big raft. You can step from one to another. They've got fenders between them, but they're rubbing their timbers away. If they don't use them soon, they'll sink where they are.'

'Are they anchored, sir?' Forster asked him.

'Indeed, 'tis likely, but I've only seen ropes that are tied to the shore.'

Forster turned back to Captain Brewster. 'With respect, sir, might it not be a good idea to cut the shore cables and any anchors we can find, to let the whole mass of barges drift away from the shore. The wind's from the north, and it'll probably stay there for a few days, so it'll take the barges well out of the reach of land-based fire-fighters and put a bit o' distance between us and the soldiers' muskets.'

'A good idea, Forster. I'll remember that you made this suggestion,' Brewster said. 'Once the barges are clear of the shore, we'll light the fuses which will set fire to the combustibles which you will take aboard.'

'Why do we use fuses, sir? Why not just set fire to the barges?' a more cultured voice asked.

This was Bainbridge, the lay preacher, determined that Forster should not outshine him.

'A good point, lad, but I'm hoping to have you all back on board *Catherine* here before the Frenchies see the flames.'

Brewster was delighted with the way it was going. Both Forster and Bainbridge were now enthusiastic and eager to please. Forster's suggestion was part of the plan of attack which he had already drawn up, but there was no harm in the man thinking that it was entirely his.

'Can't understand why the captain's brought this lot together,' Clayton whispered when the meeting was over and the men were busy preparing combustibles. 'It's a queer bloody mixture: cooper's mate, blacksmith, carpenter's mate, sailmaker. There's even one of the pusser's clerks. I can see the sense in taking the prime seamen, but he's left better men on *Adamant*.'

Lawson said nothing. Some of these men had been almost truculent when they had been sent aboard the sloop. At least three of them were rabble-rousers and lower-deck lawyers. Now, they all seemed keen and eager.

There was no need for histrionics at the officers' meeting that followed.

'Where's the Irishman?' Brewster demanded, looking around the tiny cabin set in the stern of the sloop.

'On the foredeck, sir. Shall I get him?' Clayton asked.

'No. He can stay there. I don't want him to hear any more than he needs to know. He's probably what he says he is, but there's no sense in taking chances. He knows about the mutiny but he must not learn the full extent of our isolation. The operation for tonight is intended to show our confidence to the French: a confidence which will imply to them that we have an effective force at Brest. That is the main purpose. If we are successful in destroying a single invasion barge, I shall be delighted. Can you all see the chart on the table?'

There were affirmative murmurs in English and Russian. Brewster pointed with a pair of dividers at Brest Roads.

'The naval dockyard is on the west bank of the River Penfeld. Some of the finest vessels in the world have been built there. However, over the past year they have been turning out sailing barges, crudely made but good enough for their purpose, which is to carry guns, horses, the wagons of the commissariat and, of course, men across the Channel. Now the Admiralty has known about this for some time. What we did not know was how well the barges are guarded.'

He paused and waited until Grayson had finished translating.

'This Irishman Maharg swears that they are not guarded. Except for a few old nightwatchmen, who are supposed to keep local thieves away, there would be nobody nearer than half a mile. We shall send a boarding party in the cutter. There will be fifteen men in three sections of five with a midshipman in charge of each. The cutter will set the first section, under Mr Lawson, on the eastern side of the barges, as close to the shore as possible. Once aboard, they will secure any nightwatchmen they come across and place their combustibles where they'll be most effective. Meanwhile, Mr Heward's party will have climbed aboard the southern-most barges. Their job will be to cut any anchor cables they can find. Mr Clayton will take his men to the westward side. By this time, you will likely find a few nightwatchmen trying to creep ashore, having been disturbed by the two parties already on the barges. Hold these men prisoners until you have placed your combustibles and lit the fuses. Then you can let them go. Once the barges are adrift from the shore, Mr Lawson and Mr Clayton will retire from the landward side of the barges and join Mr Heward's section on the southern edge, and there you will find the cutter awaiting you. Any questions so far?'

'What about the mooring ropes on the shore, sir?' Pocklington asked.

'Your marines will be responsible for them, Mr Pocklington. You will take your men ashore in the whaler to the east of the barges. A section of them will cut the moorings. The rest of you will hold the road to delay the soldiers who will be sent out from Brest as soon as the alarm is raised. Once the barges have drifted away from the shallows, you will disengage from the enemy, get aboard the whaler and sail clear.'

'Thank you, sir.'

'You should all be back on board *Catherine* within the hour and on your way through le Goulet before the moon is up.'

Commander Baratovski asked a question of his liaison officer who immediately translated. Brewster pointed to the narrow channel leading to Brest Roads.

'Le Goulet is no more than a mile wide. It's guarded by

72

the guns of the fort on the northern side.'

'Guns?' queried a Russian junior officer, a little man with long moustaches and worried eyes, who obviously had a fair knowledge of English.

'Their equivalent of our thirty-two-pounder long guns. You'll be well within range as you pass through le Goulet. They'll shoot three thousand yards without any bother.'

The little Russian blinked and his Adam's apple wobbled, but he nodded, his eyes riveted on Brewster's until a sharp question from Baratovski caused both him and the liaison officer to start the translation at once.

The Russian commander shrugged away the consideration of being fired upon.

Brewster continued: 'They'll not see you on the way in. It'll be very dark. The tide will be with you, running at about two and a half knots, and the wind should be nicely on your beam, so you'll have no need to tack. Getting out will not be so easy. If you wait for the ebb tide, the moon will be up and you'll be shot at all the way through. By that time too it'll be like a hornets' nest in Brest Roads. So you've got to sail out against the tide, but you should manage if this northerly breeze holds.'

Brewster waited for the translation to end and he was just about to speak further when Baratovski raised his hand.

'I see before dark,' he said, nodding his head vigorously.

Captain Brewster looked doubtful. Commander Baratovski, his eyes shining with enthusiasm, made another effort in English, then abandoned it and spoke rapidly to Grayson. Heward winked at Lawson and indicated, with a movement of his eyes, the little Russian junior lieutenant with the moustaches. Whatever Baratovski was saying found no favour there. The man looked sick with apprehension.

Commander Baratovski would like to take *Catherine* into le Goulet this afternoon, sir. He wishes to see the channel in daylight and to allow the French guns to fire at him to ascertain their position and strength.'

Lieutenant Pocklington muttered, 'Good man,' and

Mr Prendergast smiled his appreciation. The Russian commander was obviously a brave and resourceful officer. Captain Brewster considered the request for a moment, then shook his head decisively.

'No, *Catherine* could be disabled. We can't afford to lose her.' He shrugged. 'Anyway, if they see you close by in daylight, they'll probably organize a special watch tonight. You'd better keep well clear of le Goulet. Just sail back and forth across the estuary, sending signals to *Adamant* from time to time. Head out to sea at sunset, as if you were coming to join us, but we'll meet here two hours later when you will show masked lights on your seaward side to help us to find you. Hoist red, white and green in that order from your masthead. Then, we'll know it's you.'

CHAPTER EIGHT

'Are you really as calm as you look, or are you scared to bloody death like I am?' Heward whispered irritably as they crouched in the bows of the sloop, straining their eyes, looking for enemy vessels on the dark surface of the water.

'Of course I'm scared,' Lawson replied quietly. 'Anybody who isn't has no imagination. We'll be fine once it begins. You'll see all this lot perk up when we get into the cutter.'

He indicated the dark shapes crouching under the gunwales on the narrow foredeck of the sloop. This was the party that would be boarding the barges. The marines were assembled in the afterpart of the vessel. The men were quiet, perhaps brooding or dozing, or maybe praying.

'I've never been in action before,' Heward went on. 'Not the close-up stuff, anyway. I wouldn't mind the guns so much. It's the sword in my guts, or the bayonet up my arse, which bothers me. Result of my home life, I suppose.' He sighed, paused reflectively, then added, 'The gilded acres on the banks of the Severn have been paid for in blood by every generation of Hewards, Navy and Army, since Cromwell's day. Nothing seems to please my father more than to talk about it with a bunch of like-minded, one-time warriors. They get together two or three times a year, an arm missing here and a leg there, sabre cuts galore, and I had to dine with them from the age of nine. The dining room's been swimming in blood from every major battle over the last fifty years and more. Used to scare the wits out of me.'

'Well, you'll soon be able to tell 'em your own battle story.'

'Not bloody likely. If there's one thing I learned from my genteel upbringing, it's to keep my mouth shut about such things, particularly if I'm fortunate enough to have a son of my own.'

A stirring on their left reminded them that they had company in the bows. The Irishman was lying on the deck boards trying to sleep.

'What about you, Mr Maharg?' Heward asked. 'Did your father scare you with stories?'

'Never knew a father,' Maharg grunted and turned over, pulling his coat closer about him.

'Look!' Lawson hissed, pointing ahead.

'Where?' Heward demanded.

'There's a boat under sail, fine on the port bow. I'm going to report to Baratovski.'

The Russian commander nodded an acknowledge-ment to Lawson and took over the wheel from the helmsman. No word was spoken. He looked grimly ahead.

A hundred and fifty yards over the water, unaware of the approaching danger, the seventeen-year-old Ensign O'Toole huddled deeper into his coat collars and shi-vered in the cold night air. He knew little about boats, but the *major d'artillerie* who commanded the small garrison overlooking le Goulet, disliked émigré Irishmen, and someone had to be in charge of the little *tartane* that patrolled le Goulet. Left to themselves, the fishermen, whose boat had been commandeered, would either anchor and go to sleep or sail several miles to the south to tend their lobster pots. Then the impudent Russians, whose sloop had restricted fishing all day, could creep into Brest Roads unobserved, if they were mad enough.

'Move forward. We go about.' the elderly Breton at the helm of the *tartane* ordered rudely.

O'Toole moved clear of the heavy wooden tiller and

ducked his head as the boom of the lateen sail swung around the single mast. It had hit him twice during their constant tacking to and fro in the narrow channel. They had laughed the first time. When it happened again, they were ominously quiet, and the youth knew instinctively that they wanted him out of the way. So he watched the men closely, straining to hear their whispers and keeping a tight grip on the loaded pistol under his topcoat.

It was not that Bretons had anything against the Irish. They just hated everybody in authority, especially foreigners, and they placed all Parisians in that category. It had been a major blunder that had sent the 101st Regiment d'Artillerie, recruited exclusively in Paris, to Brest, O'Toole reflected bitterly. It was almost as stupid as his own involvement with Wolfe Tone and his damned United Irishmen, which had cost him dear.

His mind wandered back to happier times, as it frequently had of late. What was so special about the harvest that he should relive it so often? Probably his participation even as a small child, he mused. Helping to fill the baskets with the bread and cheese and even meat on occasions, to be taken out to the fields in the gig. Then, in his early teens, conscious of his own strength and fully aware of the pride his father took in him, he had worked as long and as hard as any of the hired labour. His eyes filled with tears as he remembered his father's face at their parting: lips trembling, ghastly pale, utterly defeated. Was it only six months ago? God! How they loved each other! But he had been obliged to hurry away, and he would never dare go back, for it would be a hanging matter if he were taken. Treason is rarely forgiven in Ireland, even for boys.

'Whist!' the man at the helm warned.

O'Toole saw the bow wave of the sloop, a splodge of grey on the dark sea. Then he made out the rig against the faint stars. Quickly he reached for the smouldering fuse in the bucket and applied it to the touchpaper of the rocket, already positioned on the transom. It spluttered and went out. It was damp. He blew at the fuse rope until it burned white and the saltpetre threw off sparks. Then he thrust the brightly glowing end into the rocket. It caught and spouted flame just as the bow of the Russian sloop cut into the *tartane*, rolling it over and under its keel. The last thing O'Toole saw before the sea closed over him was the fiery trail of the signal rocket plunging into the dark water to extinction.

On board the *Catherine*, Commander Baratovski relinquished the wheel to the helmsman and barked a sharp order that sent one of his men running forward to disappear down the hatch there. He had been told to inspect the bows for damage after the collision. Otherwise the commander gave no outward sign that he had just deliberately run down a fishing boat and probably made an end of her crew.

'A rare man is this,' Heward said admiringly. 'Do you reckon they would have seen the rocket ashore?'

'We'll know soon enough if they have,' Lawson replied, leaning over the side to bring the wake of the sloop into his vision. 'I hope that neither of our two boats back there runs into the wreckage.'

He could just see the cutter close behind. Mr Saunders would be at the helm with his eyes glued on the dark outline of the sloop's stern. The whaler was invisible from the sloop, but it would certainly be in its ordered position. Although Midshipman Atkins was nominally in charge, the captain's veteran coxswain, Mr Hampson, would be in control.

They were sailing fast over the dark sea, with the fresh breeze on their beam, when the whaler struck the submerged wreckage and almost leapt out of the water. Mr Hampson had a brief vision of part of the wreck as it rolled. There was a uniformed body entangled in the ropes. Then it was gone, and the whaler was lying bows to wind, flooded but still floating. It had been a remarkable piece of boat handling and, miraculously, no one was lost.

'Damn your carelessness,' the badly frightened Midshipman Atkins gasped. 'You could have drowned us all.'

'Get baling,' Hampson ordered.

'Are you presuming to give me orders?' Atkins yelped.

'No, sir. I'm telling the two men 'ere, but if I was you, I'd grab a bucket and help, while I makes shift to keep her bows to the weather. If the sea catches us abeam in our present state, we'll capsize.'

Atkins had enough of his wits about him to realize that his life depended upon the skill and experience of the captain's coxswain. He began to bale while the whaler wallowed in the swell and the dark waters passed within inches of the top of her gunwales.

Baratovski dropped anchor about two miles to the southwest of Brest, as arranged, and Saunders brought the cutter smartly alongside. Only then did they realize that they had lost the whaler, so vital to the operation.

Lieutenant Prendergast, who had the overall command of the task force, stared morosely into the blackness for an age. Everyone waited in silence. He consulted no one. At last he took out his watch and held it close to the light from the binnacle. Then he approached the officers.

'We can delay no longer. The incendiary parties will start. If the whaler turns up, the marines will follow immediately. Failing that, they will await the return of the cutter. In either case, you will lack marine support at the beginning of the operation. Absolute silence is now vital.' He turned to the men. 'Keep your tongues still. Make sure that your equipment doesn't lose its muffles. A musket shot will bring the enemy out of their beds in no time, so make sure that no one hears you getting onto the barges. Into the cutter with you. Good luck.'

Lawson's section scrambled down the net and took up their positions in the bows, whilst Clayton's men occupied the stern. Saunders' group filled the space between. Maharg went aboard last and sat next to the helmsman.

'Mr Maharg, the success of this venture depends upon your directing the cutter on to the barges without raising the alarm,' Prendergast called quietly down to him.

'I shall make shift to do that, never fear,' the Irishman replied cheerfully, 'particularly as 'tis my own neck that'll be lying under the guillotine if I'm caught with this lot.'

Rather an odd thing to say, Lawson reflected as the cutter was being tacked to windward by Saunders. The thought was driven from his head by another, more urgent consideration. Lieutenant Prendergast had forgotten to make alternative arrangements for cutting through the land moorings. It was to have been the marines' task but they would have to await the return of the cutter unless the whaler turned up. If the moorings were not cut, the mass of barges would not drift away from the land. The Frenchmen would board them easily, put out the fires and make an end of the British sailors there. He told the others.

'So what's the best thing to do?' Clayton asked.

'I could go ashore and cut through the moorings,' Lawson suggested, 'but I'll need more men.'

'You shall have two of mine,' Heward said. 'Forster and Bainbridge, you will attach yourselves to Mr Lawson's party.'

The lights of Brest, not many at so late an hour, could be seen to starboard, and a few lamps at the more distant fort were visible on the port bow. Otherwise there was nothing but the black void of the water on all sides. It was perfect for their purpose, so long as Maharg did not get lost.

'There's the first of the barges,' Maharg hissed suddenly. 'Can you see it?'

Saunders steered closer. Now several of the large, squat shapes could be seen slipping by on their port side and there seemed to be no end to them. It was an armada of sailing barges and no one appeared to be on watch. The French were evidently over-confident about the security of their land-locked harbour.

'I can 'ear the land: surf on t'pebbles,' a seaman said urgently.

Saunders put the tiller over, came into the wind and closed with the nearest of the barges. They were solid timber vessels, eight feet out of the water and close together. Many hands fended off and then held on to the barge's side and mooring ropes whilst Lawson's party climbed aboard. Tools and combustibles were passed up from the cutter. Maharg suddenly sprang for the barge as the cutter sailed away.

'I understood that your job was to direct the cutter,' Lawson whispered furiously.

'So I did,' Maharg replied. 'I put you on the barges like I promised. Surely they can find their own way around to t'other side. Come on. Let's get ashore and see to these cables.'

He swung away into the shadows and Lawson started after him, but his men were awaiting their orders.

'Johnson, Parker, Greenly and Webb, come with me. The rest of you will place the combustibles inside a couple of barges.'

'Combustiballs, sir? What's them?' Moody asked.

'The bloody stuff you've just unloaded from the cutter: the bags of oily rags, tarred cloth and lumps of pitch,' Lawson hissed. 'And keep your voice down. You'll arrange these materials so they'll burn well, but don't light them until I return, unless you hear shots ashore.'

'Supposing we 'ave ter set fire to the barges an' you're not 'ere, 'ow do we get orff?' the same voice whispered.

'Use your mother wit, Moody. Just run from barge to barge, away from the fire, cutting any anchor cables you can find. If we get the shore cables loose, and you and the other parties cast off enough anchors, the whole fleet of barges will drift out to the open water.'

'It'll still be on fire. 'Ow do we get orff?' Moody persisted.

'You'll find Mr Heward's party back there. That's where we all have to assemble when the job's done. Mr Saunders will take us off from there in the cutter. You were told all this back on the sloop.'

He snatched his arm away. The man had been gripping his sleeve in his anxiety. He had listened to the briefing but he had been told that a midshipman would be in charge. Now that Lawson was going off, he was scared. He lacked confidence without a leader.

'Take him with you, sir. Me and Bainbridge will do all that's got to be done here.' Forster said confidently.

'Come on, Moody. Join my party,' Lawson said.

He led the way ashore, easily crossing from barge to barge, using the wicker fenders as bridges. He took the heavy sheering tool from Parker, slung it around his neck to leave his hands free and scrambled down the mooring rope, which was as thick as a man's thigh, to reach the beach. There, he looked around him and listened. Everything was still.

'Mr Maharg,' he called softly.

There was no sound save the crunching of seashells and shingle as his men joined him. Maharg had deserted them.

'Right, my lads. We must work fast. I think we're betrayed. Find the moorings along the shore. We have to cast off every one. Where's Johnson?'

'Right beside you, sir.'

'You'll be the advanced listening post. Get along the beach a couple of hundred yards and keep your ears open. Fire one shot at 'em when they come, then retire as quickly as you can to join Forster and Bainbridge on the barges.'

'Suppose they don't come, sir?'

'They will. Depend upon it. Mr Maharg has gone to raise the alarm. However, if I don't hear a musket shot, I shall come for you when the mooring ropes are cut loose. Get off with you.'

He examined the rope they had just climbed down. It was wound around a massive baulk of timber, which had been set at an angle against the drag of the barges, and secured with a rusted iron shackle. They sheered through the shackle and cast the cable loose. It slid a few yards across the shingle and stopped. They moved on to the next, which was secured in the same way, and on to a third. Maharg had estimated that there would be six cables holding the barges on the shore, but they could no longer trust any information that had come from the Irishman.

'Dear God! Just look at that, sir,' Moody wailed, staring wide-eyed over Lawson's shoulder.

Lawson swung around from the link he was cutting and saw the falling sparks of a rocket. The sound of the explosion reached them. Now, a bell began to ring from the direction of the town. Lights were appearing over a large area, nearer than he had expected to find any houses.

'There's another rocket!' Parker exclaimed. 'They're on both sides of us.'

He was pointing to where the fort was situated, overlooking le Goulet. The gunners there were acknowledging that they had seen the signal from the town. It would be a desperate business getting out now, whether they waited for the tide or not, particularly as some of the French warships would very likely be preparing to sail away from their moorings.

As Lawson strained with the shears, he considered what he would do if he were in charge of the whole operation. Would he abandon the shore parties now that the alarm had been raised prematurely? The sloop was vital to *Adamant*'s present role. Prendergast's duty was clear. He had to sail for the open sea without delay. Even as Lawson reached the decision, he realized that Prendergast would not desert them unless he was attacked by a superior force. Apart from opposition from Commander Baratovski, who was obviously a fire-eater, there was also the very real fear of a withdrawal being misinterpreted. It takes a very special brand of courage to act in a manner which might later be described as cowardly. So it seemed likely that *Catherine* would be lost and, as a result, the chances of Brewster's bluff lasting a week would be slim.

A musket shot rang out nearby. That would be Johnson warning them of the enemy's approach. Now there was the racket of small-arms fire that must be from the French, unless the marines had landed.

'How many more cables?' Lawson demanded.

'Only one, sir and that's set well back on the beach.'

'Them there combustiballs on the barges 'ave bin lit,' Moody informed them.

'It'll do no good, because the Frenchies'll be there in a brace o' shakes, and they'll soon be amongst our lads,' Parker said.

'Grab the other end of these shears and save your breath for running,' Lawson snarled.

They ran up the beach with the shears between them, stumbling over the shingle, heedless of the noise they were making. Already the great mass of barges had slewed away from the shore by twenty yards or more at the corner they had freed. If the last cable could be released before the French reached them, the whole lot would go, and they would take some stopping, as the wind had increased over the past half-hour.

'More combustiballs on t'other side o' the barges,' Moody reported.

Lawson grunted in acknowledgement. Clayton's section would have had plenty of time to start their fires. He wondered if Saunders had managed to land the marines. If he had, how was he going to get them all back on board *Catherine*? He would need to make two journeys and there was barely time for one.

'Two of you get your hands on the shears with me. This last shackle's thicker than the others. A good grip now. Altogether, squeeze.'

It cut through. The action was repeated on the other side of the shackle and it fell apart. They seized the freed end of the cable and began to unwind it from the bollard, but it was slipping away itself. Now it was free and snaking away from them down the beach. The mass of barges was moving.

Lawson's elation was short-lived. He heard the crack of a bullet striking bone and the cry of a wounded man. Moody was on his back, kicking in agony or fear.

'We're being fired on. The bleedin' Frogs are down there by the barges where we got ashore. See 'em agen the flames. We'll never get back now,' Greenly cried, verging on panic.

'Shut up and help me with this chap,' Lawson hissed, reaching down to take the wounded Moody under the armpits. 'Heave him over my shoulder. It'll be easier. The rest of you, get up the beach and wait for me in the dunes.'

There was a volley of musket fire, followed by sporadic shots, but none seemed to come near Lawson as he struggled on with his load. He looked back over his shoulder. Fifty or more French soldiers could be seen against the light of the fires. Some were firing at the barges, but a good half of them were being dragooned into taking up the first of the cables that Lawson's men had released. They were lining up as in a tug-of-war. Lawson sank to his knees with Moody drooped over his shoulder, and watched.

The end of the cable was forty yards short of the bollard. They were now straining to close the gap, but the off-shore breeze had the barges, and the irresistible movement of the great fleet was dragging the soldiers, stumbling and cursing, over the loose shale and cobbles down the beach. Two hundred men would not have managed to hold the barges, particularly as they were being shot at. Vicious spouts of flame from muskets inside the barges indicated that someone there had organized those on board.

'Get me to a doctor, sir,' Moody whimpered.

Lawson rose and picked his way over the shingle to the clumps of marram grass beyond.

'Over here, sir,' a voice called.

Lawson carried Moody in the direction indicated and thankfully lowered him to the ground.

'I think the marines are on the barges, sir,' Greenly whispered.

'They must be,' Lawson agreed. 'Mr Clayton and Mr Heward will have their parties searching for anchor cables rather than shooting.'

He pulled open the trousers of the wounded Moody and gently eased the blood-soaked shirt out of the way. The bullet had ploughed through the bottom rib to the right.

'I bet it was our bloody marines what shot 'im, sir, 'coz the Frenchies 'ave not followed us and they would 'ave done if they'd seed us.'

'You may well be right, Greenly,' Lawson grunted as he examined the wound, 'but it won't make him bleed any the less. Get your shirt off and rip it into strips. I'll see you get a new one. As for you, Moody, you can consider yourself lucky, because the bullet's gone right through and out the back. There'll be no need for the surgeon to probe for it. In a couple of weeks' time, you'll have forgotten all about it.'

He made the shirt pieces into wads and fastened them as best as he could over the bloody holes at front and back with Moody's own scarf. Then he took his coat off and covered the trembling man with it. It had been ruined with Moody's blood anyway.

'Stay with him, Greenly, and keep awake. Webb and Parker come with me. If we can't find an untended boat between here and the town, I'll be very surprised. Don't worry about being left behind, Moody. I'll come back for you both.'

As he led the way into the darkness, the words he had used struck him like a blow. He stopped in his tracks.

Don't worry. I'll come back for you both, he repeated in his mind. God! It hurts as much today as it did then. Can it really be ten years ago?

He felt the tears start and rubbed at his eyes irritably, thankful for the darkness, which hid such human frailty from the men he had to command.

'Keep it as quiet as you can,' he cautioned and continued on his way.

Parker and Webb followed, thinking he had halted to listen for the enemy.

Lawson forced himself to concentrate on the task in hand. Childhood memories had always been a weakness. They had to be purged. A picture of his father persisted: slightly built, stooping and studious. He had been a kindly, sensitive man, too unassertive and self-effacing to be successful in the business he had inherited. Unable to cope after the death of his wife, he had gone off to make his fortune in Leeds, leaving Lawson and his sister in the care of their aunt. They never saw him again.

'I'll come back for you both,' Lawson whispered bitterly, then cursed under his breath and walked on.

CHAPTER NINE

The whaler had been taken well to the south of Brest Roads by wind and tide during the struggle to keep her afloat. Then Hampson had to tack her back against a three-knot current in a strange harbour, to try to find a sloop that was showing no lights and maintaining a strict silence on board. It was the rocket from the fort, casting a momentary gleam on the sloop's mainsail, that eventually revealed her position.

'No doubt you'll have a good explanation for your late arrival, Mr Atkins,' the worried Lieutenant Prendergast said sharply as the whaler came alongside.

'Yes, sir. We –'

'Not now, damn it. Get over to the barges and help the cutter to fetch our men off. Find Mr Clayton's party on the west side.'

'We're taking water, sir.'

'Are you sinking?'

'No, sir.'

'Then, what the hell –? Get over there. Those men will be lost if you don't take them off directly.'

As the whaler disappeared in the direction of the fires, Prendergast began to pace the narrow deck of the sloop, watched amusedly by Baratovski. It was his first independent command, and he needed so much to prove to himself that he was a worthy son of an illustrious naval family: one that had produced an unbroken line of senior

87

officers for a hundred and fifty years, except for a brief period of royal disfavour following the Restoration. Blake had been his mother's name, and Robert Blake, her great-grandfather, was generally thought to have been the most successful admiral the Navy had ever known.

Lieutenant Grayson approached him.

'Commander Baratovski would like to take the sloop in closer, sir, with your permission.'

'Thank him for his suggestion,' Prendergast said, his eyes fixed on the distant fires. 'I have considered the possibility. There are several French frigates lying within this waterway. They will now be weighing anchor to come searching for us. If we approach that fire, they'll spot us immediately.'

'She comes – the cutter,' the little Russian officer with the moustaches said, pointing into the blackness.

Saunders brought the cutter around in a circle until she was bows to wind within a yard of the sloop. A rope was thrown and they were secured alongside. Heward's party and fifteen marines were in the boat. They scrambled gratefully onto the deck above, leaving Saunders and his crew of two.

'Where is Mr Heward?' Prendergast demanded looking down into the cutter.

'Didn't come this time, sir. Thought he'd better go and look for Mr Lawson.'

'He'd no business doing so,' Prendergast said exasperatedly. 'If you find him when you go back, tell him he has to return with you. Where do you go next?'

'To the westward side of the barges, sir, to find Mr Clayton's party, and then I shall go to the east to pick up Mr Pocklington and the rest of his marines.'

'I've just sent the whaler to the western side.'

'So we'll go direct for Mr Pocklington if it pleases you, sir.'

'They should be waiting on the southern side of the barges by now. You'll find most of our men there. I'll wait for half an hour, if we're not spotted before then. Should you see gunfire from this direction, make your own way back to *Adamant*. I must look to the safety of the sloop.'

'I understand, sir.'

'Good luck, Mr Saunders.'

The cutter eased away from the side of the sloop and disappeared into the darkness, watched by the score of men who had just left it.

Meanwhile, the whaler, now plugged and bailed almost dry under the direction of the experienced Mr Hampson, had made her long starboard tack to the westward and was now being eased towards the barges with the breeze fine on her port bow. Mr Hampson was keeping outside the bright circle of light cast by the fires. Even so, they were seen by French soldiers on the beach, who shouted and pointed. A few seconds later, a ragged hail of musket balls holed the sail in many places and splintered the timbers along the port side above the waterline.

'Get under cover, you men,' Hampson shouted.

'Hold your course, Mr Hampson!' Atkins ordered, in a voice that was high-pitched and had a hint of panic.

'That I will, sir,' the old coxswain replied patiently. 'And do you keep your head down, Mr Atkins, for they'll not leave us alone now. No sense in us both being exposed.'

Atkins ignored the advice and sat up defiantly in the bows as the whaler drew nearer to the mass of barges, with its numerous bright fires, under a canopy of smoke.

'Ahoy there, *Adamant*,' the unmistakable voice of Midshipman Clayton shouted across the water.

Hampson skilfully brought the whaler alongside the barge and his two crewmen dropped the sail. There appeared to be nine men waiting in the shadows but three of them were prisoners. These were nightwatchmen who had been rounded up at the beginning of the operation. Clayton had taken them from barge to barge away from the fire. Now they had to be released.

'Do you speak French, Mr Atkins?' Clayton demanded.

'There's no time for speaking. The soldiers are firing at us,' Atkins shrilled.

'All right, you Frogs, clear off,' Clayton shouted at the prisoners and waved his arm. 'My party, get down into the whaler. Look alive.'

At that instant, a volley smashed into the group. There was the sickening sound of musket balls striking flesh and bone, followed by the screams of the injured. One of the prisoners had been swept away. Clayton was struck in the leg and shoulder. Two of his section were caught just as they were getting down from the barge. One plunged head first into the sea and was lost. The other landed in the whaler and thrashed about in the bottom gasping and crying and appealing to the Almighty in his agony and fear.

Midshipman Atkins drew back in horror from the wounded man at his feet and looked towards the shore. In the light from the fires, he saw fifty or more soldiers in two lines. The front rank had fired and the second was now aiming.

'Get aboard, you men. Jump for it, for Chris' sake,' he shrieked.

The second volley caught them all exposed. Another man crashed down into the whaler and lay still. One of the whaler's crew was struck in the neck, and his life's blood spurted as from a hose. He fell against Atkins and clung to him, drenching the midshipman's jacket before he could be pushed away.

On the barge above, one of the prisoners snatched the pistols from the wounded Clayton and pointed them over the side. Mr Hampson was the nearest target. Both were fired at him. The old man was hurled backwards to fall across the top of the rudder blade, where he lay, half out of the boat and precariously balanced.

'Push off. Get the sail hoisted,' Atkins screamed.

He stumbled over a body in the bottom of the boat and made for the tiller. The whaler was already moving away from the side of the barge and the sail was rising rapidly, hoisted by a badly frightened man. Starboard helm was needed immediately but Hampson's weight was restricting the movement of the rudder. Atkins heaved at the legs and toppled the body over the transom of the whaler into the sea.

The shock of the cold water revived the captain's veteran coxswain. Raising a hand, he shouted. Then he was gone, but not before he had been seen by the injured man lying in the stern of the whaler and the man heaving at the sail. Clayton and the two remaining men of his section, abandoned on the barge, were also witnesses.

Meanwhile, on the opposite side of the great flotilla of barges, Lieutenant Pocklington, with his rearguard of marines, was being joined by Midshipman Heward and the two men from Lawson's party, Forster and Bainbridge, who had been left on the barges to start the fires.

'Mr Lawson and his landing party have not managed to get back on the barges, sir,' Heward reported.

'Lucky man,' Pocklington said.

'Lucky, sir?'

'At least, he won't have to hold back this lot,' the marine lieutenant said, indicating the bobbing lights approaching from the direction of Brest. 'Must be nigh on twenty boats we can see, and I would wager that there'll be twice that number without a lamp between 'em. Given an average of eight to a boat, I'd say we can expect around – three hundred soldiers over the next fifteen minutes. Oh yes, young Lawson's far better off ashore.'

'Too many for us, sir?'

'Aye. Let's see if we can get out of it.' He turned to his sergeant. 'We'll move to where the cutter is expected to take us off. Don't suppose you've seen the whaler?'

'No, sir.'

The marines began to move quickly but without noise, from barge to barge, away from the landward side, until they could go no further. Then, they looked to the priming of their muskets and waited.

The first of the Frenchmen were boarding. They could be seen clearly silhouetted against the flames. Now, they were being directed by one who was waving a sword and they were moving towards those barges which were burning. Their job would be to cast them off to save the rest. The main body of the French soldiers, now arriving in strength, would be ordered to search for the saboteurs.

'Bloody 'ell! There's 'undreds of 'em,' a marine exclaimed.

'Shut up, Frazer,' a sergeant growled.

Heward had been looking the other way, over the

lightening waters of the great anchorage, and he had seen what he thought might have been the whaler, but he was not sure and, since the vessel had not closed on the barges, he thought he had been mistaken. Forster had also been watching. He whispered to Heward.

'It did look like our whaler, didn't it, sir? Could have sworn it was. That funny high prow that the carpenter put on her last year, after she'd been damaged. Can't be many like her.'

Heward nodded thoughtfully, but said nothing.

The French soldiers were now spreading across the barges. Some had lanterns and swords but most carried muskets and bayonets, which gleamed redly in the light of the fires. These men were working their way over the fenders from one barge to another, pausing with their lamps to search the gaps between and the surface of the water. Obviously they intended that no one should escape from this audacious raid. General Hoche would be furious and a few heads might be expected to roll if the enemy got away unscathed.

A whistle sounded in the distance from the west side of the barges. It seemed that the French soldiers had found something of interest there. Heward wondered briefly if it could possibly be Clayton's party. It seemed unlikely. If Clayton had not been taken off by the cutter, he and his men would surely have joined Lieutenant Pocklington.

The marines had spaced themselves in firing positions along one side of the outermost barge. It would be as good as a trench, since the bulwarks were stout enough to stop a musket ball, and they were just the right height for a standing man, who could duck below cover to reload. Heward, Forster and Bainbridge were on the seaward side of the same barge, anxiously looking over the water. There would be a desperate situation if Saunders did not arrive soon.

'There's the cutter, sir. I'll stake my life on it,' Forster said.

They followed the direction of his pointing arm.

'Have a care,' Bainbridge warned urgently when Heward reached for the covered lantern. 'There's another rig beyond the cutter and there's no light showing from it.

Can you see it, sir? It appears to be on the opposite tack.'

The moon was low on the horizon and obscured, but it was now possible to make out the loom of the land against the luminosity of the cloud and the nebulous glimmer of the sky. The topsail of the taller-masted vessel beyond the cutter was certainly not that of the whaler, so it must be French, Heward reasoned. He lowered the lantern indecisively.

'Fix bayonets,' Lieutenant Pocklington ordered in a low voice on the other side of the barge.

There was the slither of steel leaving scabbards, followed by the metallic clicks as the bayonet rings snapped onto the muzzles of the muskets. It was a blood-chilling sound. Heward's fear of cold steel caused him to shiver involuntarily. He took up the lamp again. Better to take a chance with the cutter, he thought, than be bayoneted to death by French soldiers. He stood up and opened the lantern shutter.

The light was seen by the nearest French soldiers. A great shout went up. Whistles shrilled and the men began to advance.

'Number one section, present arms,' Pocklington ordered calmly. 'Take aim. Fire.'

The racket of muskets across the water gave Saunders all the direction he needed. He brought the cutter out of the darkness, heeling steeply in the stiffening breeze as he approached close-hauled.

'Number two section, present arms, take aim. Fire.'

The sergeant's voice was now giving the commands in a manner as unemotional and unhurried as his officer's. Meanwhile, those who had just fired were reloading and the third section was stepping forward in readiness.

'She's coming too fast,' Heward said tensely. 'She's coming *too bloody fast*! Fend her off!'

Saunders misjudged the distance and rammed the bows. There was a crunch of timbers, vital ones, it seemed. They would certainly not be those of the heavily constructed barge.

'That's buggered it,' Forster groaned.

'Clumsy sod,' Heward said under his breath.

Then he realized what had happened. Someone, a

marine most likely, had cast loose their barge from the others, but only one end had worked itself out from the pack. It would have been invisible with the light of the fire above it. Saunders would not have seen it projecting until the last second.

'Tie her alongside,' Heward shouted to Forster, and jumped aboard with the lantern.

The sea was pouring into the cutter from two splintered planks on the starboard bow. Saunders placed his foot against it and pushed. It closed the gap but more water was getting in than they could possibly pump out.

'Gregory, come here,' Saunders commanded. 'Sit on top of those broken planks and brace yourself with your feet hard on the ribs. You've got to try to keep the sea out.'

'Still plenty of water getting in at the keel,' Heward said gloomily as he looked around with the aid of the lamp, indifferent to the musket balls cracking through the sail above his head.

'How many men in the party?' Saunders asked.

'Twenty-eight, I think when this attack started. Might be a few less now.'

'There'd better be, or we'll sink for sure. Just tell Pocklington that this boat's built to carry twenty, and she's keeping the sea out only by courtesy of Gregory's arse. Let him decide what's to be done. He's in command.'

'Ahoy, *Adamant*. I'm coming alongside,' came a cry from the darkness of the sea.

'Who's that?' someone exclaimed.

'Come in, Lawson. You're just in time,' Saunders shouted.

The vessel that had earlier been seen beyond the cutter and temporarily forgotten in the excitement of the last few minutes, was being eased skilfully closer. Now a rope was thrown and made secure. It was a large, single-masted, open boat which Lawson's landing party had stolen. Even with his own men already on board, including the wounded Moody, there would be room enough for all.

There was no time for explanations. Pocklington's

marines were fighting a rearguard action and ten of them under the command of the sergeant, were already jumping into the cutter, whilst the rest were still firing at the French.

'Get across to the other boat. Look lively now,' Heward shouted.

They scrambled from the sinking cutter into the stolen French boat and took up positions where their field of fire would not be masked by the flapping sail of the cutter they had just left.

'Here come our lads now,' the sergeant shouted. 'Cover the flanks and fire when you see a target.'

He had been warned by a whistle that the rear guard was falling back. Now they were scrambling down from the high side of the barge they had occupied, and jumping into the sinking cutter to the accompaniment of an increasing racket of musketry. The French knew what was happening and they were up from their cover, advancing and shooting.

Saunder's cutter, which was now knee-deep in water, was still tied, bow to stern, to the stolen boat that Lawson had brought. They were both wallowing sideways, wearing very slowly around, not sailing, but increasing the gap between them and the barges, whilst the last of the marines were still transferring.

French soldiers appeared in stark silhouette on the barges to the right. They were immediately shot at by the marines already in position. More emerged to the left, easily visible in their pipe-clayed crossbelts, bunching together as they converged upon the barge that the marines had just abandoned. The British muskets did tremendous execution, but the rest came on with a cheer, heedless of the flying bullets.

Down into the barge they jumped, jostling each other for a firing position, excited and eager to kill. The crowded boats lay beneath them at less than twenty yards, and the retreating raiders were completely exposed, many still scrambling from the sinking cutter to the larger boat beyond. Thirty or more French muskets converged upon them at a shouted word of command. A massacre seemed certain.

'Get under cover!' Lawson roared at the men near him. 'Get your heads –'

The explosion that cut short his words was devastating. The night turned into day in a brilliant sheet of flame as the barge that had held the French soldiers shattered into a thousand splinters. A fused keg of gunpowder, left behind by Lieutenant Pocklington, had blown up.

Lawson saw French soldiers hurled high above the barges, but he was too shocked to comprehend fully what had happened. The cutter was swamped and going down, but the last of the marines and Saunders would get out in time. He saw them cut it loose, and as it lurched off to its final rest, he pulled on the tiller of the stolen boat and turned away, gathering speed rapidly as the following wind filled the sails.

They had been hit by fragments of the barge. The sail was full of holes. Something had struck the top of the starboard bow and taken a great bite out of it. Several men had been injured. Some were sprawled on the boat bottom, quite still. One was crying like a child. Another shouted hysterically that he had a lump of wood through his neck. Both were roughly quietened by those nearby. Silence was essential, if they were to escape.

A wounded man lay across Lawson's feet. One of the marines had him and was propping up his head.

'It's Mr Pocklington, Sergeant,' he called quietly.

The sergeant squeezed his way through the crowded boat, stepping over the bodies and knelt by the officer.

'Caught by my own mine, Sergeant,' Pocklington said in a marvelling, dreamy sort of voice, as if he didn't really believe it. 'It feels as if I've got a few links of the boat's chain hanging out of my guts. It'll be the end of me, I think. Yes, it'll be the –' his voice sank to a whisper – 'the end of me.'

When the marines' mine exploded, the Russian sloop was just being winched up to her anchor, preparatory to moving out. They had left it late. The moon would be high and bright before they could clear le Goulet, and they would be fired upon as they came within range of the heavy guns in the fort.

Lieutenant Prendergast was angry with himself for having listened to Baratovski. He knew he should have acted on his own judgement of the situation and left both the cutter and the whaler to find their own way back to *Adamant*. *Catherine* could now be destroyed because of his stupidity. The liaison officer approached him. He looked embarrassed.

'Commander Baratovski has asked me to inform you that he is of the opinion that the explosion has ended the engagement ashore. He suggests that we move in closer to the bar —'

'Commander Baratovski is getting to be a bloody nuisance,' Prendergast interrupted harshly. 'Can he not understand that the safety of this sloop overrides all other considerations. Tell him that my orders from Captain Brewster allow no latitude for personal heroics. We're getting out NOW.'

Baratovski heard everything, as he was only a few yards away, and he must have understood that he was being reprimanded. His face darkened in anger. Obviously he would have pursued the matter had not Atkins come alongside at that moment in the whaler with seven men on board, four of them wounded. Prendergast leaned over the side and shouted down to the boat.

'You have not brought many off, Mr Atkins. Where are the others?'

'Watch out!' an English voice shrieked. 'They're going to ram us.'

A large ship was bearing down upon them out of the darkness. Baratovski shouted orders, and the Russian seamen sprang into action. The sheets were jerked tight. The helmsman spun the wheel, and the sloop paid off, crowding the whaler sideways against the sea and flooding it. Atkins leapt for the safety of the sloop. Those who were helping to get the wounded on board followed his cowardly example. The small boat rolled over and sank with two wounded men still in it.

The approaching ship was a French third-rate of sixty guns. Her captain had chanced upon *Catherine* and was attempting to run her down, but the magnificent sloop was gathering speed rapidly. Baratovski coolly steered across the Frenchman's bows and put the helm full over as he cleared with only inches to spare. The sloop scraped along the Frenchman's windward side, past the muzzles of thirty-two guns, with the leach of her sail dusting them as she went by. Not a gun fired. The French captain had not had time to inform his gunners of the situation. They did not know what was happening. Since the two vessels were sailing in opposite directions at a combined speed of thirteen knots, they had little time to think about it. Had Baratovski chosen to sail at an angle away from the Frenchman, he would have been exposed to her full broadside, and his sloop would have been battered to pieces in minutes. As it was, he was fired at belatedly by the two heavy guns mounted in the Frenchman's stern but, apart from two holes in *Catherine*'s mainsail, she was none the worse for it.

'Well done, Mr Baratovski!' Prendergast shouted. 'Now we must get clear away.'

If the Russian commander understood, he made no acknowledgement. *Catherine* gained three hundred yards in the time it took the heavier French warship to turn and present her broadside. Only the silhouettes of her sails would be visible to the Frenchmen when they aimed their guns, but those about to receive the shot watched anxiously as the bombardment commenced.

Expanding blooms of flame passed successively from bow to stern of the French ship as her guns fired. Most cannonballs fell harmlessly in the sea, but some found their target.

Two crashes aft announced hits on either side of the sloop's rudder. They would cause damage to the finely carved oak panelling in the great stern compartment where royalty had been entertained in happier days. A more serious injury was caused by a shot that bounced off the sea and ploughed through the starboard shrouds supporting the mast, leaving only one rope to do the work of five.

For the moment the mast was safe enough. The wind was blowing over the port side and there was no strain on the starboard shrouds. But the sloop had to turn around to reach the open sea. The wind would then be putting pressure on the other side of the sails. If the severed shrouds were not replaced before that happened, the remaining one would certainly break under the strain and, without support, the mast must go over the side.

Baratovski set the entire crew to replace the shrouds. Prendergast called upon *Adamant*'s sailors and marines to assist. The narrow decks were alive with activity as the men heaved new cables from the hold, up through the hatch and on to the masthead to be secured by agile top-men high above the water. Others had the lower ends of the same cables, which they were feverishly splicing onto the wooden blocks which would be tensioned at the chains. Meanwhile, the sloop gained rapidly upon the Frenchman, but she was sailing further away from le Goulet, and the moon climbed higher.

'It's getting to be as bright as day,' one of the marines fretted. 'They'll blow us out of the water when we try to get through the Gut.'

'If we get that far. Look yonder,' the man working with him said.

In the direction of Brest, two vessels, which looked as if they might be frigates, were clearly moving. The silhouettes of their sails stood out starkly against the moon-lit clouds. There was already a three-decker between the Russian sloop and the only exit from Brest Roads. Here were two faster ships moving up to close any gaps. *Catherine*'s racing qualities would keep her well ahead of them, but the crew had not finished their work and Baratovski dared not order them to change course until all the shrouds were in place and tensioned.

CHAPTER TEN

The French boat that Lawson had stolen was over-loaded with marines and sailors. It had been damaged by the explosion and was leaking badly. As a result, it was very low in the water when they sailed out to rendezvous with the sloop, but safe enough, Lawson thought, provided they indulged in no fancy manoeuvring, and the wind did not increase. Conse-quently, when they saw and heard the French ship attack *Catherine* half a mile ahead of them, Lawson changed course for le Goulet without consulting anyone.

Since Lieutenant Pocklington was lying unconscious in the bottom of the boat, there was no one of higher rank than the three midshipmen. Of these, Lawson was the senior by two months. It was doubtful that he would be held directly responsible by the naval hierarchy should anything go wrong, but if something catastrophic did happen on the way back to *Adamant*, and a scapegoat had to be found, then he was likely to be that person. Having considered these points carefully, Lawson gripped the tiller with a new determination and steered for the northern side of le Goulet.

It was darker close in shore where the water lay in the shadow of the rocks. The rest of the channel shone like silver. If they kept near to the land which rose steeply from the beach to a false crest, they would be closer to the guns but hidden from the gunners.

It would be important to drop the sail and the mast. There were four pairs of oars, Lawson had noted. He hesitated before giving the direct order that would make it obvious to everyone in the boat that he had assumed command: an order which might be challenged and even ignored by the other midshipmen.

'Get the oars out. Quietly now. Two men to an oar. The rest of you, give them room to work. We're going to drop the sail directly.'

Heward, who had been sitting well forward, picked his way through the crowded boat and joined Lawson on the stern seat, having ousted the marine who had been sitting there.

'What have you got in mind?' he demanded peevishly.

'Keeping out of sight,' Lawson replied. 'It's unlikely that there will be any soldiers close by the water as they all have their jobs to do up in the gun positions, which are two to three hundred yards back. The tide should take us quietly through the Gut, with maybe a touch of the oars now and then. If we all keep silent, we'll not be noticed.'

'Let's hope you're right,' Heward grumbled. 'Would rather have gone over to the far side of the channel myself. It's lighter but they need to be damned good to hit us at a mile.'

Those few words indicated that Heward had accepted his authority, Lawson realized. To discuss the matter further would weaken his tenuous leadership and possibly encourage opinions from the listening senior marine sergeant, so Lawson said nothing and held his course for the shoulder of land marking the entrance to the channel.

'Is Parker there amidships?' Lawson asked quietly as they drew close to the land.

'Aye, sir, here I am,' Parker whispered.

'You know the rig of this boat, since you set up the mast and hoisted the sail when we borrowed it. I want you and Webb to lower the sail, unstep the mast and stow it as we found it. Don't let's have any clatter.'

The luff of the sail was attached to the mast by quoit-like rings made of iron. Parker sensibly gathered the canvas from ring to ring, hand over hand, a yard at a time, whilst Webb controlled the speed of the descent by means of the halyard. It was accomplished almost without noise and the boat's way through the water dwindled to nothing. Their passage now to the open sea would be at the speed of the tide and it would take them at least three hours, Lawson had calculated, unless they took to rowing.

'Not a sound: not a movement, if you value your lives,' Saunders' voice cautioned in the darkness forward.

Lawson smiled his relief. Saunders had always been that bit closer to him than Heward, since they had similar backgrounds and no exalted relatives. It would have saddened him to have lost Saunders' friendship through his assumption of command, whereas he would have been ready to defend his rights vigorously against a son of the wealthy and influential Heward family.

The tide was moving fast, they discovered, as they drew nearer to the shore. They could line up the silvery semaphore tower against the dark rocks close at hand and watch it advancing. They were under the lee of the rocks themselves and could see the dull grey foam around the jagged, clutching projections of land and hear the rolling of the tide.

So it went on for an hour with the men sitting quietly and no one moving, except to give a few pulls on the oars to avoid obstructions. There was no challenge from the land. Moody had been delirious and noisy at one stage, so they poured rum into him from the keg which had been rescued from the cutter. That had quietened him. Now, it seemed likely that they would get completely clear without trouble, and Lawson's first independent command might be considered worthy of a commendation in the captain's report. He began to feel quite cheerful.

'Gunfire!' Heward said, breaking into Lawson's reflections. 'Back there, Shouldn't wonder if it is the sloop running into trouble again.'

As they watched, the dull boom of the shot came to their ears. Two more flashes were followed nine seconds later by the sounds of the explosions. It was from a ship action.

'About two miles away, according to my reckoning,'

Heward said. 'I wonder if those manning the guns ashore can make out which is friend and which is foe? They'll know their own, I suppose.'

'And they'll see clear across to the other side of the channel in this light,' Lawson said. 'Wouldn't care to be on board the sloop when they get in range of the fort.'

'If they get that far. More'n likely, whatever is engaging them out there will sink them. Look at that!'

A large warship was delivering its broadside: less than a second between each gun, and the continuous flashes were hitting the clouds and casting angry red splotches over the silver sheen of the sea. Now another ship was firing in close proximity to the first. The thunder of their combined bombardment rolled across the water. It was certainly not the sloop replying.

'It looks as if the whole French Navy is out there trying to sink our Russian friend,' Heward commented.

'I think the big ships is firing at each other, sir, begging yer pardon,' the marine sergeant volunteered.

'Firing at each other!' Heward exclaimed incredulously.

'Looks that way ter me, sir, and I've bin in a few ship battles in my time. Right now, I'm seeing the flashes from one of the ships whose guns are shooting this way. I can see the spout of the flame: the white 'eart of it. On the other, you don't see the spout. All you've got is the bloom above the hull of the ship, so it's firing away from us.' He stood up in the boat and strained his eyes. 'Must be three or four ships out there, sir. I can just make out their rigs against the sky. Yes, one of the others is firing now.'

It was now obvious to all that there were at least three ships engaged and all moving faster than the tide towards the west and the open sea. Soon they would be in line with the guns of the small fort; and one of the ships must be *Adamant*. There could be no other explanation. It was not part of the original plan that Captain Brewster should go to the rescue of the sloop, but plans are made with cool, clear heads and have nothing to do with emotions. The explosion on the barge and the earlier gunfire would have been seen and heard well beyond Brest Roads. It rather looked as if Brewster had found the waiting intolerable and had gone into the channel to see for himself.

Suddenly the guns of the fort opened fire, startling everyone in the boat by their close proximity. Lethal iron was hurtling past above their heads making a whirra-whirra-whirra sound, but they would be perfectly safe as long as they kept close in shore or until the dunes petered out.

'Evidently they know which is friend from foe,' Lawson said, 'but they're shooting from an elevated position, and they'll have telescopes in use. Even so, they're taking a chance at this range unless – you can't see the sloop out in front of the pack, can you, Sergeant?'

'Yes, I can, sir. She's hugging the far shore,' the marine answered after a moment's hesitation.

The false crest, which had concealed the fort from Lawson's party in the boat, was now falling away and they could see the building, black against the bright moonlight. It seemed certain that someone up there would soon report the presence of a small boat drifting slowly past. All were anxious, but no shot was fired at them. Evidently, every man with a telescope was closely observing the distant sloop and the sea around it, watching for the fall of the shot, the white plume of water, which would help them correct the range.

'I wonder if we could do anything to help at this stage,' Lawson whispered.

'I was thinking the same thing myself,' Heward replied. 'There's a fold in the land, which is probably a stream bed or maybe a worn cart track. We could reach the fort unseen by way of it, then use our nonexistent explosives to blow it up. Alternatively, we could try the Jericho trick, if we had a trumpet. They wouldn't be able to sight their guns very well if we made the walls fall down about them.'

'There's a building close by,' Lawson persisted.

'So?'

'What's that next to the building? Can you see it? It's rounded at the top. I think it could be a haystack. I've half a mind to go and look.'

'You're mad!' Heward breathed, but his eyes were

thoughtful. 'It wouldn't need more than the two of us,' he added after a pause.

'Oars!' Lawson called quietly. 'Forward pair only and keep it quiet.'

As the boat gained on the tide, Lawson steered for the shallows to the accompaniment of whispers and grumbles throughout the length of the boat.

'Keep your tongues still,' Saunders commanded those around him, and made his way aft. 'What's going on?'

'Heward and I are going to see if we can distract the soldiers,' Lawson told him. 'I want you to stay with the boat and let the tide take you through the channel. There's a beach just before the headland. We'll join you there. Probably be there before you.'

The boat grounded. Lawson swung his leg over the side. Heward did the same and they stood thigh-deep in water, holding the boat steady. Midshipman Saunders looked far from pleased at being left behind but he said nothing.

'Parker, you didn't use your combustibles,' Lawson said.

'No, sir.'

'Bring them along.'

'I turned my ankle back there on the beach, sir.'

'I'll take them, sir,' the marine sergeant volunteered. 'And – with respect, sir – do you think it might be as well to have the support of a section of my men, in case we get into trouble?'

'No. We'll need to run like hell once we've started the fire going. The fewer the better, I think. Leave your musket in the boat.'

Lawson, Heward and the sergeant struggled to push the boat off but it wouldn't budge. The tide was falling fast and they were firmly aground. Some of the men had to get out to lighten the boat and then scramble back as it floated into deeper water. The three men watched them moving away with the touch of an oar, back into the tidal stream, then turned and waded to dry land.

Adamant had joined battle with two French frigates. They had both been in pursuit of *Catherine* until *Adamant*

105

intervened. Now, one of them was badly damaged. Captain Brewster had cleverly outmanoeuvred its commander, and *Adamant*'s last broadside had sent it reeling off with ruined steering and shattered walls. Had there been time, they would have boarded her and taken her as a prize, but the other frigate had not given up. It was coming in for a second attack and, since her forty guns would not be a match for *Adamant*'s fifty, it seemed likely that the French captain was gallantly risking his frigate in what could only be a desperate endeavour to disable an audacious British fourth-rate.

He would shoot at *Adamant*'s masts and spars with his guns at high elevation. They would be loaded with chain shot, or dumbbell-shaped bar shot, projectiles designed to cut away part of the intricate maze of ropes that control the sails. He had to make *Adamant* unmanageable for the short time it would take the heavier French third-rates to join in the battle.

Two great belches of flame erupted and blossomed above *Adamant*'s stern, illuminating briefly the captain and the others on the quarterdeck. At the same time, the planks under their feet bucked, as if struck from below with a giant hammer. This was the effect of the sting in *Adamant*'s tail, as Madame Hanikof had so aptly described the twin guns in the captain's quarters. They had fired together. The two thirty-two pounders, which poked out of the stern on the deck below them, immediately followed. All four shots struck the frigate but still it came on, with the stiffening northerly breeze laying her over, and her decks at an angle.

There was a single long gun in the bow of the French frigate. It was the only gun that they could bring to bear upon *Adamant* whilst they were sailing directly astern. It fired. A neat hole appeared in the mizzen topsail. It had missed the mizzenmast by inches. Now the thunderous flapping of uncontrolled canvas warned them that the cannonball had gone on to cut through vital ropes tensioning several sails further forward. There was nothing for the officers to do. The top-men were already up there and they would sort it out. Meanwhile, *Adamant* was losing speed.

The frigate now began to gain on her rapidly, and it was evident that her course had been changed. The French captain intended to take his vessel to leeward. There, the tilt of the frigate's decks would give maximum elevation to her guns, enabling them to hurl their disabling projectiles into *Adamant*'s upper rigging where most of the ship's vital ropes converged.

Adamant's gunners sweated to reload. They knew that if they were disabled, they would be overtaken by the heavier French ships before they could repair the damage. Their captain, outwardly calm, watched the advance of the enemy whilst his mind registered the familiar sequence of gunnery sounds below decks: sponge-out, cartridge, ramrods, shot, ramrods, and finally the squeal of blocks and tackles and carriage wheels as the guns were heaved into their firing positions. It was a race. If they lost, the best that they could look for would be years of captivity.

The British guns roared again, two twenty-four-pounders and then two thirty-two-pounders on the deck below them. Bursting timbers, or metal, around the frigate's bow caught the moonlight as they flew. Then it was seen that the long gun that had just fired at *Adamant* was dismounted, with its barrel askew and pointing at the sky.

'Those shots will have cleared a few men off the deck of the frigate,' Trevelyan said.

'There's nae doobt that they've done a deal o' damage, and if I'm not mistaken, I –' Atherton paused, straining to see over the water – 'yes, I think we've maybe cut through her steering ropes. See how she yaws. 'Tis either her steering gear or the helmsmen that ha' been swept away.'

The frigate was no longer on course. She was briefly out of control, and the stiff breeze was in her sails, driving her around to starboard. A sensible captain would have fallen back and tried again for *Adamant*'s leeward side when he was sure of his steerage. Brewster expected that, but the frigate surged forward on her new course and began to overtake *Adamant* to windward.

'The man's a fool,' Brewster said.

The Frenchman approached rapidly, bowing her masts towards *Adamant*. Her guns, which would have been reloaded with projectiles designed for firing into the rigging, were tilted downwards with the heeling deck upon which they stood. The French gunners would not be able to elevate them enough to shoot above *Adamant*'s side.

Now it was the turn of *Adamant*'s starboard guns, the aftermost ones first, followed by one after the other, working their way forward. It was a monstrous succession of deafening roars and hellish flame, which would shrivel the hair and blacken the skin of the men who worked the guns if they got too close to the gun-ports.

It was over in less than half a minute, and *Adamant* became relatively quiet as her gun crews sponged out and began to reload. There would be no target for them by the time they had finished. The French frigate was crossing the wind, going about onto a port tack to escape into the friendly darkness. Her port side was shattered, and a good third of her men would be either dead or wounded.

Less than a dozen of the frigate's guns had fired at *Adamant* and most of these had been loaded with bar shot, much of which had not penetrated and was lodged in the stout timber. Even so, it would have caused splinters to fly inside the ship and some men on the gun-decks would have been hit.

'I'll have reports of casualties and damage from all departments as soon as convenient, Mr Trevelyan,' Brewster said.

As Trevelyan turned away to do the captain's bidding, Mr Atherton pointed across the water. There was a fire on the north shore of le Goulet, very close to the fort.

'Belay that order, Mr Trevelyan,' Brewster called after him. There's a fire ashore. It might be a furnace. If so, they'll likely be heating some of their round shot for us. Please have the carpenter send his mates around the ship to make sure there's plenty of water to hand.'

'Looks too big for a furnace,' Atherton objected when Trevelyan had gone.

'Maybe you're right. I wonder if you will be kind

enough to go below and see if the ladies are comfortable? Tell 'em we've nothing to worry about, apart from a shot or two as we pass the fort. Mind you, if the man in command there has no more experience than the captain of yonder frigate, they'll be wasting their powder. You'd have thought he'd have had more sense than come up as he did.' Brewster shook his head at the wonder of it. 'The French did themselves a grave disservice when they cut off the heads of all their aristocracy and landed gentry, for they destroyed the class which provided their experienced naval commanders.'

'I find it very interesting tae hear that ye've become a supporter o' the nobility,' Atherton chided.

'You know I haven't. Anyway, it wouldn't be the same in the British Navy if they followed the French example, would it? We've plenty of captains who came from lowly stock, and it was always so. Look at old Benbow. Then there was Drake, Hawke – Blake, to mention a few. Why, I do believe that Admiral Duncan, whose command we're supposed to be joining at Yarmouth, was the son of a Dundee tailor.'

'Nay, he was a crofter,' Atherton objected scornfully.

'And you're an argumentative old bugger,' Brewster said, patting him affectionately on the shoulder. 'Go and see to Madame Hanikof.'

It was now obvious that the fire ashore was not that of a furnace. The flames could be seen above and to one side of the long, low building that must be a fort. Captain Brewster raised his telescope. Certainly there was a house on fire and what appeared to be two or more haystacks. Between them, they illuminated the fort clearly, providing a good target for *Adamant*'s gunners.

'Pass the word for Mr Muir,' Brewster ordered.

Mr Muir was the gunner, a senior warrant officer from Edinburgh with responsibility for all the armament and the two magazines on *Adamant*. He was a strict disciplinarian who ruled his empire with a rod of iron. In this, he was assisted by Davies, an equally dour Welshman, and a bad-tempered Dublin man called Blackshaw. They were known as the unholy trinity on the gun-decks, but Muir was deeply religious and he carried a copy of the Old

Testament at all times in the right pocket of his jacket. Woe betide anyone who swore in his presence. Such a man would be given all the loathsome tasks connected with his department. Depending upon the frequency of the offence, he might be deprived of his hammock for a week or have his grog stopped. Such miscreants were sometimes compelled to attend Bible readings on Sunday afternoons when the rest of the men were taking their ease.

'Ye wished tae speak tae me, sir?'

Brewster lowered his telescope and turned to the man who had appeared from the shadows: a tall, thin person with a severe face, who was carrying a ranging triangle under his arm.

'Aye, Mr Muir. Let me have your damage report.'

'One twelve-pounder oot of action, sir: starboard three on the upper deck wi' a split trunion. I'll ha' it replaced as soon as convenient. Mair serious is a thirrty-two-pounder, starboard seven, which is cracked in the bore, and I've had it closed doon. That's the third from Dawes' Foundry, sir. I dinna trust Dawes' workmanship.'

'What about casualties?'

'Three dead and seven wounded, sir.'

'Not bad. Not bad at all, Mr Muir, and the rate of fire was excellent. Can you range on the fort yonder?'

'I've estimated the range, sir. As far as I can judge, we shouldna' have any difficulties wi' the heavy guns on a ten-degree elevation as we draw level.'

'Thank you, Mr Muir. Shoot when you consider it proper.'

He dismissed the gunner and took stock of the situation. *Adamant* was fairly in the channel and the sloop was well ahead and under orders to get clear: orders that had been ill received by the Russian commander. It seemed that the operation was to be an unqualified success, particularly as they had a distinct visibility advantage over the gunners in the fort.

Lawson, Heward and the marine sergeant were hiding behind a stone wall when the first shot from Muir's starboard battery was fired at the fort. It fell short on the shore not a hundred and fifty yards away, hurling lethal shingle high into the air. A second struck, and yet a third, all close by, but they had more pressing worries. There were French soldiers between them and the sea, searching for the fire raisers. Another detachment, spread well out, was coming from the direction of the fort. The British men had been seen, and it was obvious from the movements of the soldiers, now clearly revealed in the bright moonlight, that their approximate position was known.

The guns of the fort were shooting at *Adamant*. The projectiles, which had been taken from a furnace and were glowing with the heat, could be seen passing overhead. They were calculated to bury themselves in a ship's timbers to ignite the pitch, resin and paint which liberally covered them. The fort's rate of fire was of necessity slower. Hot shot had to be carried on cradles and coaxed into the muzzles of the guns to roll down the bore onto the thick, wet wads of felt which had been rammed in after the gunpowder to prevent a premature explosion. *Adamant*'s cold shot was pushed in by hand and rammed home, so each gun fired three shots to the Frenchmen's one.

A few had struck the fort, though what damage was done could not be seen by Lawson's group. Anyway, they were more concerned with their own dangerous situation. Not only were the soldiers on the seaward side getting very close, some of the cannonballs from *Adamant*'s guns were falling short and crashing about them.

'There's a man climbing over the wall not twenty yards away,' Heward whispered. 'If he looks this way he'll see us.'

'Don't move. We're in the shadow. There's a soldier on the other side too. He's sitting astride the wall and looking around him.'

At that moment, one of *Adamant*'s cannonballs whistled by, too close for comfort. Half a second later, another one arrived and smashed into the wall, hurling slabs of stone in all directions. The two soldiers ran for cover.

Where Lawson was kneeling there was a sheep hole,

fashioned with a heavy stone lintel above it. It was blocked by a flat slate. He slid the slate away and looked through. The moon was on the other side of the wall. By its light, he could see six soldiers carrying muskets held at the port, advancing towards them at less than thirty paces, picking their way over the large stones that covered the field. Even if they were to double away in both directions along the wall, keeping their heads down, they would still not get clear of the line of approach before the soldiers reached them. Lawson gripped his pistol, then left it in favour of his dirk. The sound of a shot would seal their fates. They had to deal quietly with the soldier who was most likely to cross the wall at the point where they were hiding.

The shriek of a shot over their heads and the sound of another striking the ground before them, announced a change in the situation. Through the sheep hole, Lawson saw the man he had taken to be the leader, either a sergeant or an officer, since he was carrying a sword instead of a musket, fall to the ground. The others, now freed from the authority that had made them set duty above personal safety, picked up his body and ran with it down to the shelter of the sunken cart track that Heward had seen from the sea. There was now a gap in the encircling net and, if they were cautious, they could escape.

Heward and the sergeant followed Lawson through the sheep hole and across the field, keeping low, but moving as fast as they could away from the fort and the burning farmhouse. Some of *Adamant*'s shot were still falling short and landing about them. Red-hot cannonballs continued to fly overhead, but the three were now increasing the distance between themselves and the bayonets of the soldiers, and their spirits rose.

Within the hour, they had rejoined their men in the boat and were sailing clear of le Goulet. Come the dawn and they would be picked up either by the sloop or by *Adamant*, for Captain Brewster would already have steered her past the narrowest part and he should make the open sea without difficulty.

CHAPTER ELEVEN

H MS *Adamant* and the Russian sloop cruised back and forth across the entrance of le Goulet for the first few hours of daylight, impudently inviting the French men-of-war to come out and fight. It was a deliberate act of bravado, designed to show the enemy that they were confident of support from the invisible fleet over the horizon. None took up the challenge, to Brewster's great satisfaction. He had obviously convinced them that the Navy was close by, and that had been the object of the exercise.

At ten o'clock he had a signal sent ordering *Catherine* to close with *Adamant* so that Lieutenant Prendergast and the others could rejoin their own ship.

Repairs were going forward at a great rate on *Adamant*'s decks and rigging, and some of the sick and wounded had been brought out from the orlop deck to the bright sunshine. The more serious cases would stay below until they were healed sufficiently to be moved or, if they were not to improve, until the sailmaker's mates stitched them into their hammocks for dispatch to the sea. Already, there were thirteen bodies laid out under a sheet of canvas on the foredeck, waiting for a sunset burial. Only eight of them had been killed by the French.

Adams had succumbed to his family weakness during the night, having coughed his germs of consumption around the carpenter's workshop for two weeks. Alongside his body, was that of his brother-in-law. The unfortunate Morgan was the victim of gaol fever, a virulent form of typhus, which had caused the deaths of four men over the last two days. *Adamant* was paying for her recruitment from the Liverpool bridewell, and neither the sulphur fumigation of the bilges nor the gallons of vinegar sprinkled on her decks seemed to be holding the sickness in check.

'A signal from the sloop, sir,' Trevelyan said, handing over a message pad. 'Mr Prendergast wishes to know if the special people are to be brought back to *Adamant*.'

'Who are the special people?'

'The first group we sent aboard, sir, the – er – likely leaders.'

'Ah yes! The mutiny problem. I'd forgotten about it. Let 'em come. God knows we need men to do work here, and maybe they'll be so cock-a-hoop over their recent successes that we'll hear no more of mutiny.'

'There's also a request from Commander Baratovski for an interview with you, sir.'

'Granted. You might ask them if they are in need of any supplies: powder, shot or whatever.'

Brewster walked over to the centre of the quarterdeck where Madame Hanikof and her two daughters were reclining in deck chairs.

'It is a lovely morning, Captain,' Madame Hanikof smiled as he joined them.

'We'll have your cabin back in order before the afternoon watch, ma'am. Then you'll be able to make up for the sleep you lost.'

'And what about *your* sleep, Captain?' she asked with raised eyebrows. 'Sit down next to me.'

She patted the vacant chair commandingly and Brewster sat on it. Victoria gave him a welcoming smile. Annette had her eyes closed. They all looked tired.

'I'm sorry that you had to suffer so much discomfort last night, ma'am.'

'The noise was *effroyable* – terrible. But now we can tell our friends in St Petersburg of our –' she looked towards Victoria – '*passer par des temps difficiles?*'

'Difficult times, *maman*,' Victoria translated.

'*Oui*, difficult times. I would not have missed it.'

'I hope that you will not have to go through it again. I think the French will stay in Brest for a few days, but they will come out when they realize that there is no fleet. Maybe, at this moment they are questioning any prisoners they might have taken.'

'Did they take prisoners?'

'I don't know yet. I'll have a report shortly. I'm no great shakes at languages, ma'am, but I noticed that you spoke to Miss Victoria in a language that sounded uncommonly like French.'

'French is the language of society in St Petersburg, Captain,' she laughed. 'We make a rule to speak it every morning. If we did not keep it up, we should be – be. What is the word?'

'*Sprachlos?*' Victoria suggested.

'*Niet!* Dumb – not able to speak. In Russia, the language of the Court is not that of the common folk. Strange, yes?'

'Why, as to that I heard tell that the King of England is more content to speak German,' Brewster grinned. 'We have a French officer held prisoner. I am going to offer him parole. You can exercise your French on him, if you wish.'

'That is very kind.'

'He was the mate on the ship that was set on fire, but he seems to have more about him than a common sailor. It might be interesting to learn something of his past.'

He smiled and stood up. Madame Hanikof rose also. Brewster bowed uncertainly, and he was about to depart, but she placed a hand on his arm. 'We shall walk together this morning,' she said.

Embarrassed, but not knowing quite how he could refuse her without offence, Brewster allowed himself to be led to the windward side of the quarterdeck. He always took a morning walk up and down for an hour, but usually it was a brooding time when he was silent and unapproachable, considering the problems and worries of his command. Now, they were walking together and talking. There were a few nudges and winks when they were first seen. Then the men went about the work of the

115

ship as normal. Brewster broke off only when Prendergast arrived with his report. He had never enjoyed his
exercise hour so much. Madame Hanikof had been
perfect company.

The carpenters were tensioning the walls of the
captain's cabin with the wooden wedges when Brewster
and Prendergast entered.

'Hurry up with that,' Brewster ordered and sat at his
desk.

Prendergast handed him a written report and stood by
waiting, but the captain indicated that he should take a
chair, one of several being brought in by the servants who
were setting the cabin to rights. The chairs and all the
furniture had been stowed below for safety during the
recent action, as had the recently stretched canvas on the
deck boards, which now concealed the scrubbed patches
of wood which had absorbed the bloodstains of two
gunners who had been wounded there. Brewster concen-
trated on the report whilst men passed to and fro
carrying out their tasks, and the carpenters hammered at
the wedges.

'So that was how the fire started! Our own midshipmen, be damned! You say it was young Lawson in
charge?'

'I'm sorry, sir, I didn't catch that,' Prendergast said,
leaning forward.

'Stop that hammering and come back later,' Brewster
ordered.

The carpenters gathered their tools and went out. The
captain indicated the paper.

'This initiative of the midshipmen, lighting a fire
ashore, will make very good reading at Admiralty. I shall
include it in my report. Gave us a well-lit target to shoot
at. In fact, Mr Prendergast, I am delighted with the part
played by all of you and you can be sure that they will
know about it in London.'

'Thank you, sir. Here is the casualty list. I'm afraid
that Mr Pocklington died of his wounds just as I was
about to leave the sloop.'

Brewster frowned as he took the paper. 'A promising
young man; better than most marines we've had lately.'

He sighed and scanned the list. 'Clayton's missing! Pity. He'd have made a good officer one day. Good God! Hampson!'

He rose to his feet, obviously shocked, and turned to the stern window. Prendergast waited. After an interval, Brewster drew a handkerchief from his pocket and blew his nose noisily.

'When I joined the Navy as a boy of thirteen, Mr Prendergast,' Brewster said, keeping his back to the lieutenant, 'Hampson was a young able-bodied seaman as lively as a cricket. He looked out for me; taught me how to stand on my own feet. I came across him again all of twenty years ago, and he's been with me ever since. I could have got him a shore berth at Greenwich, but he wanted to stay with me.' He shook his head sorrowfully. 'Send this Russian commander in.'

Prendergast left the cabin. Brewster blinked the tears from his eyes, mopped at them and turned back to his desk. He was fully recovered when Baratovski and the liaison officer entered holding their hats under their arms.

They bowed their heads. Having noted that Baratovski was in an emotional state, Brewster responded with the briefest of nods. Here was trouble, he realized.

'Commander Baratovski has a grievance, sir, which he thinks proper to bring to your notice before proceeding further,' Lieutenant Grayson reported woodenly.

'Get on with it,' Brewster said impatiently with a glance at the Russian.

'He feels that he has been insulted by Lieutenant Prendergast and he demands an apology on board the sloop in the presence of those who overheard the words spoken. If no apology is given, he – er – he intends to call Lieutenant Prendergast out, sir.'

'A duel! There'll be no duelling amongst officers under my command, damn it. Give me the details.'

Grayson recounted the events and words spoken at the time of their weighing anchor when Baratovski had suggested going closer to the action. Brewster listened in silence.

'And that's what all this fuss is about, is it?'

'That is the sum of the complaint, sir.'

'Sit down, both of you,' Brewster ordered.

Lieutenant Grayson looked astonished, but he conveyed the order to Baratovski and each took a chair. Lawson leaned forward and fixed his eyes on the Russian officer's as he spoke.

'Translate word for word what I have to say, Mr Grayson. I wish you also to write it down since it would be improper to have my clerk do it under the circumstances.'

He took a sheet of paper from a drawer in his desk and a bottle of ink which he shook vigorously before setting it down. Then he produced three pens, selected one and passed it over. Grayson drew his chair closer and prepared to write.

'Statement made by Captain Brewster on board HMS *Adamant*, six miles due south of Ushant on April the twenty-first, 1797,' Brewster began.

Grayson wrote rapidly. Brewster opened Prendergast's report and scanned the last page before turning to face the Russian officer.

'Commander Baratovski, your report is substantially the same as that given to me by Lieutenant Prendergast, but he has added a few words which should be of interest to you, as I will send the whole statement to the Admiralty and, no doubt, a copy will be dispatched to Admiral Hanikof.'

Grayson translated. Brewster thrust his finger at the page and began to read.

'*I should like to express my deep appreciation of Commander Baratovski's work throughout this operation. He is a brave and extremely competent officer. Had it not been for his superb ship handling, we should have lost the sloop and the whole of our company.*'

Brewster looked up and watched Baratovski's face as Grayson translated. The man was obviously embarrassed.

'Do you want me to add to that report, Commander?'

The liaison officer put the question to him. Baratovski blinked. His eyes were glistening.

'Thank you, no, Captain,' he said, then spoke rapidly in Russian to Grayson.

'He wishes to thank Lieutenant Prendergast, but he

feels that the restrictions placed upon him did not permit him to use the sloop to its best advantage.'

'Right! Tell him this: Lieutenant Prendergast was obeying my orders to the letter. I should have been angry if he had exceeded them. It was done as if I had been present. Rough words are occasionally spoken in action. It is likely that I should have called him something stronger than a "bloody nuisance" if he had pestered me in similar circumstances. There now, explain that to him. Wrap it up in genteel language if you've a mind to. Then ask him if he is satisfied, or if he wants me to record his complaint in the ship's log.'

Grayson translated and Baratovski replied. There followed an exchange in Russian, charged with emotion, whilst Brewster studied the casualty list, apparently taking no notice.

'Commander Baratovski is quite satisfied, sir, and he does not want you to record his complaint or this interview in the log. He wishes you to understand that he is an officer without influence in the Russian Navy and his only hope of advancement lies in his ability to demonstrate his seamanship and his – er – courage, sir. He therefore would welcome any opportunity which could be placed in his way to prove his mettle.'

'As to that,' Brewster said with a glance of approval at Baratovski, 'the Russian Navy is no different from ours. I'll see what I can do. Meanwhile, you can tell him that he is free to cruise as close in to shore as he chooses, provided he keeps *out* –' he emphasized the word with a raised finger – 'of le Goulet and sends a signal to *Adamant* every morning without fail.'

Brewster rose from his desk, took the paper that Grayson had written and screwed it up. He then shook hands with the Russian. The interview was at an end.

The afternoon was spent transferring stores to the sloop. This included powder and shot, as she had been inadequately supplied in the first place. Mr Muir, the gunner, with a face longer than usual, had a party of marines and seamen scrubbing the rust off the six-pounder shot, which had been stored deep in the hold for months. There was an air of discontent among the seamen, he had noticed, and he was listening intently for any remarks that would give him an opportunity to single out a man for punishment as a warning to the others.

Parker was among them, having been returned to *Adamant* for attention to his sprained ankle. He was in the middle of the surlier men and it was obvious from the covert glances of some of them whenever the master gunner appeared that the low-voiced discussion centred there was anti-authority.

'Put mair effort into it, Parker. 'Tis your ankle not your elbow that's supposed tae be injured,' Muir snapped angrily.

'One of these days I'll bounce a six-pounder shot on his bald head, the Scotch bastard,' Parker muttered when Muir had gone.

'Are you sure that old Hampson was alive when Atkins pushed him off the stern of the whaler?' one man asked.

'Of course I'm bloody sure. Jepson saw it happen. Says he heard him shout and try to swim after the boat,' Parker hissed viciously. 'It was murder.'

'Then the captain ought to know,' the man said flatly. 'He'd fix Atkins for sure.'

'Aye, maybe he would, seeing as how it was Hampson, but it could happen to any of us and nothing would be done.'

'Nay, I'm not having that. He thinks about us all, does Captain Brewster. Never were a better captain in my sperience – and I've served under a few,' a broad Yorkshire voice said.

Parker dismissed him with a scornful jerk of his hand.

'They treat us like animals, man; worse, in fact. Those ten sheep penned on the foredeck have more room than we have for sleeping, and they feed well.'

'Until the officers want mutton again,' another man laughed. 'Then they'll have their throats cut. In six weeks I shouldn't think there'll be one left.'

'Are you sure that *you'll* be here in six weeks?' Parker asked insidiously. 'I'm not. As to their throats being cut, you could have your neck stretched quite easily. All you have to do is to hit that murdering bastard Atkins when next he lays a rope about your shoulders. Think about it, lad. Just think about it.'

'This might be the right time to do summat,' a young man on the edge of the group whispered. 'Wi' all t'Channel Fleet in mutiny, it don't seem right that we should be 'ere anyway. We're lettin' us mates down, that's what we're doing. They're risking their necks to make things better for us and – and we're doing bugger all. We ought to join 'em.'

''Ark at the bloody landsman,' the Yorkshireman jeered. 'Not been to sea five minutes an' he's a sea lawyer already.'

'He's right though,' Parker said.

'Is 'e 'ell right. Go against the captain! I thought you were a clever bugger, eddicated and all that. You know nowt, mate, if you think that the lads'll turn against Captain Brewster. They know when they're well off, and they'll stand by 'im, you'll see. There'll be no mutiny as long as 'e's in command.'

CHAPTER TWELVE

Lawson should have slept well on the night following the attack on the barges, but the lively movement of the Russian sloop woke him during the middle watch, and further sleep was impossible. His mind was too actively recalling the events in Brest Roads. Eventually, he tossed the blankets aside, dressed and went onto the open deck for a breath of fresh air.

It took him some time to get away from the junior lieutenant on duty who wanted to while away his lonely vigil practising his English. Thereafter, Lawson kept well forward, taking pleasure in the solitude, and the movement of the narrow foredeck as the sloop heeled to the breeze and ploughed the dark sea into sparkling foam. It was so different from the staid *Adamant*. But suddenly there was something more interesting to think about. There appeared to be a sail in the distance.

Before he could be sure, it had merged again into the darkness. Perhaps he had been mistaken, he thought. Then it reappeared much clearer against a lighter patch of sky. It was a single-masted boat clawing its way northward towards Ushant – or Ireland. It had to be French: a *pecheur* by the look of it, similar to the fishing boats out of Whitby. He told the officer of the watch.

The Russian crew turned out with commendable speed and hardly any noise. The six-pounder guns were cleared of their coverings and loaded, whilst the sloop rushed along, gaining to windward and overhauling the dark outline at a great rate. Lieutenant Prendergast and the British landing party were back on *Adamant*, miles away and out of contact until the dawn. Baratovski was in command, to do as he pleased, and he was tense with excitement. It would be his first independent action.

'Can you find me something useful to do, sir?' Lawson said to Lieutenant Grayson.

'The commander will not want you to interfere with the working of the sloop. He has it organized to his liking, but it would be as well if you were to take a cutlass from the rack and make sure that your pistols are primed. I think it likely that he will board this vessel rather than use the guns. Can you make out what it is?'

'Looks like a fishing smack, sir. If it's typical of the kind which work these waters, it'll likely be bigger than the sloop, and it could be well armed, if it has been taken over by the French Navy.

Grayson went aft to inform Baratovski. Lawson found the arms rack and selected one of the sorry-looking blades to sling over his shoulder, leaving his hands free. Three of *Adamant*'s men remained on the sloop. Having been roused from their sleep by the activity below decks, they were now at a loose end, not knowing what to do. Lawson told them to take either a cutlass or pike and keep close by him.

Voices could be heard, shouting an alarm on the vessel ahead. They had been seen. Baratovski would soon know if it was friend or foe they were pursuing, and the question of fisherman or armed craft would be answered. Lawson felt a thrill of excitement and the usual touch of fear when the unmistakable squeal of protesting gun-carriage wheels reached his ears. A gun, probably mounted in the stern, and a heavy one judging by the noise, was being slewed sideways to sight on them.

Commander Baratovski had taken over from the helmsman. Suddenly he spun the wheel in an anti-clockwise direction. He had seen the glow of the fuse as the crouching gunner had breathed life into it. The bows of the sloop swung two points to port, responding like the greyhound she was, and a second later the gun fired.

They heard the heavy shot rushing by their starboard side. Then Baratovski brought his flying craft back onto its original course. It had sounded like a big gun. If so, it would take several minutes to reload. The sloop was already within fifty yards of the *pecheur*, and it was clearly visible. Now, *Catherine* surged rapidly forward. She was passing within a yard of the Frenchman's rounded stern, and the swivel gun on her poop looked down on the open deck. There was no cover for the three Frenchmen reloading the gun, and nothing to do other than surrender, but it seemed they were bent on suicide.

Baratovski left the wheel to the helmsman and leaned over the starboard side, pointing to his swivel gun and shouting a warning in French. The Frenchmen must have heard but they renewed their efforts to heave their ponderous weapon in line. The Russian commander hesitated, then shouted an order. The scatter-gun fired instantly, blasting its charge of musket balls at the men tending the gun. Two Frenchmen were hurled across the deck. The third fell backwards against the gun, writhing in agony. He still clutched the smouldering fuse.

Lawson shouted to the three British sailors and leapt across the gap onto the *pecheur*. His men attempted to follow him, but they lacked his agility and commitment. The vessels yawed apart and they were too late. Lawson was on his own.

He had sprawled on the wet deck and banged his head against one of the wheels of the gun. He was dazed and in pain, but he needed his wits. Someone was trying to stab him with a pike. Desperately, he rolled against the man's legs, unbalancing him. The point of the weapon stuck in the deck boards. It was a boathook. Lawson grabbed the pole with one hand and slashed upwards with his cutlass. The man screamed and staggered away clutching his hip. Lawson got to his feet and knocked the burning fuse out of the wounded gunner's hand.

Now the sloop was fairly alongside. Grappling hooks were thrown to bite into the timber of the *pecheur*. The Russians came aboard with their cutlasses, thirsting for blood, but there was nothing for them to do. The French skipper shouted his surrender and raised his hands from the wheel. The prize was taken, but the boarders were mad. Baratovski dashed down the blade of one of them and cursed them all. Gradually, they lost their wildness.

The sloop was scraping her timbers against those of the solidly built *pecheur* under the influence of a heavy northerly swell. Damage would result if they did not soon separate. Baratovski ordered his men back on board *Catherine*, then spoke to Grayson. The British lieutenant looked as if he were protesting, but the commander ignored whatever he was saying and crossed to his own vessel. Grayson turned to Lawson.

'You are to take over this boat, Mr Lawson, using the three men from *Adamant* as crew.'

Lawson felt a thrill of excitement.

'And the prisoners, sir?'

'We'll take the skipper and the wounded. The young Frenchman can stay and help you with the working of the boat. He'll know where things are. Search him well for weapons before you start. Right, let's get this fellow you skewered onto his feet. He doesn't look too badly.'

The man who had attacked Lawson with the boathook was propped up against a hatch cover. They pulled him upright, none too gently.

'Jasus! Have a care, will ye,' he gasped.

They looked closely at the man's face. It was Maharg.

'It'll be the hangman for you, my lad,' Grayson said grimly.

'If you don't finish me off first. I'm badly woundet and losing blood. Anyway, things are not quite as they appear. There are more ways of winning a war than shooting cannons at folk and, strange as it may seem to you both, I'm still Mr Atkinson's man.'

'You brought the French down upon us,' Lawson said.

'Not I,' he replied indignantly. 'You were seen putting your lads onto the barges by two of the watchmen and they ran for it to raise the alarm. I went after them. I managed to stop one, but t'other got through.'

'And what about firing on the sloop and then trying to kill Mr Lawson with a boathook?' Grayson demanded.

'And how did we know it was *your* sloop? We were chased out o' Brest by a bloody naval vessel that looked just like this one, but we give 'er the slip. Then you come rushing up out of the darkness. The captain of this boat is an enemy of the revolution and so are the men you've killed. If your commander had shouted in Russian or English, or even bloody Chinese, we wouldn't have fired. But no, he has to shout in French, so we thought the buggers had caught up wi' us again. We could die on this fishing boat or the guillotine. We chose to die here.'

Grayson shook his head in half disbelief. The Irishman's story seemed plausible enough.

'It's too much for me,' he sighed. 'Get yourself into the sloop and we'll see to your wound.'

Maharg climbed painfully over the side. Grayson turned to the three British seamen guarding the skipper and the youth.

'Two of you get the wounded man over by the gun and carry him onto the sloop. Handle him carefully. Come on, Captain,' he added, taking the French skipper by the arm, 'let's have you over there.'

Grayson pushed the skipper forward and he went willingly enough, until he realized that the younger man was still detained by the third seaman, whereupon he protested, waving his hands excitedly.

'Save your French for the commander,' Grayson interrupted, 'for I understand none of it.'

He heaved the Frenchman over the side onto the sloop, then followed. The seamen passed the wounded gunner over to the Russians. Then the sloop cast off and disappeared into the darkness.

It was a broad-beamed fishing boat that Lawson was left to command. He looked around it. There was a single mast with a long gaff swinging uneasily from side to side at the top of it, from which hung a mainsail. There was also a foresail running from the masthead to a bowsprit. It would be simple enough to handle. Lawson took the tiller. The men trimmed the sails, and the boat began to move forward. They followed the course taken by the sloop and searched the sea, but there was no sign of it.

'The moon'll be up soon, sir. Just like last night.'

'Was it only last night that we were in Brest Roads, Joplin?'

'It seems like a week ago, don't it? You'll be tired, sir, and your 'ead's bleeding. Shall I take the wheel for a spell?'

'Aye, do that please, Joplin. I'll have a look around.'

He ordered the other men to keep a sharp lookout and began to explore. The boat was very similar to those which fished from Whitby, and Lawson had spent his childhood playing about them. He found food in the galley. The pot-bellied stove was still burning. He would get the French youth to cook something for them all, but first, the cabin had to be searched for weapons. He found a loaded pistol and slipped it into his waistband. Then he went on deck again. The prisoner had not moved from the starboard shrouds.

'Right, lad, let's see what kind of an armoury you've got about you,' Lawson said, running his hands around the youth's waist, feeling for a dirk or pistol.

The prisoner spoke no word but stood unresisting with head bowed under a broad waterproof hood. Lawson jerked open the boat cloak and thrust his hands inside.

'Good God!' he exclaimed, withdrawing his hands as if he had plunged them into hot coals. 'You're a woman!'

He glanced over his shoulder in the direction of the wheel. Joplin was intent on his course. The other men were forward, watching out for Baratovski's sloop.

'Let's have you below out of sight,' he said, propelling her towards the cabin.

Once below she removed her hood. Lawson turned up the lamp. She was dark and slim with long hair bundled up in a kind of snood, and wide brown eyes, which would be attractive when they lost their fear. She appeared to be in her late teens.

'Put that hood back on and keep it on,' Lawson ordered, reaching out to take it.

She thrust it back on her head in a quick, nervous movement.

'Do you understand English?' he asked in surprise.

'A little.'

'Then why didn't you speak up before the others left? We thought you were a man.'

Two large tears rolled down her cheeks and her lips trembled. Lawson felt inadequate.

'Don't worry, lass. Everything will be fine. We'll have you back with your people in the morning.'

He pulled the chair close to the table for her. Her eyes closed and she swayed. Quickly he stepped forward and, taking her by the arm, helped her into it. She sat there helplessly. Lawson kept his arm around her shoulders, steadying her.

'Just hold on. I'll get you something that'll perk you up,' he said.

He turned to get a half-empty brandy bottle that he had seen when he had searched the cabin. A movement above caught his eye. It was the grinning face of one of his men at the port window.

'Get about your business, damn you,' he shouted, with an angry jerk of his head.

The face disappeared. Lawson returned to the table with a glass of brandy and water and made her drink some. Then he tossed some wood into the stove and buttoned his coat up to the neck.

'Stay below. Later, if you feel better, you can make some coffee for us all. I see you have some in the tin. If any of the men come below, shout for me. Do you understand?'

She nodded. Lawson turned and climbed the short steps to the open deck, closing the door behind him. Then he roared an order for the two men forward to join him at the helm.

'That was your nosy, bloody face I saw at the port light, Philips. Did you not understand my order to keep a sharp lookout for the sloop?'

'Aye, sir, but I saw the cabin light and wondered if any of the Frenchies were there.'

'You're a liar, Philips. Disobey orders again and you'll be up before Captain Brewster when we get back to *Adamant*. Now, as to the girl you saw below, you don't speak to her or go anywhere near her. That order applies to all of you. Steer clear of the girl. Have you got that order into your head, Philips?'

'Aye, sir. I knows better than trying to get off with an orficer's fancy.'

Lawson's fist clenched but he controlled himself with an effort.

'Philips, you oaf,' he said quietly. 'If I hear anything of the like from you again, I'll take a rope's end to you and you'll not lie down in comfort for a week, I swear. Now get for'ard and keep your eyes open. Not you, Brown. You will take that masthead lantern down, light it and hoist it aloft again. If we can't find the sloop, maybe the sloop'll find us.'

They continued on a northerly course with the wind fine on their port bow until the moon came out as bright as the night before to reveal Ushant dead ahead at about two miles but there was no sign of the sloop.

'Ready to go about,' Lawson commanded.

Baratovski would not have sailed beyond Ushant. He had to return to the latitude of le Goulet to rendezvous with *Adamant*. The *pecheur* wallowed clumsily round and placed her stern to the north star, the opposite course.

The girl came onto the deck with a kettle full of coffee and four cups.

She showed no inclination to go back to the cabin but stood alone on the starboard side long after the coffee had been drunk. After a time, Lawson walked over to join her.

'I hope that you feel better, miss,' he began awkwardly. 'Why don't you go below and get some sleep?'

'I will not sleep.'

'We'll have you back with the others in the morning. Is the captain of this boat your father?'

'*Non*,' she replied with a shake of her head. He is my – husband.'

'Your – husband?' said Lawson, wondering if her English vocabulary had let her down. The skipper they had put aboard the sloop would have been in his fifties. 'You are man and wife?'

'Man and wife, yes. He is my husband for two days only, and now we go to England because they would send him to the guillotine.'

So Maharg was telling some of the truth, Lawson thought. Aloud he said, 'You and your husband will get to England safely enough, ma'am. Why not go to bed and make yourself comfortable for what's left of the night?'

'Sloop ahead!' Philips called from the bows.

Lawson found it emerging from an area of sea darkened by the shadow of a cloud. It appeared to be racing towards them with white water at her forefoot. Baratovski had seen the masthead light.

'Won't be long now, ma'am. You will be with your husband shortly.'

She smiled and they stood together watching the approaching vessel. It was making a wide sweep, two hundred yards off their port bow, putting the wind behind her to join the *pecheur* on a southerly course. Now her rig was starkly revealed in silhouette against the moon. Lawson tensed. It was not quite the same as that on *Catherine*. Suddenly the woman clutched his arm.

'It is the ship which followed us!' she cried, her eyes wild with fright.

'Man the gun!' Lawson roared.

He ran aft, but even as he reached it, he realized that there was nothing they could do. The French sloop was eating up the space between them and they would never skid the great cannon around in time. Anyway, there was no burning fuse and it was an old piece that did not have a flintlock.

'Belay that last order, you men,' he said bitterly. 'Walk slowly forward and throw down your cutlasses. We shall have to surrender.'

The French sloop ran alongside and a score of armed men came aboard at a rush. The four Britishers and the woman were herded close by the wheel, circled by steel blades, which parted at the command of a French naval officer.

He was tall and thin, holding a sword in one hand and a dirk in the other. He slid the dirk into its sheath, handed the sword to a sailor and advanced to inspect the prisoners.

'Midshipman Lawson of the British Navy. I am in command of this vessel,' Lawson told him.

'*Anglais! Est-il possible?*'

The officer shook his head in disbelief, looked around at the rig of the boat, gestured his amazement and passed on to inspect the rest of the prisoners, peering closely at each face, until he reached the French woman.

'Ah! Madame Lorette!' he exclaimed with a mock bow.

His voice sounded relieved. Obviously, until that moment, he thought he had captured the wrong boat.

CHAPTER THIRTEEN

General Lazare Hoche, commander in chief of the invasion forces stationed at Brest and Boulogne, was twenty-nine years of age but old in experience. He was a typical officer of the Revolution; hard, ruthless and skilful. He had several victories to his credit, in addition to the cleverly managed defence of Dunkirk against Frederick, Duke of York, the soldier son of George III of England. This last had filled him with a burning desire to meet the royal general on English soil, but there was the barrier of the sea between him and his ambition. The new barges were essential if he were to land an army and all their supplies.

The raid on Brest had left him furious. Fourteen of his precious transports had been destroyed and thirty-one were in need of repair. Then there was the damage to the frigates. One was sunk in the shallows and would probably never sail again. Others would have to be repaired by the skilled men who were needed to build the wide-beamed invasion craft.

The commander of the battery and the officer in charge of the barges had been arrested for negligence. Two regiments of artillery had been turned out of their comfortable billets in the town to take up concealed positions along the southern shore of le Goulet.

It was not that the general expected a second raid. A master of surprise tactics himself, he knew well the folly of attempting a similar venture, and he had the greatest respect for the commanders of the impudent British ships that cruised so close to the shores of his homeland. Consequently he was astonished when he was awakened shortly after dawn with the news of a running battle taking place inside the channel leading to Brest Roads. The vessels involved were a local fishing boat, a *sloop-de-guerre*, and a foreign sloop of similar size, flying the flag of Imperial Russia. He ordered his horse to be saddled immediately.

The Russian sloop had been five miles to the north-west of le Goulet when the officer of the watch had reported two vessels silhouetted against the grey rim of dawn, hugging the coast and obviously making for Brest. They could only be French.

Baratovski, from his bed, had ordered immediate pursuit and hurried on deck, pulling on his clothes as he went.

The light was at first too poor for them to recognize the *pecheur* that they had captured during the night, but the possibility that one of the two vessels could be their prize must have occurred to all, as they were sailing from the north. Baratovski was not the man to indulge in speculation with his Russian subordinates. He might have discussed the situation with Crayson had not a temporary coolness arisen in their relationship. There was a difference of opinion about leaving the prize to fend for itself whilst the sloop sought fresh glories. As it was, Baratovski had remained aloof and unapproachable whilst they were drawing nearer to the land and it was becoming obvious that they would not reach the entrance to le Goulet in time.

He had strict orders from Captain Brewster that he must not risk approaching the guns of the fort. The man was no fool. He would never have attempted pursuit had the fast French *sloop-de-guerre* been alone, but the *pecheur* was positively identified as the light improved, and he knew it for a sluggish fishing vessel that he should overhaul easily before it could reach the protection of the shore batteries.

He had tried ranging shots as the gap shortened. Both

the sloop and the *pecheur* had replied. Those first shots of the engagement had travelled far on the still morning air. They roused the two regiments of artillery hidden in the woods on the south side of le Goulet. The senior colonel had immediately sent a galloper off to inform General Lazare Hoche. Then he had ordered the guns to be loaded, promising a flogging for any man who made too much noise about it. Now the camouflage had been replaced and the gunners were waiting in concealment, eager and excited.

The *sloop-de-guerre* was clearly visible to the gunners. She was in the lead. Astern of her, the fishing boat was falling further behind, pitching over the turbulent water where wind met tide at the entrance of the channel, and making very heavy work of it. Beyond, on the open sea, the Russian sloop was still holding her course, tossing twin arcs of white water from her forefoot as she sped along. Clearly the enemy commander was going to risk entering the channel and, judging by the speed of his approach, he would not have to penetrate far to capture the badly handled fishing boat. Slowly, reluctantly, so it seemed, the French warship came about and sailed back to protect it.

The *pecheur* was not defenceless. The great gun poking over her stern was bigger than any on either of the two warships. Intended for use in the fortress, where it had served for over twenty years, it was clumsy and too heavy for a vessel of this size but, in reasonable weather, it was effective. Certainly, it had the range, and the French prize crew had hit the sloop several times whilst the Russians' six-pounder shots were still falling short.

One of its huge cannonballs ploughed a furrow along *Catherine*'s deck, shattering the raised hatch cover amidships. Another took away a section of the starboard bulwarks. But the gun was worn and inaccurate, and the Frenchmen were not familiar with it and therefore slow in reloading. Otherwise, the beautiful sloop might easily have been smashed to bits before it entered the channel.

The distance between the three vessels shortened rapidly. Now the sloop's six-pounders were hitting the *pecheur*, but they were aimed at the single gun. Baratovski did not wish to destroy the rigging. He would need to sail the boat away once he had recaptured it.

The *sloop-de-guerre* was now able to intervene. She passed protectively around the stern of the *pecheur* and presented her port-side guns to the Russian sloop.

Several men died from that broadside of six-pounders, but Baratovski had no intention of withdrawing from the action. He could not bear the thought of losing the only prize he had ever taken, and he was confident that he could hold off the French sloop and board the old fishing boat before it reached the protection of the fortress.

Catherine's guns engaged the *sloop-de-guerre*, causing great damage to her structure. She turned abruptly away from the engagement and followed the *pecheur* towards the safety of Brest harbour. Baratovski smiled triumphantly.

A more experienced commander might have anticipated a change in the defences of the channel after the successful raid on the barges. Baratovski did not. Nor did he see any significance in the *sloop-de-guerre*'s course, which would take her very close to the southern side of le Goulet. The efficient Russian sailors had trimmed *Catherine*'s sails and she was handling like the thoroughbred she was. Her guns were being fired accurately at a great rate. The enemy vessels were running away from him. Baratovski felt elated, intoxicated almost, like a dog chasing sheep, and his men shared his excitement.

It was Grayson who first saw the blue-coated soldiers less than two hundred yards away on the shore. They and their guns had been camouflaged. Now the saplings and greenery were tossed aside. Mounted officers with drawn swords were shouting orders which could be heard clearly over the narrow strip of water. The commander of the *sloop-de-guerre* had lured them into a trap from which there could be no escape.

Baratovski shouted an order and the helmsman spun the wheel. *Catherine*'s bows came round to wind whilst cottonwool blooms of smoke appeared like magic all along the shore and from the woods beyond. The two regiments had fired their first salvo.

Catherine never did complete her manoeuvre. First the wheel turned uselessly in the helmsman's hands as the rudder cables were shot away. Then the wheel itself was gone and the man with it. The calm water boiled around the sloop. Balls of iron tore through her planking at, and below, the waterline. Her timbers were smashed to matchwood and the blood of the men who had crouched behind the gunwales ran freely through the scuppers.

Grayson knew it was the end before the mast came crashing down. Dumbly, and without any visible emotion, he bent over the only undamaged gun and picked up the burning fuse from the hand of the dead Russian gunner. He knew that Baratovski, with his complexes and ambitions, would never surrender. There was nothing left for a British liaison officer to do – except die.

Lawson and his three men had been shut up in the small storage compartment set in the stern of the *pecheur*, under the ancient long gun, before the battle had begun. They had been in complete darkness, lying on nets and rope that stank of fish and oil, where they could only guess at the vessel's position and the identity of the attacker.

'Christ! That bloody gun is going to fall through the deck on top of us,' Philips exclaimed.

The cannon above their heads would have weighed five tons. They seemed to be using too much gunpowder, since it was leaping clear of the deck boards with every recoil. The timbers of a fishing boat were not usually called upon to bear such a strain. The prisoners in the lazaret had actually seen daylight between the planking with the last crash.

'We'll get out of here,' Lawson said. 'I can feel metal under this rope. Yes, I think it's a boat's anchor. Help me to get this gear off it and we'll use it to knock the door down.'

The four men scrabbled on hands and knees in the pitch blackness, pulling at the tangle of netting and ropes. The sounds above them – the squeal of gun-carriage wheels, the dull thuds of a ramrod, the rumble of a heavy iron ball rolling down the bore of the gun, told them to hurry. There was not much time before the next explosion. Now, there was the sound of creaking block and tackle and the protesting screech of the gun being hauled sideways. Then all was silent, and they knew that it needed only the application of the linstock to the touch-hole to fire the charge.

'Crowd up against the rudder post,' Lawson shouted suddenly.

If the gun crashed through the deck boards, the aftermost part of the lazaret, with its heavy main beams supporting the rudder post and outer planking of the vessel, might offer some protection. As it happened, the gunner did not have time to shoot. There was the brief whistle of an approaching projectile, terminated by a monstrous crash that shook the rudder post. Now screams dominated all other noises for a space of ten seconds, subsiding into gasps and groans and finally silence. A man had died just above the prisoners' heads.

'That's the gun out of action, I think,' Lawson said in awed tones.

'And we'll be next,' Philips cried out in panic. 'Let's get out of here. We've got the anchor free. We can knock the door down with it. We'll all be killed if –'

Daylight exploded into the lazaret as a section of the rounded timbers, above the heads of the three crouching by the rudder post, shattered into smithereens. Philips had been on his feet and he must have died instantly, torn by jagged splinters and perhaps the cannonball as well. His body was hurled up against the door. Lawson gave it a cursory glance, then turned to the hole in the stern through which the Russian sloop was clearly visible. He was just in time to see the beginning of the attack by the field artillery.

'Come on, my lads. We're taking over the boat. Grab something suitable as a weapon,' Lawson ordered.

The hole was less than a yard wide. Lawson slid through and gripped the iron bar that passed through the rudder and to which the steerage cable was attached. It would serve as a ladder for agile seamen. Seconds later, he was looking over the stern bulkhead and he could see the length of the *pecheur*'s open deck. He climbed aboard, carrying a short piece of chain from below.

Three bodies lay around the gun and there appeared to be only the helmsman still alive. He was looking ahead. Lawson quietly advanced, intending to take him from behind. He could see that the man was armed. The wheel jerked. One of Lawson's men had evidently put his weight onto the steerage cable instead of the iron bar and it was pulling at the wheel. The helmsman glanced back over his shoulder looking for obstruction and saw Lawson bearing down upon him. Agilely he leapt clear, leaving the wheel to spin freely, snatched a pistol from his belt and fired in one movement. Lawson felt a blow, as from a hammer, just below the collarbone. It knocked him backwards, but he was on his knees in an instant and hurled the chain. It struck the man in the face, sending him staggering and causing him to drop a second pistol, which he had just pulled free. Now Lawson's men were running forward. The Frenchman snatched up the pistol from the deck and aimed it, calling upon them to halt. They hesitated, then Joplin charged with a roar. The man squeezed the trigger but the pistol misfired. He hurled it at Joplin's head and leapt over the side into the sea.

'Are you all right, sir?' Joplin asked anxiously as he helped Lawson to his feet.

'I'll do,' Lawson grunted. 'Grab that bloody wheel and hold a course while I see what's to be done.'

He looked around. In the short time since they had escaped from the lazaret, the Russian sloop had been reduced to a mastless wreck. It was being carried by the ebbing tide towards the open sea, sinking and not worth the boarding. The field guns were silent, except for three, hidden in the woods, which were using the wreckage for target practice. The French *sloop-de-guerre* was now a mile away inside Brest Roads.

'Bring her around and head out to sea. Maybe the gunners ashore will think that we're on an errand of mercy. I suppose they might expect someone to try to bring off any survivors.'

'What if they don't think that, sir? What if the *sloop-de-guerre* turns round and comes after us?'

'Then we'll finish up like *Catherine*. At this moment they believe we're on their side and they'll still have doubts right up to the moment when that chap who jumped over the side reaches the shore.'

'Let's hope he drowns, sir,' Brown said, looking over the water at the bobbing head of the swimmer, now fifty yards distant. 'Maybe we should try a shot at him.'

'That would draw their attention to him. As things are, I don't think anyone saw him jump. Anyway, we've nothing more than a pistol and he's well out of range of that. Stand by to take that foresail over as she comes about, and you'll have to sail this boat between you for I don't think I'm going to be much help, the way I feel just now.'

He staggered, clutched the man's shoulder for a moment, then made his way over to the port side as the bows of the *pecheur* turned back to the sea. He was feeling sick and dizzy, but he held on to the ratlines, determined to keep his senses. As they settled on the opposite course he waved at the watching gunners and pointed deliberately and repeatedly at the drifting wreck.

'Dip the colours when convenient, Brown,' he shouted. 'Do it three times; nice and easy, then hoist them back to the masthead.'

They were sailing slowly with the failing northerly breeze on their beam and the tide in their favour. With luck they would round the headland and be blocked from the artillery's line of sight. Then providing the *sloop-de-guerre* did not give chase, they should make the open sea. But the swimmer had almost gained the shore. There was also a great deal of activity among the mounted artillery officers. However, there was a group of three, which Lawson guessed were the colonel and his aides, and these seemed to be content to watch through telescopes and do nothing. The generals produced by the Revolution did not extend a gentlemanly hand to subordinates who committed blunders. The fishing boat under the regiment's guns was flying French colours, and the colonel might be afraid of the consequences if he fired upon it, Lawson hoped.

Joplin was steering a course for the wrecked Russian

sloop, which was clearly being kept afloat only by the air trapped inside her. The tide was taking it at three knots towards the projecting headland, but the fishing boat was not doing much better. She needed a stronger breeze to drive her forward.

'Look at that, sir,' Brown said, pointing at the shore.

Lawson pulled himself upright, gasping with the pain, and looked back at the batteries. Soldiers were heaving at the spokes of the wheels, turning the guns. No longer were they directed at the wrecked sloop. Every one seemed to be sighting on the *pecheur*. It needed only an order from the colonel in command for the bombardment to begin.

CHAPTER FOURTEEN

Two horsemen could be seen approaching from the direction of Brest. They were at a gallop, one behind the other, taking hedges and ditches in their stride. When they were close enough to be recognized positively, a trumpeter from the battery on the extreme right flank began to sound the general salute. Then all eyes were turned towards the riders. Soldiers who had been taking their ease were getting to their feet, tapping out their pipes, fastening tunic buttons and setting their caps straight. Now the officers, whom Lawson had taken to be in command of the artillery, spurred their horses and cantered off to meet the visitors.

'I should think that the leading horseman is General Hoche,' Lawson told Joplin. 'See, the colonel is saluting him. Now the general will be giving orders either to blow us out of the water or to leave us to look for survivors on the wreck before it goes down.'

General Hoche would certainly have ordered the sinking of them without any qualms, but it seemed that whoever had the fishing vessel was trying to rescue someone on the wrecked sloop. The general wanted a Russian prisoner. He needed positive proof of Russian involvement in the Brest area. The fools in Paris had chosen to cast doubts on his reports of a powerful enemy presence. They would have it that every ship in the British Navy had mutinied, and it had taken a landing by marines to persuade them otherwise. Even so, they were so obsessed with their plan to invade Ireland that they would easily decide to take a chance on there being no British warships in the Channel.

The *colonel d'artillerie* expressed the opinion that the fishing vessel had been retaken by the monarchist Frenchmen who would have been locked up below. General Hoche waved a dismissive hand.

'It is of little importance. They are only guillotine fodder to keep the mob happy. Anyway, they will not escape. See.'

He pointed at the French *sloop-de-guerre*. It had gone about and was gaining on the *pecheur*. The general ignored his subordinate's suggestion that they should fire a warning shot across the bows of the fishing vessel, but he did not deign to explain his reasons, and the colonel was too much in awe of his harsh, autocratic commander to enquire.

General Hoche calmed his fretful stallion, raised his telescope and examined the wreck. He saw someone moving about. At least one of the Russians had managed to survive the bombardment. With luck he would be an officer with some knowledge of what was happening to the British Navy. Damn the stupid commanders of the two regiments of artillery for continuing firing after the sloop had been dismasted. As to the captain of the *sloop-de-guerre* – he would face a court martial for cowardice, or stupidity, if he lost the *pecheur*.

Suddenly the general snapped his telescope shut, wheeled his horse away from the group and galloped towards the headland. His aide-de-camp shrugged his shoulders expressively and spurred after him, leaving the gunners impatient but impotent. No one would now dare give the order to fire until the general returned. Meanwhile, both the wreck and the fishing boat were slowly increasing the range between them and the guns, and getting closer to the jutting land that would screen them.

'There's someone alive on the Russian sloop, sir,' Brown exclaimed. 'He's up in the bows. I can see him waving.'

Lawson forced himself to consider this information.

The pain in his shoulder was abominable and he was weak from loss of blood. All he wanted to do was lie on the deck and pass into the oblivion of merciful sleep, but now he had another decision to make.

'We'll try and rescue him,' he said after an interval. 'Approach the wreck from the leeward side, Joplin.'

'Aye, aye, sir. Do we tie up fore and aft?'

Lawson marvelled at Joplin's cheerfulness. The man was either completely without imagination or an irrepressible optimist. There was good sense in his suggestion, however. To lie alongside the wreck would support the belief that they were on an errand of mercy. Also, if the sloop retained its buoyancy and they kept it close by them, its bulk would provide some protection from the guns, although it would reduce their speed to that of the ebbing tide.

The headland was still half a mile distant, but the wind was dropping away, and it was probable that the French sloop, which was pursuing them with a full spread of canvas, would not be able to make more than one or two knots better than the ebb. With luck they might even clear le Goulet before the French sloop reached them. Then their pursuers might be in trouble. *Adamant* should be lying just outside, waiting for the errant *Catherine*. The dawn signal had not been made and the sound of the guns must have travelled far over the water.

'Brown, help me across to the wheel,' Lawson called urgently. 'Then you and Joplin can look out some suitable rope to tie up; something just strong enough to hold us. Don't use heavy cable in case the sloop sinks.'

The French sailor who had jumped over the side of the *pecheur* had lain exhausted on the edge of the water for fifteen minutes before he had been able to crawl up the beach. The movement had then attracted the attention of an idle gunner, a slow-witted soldier, who had dithered indecisively until the man was out of sight among the gorse before telling his sergeant about it. This had resulted in further delay because the sergeant needed to be sufficiently convinced to report the incident to his officer. By the time they had found the sailor and taken the information to the colonel that the vessel was in enemy hands, it was already beyond the angle of the guns situated in the woods and almost out of range of those near the shore. Even so, the colonel felt obliged to send a galloper after General Hoche to warn him of the changed situation and to request his permission to engage the *pecheur*.

Lawson was easing the fishing boat up to the wreck when the first ranging shots were fired. He felt a curious detachment. He was not in full command of his senses and all his attention was needed to get alongside gently. The Russian sloop was listing, with most of her starboard side under water. Her bulwarks were shattered. Splintered furrows crisscrossed her deck boards. Two regiments of artillery had engaged her, and probably every gun had fired five or six times. She must be full of shot holes below the waterline, precariously held up by buoyant materials and trapped air, which might well spill out if the wreck were rocked by violent contact.

Three Russian sailors were on the open deck. They had thought that they were being taken off by the French and were resigned to becoming prisoners of war. Now they shouted with delight as they recognized their rescuers and scrambled excitedly along the heeling deck of the sloop to get aboard the *pecheur*.

The distant roar of guns warned them that they were still in line of sight from some of the artillery. Twin spouts of water close astern and a pattern of strikes one hundred and fifty yards away indicated that the French were having difficulty finding the range. The sooner they cast off and sailed with the ebb, the safer they would be.

One of the Russians pointed at the main hatch on the sloop and spoke urgently. None of them had any English. Lawson guessed he was saying that there was someone still aboard.

A shriek of a cannonball overhead, and the sharp crack as it passed through the belly of the mainsail, warned them that one gun, at least, had the range. It was not from the artillery, Lawson realized. The French sloop was getting closer. Even so, they had to search for any survivors.

There was a cry from under the deck boards on the

high side. It was an unmistakable Irish voice. Maharg was trapped inside the wreck.

'Get down to the hatch, both of you. See if you can get him out,' Lawson ordered.

Brown and Joplin skated down the inclined deck, using a rope that had been secured to the *pecheur*, and swung their legs over the edge of the hatch.

'There's no way, other than cutting through the deck, sir,' Brown shouted. 'It's flooded down here. He'll be in a pocket of air and that'll be getting smaller every minute. Look!' he exclaimed.

From the hatch belched a huge bubble, followed by smaller ones as the wreck rolled, spewing bits of debris. She seemed to be settling. Clearly there would be no time to hack through four-inch planking even if they had suitable tools, and neither of the two men could be expected to swim into the darkness of the 'tween decks to help the wounded Irishman.

Maharg! Lawson roared. 'Can you see the light from the hatchway?'

'Aye, I can see it. I've been lookin' at nuthin' else for the past two hours.'

'Then why the hell don't you swim for it?'

'And if I could swim do you think I'd be sittin' here?'

The Irishman's voice, muted by the timbers, seemed to be coming from close by the bulkhead at the highest part of the heeling wreck, and probably only twenty feet separated him from the open hatch. Lawson remembered that the Russian seamen slept in this area.

'Feel about above your head. You'll find hammock rings screwed into the planking. The rows are about a yard apart. Pull yourself from ring to ring and you'll reach the hatch in no time. We'll be waiting for you.'

'I've found the rings,' Maharg shouted, after what seemed an age, 'and I'm going to try it. See that you are waiting, for I've never been under water in me life at all.'

Joplin tied the rope around his waist and lowered himself into the water. Brown remained on the edge of the hatch, holding the rope to support him.

A belch of air, larger than the last, warned of a change in the situation. The wreck had rocked violently. Brown heaved himself clear of the hatch, halfway up the sloping deck, his eyes wide with alarm.

'We grounded then, sir,' he shouted in justification.

'Get back and help Joplin, damn you.'

Lawson realized what was happening. The flooded sloop was lying deeper in the water than the *pecheur* and there was nothing he could do to get it away from the shallows. If Maharg did not reach the hatch quickly, he would have to bring his men off and sail clear. He dared not risk going aground on a falling tide.

There was a grinding of timbers and the wreck shuddered. The sea rolled up behind Joplin, engulfing him completely for a moment. The hulk was aground and no longer moving with the tide. More air spewed out in a huge noisy bubble, and with it came Maharg. Joplin gripped him, passed the rope under his arm and shouted for assistance. It was the work of a few moments for the two of them, now helped by the Russian seamen, to get the half-drowned Irishman onto the deck of the *pecheur*.

'Cast off and trim the sails,' Lawson ordered.

It would now be a race for the open sea with a chance of a shot from one of the two bow chasers on the *sloop-de-guerre* dismasting them, but the odds were certainly better than they had been. As they squared around on their course and took the light breeze on their beam, Brown and Joplin grinned at each other and the Russian seamen became quite cheerful. Then a sharp crack above their heads warned them of the accuracy of the long guns mounted in the enemy's bow. There was another shot hole in the foresail close by the mast.

'Shall we see if we can do anything with our gun, sir?' Joplin asked.

'Garn! It nearly went through the bloody deck, man. Have you forgot?' Brown ridiculed.

'Better our gun through the deck than one o' their cannonballs knocking us into t'middle of next week: and if they dismast us, they'll not take us prisoner a second time.'

Joplin drew his finger across his throat. The movement jerked Lawson out of his lethargy. His men had been arguing as if he had not been present.

'That's enough,' he growled. 'Brown, take the wheel. Joplin, lend me your shoulder and help me to the gun.'

'I'll see to it, sir. Why don't you lie down?'

Lawson turned to the Russians.

'Pa-ma-gee-tye mnye pa-zha-loo-sta,' he said. ●

Joplin's eyes were wide in surprise and the Russians looked astonished, but they moved aft to help. One of the few phrases that Lawson had learnt from the Russian junior officer in exchange for his English conversation had paid off.

They gathered around the gun. It did not appear to be damaged at all. Jagged splinters from the bulwarks had killed the French gunners. They found a wooden case that contained five serge-wrapped cartridges, but the gun was already loaded, Lawson remembered. It needed only a burning fuse at the touch-hole to fire it.

'Take aim,' Lawson ordered, and began to look around for a piece of fuse rope.

The one in the bucket had burned away to ash. He searched the bodies of the gunners. One of them had several fuse ropes looped through his belt. There was also a wooden pin with a piece of flint set in it. Lawson took the man's knife and flicked sparks from the flint until the fuse rope caught and smouldered. Then, he blew gently to coax it into full glow before dropping it into the fuse bucket and replacing the lid.

Joplin had managed to get the Russians to do his bidding, with no language other than broad Lancashire to explain his gestures. Perhaps they had used the same signals on the sloop to lay the guns on target. Certainly they were attentively watching his pointing fingers and clenched fist as he had them adjust the bearing of the great gun to line up on the pursuing *sloop-de-guerre*.

'Would you like to check my aim, sir?' he said, stepping back from the gun.

Lawson bent to look over the sights. The gun was on target. He took the fuse from the bucket.

'Stand well back, all of you,' he ordered.

If the gun were to crash through the deck to the lazaret below, it would be better if Lawson were the only one to go with it. He blew at the fuse until the saltpetre threw off sparks. Then he applied it to the black powder in the pan of the touch-hole, stepping hurriedly back as it fizzled through the thickness of the metal to the charge in the breach: two seconds' grace that saved him from serious injury. The gun bucked clear of the planking with the recoil and crashed back, shattering its own cast-iron wheels and the timbers beneath them. It was now half on its side with its breach buried in the deck above the lazaret where they had been imprisoned.

'That's the gun out of action for a time, sir, but it's done a bit o' damage yonder. I'll swear I saw the timbers fly,' Joplin cried excitedly. 'Yes, we caught the bowsprit. See her foremast canvas. It's in ribbons.'

Lawson nodded in satisfaction. The loss of any canvas on the *sloop-de-guerre* was to their advantage, particularly if *Adamant* were not waiting just outside the estuary. The *pecheur* would surely be overtaken well within the hour. The odd thing about the activity with the gun was that he felt better for it. He had been almost out on his feet: now he felt stronger and could think clearly.

'Very good, Joplin. I'll see that you are commended to Captain Brewster for the work you have done. Now see if you can find some suitable timbers to set up jeers over that gun and hoist it back on deck. We may need it again directly.'

He left Joplin with the three Russian sailors and walked back to the wheel, noting that the sails were filling. It certainly seemed that they would clear le Goulet and reach the open sea if they were not struck in a critical part of their rigging by the shot from the *sloop-de-guerre*'s bow chaser.

'What would have happened to the young woman, sir?' Brown asked when Lawson joined him.

'The young woman? God! I'd forgotten all about her. She'll probably be on board the French sloop: but you'd better search below to see if she's here. Let me take the wheel.'

Maharg was propped against the starboard bulkhead, clutching his wounded thigh and looking very ill, but he managed to leer at Lawson.

'Shouldn't ha' thought that a fine, big feller like

yourself, even if you are woundet, wouldn't have scratted around to see if he had a pretty girl on board.'

'We don't know that she is on board. Anyway, she's a married woman,' Lawson said severely.

'Hoots! A trifle like that would not have worried young blood in my day. As to being married, she changed to a widder a short time ago.'

'Her husband is dead?'

'Killed, sitting right alongside me at the beginning of the bombardment. Cannonball passed between us and left me none the worse, but it drove an iron bolt from the ship's side into the back of old Lorette's neck. He died cussing his luck, for he never got the chance to bed his wife. Maybe 'twas the work of providence, for there were o'er forty years' difference in their ages, and most folk thought he should have given the girl time to look at the world from outside the convent walls before he –'

He paused mid-sentence. Lawson had evidently seen something and was not listening.

'What is it?' Maharg demanded, striving to brace himself up to look over the bulwark.

'There's an open boat hugging the shore on the north side of the channel and they seem to be rowing it towards the sea. Four pairs of sweeps working and maybe there are ten men aboard.'

'French soldiers, would ye say?'

'Don't think so. I'm hoping it's one of *Adamant*'s boats. Captain Brewster will have been trying to find out what's happening. With a bit of luck, *Adamant* will be waiting just around the headland with all guns loaded and run out.'

He turned the wheel to starboard to bring his boat closer to the north side of le Goulet.

Brown appeared through the forward hatch and turned around to offer assistance to someone behind him. It was Madame Lorette, dirty and dishevelled, but otherwise apparently unharmed. At that moment a shriek overhead caused them all to duck involuntarily. A cannonball had passed low across the deck and punched a hole in the foot of the sail. Another raised a plume of water just ahead and a little to the left of them. The slight change of course had likely saved their mast.

'Pleased to see that you are safe, ma'am.' Lawson said with a smile. 'Lower the French flag,' he ordered Brown.

It was not fooling the pursuing *sloop-de-guerre*, so it would be as well to drop it whilst they were still in sight of the men in the ship's boat. Lawson was now convinced that they were from *Adamant*.

Slowly, the *pecheur* crept towards the headland whilst the shots from the two bow-chaser guns on the Frenchman were becoming increasingly accurate with the shortening range. They were hit repeatedly above the waterline but miraculously, it seemed, no one was hurt. The mast remained standing, gouged and scarred though it was, supporting the tired old mainsail, which was now so full of holes from bar-shot and chain that it would have disintegrated immediately if the breeze got up.

At last they reached the shoulder of land and were able to see that which was still concealed from the *sloop-de-guerre*. *Adamant* was anchored fore and aft with the whole of her port-side battery presented to the estuary mouth. When the Frenchman emerged, he would be within two hundred and fifty yards of those terrible guns. Lawson held his course for the open sea, praying that a breath of wind would get the *pecheur* out of the line of fire before his pursuer appeared.

The French commander would have expected to find a British ship somewhere in the vicinity, but he was in a desperate situation already for his failure to escort the fishing vessel into Brest harbour. He knew that General Hoche would have him shot if it escaped, so even had he guessed that *Adamant* lay in wait, he would probably have pursued the *pecheur* to the open sea. Nevertheless, it came as a shock to find his small craft under the guns of *Adamant* at point-blank range, with not enough wind to sail back into the channel against the ebbing tide. He struck his colours immediately.

CHAPTER FIFTEEN

Lawson slept for two days, then awoke to find himself in a strange bed, situated in a small cabin that was certainly too grand for a mere midshipman. It was faintly illuminated by a glass bull's-eye set in the wall of the ship. So it was above the waterline, unlike the midshipmen's berths. He lay for a few minutes feeling the movements of the ship to ascertain the position of the cabin. He had just decided that it must be on the port quarter, when he became aware that he was not alone.

There were two people in the shadows. They rose simultaneously as he lifted his head. Madame Lorette placed her hand on his brow. The other person turned up a lamp hanging from the deck beams above. It was Victoria, the younger daughter of Madame Hanikof.

'I hope you are feeling better,' Madame Lorette said.

Lawson looked from one face to the other, pale in the lamplight. He smiled uncertainly. This was not real. It was another dream. Soon, the faces would change. They would become the hideous spectres who had pursued him with cauterizing irons. His shoulder throbbed and he could still smell the burned flesh and the laudanum, the rum and the vomit.

'You are going to be strong again,' Victoria told him, moving closer. 'The doctor says you must eat and I have broth here.'

She held a dish with a lid. Hesitantly, doubting his

senses, Lawson raised his hand to rest on hers. She did not move and smiled down at him, a wonderful tender smile that would have had his pulses racing if he had believed it really was happening to him. He stroked her arm. She became attentive, her lips slightly parted. Her arm was soft and warm. Suddenly he realized she was real. It was not a dream. He withdrew his hand hurriedly. The spell was broken. Victoria was startled.

'You must try to eat,' Madame Lorette said, intervening briskly.

Lawson's mind was in a turmoil. Two real, attractive young ladies with him and he in bed, unable to help himself. His immediate needs were not food, and they were too embarrassing to speak of in the present company.

'Will you please pass the word for the loblolly,' he pleaded.

'Lob-lol-ly?' Victoria queried, her large blue eyes puzzled.

'The surgeon's mate, ma'am – the medical orderly – the nurse. Send him in as you go.'

'*Oui*,' Madame Lorette acknowledged with a business-like nod.

She bustled the younger girl towards the door and cut short her farewell smile by pushing her through. A few minutes later the loblolly arrived.

'I want to go to the heads,' Lawson said.

The man took up a bedpan. Lawson waved it away and tried to get out of the bed, but he was too weak. He groaned and lay back. The orderly slipped in the bedpan and helped him up.

Ruthven, the ship's surgeon, a likeable Scot from the Edinburgh Medical School, came to see Lawson shortly after the loblolly had departed. He grinned at the patient as he entered, poured water into a bowl set in an oak frame and scrubbed his hands. He was a small man in his early twenties.

'I've been busy below,' he said as he washed. 'Ten more puir devils with the fever and two dying of consumption. I thought when I took service with the Navy that most of my patients would be suffering from gun-shot wounds, but they're very much in the minority on the good ship *Adamant*, despite the fact that we have been busy fighting and getting shot at over the last week.'

'It's always been the same,' Lawson shrugged.

'Aye, so it has,' Ruthven sighed, as he eased Lawson's nightshirt back from the wound in his shoulder. 'But why don't we do something about it, eh?'

He unfastened the dressing and examined the sutures, probing gently with his fingers and sniffing at the healing flesh on both sides of the injured shoulder.

'You've been very lucky, you know. The bullet went right through you as far as the shoulderblade, and there it was, like a great carbuncle that needed only a nick or two with my scapnel to extract it. There were wee bits of your coat and shirt with it, as would be expected, but I managed to get 'em all out. In two or three days you'll be up and about — especially with the ladies to look after you,' he added with a grin.

'The ladies?'

'Special privilege for Midshipman Lawson. Madame Lorette said she wanted to nurse you. The idea tickled the captain's fancy, and he agreed. Then the Russian lass got jealous and asked if she could assist.

'Jealous!'

'Oh yes, she likes you.'

'She's a child.'

'She'll be seventeen next week, I'm told. Young Atkins is besotted by those big blue eyes. Follows her about, when he gets the chance. Madame Lorette appears to interest your friend Mr Heward. Must be those dark, tragic eyes of hers. She's an intelligent woman too, and she has a bit of medical knowledge that she gained from the nuns.'

'Well, Heward is welcome to her and her medical knowledge. I'll have the loblolly to look after me, if you don't mind.'

'I don't mind at all, laddie, but she's looking after you in accordance with the captain's orders, so that's the way it'll be, unless you can get those orders changed. If I ask anything of the captain in his present mood, he's bound to do the opposite.

'What's the trouble?'

'I'm to blame for the ship's fever and the consumption, don't you know?' Ruthven said bitterly.

'And aren't you?' Lawson smiled.

'No more than you are. I didn't know about that last batch of men that you took from the bridewell until we were two days at sea. They were brought into the ship whilst I was ashore collecting medical stores. No one told me about them.' He shrugged. 'Anyway, all naval ships have consumptives on board. Can't expect anything else in such abominable conditions.'

Lawson sighed. He had heard Ruthven's views many times, but the doctor was on his favourite hobbyhorse and not likely to be stopped.

'Conditions worse than you would find in the most wretched parts of Edinburgh. Crowded like beasts in damp quarters; coming in wet from watch, and nowhere to get dry; getting into bedding that's damp and mildewed. Then there's the water in the drinking casks. It was stinking before we left Liverpool. Even the fresh water that Trevelyan had brought aboard was stored in casks that have been used for meat.' He pulled at his ginger side whiskers irritably. 'It's criminal folly and unforgivable. Back home, I would not give such water to my father's horse. She wouldn't drink it, most likely.'

'Naval ships are always overcrowded. It's part of life.'

'It's stupid and wasteful, lad,' he said fiercely. 'That's why the Navy loses more men from sickness than from any other cause – even in wartime. Ship fever, or gaol fever – call it what you will – consumption, scurvy and the pox.' He ticked them off with his fingers. 'Those four complaints kill more men than the enemy and the hazards of the sea.'

'And what can be done about it?'

'Well, as to the scurvy, we've known for forty years how to prevent it, but the Admiralty will not issue the lemons and fresh vegetables that are needed.'

'Costs too much,' Lawson shrugged.

'But they don't count the cost in men's lives. Then there's the issue of soap so that the men can keep themselves and their clothes clean.'

154

'They've just issued soap to the Mediterranean Fleet, I hear. So maybe our turn will come. Will it make much difference as far as disease is concerned?'

'I think so. There's a Dr Blane who believes that lice spread the fever and I'm sure he's right. There's not a man who can keep himself free of lice in the crowded conditions below decks, no matter how hard he tries.'

Lawson grinned ruefully and scratched at his back. 'The lice don't confine themselves to the people. You think soap would get rid of them?'

'It would be a start. I'd have every man's hair cut short, especially those with tarred pigtails.'

Lawson looked at Dr Ruthven in astonishment. 'You'd cut off their queues? That would be unpopular. Some take great pride in having a fine rope of hair.'

'It wouldn't be so bad if they combed it regularly before they plaited it.'

'Some do. They plait each other's.'

'But most of the common seamen just stick the tip of the plait into pitch and it's not combed from one month's end to the other, and you'll find a colony of lice living in the roots.'

Lawson grinned. 'I shouldn't mention it to Captain Brewster. He used to have his hair in a tail, according to old Hampson. He only changed to the curled wig he wears now when it started falling out.'

The door opened and Captain Brewster entered. There was not a lot of room for the two men to be standing, especially as the captain had to bend his back to avoid banging his head on the deckboards above. He looked at Dr Ruthven disapprovingly.

'You finished?' he demanded.

'Yes, sir.'

Brewster jerked his head in dismissal. Ruthven took up his bag and left the cabin.

Glad to see you looking better,' the captain said when the door had closed. 'Wound bothering you?'

'It throbs a bit, sir, and it's itching.'

'Give it a day or two, lad, and it'll be fine – until you get to my age. Then it'll ache every time the weather's cold and wet.'

'Joys to come, sir,' Lawson grinned.

He, alone of all the midshipmen, felt easy and comfortable in the captain's company during his off-duty moments. 'The old man treats you like a son, and you talk to him as if he were your father,' Heward had once complained after a trying dinner at the captain's table.

The captain eased himself onto the stool at the foot of the cot and beamed at Lawson.

'Aye, lad. Joys to come: when the war's over and you're sitting on that grand stone quayside of yours at Whitby, smoking your pipe and telling your grandchilder how you thrashed the frogs in their own harbour.'

'Do you know Whitby, sir?'

'I did. Went there first when I was a boy. Wanted to go off with the whaling ships, but I missed 'em. They were all away and I couldn't wait a year for 'em to come back. Then, I visited again when I was a young lieutenant of twenty-five. That would have been in '78. Brought a cutter in with dispatches and mail from the Fleet. Got held up for the best part of a week by the weather. The folk were very friendly and hospitable – but the Navy don't help a man to keep friends.' He paused reflectively, then sighed. 'There was a lass took my fancy. I went back to see her when I was paid off from Leander a couple o' years later. I'd done well in my share of the prize money so I hired me a pony and trap in Malton and drove over the moors in style. I wanted to marry her, but she was already wed, with a child – a fine-looking boy. I've not been there since.' He paused, then looked keenly at Lawson. 'I've decided to make you up to acting-lieutenant, and recommend you for immediate promotion – as soon as you've satisfied the Board of Examiners that you are competent in your seamanship and navigational studies, of course.'

'That's very kind of you, sir.'

'It's no more than you deserve, lad. You've done well. Get yourself fit and you'll take over our new prize, the French *sloop-de-guerre*. Lieutenant Trevelyan is commanding it at the moment.'

'Thank you, sir. A couple of days is all I'll need, I think.'

'Don't rush it,' Brewster said drily. 'Let these lasses fill you with their broths and jellies and God knows what preparations they've been cooking. Can't get into my own pantry for them.'

His eyes had been twinkling as he rose to go, but when he reached the door, his face became serious.

'I don't suppose, Mr Lawson, that you know any of the details attending the death of my coxswain, Mr Hampson. I know you weren't on that side of the barges, but I wondered if perhaps you had heard from – any seaman what exactly happened.'

'No, sir,' Lawson replied, looking very surprised.

'Oh well! Enjoy your fancy victuals while you can. I think I heard the lasses outside just now.'

He nodded and left the cabin, leaving Lawson wondering why the circumstances of Hampson's death were being questioned. Obviously something was wrong with Atkins' report. He had no time for further thought on the subject. There was a tap on the door and then it opened. His two visitors were smiling on the threshold.

Madame Lorette carried a basket over her arm and she held the door whilst Victoria came through with a tureen. Clearly it was her intention to spoon-feed the invalid, but Lawson was determined to manage himself. He smiled and took the tureen from her hands.

'What is it?' he asked in wonder, after he had tasted the contents of the dish.

'You like it?' Madame Lorette asked with an anxious smile.

'It's delicious.'

'It will make you strong again,' she told him, nodding her head sagely.

'Obviously it didn't come from the ship's galley. How did you cook it?'

'Madame Hanikof allowed me to use her stove, and she has –' her brow wrinkled perplexedly, – 'er – *un coffret des fines herbes.*'

Lawson looked puzzled.

'A box of herbs for cooking,' Victoria translated. 'Madame Lorette is very clever with these things.'

Lawson cleared the dish, marvelling that Captain

Brewster had allowed the girls so much freedom on behalf of a lowly midshipman. Apart from the inconvenience of having them cooking outside the galley, there was definitely chicken in the concoction, and the only person with any poultry left on board was the captain. The coop that had housed the few hens bought by the lieutenants and the midshipmen in Liverpool had been washed over the side during the storm in the Irish Sea.

Madame Lorette's basket held calf's-foot jelly, liver-brawn, honey and other delicacies, each contained in a round pot about four inches high. There was also a metal box full of sweet biscuits. They were obviously from Madame Hanikof's chest, since the labels were in Russian script, but Victoria generously gave Madame Lorette credit for having selected them for their recuperative qualities. If she were jealous of the French girl, as Ruthven had said, she was certainly not showing it.

There was a tap at the door and Heward entered breezily, immediately changing his expression to one of feigned surprise when he saw the girls. He fooled no one. Victoria smiled surreptitiously at Madame Lorette who responded with a twinkling of her eyes, whilst Heward went through the necessary formality of asking Lawson how he was getting on.

'The sooner you get fit again, the better I'll be pleased,' Heward said as he pulled a stool close to where Madame Lorette sat. 'Midshipmen available for duty are in short supply. I'm just about worn out. Saunders has gone on board the *sloop-de-guerre* with Trevelyan.'

'What's the French sloop doing?' Lawson asked.

'Same as *Catherine*,' Heward said with a shrug, 'but there's talk of Trevelyan being sent into Brest under a flag of truce to see about an exchange of prisoners, if they have any of our men.'

'That should be interesting,' Lawson said.

Heward was not listening: he had turned exclusively to Madame Lorette.

This development obviously suited both of the girls. Victoria moved her chair a little further around so that she faced Lawson directly. Thereafter, the two conversations were completely independent of each other and almost private. After his initial embarrassment, Lawson began to enjoy himself. Victoria was the most entertaining and attractive girl he had ever known.

Meanwhile, up on the foredeck, Midshipman Atkins was well aware that Victoria was with Lawson. He had seen the two girls take the food below when he had first come on duty with Lieutenant Prendergast and he had noticed Heward, all spruced up within fifteen minutes of being relieved from the morning watch, creeping after them. That had been two hours ago, and they were still there.

'Look alive there, you lazy swabs, or I'll smarten you up when you get down here,' he screamed at the men on the foremast.

They were setting a new sail on the fore topgallant yard, replacing the one that had been damaged. There had been no need for great urgency, but Atkins had used his cane nevertheless and a few eyes smouldered in resentment.

Captain Brewster paused in his afternoon stroll around the quarterdeck with Madame Hanikof and spoke to the officer of the watch.

'Yes, sir,' Prendergast replied. 'I had intended to have a word with him when the job is finished. I don't know what is wrong with Atkins this morning. I've had to reprimand him twice for not having his wits about him.'

Brewster walked on. He would have spoken to Atkins himself had it not been for the anonymous letter he had received, accusing Atkins of cowardice and causing the death of old Hampson. Until the matter was fully investigated, he would give his most junior midshipman a wide berth.

'You seem troubled, Captain,' Madame Hanikof said with an inquisitive smile.

'Yes – yes, I am.'

'Perhaps, I can – to help?'

'No, I think not, ma'am.'

'Ma'am!' she mocked. 'You promised to call me Christina.'

He stopped and turned to face her. 'Christina,' he said

with a slow smile. 'Christina it shall always be – in private.'

'And now will you tell me what is causing the creases in your brow?' she asked. 'It is good to share worries. How do you say it? A problem shared is a problem –?'

'Halved?'

'*Oui*. A problem halved: but I know it is difficult for the man in command. Yet, if he keeps everything locked up here,' she clutched at her breast, 'it is bad for him.' She shook her head sadly. 'Very bad for him – and for those he loves. He builds a wall around himself and hides inside with his secrets. Then, over the years, he finds that he cannot live outside that wall: cannot share his life. The warmth goes out of him and he becomes – becomes –'

She extended a hand and slowly drew in the fingers like the closing of petals.

'Shrivelled?' Brewster suggested.

'Yes.' She nodded emphatically, her face sad. 'Shrivelled and hard. Like my husband.'

They walked a few steps in silence, then she gripped his arm and smiled brightly. He looked down at her.

'It must not happen to you,' she said with mock severity.

'If I had you to confide in, Christina, I should consider myself very fortunate. As it is, I usually discuss things with an old and trusted friend.'

'Mr Atherton?'

'Yes.'

As they continued their walk, he told her about the anonymous letter.

'What will you do about it?' she asked.

The two officers from the French sloop, who had been given the freedom of the quarterdeck for exercise, raised their hats to Brewster and Madame Hanikof as they passed by. Lawson jerked his thumb at their backs.

'I shall send them ashore in exchange for any prisoners from *Adamant*. Midshipman Clayton is alive and not too badly to be moved. He'll give me an account of what happened. Until he is returned, I shall do nothing. It would be bad for discipline to question the men who were present in the whaler at the time, so I'll leave the author of my letter in doubt as to the success of his unorthodox postal service.'

'How was this letter sent to you?'

'We have a few light-fingered men on board,' Brewster grinned. 'My clerk found it in his pocket.'

CHAPTER SIXTEEN

'Well, I'm envious of you, I don't deny it, but I'm damned pleased just the same,' Heward said as he examined Lawson in his bright blue coat with its white lapels and cuffs and brass buttons. 'Jolly decent of Prendergast to let you have it, and the tailor's made a good job of the alterations. Lieutenant Lawson! I'll have to call you "sir" now.'

'Acting-Lieutenant,' Lawson reminded him. 'I'm neither fur nor feather. I must move out of here,' he said, looking around the midshipmen's mess, 'but I can't see that I'll get much of a welcome in the wardroom from the senior officers and greybeards, although the surgeon is always friendly.'

'You should have stayed in your bed a few days longer. If you'd waited until Trevelyan completes this business with the French, you could have gone straight out to take over the sloop. We'd have had a few more days with the ladies too. Now we'll rarely get the opportunity to talk to them with any degree of privacy.'

Lawson smiled. He was far from recovered, and he could have well done with more time off before declaring himself fit, but lying abed did not suit his temperament, even though it had given him the opportunity to spend a lot of time in Victoria's company, and she was becoming important to him. He must find some opportunity to talk to her again before leaving *Adamant*.

'Victoria's birthday tomorrow,' Heward said, as if reading his thoughts. 'Have you anything for a present'

'I might find something,' Lawson grunted non-committally.

'The old man's becoming very paternal towards her, have you noticed? I have a sneaking suspicion that this shooting competition and dinner that are planned for tomorrow, might have been arranged on account of her birthday. Mind you, the men are in need of some kind of diversion. This sailing up and down within sight of the French coast is enough to bore everyone to death.'

There was a tap at the door and one of the mess servants, an old seaman called Leach, came into the low compartment with two youths at his heels. He indicated the iron-bound oak chest lying on the deck with the name J. Lawson burned into the lid. They picked it up and carried it from the midshipmen's mess. It was an historic moment: the departure from life as a midshipman and entry to the officer class. It was the first step of a ladder that could elevate him to the rank of captain, and place him on better than equal terms with the most pretentious of his mother's relatives in Whitby, the Reverend Herbert Spencer-Jerome.

Lawson had often indulged in fanciful thoughts during the miseries of his first two years at sea. Always he had seen himself as the one who would restore his sister, Jane, to the position in society that they had known prior to their mother's death and the subsequent excessive drinking and financial ruin of their father. He would go back to Whitby with prize money. Fabulous amounts were being paid, according to the newspapers and the recruiting posters. He would buy back the family house and re-establish Jane and his father's poor sister in circumstances that would compare with any of his mother's family.

Lawson smiled at his own presumption as his mind flashed over the familiar fantasies. He would find himself back in the midshipmen's mess if he failed to satisfy the board of examiners, or if Captain Brewster's recommendation did not meet with approval at Admiralty. Unlike Heward, who had relatives highly placed in the naval hierarchy, and a family tradition of naval service going back to the time of James I, Lawson had no one to look after his interests.

'Will there by anything else, sir?' Leach asked.

'Not at the moment, thank you. See me later when I am settled in my new quarters.'

He would have to give Leach a gratuity now that he was leaving the mess but the most he could afford was two shillings and he did not care to hand over such a small amount in the presence of the wealthy Heward.

Davies, one of the two gunner's mates, appeared in the doorway as Leach left. He had his hat in his hands.

'Mr Muir would like to see you, sir, when it is convenient,' he said in a voice that had lost none of its Welsh lilt, for all his years at sea. 'He wishes to speak to Mr Heward as well.'

Lawson experienced a thrill of excitement and pleasure at the choice of words and the man's changed mien. Yesterday the message would have been a peremptory, 'Mr Muir wishes to see you,' and the man might have added, 'immediately'. He had not concerned himself with Heward's convenience, an omission which brought a twisted smile to Heward's face, as it clearly emphasized the difference in rank and the inevitable barrier that must now exist between former shipmates.

The half-hour allowed for breakfast had just ended and the lower gun-deck was teeming with men moving briskly, each to his allotted task, when Lawson and Heward arrived. The legless tables, suspended on ropes in between the guns, were hoisted out of the way. Benches were being secured down the middle line of the deck. The wooden mess kits, together with other utensils, were disappearing rapidly up the gangway to the open deck, where they would be scrubbed and stacked.

All the men worked without speaking, from the deft, able-bodied seamen conditioned by years of hustle, to the clumsiest of the most recently recruited landsmen. They were supervised by petty officers strategically placed, and each with a rope's end or a cane held threateningly in his hands, but these were anxious men themselves whose eyes occasionally darted in the direction of the stairway leading down to the magazine below the waterline. This was part of Mr Muir's kingdom and he drove everyone in it as hard as he drove himself.

'Mr Muir will not have finished inspecting the magazine, sir,' Davies said after he had looked around. 'Will you wait here until he arrives?'

'We'll join him below,' Lawson said.

As he moved in the direction of the gangway, he saw a man, a poor pathetic creature, who was wearing clothes much too big for him, accidentally knock a round shot out of the rack with the bench he was handling. Now he scrambled frantically after it as it rumbled along the deck, and he was getting cursed and cuffed by those he bumped into. Lawson snatched a leather fire bucket off its hook, tossed out the water and held the bucket on its side in the path of the shot. It ran into it, jerked the bucket into an upright position and came to a halt. The man approached Lawson with his lips working nervously and his eyes frightened. He was unable to speak.

'All right, take it away,' Lawson said patiently. 'See that the bucket is refilled after you have finished your present duties.'

'Th-thank you, sir,' the man stammered in relief.

He took up the thirty-two-pounder shot with difficulty and carried it back to that part of the long rack from which it had been dislodged, by which time Lawson and Heward were descending to the lower deck, but they heard the crack of the rope's end and the yelp. Lawson paused just long enough to note that the Irish gunner's mate, Blackshaw, was punishing the man for his carelessness.

'That was not only unnecessary, it was stupid,' Lawson said to Heward. 'The man will not be made less clumsy for having been struck. It was probably fear of punishment that caused the accident in the first place.'

Davies, who was walking behind, heard the remark and grimaced. The sentiments would be well discussed by the warrant officers over their grog. Heward pursed his lips and made no comment. So far as he was concerned, 'starting' the men with a rope's end or a cane was standard practice and always had been in the Navy.

Yesterday, he would have debated the point with Lawson; now there was the barrier of rank between them.

'Mr Muir will be inside the magazine, sir,' the Welshman said. 'If you want to go in after him, you'll have to wear slippers.'

'Of course,' Lawson replied. 'Please find a pair for Mr Heward and me.'

There were two magazines set in *Adamant*'s hold: a large one just forward of the mainmast, where all the barrels of gunpowder were stored and where the cartridges for the guns were filled, and a much smaller compartment in the stern where prepared cartridges for the eighteen- and twenty-four-pounder guns of the upper gun-decks lay on shelves. Mr Muir was in the main magazine, which was divided from the rest of the hold by walls of stout timber lined with thin sheets of copper. The door was guarded by a sentry who snapped to attention as Lawson approached.

'Here you are, sir,' Davies said, handing over a pair of floppy felt slippers, which he had taken from a rack at the side of the door.

They were big enough to pull on over the buckled shoes that Lawson wore, but there were strict regulations forbidding the wearing of any kind of shoe capable of causing a spark, and Lawson's shoes had metal heels and tips. He slipped them off and Heward did the same.

The interior of the magazine was almost dazzlingly bright after the gloom of the hold, yet the light came only from oil-lamps set in the walls at various points with polished metal reflectors behind them. None of the lamp clusters could be reached from inside the magazine since the lamp rooms, as they were called, were sealed off from the magazine by small, thick panes of glass set in oak frames.

Mr Muir looked up over iron-rimmed spectacles from the book he was examining as the party approached.

'I hadna' expected ye sae soon, Mr Lawson,' he said, rising from his seat and removing the glasses. 'I wonder if ye'll be kind enough to gi' me a few mair minutes whilst I check these figures. Perhaps ye'd care tae look aroond the place? Mr Davies will be ready tae explain things tae ye.'

Probably Muir would have interrupted his examination of the books for no one short of the captain, unless directly ordered, Lawson reflected as he turned away. As it was, he welcomed the opportunity to look around. His duties had never taken him into either of *Adamant*'s magazines, and the master gunner would never have allowed an idle midshipman inside.

Just then, Blackshaw arrived with five bare-footed men, part of the large labour force of unskilled, inexperienced crew who were daily set to various tasks about the ship and would never normally enter the magazine. The man who had dropped the round shot was among them.

'They've come to turn the powder barrels,' Davies explained, noting Heward's curiosity. 'Admiralty orders: they have to be turned every four weeks to prevent the separation of the nitre from the other ingredients.'

'Yes,' Lawson replied, then added to Heward, 'This was a job I had to supervise in my frigate days, but we never had more than twelve barrels on *Wakeful*.'

'Must be fifty or sixty stored here,' Heward said.

'Seventy-seven, sir, but they'll be taking out the oldest powder casks for use in the shooting practice tomorrow,' Davies informed him.

They stood watching the magazine staff as they filled the serge bags, using scoops similar to those a shop-keeper would have for measuring his sugar or flour. A full scoop was a pound of gunpowder, and they needed ten to hurl a thirty-two pounder shot one and a half miles. Further along the table, other men were stitching the end of each filled bag and stacking the finished cartridges on racks which had the size of the gun, for which they were intended, clearly marked in chalk.

Lawson and Heward were inspecting the hoist used to send the cartridges up to the orlop deck when there was a great crash of bursting timbers followed by a string of oaths. A powder barrel had been dropped from the height of the top tier and, landing on the belly of another barrel, had burst them both. Now several of the men, looking very apprehensive, were ankle-deep in black gunpowder, which had spread across the deck. Muir walked to the edge of the pile of powder and looked up at the place from which the barrel had been dislodged. There were two men there. The man with the rope of the winch in his hands was the one who had been beaten earlier. He was frozen in terror.

'Mr Blackshaw,' Muir said in a voice that was a little above a whisper, 'ye'll be fully aware by noo that I canna' abide foul language in my department.'

'I'm sorry, sir. I – I lost my temper over their carelessness.'

'Was it carelessness,' Muir asked, taking up the sling suspended from the winch, 'or was it – inexpeerience? We shall discuss it later. Meanwhile, I should be obliged if ye'll personally check every sling before a barrel is hoisted.'

He turned back to the tiny desk where he had been working earlier, took up a paper from it and approached Lawson.

'I'm sorry aboot the accident, sir. Noo, if ye'll be guid enough tae examine this paper, ye will see the arrangements, approved by the captain, made for tomorrow's gun practice, and the competition that is tae follow. The officers and midshipmen will each take over a section o' guns, as specified on this paper. The senior officers, including the captain, will be responsible for the thirty-two-pounder guns on the lower deck. I believe that Captain Brewster intends tae sight one o' the guns himself.'

'Can we do the same?' Heward asked excitedly.

'If ye wish,' Muir replied drily, 'but I've nae doobt ye'll be unpopular amongst the misguided men who will be laying wagers on the outcome o' the competition, if ye don't leave it tae the reg'lar gunners; unless, of course, ye've acquired some expeerience unbeknown tae me. Captain Brewster kens what he's aboot in the matter o' guns.'

'What about targets?'

'The heavy guns are going tae sink that fishing boat ye captured.'

'Sink her!' Lawson exclaimed.

'Aye, sir,' Muir replied sympathetically. 'It seems that

it wouldna' be practical tae keep her. Her main timbers were badly damaged in the action and she'd likely founder in the next bit o' weather, so the carpenter informed me. The heavy guns will engage her at a mile and a half. They'll fire one section at a time, and the fall o' the shots will be obsairved and duly credited by you and Mr Heward.'

'Are we the only judges?'

'In this part o' the competition, yes. The captain and I shall judge the performance wi' the lighter guns.'

'I suppose we'll be shooting at those barrels that have been brought out of the hold and are now cluttering up the foredeck?' Heward said.

'That is correct, Mr Heward. Old beef barrels for the most part, which the surgeon has condemned because they are – noo what was the worrd – impregnated? Yes, impregnated with filth.'

'The purser will not be very pleased about that,' Lawson said. 'Doesn't he get an allowance for every barrel he returns to the victualling yard?'

'He does indeed, sir,' Muir replied. 'Now as tae the judging o' the competition, which is the reason I asked ye tae see me, Captain Brewster is most insistent upon a high standard, and the points scored will be as follows . . .'

Whilst Muir was explaining the points system, Lieutenant Trevelyan and Midshipman Saunders were awaiting the arrival of a boat being rowed out to them from the shore, in which sat a French artillery officer. They had taken the captured *sloop-de-guerre* into le Goulet under a flag of truce and anchored before the guns of the fort in accordance with Captain Brewster's orders.

It was at a time when the courtesies and conventions of war were observed strictly, and Trevelyan was as safe in le Goulet under a white flag as he would have been in the Thames. He was nevertheless anxious. He could see through his telescope that the gunners in the fort were manning their heavy ordnance, and it gave him little consolation to know that any French officer who gave the order to open fire would be court martialled. At four hundred yards, the guns in the fort would have sunk the small sloop instantly.

Trevelyan could speak French fairly fluently, which was why Captain Brewster had entrusted him with the task of negotiating for an exchange of prisoners, but there would be little for him to do. The proposals, set out in the letter that he carried, were so favourable to the French that they could hardly be refused.

CHAPTER SEVENTEEN

Annette, Madame Hanikof's elder daughter, had always preferred to lose herself in a book rather than socialize, until Lieutenant Grayson had joined the Russian sloop as liaison officer. Since his death, she was reading more than ever, devouring Prendergast's volumes of poetry and the collection of old tomes that Mr Atherton had gathered over the years. Consequently, Victoria found herself more and more in the company of Madame Lorette, particularly as the girls' mother seemed to be increasingly occupied by Captain Brewster.

Madame Lorette, or Eleanor, as she was now called by the Hanikof family, was twelve months older than Victoria, but she had spent all her life shut away from the world, whereas the Russian sisters had travelled widely and had been allowed much more freedom by their emancipated mother than most young females of their class. As a result, apart from the tending of the sick where the French girl had special experience, Victoria was the more knowledgeable and sophisticated of the two.

'I think,' Victoria said thoughtfully, holding up an elaborately frilled, yellow dress for inspection, 'that you will look so charming in this.'

It was the morning of Victoria's seventeenth birthday. Beyond the cabin walls were the sounds of the ship: squealing gun-carriage wheels suggesting the exercising of the ship's main armament, cheerful voices calling from aloft, the cracking of stiff canvas as the mainsail on the mizzenmast was brought into use and, in the background, subdued but continuous, was the slither and scrape of thirty or more 'holystones', sandstone blocks, being pushed back and forth over the wet deck boards by the kneeling, unskilled labour force of the ship.

The girls heard none of the outside preparations for the gala day. Eleanor took the garment, held it against her body and examined herself in the mirror set in the lid of the wooden trunk. Her face was flushed with excitement. She had never worn anything other than plain greys and whites in her life.

'It is beautiful,' she said, turning left and right.

'Try it,' Victoria urged.

The French girl hesitated, indecision clearly in her eyes, then she shook her head regretfully.

'I cannot wear this beautiful dress at your party. I am in – in – *en grand deuil*. My husband is dead.'

The two girls had agreed to speak only English in order to improve their proficiency in the language. '*En grand dueil*' was a phrase that Victoria had not heard before. She guessed it meant 'in mourning', and she exploded into a string of Russian that was obviously censorious and unladylike, but totally incomprehensible. She returned to English.

'You did not *know* him,' she exclaimed, gesticulating excitedly with her hands. 'He was – husband in name only. You did not go to bed together.'

'But I married him,' Eleanor said simply.

'Poo! It should not have been permitted. A guardian who uses his – his power – his position to make his ward marry him does not deserve any good thoughts.' She snapped her fingers in dismissal. 'I would dance on his grave.'

Eleanor looked shocked for a moment, then she smiled wistfully, shook her head and handed the dress back. Victoria sighed, shrugged her shoulders, then delved again into the trunk. Eventually she produced a black dress and held it at arm's length for inspection. It was creased and obviously had not seen the light of day for some months.

'This is Mama's, but she does not want it again, I think. I shall ask her. We shall have to alter it a little, but that will not be difficult. Please try it on.'

On the upper gun-deck, Lawson, Heward and Atkins were busy exercising the crews of those guns that had been assigned to them. Lawson had the first four guns on the starboard side. Heward was in charge of starboard five to eight. Atkins had been given the advantage of the extra gun in that he was allocated nine to thirteen to allow every twenty-four-pounder in the starboard battery to take part in the competition. They would have the same numbers when it was the turn of the port-side battery, and they were making sure that no time would be lost in reloading because of poor gun drill.

'Faster, damn you. Put your backs into those side tackles. Heave, you idle swine, Jacobs.'

Atkins brought his cane down hard on Jacobs' buttocks. His five guns were not being served as efficiently as those in the other two sections, and his voice, louder and half an octave higher, was irritating everybody on the deck. The competition meant a great deal to Atkins. Victoria was to present the prizes.

Lawson and Heward hardly raised their voices as they drilled their gun crews, but the men were dripping sweat with their efforts and obviously tremendously keen.

'Can we go through it just once more, sir?' Riley, the senior gunner asked, after Lawson had called enough. 'Five of the men are new to the work and it's important that they get the sequence right, for it'll be the rate o' fire that'll decide it, more'n likely, 'specially if we gets down to point-blank range.'

Each section of these guns would have three barrels to sink at a range of five hundred yards – no mean feat from a moving ship with the targets bobbing up and down in the swell. If they were unsuccessful in the time allowed by the captain and Mr Muir, *Adamant* would close to point-blank range which, for this size of gun, was up to two hundred and seventy yards. All the gun captains were anxious to avoid this as it was generally reckoned that any fool could score hits at point-blank range, where no elevation was required, but it took a skilled man to estimate the correct angle for distances beyond.

'All right, Riley,' Lawson agreed. 'Once more then. Guns one, two, three and four, load.'

They went through the drill again. Riley was still not satisfied but it would have to do. It would soon be time for Lawson and Heward to prepare for the judging of the lower deck guns and, since the captain and senior officers were involved, they had better be ready for them. Anyway, Riley and the others would be kept busy enough preparing for Mr Muir's inspection before the competition began. If the master gunner saw any signs of wear on the ropes used to restrain the guns as they recoiled, or on the side tackles, which enabled the men to heave the fifty-hundredweight weapon back into position after it had been reloaded, he would withdraw that gun from the competition and charge the gun captain and crew with negligence.

The ship's whaler was ready to be hoisted over the side. The boat was to be used by Lawson and Heward when they went out to judge the shooting of the heavier guns. The crew, standing in readiness, looked far from happy. They would be obliged to sail close to the target, taking care to keep out of the line of fire. It was safe enough, Lawson thought, provided the gun captains knew what they were doing and there were no accidents.

Lawson turned from his inspection of the whaler to see two young ladies approaching. Heward grinned and swept off his hat in an elaborate bow. Victoria fell in with his mood and responded with an equally elaborate curtsey, but her eyes were really for Lawson, who had merely raised his hat and smiled.

'I do hope that you have a very happy birthday, Miss Victoria,' he said softly.

'Oh yes, many happy returns,' Heward said breezily, tearing his eyes away from Madame Lorette.

Every eye on the foredeck had noted the arrival of the two girls, and a pretty sight they were in the bright morning sunshine, holding on to their bonnets and voluminous skirts against the freshening breeze. Some men were openly envious, and one turned away to mutter

174

lustful comments to his neighbour, but the most covetous person of all, jealousy and hatred in every part of his being, was Midshipman Atkins, who was viewing the encounter across the waist of the ship from his position on the quarterdeck. Parker, who was working under Atkins' supervision, stopped what he was doing and followed the direction of the detested midshipman's eyes. Then he leered and nudged the fellow next to him, who in turn drew the attention of another man until the party of six men had stopped work to enjoy Atkins' obvious torment.

'Well, Mr Atherton, are we going to have a little bet on the outcome? Just you and me, your guns against mine?' Captain Brewster said affably.

'Ye consider yourself guid enough tae compete against me, do ye?' Atherton replied, the dourness of his expression relieved by a twinkle in his eyes. 'Well, I wouldna' say no tae taking a guinea from ye, sir. That's for scores by the four guns sighted by yourself or regular gun captains. Then I'll take another guinea, if ye've a mind, on the result of oor personal shooting. Surprised, sir? I ken ye used tae fancy yourself in the auld days, but it was a long time ago.'

'You're on,' Brewster growled. 'It's time you were taken down a peg or two. We'll sight our own guns after the main events – just the two of us. It should amuse the men and they need a bit of a boost. We'll see if we can sink any of the barrels that the twenty-fours can't hit.'

'Time we were away, sir,' Warrant officer Davies, the Welsh gunner's mate, called from the waiting whaler.

'I have a small present for you,' Lawson said quietly to Victoria. 'I'll let you have it when we get back.'

Her eyes were shining as he turned away to supervise the launching of the whaler. Then she and Madame Lorette stood together watching as the whaler was hoisted over the side to the sea and rowed out to the distant target.

There the whaler was left to drift slowly to leeward, keeping pace with the doomed *pecheur* which, abandoned, lay a hundred yards away, awaiting the first of the heavy cannonballs that would complete her destruction.

Lawson and Heward, assisted by the experienced Mr Davies, who would have been well briefed by Mr Muir, were entrusted to note and record the shots from each section of four guns as they fired, with an interval of two minutes between groups. Every shot striking any part of the vessel would credit one point. Shots striking within three feet of the waterline were worth one and a half points.

'There's the signal flag broken out, sir,' Davies said, lowering his telecope.

'For what we're about to receive,' Heward breathed, his glass on the distant *Adamant*, from which tongues of flame spat, to be immediately engulfed by smoke.

His head jerked around to watch the target that Lawson and Davies already had under observation, but there was plenty of time. The cannonballs must travel in a high trajectory and would take ten seconds to arrive. The noise of the guns would reach them earlier.

Two spouts of water rose before the *pecheur*, to be immediately followed by another beyond. No one saw the fall of the fourth shot but it certainly had not struck the target or they would have heard the crash.

'Probably a misfire, sir,' Davies said.

As if to confirm his opinion, the fourth shot whistled across the distance and struck the target. Obviously the flintlock mechanism, which was still very new in the Fleet and not popular with the older gunners, had failed. There would have been a delay whilst the gunner had cocked the mechanism again and perhaps, in the end, turned to the bucket that contained a glowing length of fuse.

'That's one point scored for the first section,' Lawson said, making a mark on his pad. 'Now we'll see what the next group will do.'

'Whose is it?' Heward asked.

'Mr Atherton's.'

They watched the four blooms of white smoke, which looked for all the world like the heads of cauliflowers, appearing in quick succession, to be dispersed by the breeze. Then the iron arrived. Two hit the target and one plunged into the sea a hundred yards short. The fourth passed over their heads making a sound not unlike a flurry of pigeons' wings on being released from the racing basket. Everyone ducked.

'Bloody hell!' someone exclaimed.

'There it goes, be damned,' Heward shouted excitedly, following the track of the descending projectile into the sea beyond them.

'What do you make of that, Mr Davies?' Lawson demanded urgently.

'Most likely the cannonball has split, or maybe it's not perfectly round, so the air resistance is greater on one side than the other, causing it to skid out of line. It's not uncommon, sir.'

He had delivered his explanation as if he were in front of a class. Training gunners was one of his duties. Lawson's startled eyes sought Heward's. Heward grimaced.

'We're probably a bit too near then, Mr Davies?' Lawson queried sharply.

'We are indeed, sir.'

'Get rowing!' Lawson ordered abruptly.

The six-man crew needed no urging. They had all looked scared when the shot passed overhead. Now they were putting their backs into the sweeps and the bow wave was foaming white away from the *pecheur*.

'Why on earth didn't you tell me, Mr Davies?' Lawson hissed exasperatedly.

Davies looked uncomfortable. 'Indeed, it did occur to me, sir, but not every officer would welcome being advised – unless asked. Mr Trevelyan has been most particular on the subject.'

'Particular? What do you mean?'

'He said that unasked-for advice is impertinence, sir.'

'How long have you specialized in gunnery?'

'Twenty years, sir.'

'Before I was born!' He tapped Davies on the shoulder. 'If at any time you see me making a fool of myself in the matter of guns, just let me know.'

'That I will, sir.'

'Me too,' Heward said fervently.

Captain Brewster's section of guns registered two hits on the second round, both plunging shots that probably went out through the bottom. Then Mr Atherton's section managed another two hits, but before it was Captain Brewster's turn again, the *pecheur* lurched and began to settle by the stern. Now there was only a triangle of timber above the surface. The sea boiled around it but none of the shots registered a hit. Slowly the boat slid beneath the surface.

'It looks as if Mr Atherton has won,' Lawson said, totting up the points. 'Mr Prendergast and the captain share second place.' He was making a show of briskness, but his eyes were sad and he kept them averted, looking at the paper.

'Miserable business, seeing your first command going to the bottom,' Heward said sympathetically.

Lawson nodded and smiled.

The midday meal had been served when the whaler returned to *Adamant*. Lawson made sure that his boat crew got their rations. He was about to go to the wardroom, when he received a message to join the captain's table. He washed hurriedly, changed his boat gear for the jacket he had been given by Prendergast, and entered the cabin. To his surprise, Heward was already there, seated between Victoria and Madame Lorette and grinning broadly at Lawson's obvious astonishment. There was an empty place on Victoria's left to which Lawson was directed. The only other people at the table were Madame Hanikof and the captain. It was like a cosy family affair, except that Annette was absent.

'Sorry I didn't give you notice,' Brewster rumbled. 'Last-minute arrangement. Nothing to do with this evening's party. Just wanted to hear what you thought about the shooting.'

Since Brewster never said another word about the morning's work, he was obviously not in the least interested in what either Lawson or Heward thought about it. It was evidently a contrived situation, an additional concession to Victoria's birthday through the influence of Madame Hanikof. No one had ever been known to dine with the captain at midday, and indeed, it was a curious social occasion in which three separate conversations were going on most of the time. Lawson shyly and surreptitiously slipped a beautiful enamelled brooch into Victoria's hand. The men saw nothing but no woman could have failed to note the love in Victoria's eyes as she accepted the gift.

The gun crews were standing in readiness by the twenty-four-pounders when Lawson and Heward arrived on the gun-deck. Atkins had been there for some time, wooden-faced and unresponsive to Heward's cheery grin. He had dined alone in the midshipmen's mess and, of course, he knew where the other two had been.

As Muir had predicted, there had been heavy betting on the results of the twenty-four-pounder competition, and the gunners were excited. In fact the whole ship had an air of festivity about it, which had been heightened when the story got around that Captain Brewster and Mr Atherton were to compete against each other after the main shoot.

Not many naval captains would have risked their precious dignity in such a public display. Whatever the officers thought about it, the men were delighted. Brewster could sense their high spirits, and feel their friendship towards him. It pleased him immensely. He beamed at Atherton.

Do you think we might have a concert after grog has been issued this evening?' he asked genially.

'I shouldna' be surprised, sir, especially if ye offer a few ounces o' 'baccy tae every man who performs,' Atherton replied.

'See to it then, will you? Ask the bo'sun if he will be good enough to organize it again. Tell him it can be just like he did it last time: lots of songs where they all sing the chorus. That's the sort of thing that goes down well.'

'The bo'sun is just below, talking tae the purser. Would ye not rather ask him yourself, sir?'

'I haven't your charm, Mr Atherton,' he smiled. Then added, 'I'd rather you spoke to him because he'd take it as an order if it came directly from me.'

Captain Brewster looked down over the hammock

rack that served as a safety fence on the forward end of the quarterdeck. The bo'sun, a man of above average height, all bone and muscle, with a face like chiselled granite, was looking over the shoulder of a fat man in his early fifties, who was pointing to some item in the ledger he held. Both wore the same type of coat, blue kerseymere with brass buttons, and yellow nankeen trousers, but whereas the bo'sun had a glazed, shortened top hat jammed hard on his head, the purser wore a three-cornered hat over his wig. As pursers were usually of more gentle breeding, they cherished this concession in the matter of headgear, even though the bo'sun was their equal in rank.

'Since the purser's there, you can ask him to release enough beer from store to allow every man to have a pint – no damn it, a quart – at the same time as he issues the grog.'

Atherton whistled his surprise. 'What shall we say th'occasion is? He'd better not write Miss Victoria's birthday in the victuals book.'

'It's the national saint's day. Did you not know?' Brewster said, with a raising of his eyebrows.

'Which saint is that?'

'Miss Victoria shares an anniversary with the good St George.'

'It's tae be hoped that ye'll show the same conseederation for St Andrew when his turn comes along,' Atherton said with mock severity as he went off.

'Mr Atherton!' Brewster called after him.

'Yes, sir?'

'While you're down there, just tell Atkins to shut up,' the captain said quietly. 'I can hear his stupid voice from here. Like a bloody fishwife screaming at the men.'

On the upper gun-deck, Lawson pointed out to sea. The whaler was being rowed past, and the men in her were tossing barrels off, in groups of three, over the stern.

'There they are, my lads. The last three they put into the sea are ours. There are two fathoms of rope between each barrel, so they'll keep together. All we've got to do is sink them before the other gun crews sink theirs.'

The crews of Lawson's four guns crowded around their gun-ports. Black spots could be seen dancing up and down on a sparkling sea. The chances of any section sinking its three barrels at five hundred yards were small. In fact, the ship's bookies offered odds of eight to one against, and there were not many takers when it was learnt that the captain was allowing only five minutes' shooting at this range. Much of the money placed was on which section would sink the most barrels, and Lawson's was the favourite. However, the competition that had caught the interest of the whole ship's company was the one to follow between Captain Brewster and Mr Atherton. Everyone had bet on the outcome. It was common knowledge that they had both been gunners in their youth, and most were aware of their friendship.

'Stand by tae commence firing,' Mr Muir shouted.

He had his watch in his hand. Blackshaw gripped the rope of the bell clapper. Davies, who was the more senior gunner's mate, had been sent aft to keep an eye on Atkins, but when Mr Atherton came below, he moved further forward towards Heward's section and watched unobtrusively. The master's presence near the after-gangway would surely quieten the midshipman.

The harsh clanging of the bell started the action. Some of the gunners foolishly jerked their flintlock lanyards immediately, their reflexes triggered by the sudden noise. The others checked their sights again, ignoring the roars and smoke about them, before they fired. Mr Atherton took a pair of earplugs from his pocket and swiftly inserted them.

Speed in reloading was important. Some of the guns would fire seven shots in the time allowed. The badly served ones might manage four. It soon became obvious to Midshipman Atkins that the guns commanded by Heard and Lawson were being much more efficiently handled than his. He was livid with rage, particularly after one of his guns misfired and another lost its flint, but he had to control himself with Atherton obviously watching him.

'This gun sounds as if it's cracked, sir,' the gun-captain on number thirteen shouted urgently.

'Carry on, damn you,' Atkins spat viciously, his threatening, clenched fist concealed from Mr Atherton.

The gun was reloaded in brooding silence by the men who attended it. They all knew the danger. The gun captain had been darting worried glances from the supervision of his work at the youth in the long blue coat of authority. Atkins was too busy mouthing threats and shaking his stick at the other gun crews to notice. The carriage wheels squealed over the deck boards as the heavy gun rolled forward to thrust its muzzle through the side of the ship. The gunner primed the pan and cocked the flintlock mechanism. Then, indecision gave way to determination. He strode over to the midshipman.

'I'm sure the barrel is cracked, sir,' he said doggedly.

'You insolent swine,' Atkins screamed. 'Get back to your gun and carry on.'

He lashed out with his cane. The man took the blow on his shoulder and returned to the gun, obviously seething with rage. Atherton saw the incident and approached curiously, removing his ear plugs. Davies also noticed that something was amiss but, like Atherton, he had not heard what had been said. He too moved closer.

The gun captain's gestures to his crew, and the furious 'damn-them-all-to-hell' expression on his face as he seized the lanyard, suddenly made it clear to both Atherton and Davies what the situation was.

'Stop!' Atherton shouted as he hurried forward. 'Stop, I say!'

He barged Atkins out of the way in his eagerness to reach the gun, but he was too late. The gunner had probably not heard the order in that bedlam of noise, or maybe he was too consumed with rage to heed it. As Atherton's hand gripped his shoulder, the man jerked the lanyard. The flint sparked. The priming powder in the pan ignited in a puff of flame, and the gun blew itself to bits, instantly killing the gunner, one of his crew and Mr Atherton.

CHAPTER EIGHTEEN

The sun, wreathed in wispy clouds and glowing red, was sinking to the horizon when Lieutenant Prendergast knocked on the door of the captain's quarters and entered. He found Captain Brewster slumped at his desk staring blankly at the bulkhead and showing no indication that he had seen or heard his second-in-command.

'The men are assembled for the burial service, sir,' Prendergast said quietly, 'Rather a lot present, too, sir,' he added significantly.

'Yes, they had expected a concert at sunset,' Brewster mused, with no change in his expression.

'Will you attend the service, sir?' Prendergast asked, after an interval in which the captain had made no further comment.

Brewster sighed, rose from the desk and took up his hat.

'Yes, Mr Prendergast, I shall. Did you instruct the chaplain to make it brief?'

'Yes, sir. I also informed him that you would not be speaking.'

Captain Brewster nodded, slipped a small red book into his pocket and walked out onto the quarterdeck. Prendergast followed, but stepped aside to speak briefly to the senior marine sergeant who had obviously been waiting for him.

Attendance at the burial service was not compulsory, but the foredeck, welldeck and rigging were crowded with silent men, bare-headed in the evening breeze. Brewster halted, surprised.

'I don't like this, Mr Prendergast,' he said, his eyes taking in the two to three hundred grim faces. 'A half, maybe two-thirds of the ship's company here. In an ugly mood too by the look of them. Have you got Atkins somewhere safe?'

'Yes, sir. He's in Mr Trevelyan's cabin. There are two marine sentries posted outside, and I have just given orders for the whole marine force to be ready in case of trouble.'

Brewster straightened himself, set his cocked hat firmly on his head and walked to the forward edge of the quarterdeck. There he removed his headgear, cradled it in the crook of his arm and nodded to the chaplain. Before and below him on the welldeck, a hatch cover had been set up with one end resting on the bulwarks and projecting over the sea. The inside edge of this makeshift platform was supported by a trestle. It was the traditional naval bier, covered by a flag that did not conceal the shapes of the three bodies beneath. Brewster gave the preparations a cursory glance, looped his spectacles around his ears and looked down at his Common Prayer book, which had the ship's repertoire of suitable hymns pasted in the back.

There had been three burial services over the past week, each attended by no more than fifty men, and the hymns had been the same in every case. Now, it seemed that the size of the congregation had stimulated the chaplain to find something different. The little group of instrumentalists struck up with 'Fanad Head', an Irish melody which was well known, but for different words than those in Brewster's book.

They are all gone into the world of light,
And I alone sit lingering here.
Their very memory is fair and bright
And my sad thoughts doth clear.

Eventually, they reached that part of the service where the bodies are dispatched to the sea. Thirteen had been buried as one only a few days earlier. Now there were only three, but the drama of the situation, starkly revealed in the faces of the men, was more acute than it had ever been.

The chaplain's voice could be heard clearly over the silent decks: 'And so we commit these bodies to the deep.'

He bowed his head. The burial party hoisted the hatch cover to the full extent of their arms. The great ensign rippled as the three grey shapes slid from under it. The silence was intense: even the ship seemed to cease its creaking, and the air was still. The sound of the bodies striking the water was heard by all.

'That bastard Atkins ought to be pitched over with 'em.'

Most of the faces jerked in the direction of the concealed man who had shouted. Then they turned back to fix their eyes on Captain Brewster who, in turn, glared at the shocked chaplain, willing him to carry on with the service as if nothing had happened.

'Do you wish me to find the man who shouted?' Prendergast asked when the service had ended.

'No. We should have to punish him, and that could be dangerous in the present situation. Anyway, I recognized his voice. At least, I think I did. It was that bloody Parker, I feel sure.'

'I see. What are your orders regarding Midshipman Atkins, sir?'

'I'd like to take a rope's end to him,' Brewster said in an angry undertone. Then added, 'You'd better leave him where he is for his own safety. If we see a British ship homeward bound, we'll get him aboard it. He'll never do any good now on *Adamant*.'

'What about putting him on the sloop when Mr Trevelyan returns, sir?'

'No. I want shut of him.'

After Prendergast had left, the captain wrote up the log, then drafted a report of the incident to be copied by his clerk for dispatch to Admiralty at the first opportunity. This was his usual occupation in the early evening, normally followed by a pipe and a bottle of wine, or maybe something stronger, with Atherton. Now, he was alone and, since he had declined an invitation to join the Hanikofs at dinner, using the excuse that he had too much to do, he could hardly invite them to share his evening.

He went out onto the quarterdeck, palely lit by the moon, and looked around. Lawson was in charge of the watch in his new capacity as acting lieutenant. Brewster buttoned his coat to the neck and began to pace the windward side with his hands thrust behind him, obviously seeing and hearing nothing, brooding and unapproachable. He kept it up until four bells, having noted the lights in the officers' accommodation go out one by one, then he returned to his quarters, saying goodnight to the marine sentry posted at the door.

Brewster had surrendered his night cabin to Madame Hanikof rather than oust any of the lieutenants from their quarters. Now he had a bed set up in the small compartment formerly used for the captain's special stores when *Adamant* had been commanded by men with more fastidious tastes than Brewster's. It was adjoining the night cabin, and Brewster had often wondered if his snores had disturbed Madame Hanikof. Quietly he removed his boots, hung his clothes in the cupboard and put on a thick flannel nightshirt. It was half-past ten. Apart from the men on duty, all the ship's company should be in their beds.

Sleep was denied Brewster. He lay tossing and turning, with the bed creaking under him. He heard eight bells and the change of the watch, and he knew that he would not sleep that night. He was just about to get out of bed when the door slowly opened. It made no sound, but it admitted the light from the lantern that Brewster had left burning on a low wick in the main cabin. He tensed, ready to spring for the cutlass hooked onto the bulkhead, then relaxed, hardly able to believe his senses. Madame Hanikof was outlined in the doorway. She came to him quickly and kneeled at the side of his bed. She took one of his hands in hers and smoothed his hair.

'I do grieve for you,' she whispered.

He reached out to her and she went to him in close embrace. Her cheek against his was wet with tears.

Lieutenant Trevelyan brought the captured *sloop-de-guerre* out of le Goulet before noon on the following day with four newly released British prisoners of war on board, including the wounded Midshipman Clayton. For these he had handed over all the officers and men from the French sloop, except the commander. This gentleman thought he would be shot if he went back, and he had used his conversation opportunity with Madame Hanikof to tell her of his fears, so Captain Brewster had agreed to keep him.

'Well, there's your future command,' Heward said to Lawson as the vessel sailed towards *Adamant*. It's not as big as the Russian sloop but it's fast. Just look at that bow wave. Must be doing all of twelve knots and we can hardly feel the breeze here. What's the figurehead supposed to be?'

'It'll be a greyhound. That's what her name is anyway, so I'm told: *Le Lévrier*,' Lawson said.

'We learn something every day,' Heward said drily. 'If I'd known that I was destined to spend so much of my life sparring with Frenchmen, I'd have made shift to get my tongue around more of their language. God knows, we had plenty of opportunity as children in the Heward household. Mother was forever taking in French refugees when the guillotines were at their busiest.'

'Now you have another French refugee to help you,' Lawson reminded him with a grin.

'Are you ready for off, Mr Lawson?'

They spun around, startled. Captain Brewster had approached and was standing just behind them. He had a red canvas bag in his hand.

'Yes, sir.'

'Well, you'd better not go without this,' he said, handing over the bag.

Lawson nearly dropped it. It was surprisingly heavy. He looked puzzled and Brewster smiled.

'It's a copy of Kempenfelt's signal book. Always keep it tied up in this bag. There's a pound of lead stitched into the bottom of it. If there's any chance of being captured, you'll toss it over the side.'

'Yes, sir.'

'You'd better go and lock it in your sea chest,' the captain said, raising his telescope to take in the approaching sloop.

'I'll help you,' Heward said, eager to escape.

'I need you here, Mr Heward. Your eyes are younger than mine and I'd like your opinion. Now what d'you make of the Frenchman's lines? Do you reckon *Le Lévrier*'s finer built than the Russian sloop?'

He prodded Heward with his telescope in a semi-jocular manner, inviting him to use it. Heward looked surprised as he took it.

Lawson's cabin was the smallest private accommodation in the whole ship, being nothing more than a walled-off section of the enclosed space where small arms were stored, but it was heaven compared with the shared midshipmen's berth.

The marine sentry, who stood guard over the armoury, crashed to attention, but he seemed to be amused about something, Lawson noted. Could it be that there was anything amiss with his dress? He would examine himself before returning to the upper deck. He scowled at the man, seized the handle of his door and entered. Immediately, he knew the reason for the smirk on the marine's face. Victoria was waiting in the tiny cabin – alone. He hurriedly pushed the door shut behind him.

'I had to see you before you go away, John,' she said, rising from the corner of the bed, her eyes seeking his anxiously.

'But not here,' Lawson breathed. 'The man out there will talk. The story will be all over the ship by –'

There was barely room for a chair between the bed and the bulkhead, and they were very close. It was inevitable that she would be unbalanced in such a confined space. Lawson raised his arms to steady her and she swayed inside them. Now, he looked down at her: attentive blue eyes, long copper-coloured hair, full red lips slightly open. Her hands slid from his lapels to his shoulders, and her fingers caressed his throat. Trembling with desire, he drew her to him. Her vibrant body moulded into his as he clumsily crushed his lips upon hers. He could feel her firm breasts and urgent thighs pressing, fusing against his. The inhibitions built of his lowly situation crumbled under the overwhelming pressure of his desperate need to become one with her: but it was not to be.

It was the first time that he had kissed and embraced a passionate girl. Never had he experienced such heights of ecstasy. It overwhelmed him, took over his self-control, and he was unable to delay the surge of his virility. Now, he stood holding her, trembling slightly, not responding to her demanding body. She looked up at him, misunderstanding the change, anxiety, perhaps fear, in her eyes. He held her gently to him and stroked her cheek. Her tears were hot on his hand.

The stately East Indiaman, wallowing in the southwesterly swell towered over the captured French *sloop-de-guerre* now commanded by Acting Lieutenant Lawson. Captain Bramley, a large bewhiskered Yorkshireman in his early fifties, looked down from the height of his main deck. He would probably not have stopped willingly had the encounter been in the English Channel. There he would have been expected to yield some of his crew to be pressed into the Navy. South of Brest, he had no such fears. It was illegal. He had no fears either that *Le Lévrier* might be French, masquerading under the British flag. He had seen *Adamant* clearly before the mist had shut her off from view. Even so, he had ordered the guns of the Indiaman to be loaded and run out, to be on the safe side. Now he watched through his glass as the boat was rowed over from the sloop, carrying a young-looking officer.

'Look lively if you're coming aboard,' he shouted down impatiently as the sloop's boat made a second clumsy attempt to grapple the boarding ladder that had been unrolled down the curve of the ship's side.

Lawson sprang for the rungs, cursing as the roll of the ship brought the sea up to his waist in full view of the idle passengers crowding the bulwarks.

'Haw, haw, damned fellow had a bath there, I think,' an extravagant accent proclaimed from above.

Lawson seethed as he climbed. Those on the upper deck would be company officials in the higher grades, and Indian Army officers together with their wives and broods. He had met the like before: people full of their own importance, all keenly aware of their position in the Anglo-Indian society and determined to maintain the pecking order of things, so far as those below them were concerned. Quite a few of them viewed Lawson with veiled contempt, or so he fancied, when he doffed his hat in the presence of Captain Bramley.

'A request from Captain Brewster of HMS *Adamant*, sir,' he said passing over the letter, which had narrowly escaped being immersed in the sea.

The Indiaman's captain ripped open the envelope, read the contents and handed it over to a senior officer.

'We are requested to carry dispatches for Admiralty and several bags of private mail. We are also asked if we can give a midshipman passage to London. Please get the purser to write a confirmation. Tell him to file this letter with a copy of our reply, or we'll never get a brass farthing out of the government.' He turned back to Lawson. 'Perhaps you would care to take refreshment whilst you are waiting.'

Captain Bramley led the way to his sumptuous quarters. The ship had not touched land since the Cape and he was eager for news. He poured generous measures of brandy into two glasses and passed one over to Lawson. They sat comfortably enough until the letter arrived for signature. By then, Lawson had given Captain Bramley an account of the news up to the time of their departure from Liverpool, and also the latest developments in the Navy.

'Mutiny in the Fleet! What is the world coming to?' the captain said with a sad shake of his head. 'We'll be following the French fashion next. You mark my words, young man.'

He opened the door and walked with Lawson over the scrupulously clean deck boards towards the entry port.

'Your speech suggests that your home is not very far

from where I shall be going next week,' he said.

'Whitby, sir,' Lawson replied eagerly.

'Thought you were from thereabouts. I'm going to Pickering. If you're writing home, let me have it. I'll see that it's delivered.'

'Thank you, sir. That is most kind.'

Atkins' face was wooden but his eyes were murderous as he descended below the level of *Adamant*'s deck to the sloop's boat. He was being sent home like an expelled schoolboy. Brewster did not regard him as sufficiently important to merit an escort of equal rank, even though an official report was being sent to Admiralty, charging him with conduct unbefitting of a midshipman. His career would be ruined on the strength of a testimony given by Clayton, a coarse, common fellow who should never have been rated midshipman. It was an affront to an honourable naval family.

He said nothing to Lawson as he climbed aboard the sloop, and he maintained his silence as the distance closed between it and the Indiaman. Lawson's promotion was the sort of thing that could be expected from an ill-bred fellow like Brewster. As to the girl, Victoria, she was a slut from all accounts. Lawson and she would be well matched.

Lawson had Saunders as his second-in-command and he had been given the three surviving Russian sailors, at his own request, and also Joplin and Brown who had served so well on the *pecheur*. Additionally, he had the pick of the keen young top-men and a few sensible older men as well. In all, a company of twenty-two.

Three days after the Indiaman had sailed off to England with Atkins and *Adamant*'s mail, Brown woke him at dawn.

Mr Saunders asked me to tell you that we've picked up some company during the night. British frigates, sir. There's a brace of 'em close in shore, and a big ship's been seen to the nor'ard: maybe three or four miles, sir.'

Lawson had kept the middle watch and he'd been in bed less than two hours, but he tossed the blankets aside and wrapped his boat cloak around him.

The sea was grey in the early dawn light, and a cold stiff breeze had whipped it into a turmoil of white tops and spindrift. Lawson drew his cloak closer and looked around. The frigates were clearly visible. The bigger ship, which Saunders had seen to the north, had disappeared behind a curtain of rain. *Adamant* was hull up to the westward and approaching.

'Looks like the mutiny's over,' Saunders suggested.

'Yes, it does. *Adamant* will have seen this lot, but we'd better hoist a signal to be on the right side, and we'll keep our eyes skinned for any messages from Captain Brewster. I'm going to get shaved. You never know what the day might bring.'

He yawned and went off to his quarters. There he noted that his newly acquired servant was making coffee on the stove. He flopped into the leather-upholstered chair and looked around the luxurious appointments of the small cabin with immense satisfaction. This was comfort such as he had never known. It would be hard to return to the spartan accommodation of the midshipmen's berth, should his appointment as lieutenant not be confirmed.

By noon, seven ships had assembled between Ushant and Brest. The rest of the Channel Fleet would be dispersed eastwards, covering the French coast as far as Dunkirk. Clearly, *Adamant*'s vigil had come to an end. After Brewster had paid his respects to the rear admiral commanding the Brest squadron, it would be time to sail for Yarmouth to join Admiral Duncan's North Sea Fleet. A string of bunting danced at the masthead of the flagship.

'A signal from Rear Admiral Seymour, sir,' Prendergast said, handing over a folded piece of paper a few minutes later.

'Can't be all that bad, Mr Prendergast,' Brewster smiled, noting the lieutenant's worried expression.

He opened the message and read it. The rear admiral had invited him to dinner at one o' clock. He was to bring with him one of his lieutenants and Midshipman Atkins.

Brewster stared morosely across the deck. He then

became aware that Heward, who would have received the message and was waiting for a reply, was watching him attentively from the signal hoists.

'A special relationship, is it?' Brewster asked quietly.

'Midshipman Atkins is the rear admiral's nephew, sir,' Prendergast replied sympathetically.

'Oh well,' Brewster shrugged. 'He would have learnt about it sooner or later. It'll put a damper on the conversation at dinner. Please join me, Mr Prendergast, and tell Heward yonder —' he jerked his head in the direction of the signal midshipman — 'that he'll be going in place of Atkins.'

Adamant was detained for two days by Admiral Seymour, during which time he studied a copy of the report on his nephew and examined witnesses. Lieutenant Trevelyan spent many hours on board the flagship, and he dined with the admiral on the last evening before departure, a courtesy not extended to his captain.

CHAPTER NINETEEN

Le Lévrier was under orders to sail to Portsmouth
with mail from the Channel Fleet and dispatches
for Admiralty. There she would be assessed by a
board of officers and possibly purchased by the Navy.
Failing that, the sloop would be put up to public auction.
In either case, *Adamant* would get the prize money, after
the Admiral of the Channel Fleet, who had been shore-
bound in Portsmouth when the sloop was captured, had
deducted his customary one-eighth share.

Lawson was not thinking about the prize money as he
entered the Solent, with the Needles behind him on the
starboard quarter. It was his first command and there was
no one other than himself to be held responsible if they
were to go aground on the spit or accidentally run down
any of the numerous small boats plying between the
mainland and the Isle of Wight.

But it was a glorious day with the bright sun gleaming
on the water, and there are few pleasures to compare
with those of taking a boat into harbour after weeks at
sea. All on board were happy and cheerful, although
Lawson's delight was dulled by the gloomy prospects of
what was to follow. There would probably be a delay of
weeks before he could leave the sloop. Then he would
have to travel overland to Great Yarmouth to rejoin
Adamant. By this time, Victoria must certainly have gone
back to her people and he would never see her again.

Saunders had the chart clamped to a table on the open deck. Together, they pored over it, checking landmarks as they passed by them and taking compass bearings of those ahead. They kept close to the island until they had left the great guns of Cowes' fortress behind them, and they could see the broad, busy expanse of Southampton Water on their port side. Gosport now lay ahead with Portsmouth just beyond. Clearly visible were tired old warships lying at anchor, with their masts removed and smoke rising from their numerous chimneys. These were the hulks where the Navy accommodated its prisoners of war.

The fresh southwesterly breeze that had brought them so smartly through the Solent against the ebbing tide had been getting stronger for some time, but it had hardly been noticed whilst it blew from behind them, and they had level decks. As soon as they changed course for the entrance to Portsmouth Harbour, they felt the full force on their beam. They were carrying far too much canvas.

The sloop heeled violently over, with her leeward side almost awash and the wildly tilted guns straining at their tackles. One frayed rope there and a gun might go squealing across the deck to smash its way through the opposite side, possibly killing somebody on the way.

'All hands to shorten sail. Helmsman, bring her bows to wind,' Lawson shouted urgently.

He ran to assist the helmsman. Together, they strained at the wheel. Saunders joined them and put his weight behind it. Slowly, the deck levelled and the sloop lost her speed as her bows turned to the wind.

The men clawed in a great reef on the mainsail and took in the flying jib, whilst the ebbing tide carried the sloop back over the course they had just sailed. Lawson knew that there would be telescopes in plenty directed at the sloop from Southsea Castle and from the two forts, Gilkicker and Monckton, guarding the approaches to the harbour. His main area of concern however was the huge man-of-war anchored to the west of the harbour entrance. Its quarterdeck was thronged with officers taking their exercise, and they had watched the approach of the sloop with professional interest, obviously noting that she was French and therefore a prize. Now the same officers were witnesses of his bad seamanship.

'I made a bloody mess of that,' Lawson said ruefully when they were back on course.

'Aye, lad, you did,' Saunders mimicked with a grin.

HMS *Adamant*, which had continued on an easterly course after *Le Lévrier* had left her, made very good speed from the same wind that had caught Lawson unawares. She had rounded Beachy Head at sunset and left the South Foreland behind at dawn. It was a remarkable performance, but it brought no pleasure to either Captain Brewster or Madame Hanikof. This might well be their last day together, unless *Adamant* were delayed.

Dr Ruthven had condemned most of the water and much of the beef whilst they had been patrolling off Brest, so supplies were needed urgently. Now Ruthven was laid low with the fever, so it seemed that the many sick men should be sent ashore for treatment.

'Mr Prendergast, you'll be aware that we are now without a surgeon,' Brewster began.

'There are two assistants, sir.'

'But neither has served the required three years to qualify as a full surgeon. Anyway, they don't seem able to cope with the fever. There are ninety-four poorly, according to the returns. There'll be more accommodation for the sick at Chatham than at Yarmouth, and we'll stand a better chance of getting a replacement surgeon for Ruthven there.'

'It's over thirty miles off course, sir,' Prendergast cautioned.

'Aye, it is, but we'll anchor off Sheerness, and then I'll send a dispatch overland to Admiral Duncan. He will have it in the morning. With luck we should also be able to get reinforcements for those we send ashore. Is that hell-ship still there, the one they use to accommodate pressed men and recruits?'

'HMS *Sandwich*, sir?'

'Aye, that's the one.'

'It's at the Nore, sir.'

'Well, there we are then. We're no use to the North Sea Fleet without seamen, and we might pick up enough replacements from *Sandwich*. Then there's this Irishman, Maharg. He's been pestering me to let him go to see his Mr Atkinson at Admiralty to acquaint him with the situation amongst his fellow spies in France. I'll send him into Chatham with Heward and two of the master-at-arms' mates as escorts. Then, the port admiral can worry about whether he's genuine or not.'

'I'll set a course for Sheerness, sir.'

Prendergast looked concerned when he gave the order to the officer of the watch. Trevelyan noted the change of course and the time in his little pocket diary. He had made many such notes since his dinner with Admiral Seymour.

Adamant anchored just inside the mouth of the Medway. After a time, several hoys came alongside carrying water and supplies of meat. The same vessels took off forty-seven seriously ill men, whose chances of survival in the hospital ashore would be about even. They knew it, but they were happy to go. The conditions there would be better than in *Adamant* and, as well as the wonderful feeling of being on dry land again, it would be easier for friends and family to visit.

Ruthven was not among those sent ashore. Hearing that he was to be replaced, he rose from his sick bed with a face like a corpse, dosed himself liberally with the same concoction that he had been prescribing for the fever and managed to stay on his feet. Thereafter he grew stronger. Other sick men, perhaps taking heart from the surgeon's remarkable recovery, began to improve also.

An elderly lieutenant from HMS *Sandwich* came aboard on the second day. He was greeted affably by Captain Brewster and escorted to the great cabin where he was made comfortable with an easy chair and a glass of brandy.

'How many men do you need, sir?' the supply ship's lieutenant asked.

Brewster consulted his list. There was no chance whatsoever that he would receive either the numbers or the tradesmen he required from HMS *Sandwich*, but he had to ask.

'Let me fill your glass, Mr Benson,' he wooed, tilting a bottle.

Lieutenant Benson, well used to obsequious captains when it came to the question of obtaining men, held out his glass and kept it under the neck of the bottle until he had a good measure of brandy.

'Would forty-five be enough, sir?'

'I was thinking of more like a hundred and forty-five, with a good half of them trained seamen,' the captain countered.

Benson smiled in a manner which suggested that Captain Brewster was joking. Then he pulled a notebook from an inner pocket and consulted it.

'We can certainly let you have as many as you've sent ashore to the hospital, sir, and we might –' he made some calculations, scribbling busily with his pencil – 'yes, we might be able to let you have another twenty, a mixed bunch of landsmen and ordinary seamen, particularly if you can help us, sir.'

'In what way?'

'We need an experienced seaman with a fair education: not a clerk, someone who knows a jib boom from a starboard lanthorn. The Impressment Service is very busy just now, and they're bringing in so many that we're having difficulty categorizing them.'

'So you need a man who knows his seamanship, who is also capable of questioning men on their ability and able to write it down?'

'That's about it, sir. If he's also good at figures, so much the better.'

'I will let you have an able seaman who used to be a lawyer's clerk, if you can make your mixed bunch up to thirty,' Brewster said, pouring more brandy into the lieutenant's ready glass.

'Your very good health, sir,' Benson said, raising his drink. 'I'll see what can be done.'

'Please arrange Parker's transfer to HMS *Sandwich*, Mr Trevelyan,' Brewster said after Lieutenant Benson had gone. 'Ensure that he is ready to move with all his kit packed by the end of the afternoon watch.'

Heward was related to Admiral Wren, so it was not very difficult for him to get past the permanent barrier of lieutenants and senior officers who would normally shield the port admiral from the lower stratum of society. He was conducted to a large, handsome room with a magnificent view of the Chatham water. A tall man with a sharp, hawk-like nose turned away from the window as he entered and made an effort to be affable.

'Hello, Willy. Glad to see you,' he boomed.

Heward, who had winced at the use of his childhood name, shook the admiral's extended hand, noting, not for the first time, the steely blue eyes and high cheek-bones. These facial characteristics, together with the aristocratic nose, were dominant on the maternal side of his family.

'Don't suppose you've seen your mother since I was there in December?'

'No, sir. I've not been home in twelve months,' Heward replied, resisting the urge to compare his own features in the mirror set on the wall with those of his uncle. They were supposed to be very much alike.

'And you're wanting to go home, eh? That why you came to see me?'

'Just to pay my compliments, sir, having come ashore to escort the spy Maharg.'

'Damned funny business, that,' the admiral grumbled. 'Mind you, this Atkinson at Admiralty is a damned funny sort of a feller. I knew him as a lieutenant: half Frog, y'know. Supposed to be of good family, but you never can tell with these foreigners.' He shook his head doubtfully. 'I'm sending the French filly with Maharg for Atkinson to sort out. Don't see why he shouldn't do something for her.'

'I was wondering about Madame Lorette, sir,' Heward said hesitantly. 'She's not a spy. She's just a girl who was more or less forced into marriage with one of Atkinson's agents. She's a refugee, in fact, and if she's sent to Atkinson he'll push her into the network – Calais, Boulogne, somewhere in France – and she'll wind up being strangled in a prison cell for a cause that means nothing to her.'

The admiral extracted a snuff box from the tail of his coat, took a pinch and looked at his nephew speculatively.

'Attractive young woman, is she?'

Heward shrugged his shoulders and pursed his lips, a masquerade of indifference that brought a momentary gleam of amusement into his bachelor uncle's eyes.

'What would you have me do with her?' the admiral asked.

'I thought perhaps that, er – mother might take her. She's had any number of refugees.'

Admiral Wren considered the proposal whilst examining the broad expanse of his domain through a brass telescope.

'You'd better go and ask her then, hadn't you?' he said at last, closing the telescope and placing it on the wide window ledge. 'She's been in town these last three weeks, and I think she plans to stay another month. I'll send you to Atkinson with Maharg and the girl. You can call on your mother after you've handed over the Irishman. The town house is only a stone's throw from Admiralty anyway.'

'Er – what about *Adamant*, sir?'

'You'll not be missed there. Matter of fact, I have six idle midshipmen pestering for berths. I'll give you a letter for Captain Brewster.'

'I don't wish to lose my place, sir.'

'Nor shall you. If *Adamant* has weighed anchor by the time you get back from London, I'll send you out on one of the victualling hoys to rejoin her. Do you – enjoy serving under Captain Brewster?'

'Indeed yes, sir. He's a very good commander.'

'Hm! Is he?' The admiral rubbed at his chin thoughtfully, walked across to the window, and looked out. 'Captain Brewster has to be questioned over a rather odd business.' He turned back to Heward. 'Wouldn't have mentioned it if you were not family, of course, and I couldn't trust you to keep it to yourself. Fact is, I've reported *Adamant*'s presence here, and I'm half expecting to conduct an enquiry soon, or to send Captain Brewster up to London. Seems there was some trouble with the civilian authorities in Liverpool. A brothel-keeper got robbed and killed.'

'I know all about it, sir.'

'Do ye, be damned!' the admiral exclaimed, waving Heward to a seat and lowering himself into the large leather-covered chair behind the oak desk. 'Tell me about it.'

Heward gave his uncle the details of Tom Thumb's murder and the stolen money. Admiral Wren nodded his approval over *Adamant*'s immediate departure from the Mersey. Obviously Brewster had acted as he would have done in the circumstances.

'You were not there when the blow was struck?'

'No, sir, but I've heard that side of it from Lawson and Saunders.'

'And they are now in Portsmouth, you say? What of the other witness, Mr Atherton?'

'He's dead, sir.'

Admiral Wren drummed his fingers thoughtfully on the desk, rose and walked over to the window again. The view of the harbour was like a magnet to him, it seemed, but he was thinking of other things.

'Can't understand what all the fuss is about,' he mused. 'Your account is much the same as the first letter that went out from Admiralty. It was nothing more than a request to obtain a statement from Captain Brewster, should he arrive within our jurisdiction. You know the sort of thing: copies sent to Plymouth, Portsmouth, Chatham: nothing important. Then, a couple of days ago, another letter was sent out, signed by Admiral Atkins, and it seems that the whole business has assumed a new significance.'

'Admiral Atkins!' Heward exclaimed.

'Yes, permanent now on Admiralty staff. You know the family – Sir James and Percy, all well placed in the navy. Percy married a Seymour. Now, his brother-in-law has just been made up to rear admiral. He probably relieved you at Brest.'

'He did indeed, sir,' Heward breathed. 'Let me tell you the rest.'

He told him why Atkins had been sent home, adding that if he had been captain, he would have clapped him in

201

irons. Then he spoke of the signal that had been received from the flagship when Atkins had been invited to dinner, and of Admiral Seymour's subsequent rudeness to Captain Brewster.

Sitting at the table in the commander's quarters on *Le Lévrier*, a middle-aged lieutenant wearing shoes with odd buckles, a work-stained smock and trousers which, by their appearance, suggested he might spend much of his time crawling about in the bilges, signed a sheaf of papers and passed them over to Lawson.

'There you are, my lad. Sign each paper as I have done. It's just to confirm that the shipwright and carpenters have made a thorough examination in your presence.'

Lawson took up the pen and scanned the first page. It referred to the main timbers of the sloop. He had seen the men going over them, yard by yard, with sharp spikes in their hands, testing for rot. They were pitch pine and as sound as they would have been on the day they were laid. He signed and passed on to the next page.

'Will you be recommending purchase for the Navy, sir?'

'Oh the Navy will certainly buy her. She's very satisfactory, and they're crying out for this type of vesel in the North Sea. I shouldn't wonder if she's on her way to Admiral Duncan within twenty-four hours. His position will be desperate now that the Russians are going away.'

'The Russians are leaving the North Sea Fleet!' Lawson exclaimed.

'The last I heard, Admiral Hanikof was waiting only for a favourable wind, with no thought at all for the Dutch who are building up their Navy's strength to invade us. The wind got away from the northeast yesterday, so they could be well on their way home by now. Bloody cheek when you think about it. We've been feeding them all winter and providing materials to repair their ships. Then as soon as the Baltic ice melts, this new Russian Emperor wants his ships back home. Wouldn't surprise me if he joined up with the French, for there are pressures on him to do so, and I think that Emperor Paul takes after his spineless father. Pity he lacks the spirit of old Catherine.'

Lawson was later to reflect upon the unexpected political awareness of an officer who had obviously risen from common seaman and, due to the nature of his work, would rarely mix with people who were at the centre of affairs.

Right now he was brooding over the consequences of the Russian withdrawal, as it affected him. *Adamant* should have joined the North Sea Fleet several days ago. The Hanikof family would have been reunited. He caught a momentary, vivid picture of Victoria: bright hair, blue dancing eyes, and a personality more vital and compelling than any he had ever known. He loved her with all the passion of youth. There was nothing he would not have sacrificed to be with her. They could never meet again, it seemed.

'Do you want to come ashore with me?'

Lawson jerked out of his gloomy reverie. 'I'm sorry, sir. I missed that.'

'If you come with me, and I get the bill of sale signed immediately, you can report to the admiral for orders as the acting commander of the purchased vessel. Then, provided there's no senior lieutenant they want to get rid of, and no junior officer with influence, who's been promised a small vessel of his own, you might get orders to sail. The longer you delay, the more likely it will be that they'll find someone else for the job.' He smiled. 'Especially if the powers that be learn about the manner of your approach to Portsmouth Harbour.'

'Thank you for your advice, sir. I am most grateful for it,' Lawson said.

'That's all right, Mr Lawson,' the ship surveyor replied affably, gathering his papers from the table. 'Let's get on. If we're quick, we'll maybe catch the purchasing officer before he goes off for his dinner.'

He paused in the doorway. His eyes, now serious, looked into Lawson's.

'If you do get the command, you'll remember to check your stores before you leave harbour. See that you've plenty of good, dry gunpowder. The French privateers

203

have been pretty busy in the Channel just lately. Lay in enough food and water for two months at least. Many a promising young feller has come to grief on his first command by forgetting to victual. Oh, and if you have any bad buggers on board, get rid of 'em ashore. A rotten apple'll turn the rest, and men are no different in my experience, particularly when the commander is as young as you.'

CHAPTER TWENTY

When Heward took his party to London, the morning was bright and sunny, so Maharg asked to ride on top of the coach with the two seamen who were serving as escorts. This suited Heward admirably. Madame Lorette and he would now have the inside of the coach to themselves. Off they went, through the streets of Chatham and out onto the smooth toll road beyond, with the pair of horses, in tandem, thrusting energetically against their collars and kicking up a fine dust which rose behind them in a cloud.

On the road a few miles beyond Rochester, one of the seamen began to vomit, so Maharg stopped the coach. Heward recognized the symptoms immediately. The man was suffering from the same sickness that had carried off so many of *Adamant*'s people. They found a doctor. He confirmed that the sailor was very poorly, so they left him behind with a woman recommended by the doctor as a 'sober, caring body' with some experience.

Three hours later, just before Bexley, Maharg hammered on the roof of the coach. Heward opened the window and looked up.

'What is it now?' he asked testily.

'You'd better find a doctor for this feller too,' Maharg shouted. 'Seems to me he's going the same way as his mate.'

They helped the man down to the road and bundled

him inside. There was no assistance from the driver. He stood by the head of the leading horse and wouldn't go near them. His eyes showed the fear he had of the plague, and clearly he was not very happy when they laid the sick man on one of the upholstered seats of his coach. Heward told him to drive to the nearest coaching inn.

The midshipman paid two guineas for medical attention and accommodation in Bexley and promised, like the Good Samaritan, to settle for any extra on his return. Then he ordered dinner for them all.

It was obvious that the other diners knew about the sickness. Two left the room as soon as Heward's party entered. The remaining four hurried through their food and departed without a word. Evidently, the coach driver had been talking.

'Odd that the fellow has not come in for his dinner. I told him that I would buy it,' Heward said.

'Sure, he'll be having it in the kitchen,' Maharg shrugged, stuffing roast beef into his mouth.

Heward pushed back his chair and went to look for him. The man was not in the tavern. The tandem coach had gone from the yard. Their baggage had been dumped by the wall of the stable. The driver must have been terrified of the fever to give up his dinner and lose his fare.

There was no private vehicle available in Bexley before the morning. The stage, which was due to stop for a change of horses at seven o'clock that evening, would almost certainly be booked right through to London. There was nothing for it but to stay the night. Heward shared a room with Maharg. Madame Lorette had the room next to it.

She slept badly and was wide awake long before the knock on her door early the following morning. Maharg was on the threshold. He placed a finger on his lips, then beckoned her to follow him into the adjoining room. Heward was tossing and turning on his bed, his face and chest streaming with sweat. She hurried to him, placed a hand on his brow and felt his pulse. He appeared to be suffering from the same illness that had taken his men.

Maharg brought the doctor to the tavern. He examined Heward and suggested that they should send him to join the seaman who was lying sick in the town. Madame Lorette was determined to nurse him herself, so he told her how to go about it and took his fee. Later, he arrived with a supply of medicines. By this time, Maharg had gone, having extracted two guineas from Heward's purse for expenses.

'I'll see that the Navy is informed, me dear,' he said as he departed. 'I can't be waiting here, for much depends upon me gettin' in touch with Mr Atkinson.'

That was the last she saw of him, and no one, other than the doctor, came anywhere near the room until Heward was able to sit up in bed, a ghost of his former self, three weeks later.

HM Sloop *Greyhound* sailed out of Portsmouth ten days after her arrival, with the paint of her Anglicized name still wet. There had been no ceremony in the renaming of the prize. A few brush strokes had obliterated for ever the elaborate gold script of a French artist. Then the drunken sign-writer from the Admiralty dockyard had daubed on her new name in white paint, upon a background of black that was not yet dry. Consequently, the latest addition to the British Navy was sent to join the North Sea Fleet with weeping, grey lettering that was washed off before they cleared Dover Strait. This caused a suspicious frigate captain to send a boarding party to examine their papers when they had reached the latitude of Foulness Island.

'Your parent ship, *Adamant*, left London River on the morning tide yesterday,' the frigate's lieutenant said when he had satisfied himself that the sloop was British. 'She's been lying in the Medway for the past week.'

'Then she has not yet joined Admiral Duncan!' Lawson exclaimed, struggling to contain his excitement. 'What has happened to the Russian ladies who were on board?'

'I don't know about any Russians. Maybe they were sent ashore when Captain Brewster left *Adamant*. Oh yes, you won't have heard about that either,' he said, noting the incredulous expression on Lawson's face. 'Your captain's gone off to Admiralty for an enquiry into something that happened in Liverpool. Captain Hotham is acting commander of *Adamant*. Anyway, I doubt if it will affect your future. A small sloop such as this will be ideal for work in shallow waters. I should think that Admiral Duncan will send you off to join the others in the vicinity of the Texel.'

Lawson was no longer listening. He knew that *Greyhound* was destined to be one of the eyes of the Fleet. There was little else that she could do, other than deliver dispatches. His mind was full of the news he had just received, and he wanted to discuss it with Saunders. If the boarding officer had expected a glass of something to comfort him on his journey back to the frigate, he was disappointed.

Admiral Duncan flew his flag aboard HMS *Venerable*. She was a leaking, seventy-four-gun, third-rate: a ship well known to Lawson since he had spent the first six months of his naval career on her rat-infested, stinking, orlop deck. As he approached the old warrior, wallowing tiredly at anchor, the misery of that time came flooding back to him. For a moment he was barely thirteen years old again, homesick and frightened, apprehensive at the thought of entering her.

Saunders, who had joined Lawson on *Venerable* at the same age, had been watching her signal flags. Now he lowered the telescope and briefly consulted the signal book.

'You are to report aboard, sir. They'll send a boat,' he said briskly.

'Acknowledge, please,' Lawson replied, noting with mixed feelings that Saunders had said 'sir' for the first time.

Lawson worked the single-masted sloop to within a cable's length of *Venerable* before bringing her into the wind and dropping anchor. He was well aware, as were all those serving on *Greyhound*, that their seamanship would be under the scrutiny of many telescopes, and the critical eyes of all idle seamen in the vicinity. There was also *Adamant* anchored to windward of the flagship, and her people would certainly be interested in the handling of their prize.

Lawson had expected that he would be given his orders by one of the staff officers. He was therefore most surprised when the spruce, fresh-faced, young lieutenant who met him at the entry port, told him that Admiral Duncan wished to speak to him.

'Personally?'

'Those are my orders. I'll take you to him.'

He led Lawson up the gangway to the quarterdeck and then aft to the spacious accommodation set in the stern of the ship. Lawson looked around him with interest, but there was little he could see of his past. It seemed a lifetime away since he had walked these same deck-boards. Could it be only five years?

Admiral Duncan, at the age of sixty-six, was a man of some influence. Quite apart from his own record, which was impressive by any standards, his wife's relative, Henry Dundas, had become Treasurer to the Navy and Secretary of State for War. It was generally known that the admiral had been offered the command of the more prestigious and much better-equipped Mediterranean Fleet, but he had declined it, believing that the warmer climate would awaken the West Indian fever that had plagued him for years. The gulf in rank and experience between Admiral Duncan and Acting Lieutenant Lawson was enormous, yet the elderly officer rose to his feet and extended a welcoming hand across the desk to his diffident visitor.

'Delighted to make your acquaintance, Mr Lawson,' he said with a smile. 'Please take a seat.'

Lawson thanked him and perched uneasily on the edge of a large, leather-upholstered chair. Never had he seen such a man. Apart from his high rank and eminence, his courtesy and charm, the admiral was six and a half feet tall, with shoulders to match.

'I see that you have a report for me,' Duncan said, indicating with a nod the package in Lawson's hand. 'Just tell me about yourself. I already know the orders you were given in Portsmouth. We have a fast overland mail system between here and London. How long have you been in the Navy?'

'Five years, sir.'

'Right. Just go on from there. Where did you live? How old were you? Just talk to me. Tell me all about yourself.'

Hesitantly at first and prompted from time to time, Lawson described his life and, although he had never heard of such an interview, he knew instinctively that the admiral's purpose was to assess his character. This was confirmed by Admiral Duncan's opening words when Lawson had finished.

'Mr Lawson, I have a very special task for you and your –' he smiled – 'nameless sloop.'

'I'm sorry about that, sir.'

Duncan waved the triviality aside. 'I will have a painter sent out to you to put the matter right. Your task is somewhat delicate – politically – and if Mr Fox were to hear of it he would cause the Prime Minister no end of embarrassment. The fact of the matter is that the Navy is under an obligation to facilitate the return of a certain lady and her daughters to their homeland.'

Lawson tensed. Duncan looked at him keenly, then nodded.

'Yes. The unfortunate Madame Hanikof and her daughters are stranded here, because the Navy commandeered the Russian sloop *Catherine*. Her husband left for the Baltic under orders from St Petersburg, believing that his errant sloop would follow the fleet once his wife had learnt of his departure from these waters. He, like us, had no means of knowing that *Catherine* is destroyed and gathering silt in le Goulet.'

The admiral rose from his chair and walked over to the wide window casement where he looked across the water at *Adamant*.

'Obviously, the ladies cannot travel overland through enemy territory, so we are morally obliged to send them by sea. Mr Pitt has enough troubles in parliament without our adding to them. There would be uproar if it was discovered that we had weakened the North Sea Fleet by the removal of even one vessel, particularly as I have been demanding reinforcements for the past six months.'

'And my sloop would not be missed, sir?'

Duncan turned away from the window and smiled. 'Your sloop does not exist, Mr Lawson. The paperwork and possibly *Adamant*'s prize claims, will be filed by a careless clerk in Portsmouth. I shouldn't think they'll know about the transaction in London for twelve months at least. Certainly not before you get back from the Baltic.'

'And since I am still a midshipman, as far as Admiralty records are concerned –'

'You would not be missed either,' Duncan finished for him. 'But don't worry, Mr Lawson. I'll look after your interests.'

Admiral Duncan rose and smiled. The interview was evidently at an end. Lawson felt his hand gripped and a pat on the shoulder. Then he was outside, with the questions he had wanted to ask unspoken. Such is the effect that a charming, high-ranking officer has upon a lowly subordinate.

Lieutenant Crompton, the administrative officer who gave Lawson his orders, was professional almost to the point of coldness. Certainly, the personality he presented to an acting lieutenant was not likely to invite questions unrelated to the matter in hand, but Lawson was very worried about Captain Brewster's court of enquiry at Admiralty.

I really don't know,' Crompton replied, with a frown of impatience. 'One hears rumours, but –' He shrugged the matter away and bent once again over the chart.

'I believe that the matter is connected with a murder investigation in Liverpool, sir,' Lawson persisted. 'I should like you to make a note of the fact that Mr Saunders and I are the only surviving witnesses.'

'I will duly note what you have said, Mr Lawson, but I think it likely that Captain Brewster would have informed the admiral if he'd felt that this court of enquiry would want to hear your evidence.'

'Like a bloody cold fish,' was how Lawson described the staff officer to Saunders an hour later.

'So now we're both off to Russia? How wonderful! I've always wanted to see St Petersburg.'

'I doubt if we'll be so lucky. It's expected that we'll find the Russian fleet at Copenhagen. Failing that, we set a course for Riga. Anyway, Madame Hanikof will be able to advise us. She's coming aboard after dark. The Navy wishes to make sure that its right hand doesn't know what the left is up to.'

HM Sloop *Greyhound* slipped away from the fleet in the middle of the night with her passengers. Madame Hanikof retired to her bed immediately, obviously distressed. The older daughter did not speak. Even Victoria was subdued and had barely responded to Lawson's fond smile as she came aboard. They were depressed, Lawson realized, by the furtive manner of their departure. They had been feted guests. Now they were an embarrassment.

Dawn found them spanking along under a fresh southwesterly in an area that was busy with fishing boats. They were single-masted vessels for the most part; a few of them were very similar to the French *pecheur* that had been sunk in the gunnery practice. Lawson examined them through his telescope, hoping that he might recognize one from his home town of Whitby. He had not found time to write since he had received his orders to sail for the Baltic and there would be little chance of sending a letter once they had passed through the Skagerrak.

'Fish for breakfast, is it?' Saunders asked as he came yawning up to Lawson, ready to take over the morning watch.

'If I see a boat that I know, but most of these seem to be from Scotland.'

They slipped rapidly through the herring fleet, attracting a cheery wave from a few boats, but no one offered fish. No skipper would encourage a naval vessel to come too close, if he had young men on board. Fishermen made good sailors and were therefore particularly valuable to the Navy. The fishing fleet would very likely be raided by Admiral Duncan's ships if they followed the herring much further south. Then they would scatter in all directions, unless their crews consisted of men considered to be too old to serve.

'I'm going to turn in for a couple of hours,' Lawson said when he had satisfied himself that he could not identify a Whitby boat. 'I feel I could sleep for a week.'

He went to his cabin, made an entry in the log about the fishing fleet, noted the rim of the sun climbing out of the sea to the east and prepared for bed, reflecting as he did so that Victoria would be sleeping just a few feet away on the other side of the bulkhead.

Captain Brewster soon realized that he had been ordered to London on a pretext. The Liverpool magistrates had long lost interest in the Tom Thumb affair, having been convinced by their informers that the doorkeeper, whose body had been found with its throat cut, had been murdered for the money that he had stolen from the brothel. This much Brewster discovered whilst he was waiting for the Admiralty to start their enquiry. Rear Admiral Neilson-Clare, who had been commanded to conduct it, was sick and did not appear for a week.

Brewster had expected to be away from *Adamant* for three days at the most. His innocence would quickly be established by the evidence of Lawson and Saunders. Consequently, he had not taken his leave of the Hanikofs and he had no clothing other than the uniform he wore and a few shirts and socks. He became convinced that he was the victim of a conspiracy to keep him off his ship, when his two witnesses could not be found.

He had sent them into Portsmouth with the captured French sloop, *Le Lévrier*, but there was no record of their ever having been there. Could they possibly have sunk without trace? Then there was the mysterious disappearance of the only other person who could have testified. Midshipman Heward and his party had not been seen since they left Chatham.

Rear Admiral Neilson-Clare turned out to be an old dodderer in the first stages of senility. It was necessary that any enquiry should be conducted by an officer of equal or senior rank. Neilson-Clare satisfied this condition, but he was an alcoholic. He was unable to retain much of what was being said. Most of the questions were prompted by a shrewd-looking civil servant called McDonald. The enquiry was not finished at the end of the morning. Nor was it resumed in the afternoon. The old gentleman had taken to his bed again, having been indulged in his weakness for good brandy by a naval officer of his acquaintance who had 'chanced' to join him for lunch.

Two days later, Brewster was furious to learn that *Adamant* had been ordered to join the North Sea Fleet without delay. She had sailed with a temporary commander who had been sent down from Admiralty for the purpose. Brewster's complaints were met by bland assurances that he would resume his command as soon as Rear Admiral Neilson-Clare was well enough to complete the enquiry.

Brewster knew instinctively that the Atkins family was responsible, but he could prove nothing. Even if he discovered cast-iron evidence of their involvement, the only access he had to the Admiralty Board would be through the ineffectual Neilson-Clare.

After another week of delay, during which time rumours of a second mutiny reached London, Captain Brewster was informed that the enquiry into the Liverpool murder would be conducted by another senior officer as soon as one could be found. Meanwhile, he would be obliged to attend a court of enquiry into the loss of the Russian sloop, *Catherine*.

CHAPTER TWENTY-ONE

The Batavian Republic, as Holland was called in 1797, was a French ally. Her fast frigates were always on the look out for saucy British sloops. Such vessels would either be carrying dispatches to and from London, or spying on the home fleet. Lawson had followed his orders to keep well clear of the Friesian Islands on his passage to the Baltic Sea. Consequently, he had no real anxiety about the frigate that appeared to the west-northwest of him at dawn on the day after they had left the herring fleet behind. His confidence waned during the morning, as the frigate seemed to be on a course that could bring it within gun-shot of *Greyhound*. At midday he made his anxiety obvious to all when he ordered more sail than would be comfortable in such a stiff breeze.

'Could be heading for Heligoland,' Saunders suggested.

'Sail on the port bow, sir!' one of the seamen on look out warned urgently.

Out of the haze and the rain squalls to the northwest, at less than four miles, a second frigate had emerged. It appeared to be a two-decker.

'Are you sure she is Dutch?' queried Madame Hani-kof, when Lawson had changed course to the eastward.

'No, ma'am. I'm not sure about either of them. I'm taking no chances. We've just got to keep out of range.

They'll be faster than the sloop with this sea running,' he said, indicating the heavy swell bearing down astern of them, 'so we can't escape to westward. With luck, we'll run ahead of them until dark and then lose them.'

'If you don't run out of sea first. How far are we from Holland?'

'Hopefully, about twenty miles.'

She laughed delightedly. 'Hopefully, Mr Lawson, you are right.'

Victoria had kept aloof from the midshipmen since she had joined the sloop, obviously avoiding them. Now she remained holding onto the rail over on the weather side, within a few yards of Lawson after her mother had walked away. He smiled at her, but she did not respond. Her eyes were fixed on the nearer frigate and her face, normally so animated and vital, was expressionless.

'Don't worry about it,' Lawson said with false heartiness. 'We'll be well clear after dark.'

'I am not worried about the two ships,' she said, still looking over the water.

Lawson moved to her side and waited. She kept her eyes on the sea, needing him to prompt her.

'What is wrong, Victoria?' he asked gently.

She swung around to face him. They were close enough to touch each other, but the helmsman was there and certainly watching. She turned her head back to the sea and thrust her hands deep into her pockets. There were tears in her eyes.

'What must you think of me?' she whispered.

'I think you are the most wonderful person I have ever met.'

'But I behaved so – so – like a whore.'

Lawson was startled. In his circle, the word would never be spoken in the presence of ladies and definitely not used by a lady. Victoria's society was evidently different. Certainly, she was in no way diminished for having expressed herself in such an unEnglish manner. Now she was watching him anxiously, willing him to deny it. His eyes met hers and he smiled. There was no need for him to speak. The message that passed between them was enough. They were in love with all the intensity of young people experiencing such a relationship for the first time in their lives.

Saunders destroyed the magic moment by approaching with a piece of paper in his hand. Completely insensitive to the situation, he smiled briefly at Victoria and handed to Lawson the pencilled results of his navigation exercise.

'That's the best I can do,' he said with brisk confidence. 'According to my reckoning, if we hold our present course, and the wind doesn't change, we'll be in amongst the West Friesian Islands by dusk.'

'Let's look at it on the chart,' Lawson said, including Victoria in the invitation.

They gathered around the chart table where Saunders explained his calculations with great conviction and enthusiasm, but Lawson could follow with only a part of his attention. Under the table, Victoria had twined her fingers through his.

'Well, there's nothing for it but to hold our course and hope for the best,' he said when Saunders had finished. 'Meanwhile, we'll ask the cook to bring dinner forward an hour, if he can do it without spoiling it, and tell him to give extra rations today. If we're going to be taken prisoner, we'll have full bellies.'

They went out on deck and looked over the sea. Both frigates were much nearer. They were wearing full canvas and converging. If they were enemy, as now seemed likely, they could be clearing their decks for action. Each vessel might carry four times as many guns as *Greyhound*. Their heaviest, the equivalent of the British thirty-two-pounder, would be able to sink them before the sloop's six-pounders were in range. There was nothing to do other than sail eastwards.

'They're hoisting their colours,' Saunders called half an hour later. 'Frigates of the Batavian Republic.'

'You're wrong,' Lawson said as he examined them through his glass. 'The one to the nor'ard is flying French colours.'

'Same stable. Which country is to be recommended for the way it feeds its prisoners of war? We've still got time to choose which ship captures us.'

'We might still keep out of range until dark,' Lawson grumbled irritably. 'Especially if the helmsman will steer straight,' he added in a louder, angry voice as the sloop yawed off course under the surge and lift of a huge following wave.

The helmsman, an experienced seaman, heard the criticism, as he was intended to. It was unjust. He was struggling. The sea had been rising for some time and Lawson ought to have doubled the hands at the wheel earlier. The commander was at fault, not the helmsman. Lawson stepped in to help him, full of remorse and ashamed of his anger. He did not apologize, but the man understood and smiled to himself.

One of the Russian seamen came running to relieve Lawson. He stepped back and examined the spread of sail above them.

They were rushing along, accelerating in wild leaps down each successive sea, steadying briefly in the troughs and being borne onwards. The standing rigging had taken on a new keening note, higher than before, and the single mast groaned under the stress. The sloop had a sensation of weightlessness about her, and was not fully under control. They had to reduce sail without delay or there would be more immediate troubles than the enemy.

'All hands to shorten sail,' Lawson shouted.

The men turned out with a rush. Obviously they had been waiting for this order, he realized with some embarrassment. The petty officer would have known the danger and mustered the others in readiness.

What a bloody fool I am, Lawson thought furiously.

Quickly the crew hauled down the topsail and reefed the main course, some of them casting apprehensive glances over their shoulders as they worked. The two converging frigates, each with its three masts still well-clothed in grey canvas, came inexorably on. The heavy swell was not worrying them. It seemed that there could be no escape.

Throughout the afternoon, the gap narrowed between the sloop and her pursuers. They were in range, but no shots were fired. Evidently, they were not wanting to damage their prize, which must soon surrender. The island of Terschelling stood clear ahead, presenting its narrow, western end. On the starboard bow lay Vlieland. The Dutch Fleet normally sheltered just beyond these islands in the Waddenzee. At this rate of approach, the sloop must be amongst them long before dark. There were still three hours before sunset.

The Dutch frigate fired two warning shots when it had approached within half a mile and when Terschelling was near enough for the green of the grass and the yellow of the gorse to be seen clearly. Both cannonballs struck the water ahead of *Greyhound*, one to the right and one to the left.

'They could have hit us with either of those, without any bother,' Saunders observed. 'They want to capture us before we reach the Dutch Fleet on the other side of the island, so they won't have to share the prize money. Do we surrender now or wait until they've knocked the mast out of us?'

'We'll carry on. Have the men clear away the aftermost guns. If the Dutchman continues with warning shots, we won't fire. If he hits us, we'll reply. Our six-pounders will shoot that distance.'

Saunders looked at him in amazement, but he said nothing and went off to give the orders to the gunners.

He's probably right, Lawson mused. A shot amongst them would likely kill a few men and he would be responsible for their deaths. But the alternative was to surrender without a fight. What would the British Navy think of that? He, the commander, would be up for court martial, not Saunders. Madame Hanikof, Annette and Victoria appeared, all brought out by the squealing of gun-carriage wheels over the deck boards above their heads. His decision to fight could also result in their deaths or disfigurement. Could he live with himself after such a tragedy of his making?

'Bloody hell! Will ye look at that?' a voice exclaimed from over by the wheel.

Lawson spun around. Dead ahead, coming around the heel of Terschelling, was a three-decked man-of-war, her guns run out. With two frigates behind them and a first-rate in front, and the three-decker almost as close as the nearer frigate, it was merely a question as to which vessel they should surrender. The Admiralty could hardly complain if he struck his colours now.

'Belay that last order, Mr Saunders,' he shouted. 'Stand by to bring her into the wind and heave to. We're going to surrender.'

A hand clutched his arm and shook it urgently. It was Madame Hanikof's.

'That is my husband's flagship.'

'Are you sure?' Lawson demanded incredulously.

'*Oui*. I am sure,' she said, nodding her head vigorously. 'She is *Sophia-Augusta*. I know her well.'

Madame Hanikof showed no enthusiasm at the prospects of being rescued by her husband, Lawson thought. Now as he watched spellbound, the Imperial Russian flag was broken out from the backstay of her mizzenmast. At the same time, another large ship came into sight behind *Sophia-Augusta*, followed by yet a third. Lawson turned and looked astern. Both the Dutchman and the more distant French frigate were already heaving to, pausing to make sure that this really was happening to them, before taking refuge in flight.

It had been the hankering for a little glory and perhaps a few prizes that had persuaded Admiral Hanikof to delay his return to the Baltic. Neither hope had been realized, and he dared delay no longer. The two frigates could have been his had he been patient for another hour. He had heard the guns and foolishly rushed out from cover too early. Now the enemy vessels were beyond his reach and he was left with nothing.

The admiral was astounded when his wife and daughters, escorted by Lawson, were rowed across to the flagship. This might have accounted for the lack of emotion at their reunion, but he was livid with rage when he learned about the loss of the royal sloop. Lawson was ordered to attend an immediate court of enquiry, but he was then kept waiting for an hour outside the closed doors of the admiral's office.

'You understand, Mr Lawson, that your sloop was in the hands of the enemy when we came to take it from them,' the Russian interpreter said when the investigation into the loss of *Catherine* had ended.

Lawson looked from the dapper little man with the gesticulating hands, who spoke perfect English, to the fat, bearded Admiral Hanikof sitting behind a desk.

'I had not surrendered,' he said defiantly.

The admiral shrugged his shoulders, spoke rapidly in Russian, then turned rudely away to look at some papers held by a clerk on his right. Obviously, the matter was closed as far as he was concerned. Lawson waited for a translation, knowing perfectly well that whatever he had to say would be ignored. The interpreter cleared his throat and chose his words carefully.

'In the admiral's opinion, the sloop which you commanded was being driven into enemy coastal waters by hostile frigates and there was no way that you could have been saved from capture, had it not been for the intervention of the Imperial Russian Navy. Apart from that, since the British Navy has lost the Russian sloop *Catherine*, which it took without permission from its lawful and legitimate duties, the admiral feels that he must take, in exchange, the French sloop, *Le Lévrier*.'

'But – but he has not the –'

'Particularly,' the little man interrupted, raising his hand to silence Lawson, 'as the Russian seamen who survived the destruction of their sloop have sworn on oath that the Imperial sloop *Catherine*, under the command of Lieutenant Baratovski, was the only naval vessel which actually exchanged shots with *Le Lévrier*.'

The Russian seamen knew that the *pecheur* had fired at the sloop – and hit it, Lawson reflected, but it had nothing to do with the legality of the case. The French commander had surrendered to *Adamant*. However, it was obvious that Admiral Hanikof intended to take the sloop, and no arguments advanced by an acting lieutenant were going to influence him. He was guilty of piracy, but the points he had raised in justification of his action would probably be enough to keep a visiting foreign admiral out of the criminal courts should he ever return to Britain.

'What about my men?' Lawson asked coldly.

'The admiral is prepared to detach a frigate from the fleet to convey you and your men to the fishing ground known as the Dogger Bank. There they will place you on board a fishing boat and you can make the fishermen take you to where you want to go.'

Lawson bowed, turned and left without a word.

Madame Hanikof was waiting as Lawson left the admiral's presence. She had been standing in the passageway that gave access to the administrative accommodation. Now she moved to meet him.

'Mr Lawson,' she said sadly as she took both of his hands in hers, 'I am deeply sorry, and I feel so ashamed, but there is nothing I can do.'

'My deepest regret, ma'am, is that I shall soon be saying goodbye to you and – and your daughters.'

'Yes,' she whispered, nodding her head and watching him intently. 'I do believe that. But you are young. Victoria is also young. You will both find someone else one day. Go to her, for a moment only.'

She opened a door and smiled at him sympathetically. He entered a small office. Victoria rushed into his arms as he closed the door behind him and leaned upon it. Too soon the discreet tap from outside warned them that their time together was over.

'I shall always love you, my dearest,' she whispered, her blue eyes glistening as she looked tenderly into his.

He smiled sadly down at her, then kissed her hair and held her close to him.

'If we love each other enough, we shall find a way,' he said gently.

There was a second tap. They kissed urgently, passionately, each knowing deep down that it must be forever. Then she pushed her body away from his, walked quickly across the small chamber and stood with her back to him.

'Please – please go quickly,' she pleaded tearfully.

He opened the door, looked back at her for the last time, and left. Her head had been bowed. Now she collapsed into a chair sobbing.

Less than an hour later Lawson, Saunders and the British seamen had been transferred to the frigate *Eudoxia*, the most disreputable and worn-out vessel of the entire Russian Fleet. They took only their personal possessions, and even these had been searched by their allies to make sure that they had nothing belonging to the sloop. Lawson's baggage was examined more carefully than the rest, but he had already dropped the red bag containing Kempenfelt's signal book over the side. A letter that Madame Hanikof had slipped to him addressed to Captain Brewster was secure in an inside pocket of his jacket.

It was now quite dark, so they saw nothing beyond the deck of the frigate as they left the Fleet. They were all conscious of the clacking and sighing of the pumps, which worked unceasingly, and the stink of fetid air escaping through the grated hatch from the crowded deck below. They also noted the rags worn by the common seamen and the haughty, contemptuous attitude of the officers towards their underlings. Three men were beaten unmercifully to the deck boards by officers and petty officers before they had been an hour on their way. It was perhaps a useful experience for Lawson's men, who had been so near to mutiny on *Adamant*. The Royal Navy was harsh, but the Imperial Russian Navy was hell.

They slept on the top deck, preferring the May night in the open to the foul air of the covered decks below. The wind had dropped and the sea was subsiding. For the first time in over a week, they were able to sleep for more than four hours at a stretch, so perversely, they were all wide awake long before dawn, cursing the hardness of the boards under them. They got up in twos and threes to walk around the foredeck and piss surreptitiously in the scuppers. It was a British seaman who first saw the enemy frigate's bow wave against the blackness of the sea.

'There's a ship o'er on t'starboard beam, sir,' he reported when he had found Lawson. 'Seems to be uncommon near fer comfort, and she's showin' no lights.'

Lawson sprang to his feet and peered into the darkness. He saw the barely discernible silhouette of a ship's rigging and drew the attention of the watch-keeping officer to it by pointing silently.

The officer was in a panic of indecision. He knew his duty, but it was obvious that he was afraid to disturb his aristocratic young captain. There had been a wild party, which had lasted until the small hours and had kept many of the men awake. The enemy helped the deck officer out of his dilemma. They fired a broadside of twenty-two guns at the Russian frigate, and that woke everybody.

Eudoxia was doomed before her guns could be manned. Worm-eaten and rotten, several of her main timbers collapsed, and the sea flooded her lower decks in minutes. She heeled steeply to starboard. One of her guns fired, hurling its shot uselessly into the water a few feet away. Then there was chaos below as heavy cannon broke free of their tackles under the strain of a fifty-degree list, and squealed their way across wildly tilted deck boards to add their tonnage to the battery on the other side. *Eudoxia* lurched further over, bowing her masts to the enemy, as if acknowledging her defeat and praying to be left to die in peace.

'*Adamant* to me,' Lawson called.

'Some of us is with you, sir,' Brown replied close by.

'There's a boat here. I want you all to gather around it,' Lawson told him.

Eudoxia was lying tiredly on her side with her timbers groaning: her lower yards almost touching the sea. One of the ship's boats had been secured to a cradle close by the base of the foremast. Now the cradle was gone and the boat was swinging and thumping against the steeply sloping deck, held by its lashings at one end only. The problem would be to lower it to the water the right way up. In its present precarious situation, it could plunge like an arrow and be lost.

'Mr Saunders, are you with us?' Lawson shouted.

'Right alongside you.'

He sounded less than six feet away, but it was too dark to identify or even count those who were near.

'We need ropes to pass around the mast, and blocks and tackle to lower away. Just feel around inside the boat,' Lawson ordered.

'Here we are, sir. I've got 'em,' Brown shouted.

Lawson took one of the wooden pulley blocks that they

passed up to him and lashed it to the frigate's mast, which now stretched almost horizontally just above their heads and parallel to the water. There was little time left for *Eudoxia* and the men knew it. They worked frantically securing the tackle on bow and stern until finally they were ready for hoisting.

'Take the strain.'

The men heaved at the ropes under Lawson's direction. The lower end of the boat rose. When it was horizontal, all scrambled in. They lowered themselves to the sea and cast off, not a moment too soon. With a great noise of rending timbers and belching air, the ship rolled over and began to settle deeper in the water.

There had been four hundred and forty men living in *Eudoxia* and probably a half of them were trapped on the lower decks. A hundred or more swarmed around the main cluster of small boats still tied down amidships. The rest were either in the sea or clinging to some part of the sinking frigate. No sooner had Lawson's boat got under way than it was stopped by desperate, terrified swimmers who clutched at the oars and clawed themselves aboard.

'No more. They'll capsize us,' Lawson commanded.

The boat was already too crowded to survive for long. Now British and Russian hammered at the fingers and heads of the unfortunate seamen who were still struggling to get out of the water. At last they rowed clear and disappeared into the darkness with the pitiful entreaties and the curses of their doomed shipmates ringing in their ears.

The Dutch frigate that had sunk *Eudoxia* was the same that had pursued Lawson in the sloop the day before. The French frigate was also in the vicinity. During the early morning they took between them seventy-four survivors into captivity. Eighteen of them were *Adamant*'s men. Lawson had lost only one.

CHAPTER TWENTY-TWO

HMS *Sandwich*, lying at the Nore in the mouth of the Thames, had been a seething bed of discontent long before Parker's transfer from *Adamant*. She had been moored there for two years. Her timbers were rotting. The foul stink of decay from her bilges was always present; yet she was considered to be good enough accommodation for men who had volunteered or been caught in the Navy's net.

There were over six hundred living aboard her at the beginning of May 1797, most of them awaiting postings to active warships. There were clean-living men, taken from the streets and the merchant ships by His Majesty's Impressment Service, living on crowded decks in the company of thieves from the magistrates' courts, able-bodied vagrants turned out of the workhouses and the lousy sweepings of the Thames-side gutters, half naked and filthy.

Parker was not affected by this overcrowding. He shared a cosy, semi-private area with four other clerks, close by the purser's store. He was much better off than he had been on *Adamant* in that he stood no watch and his duties took him ashore. In fact, he was more comfortable than at any time since he had joined the Navy. Certainly, there was no reason for him to take part in the mutiny that broke out a week after he had joined the ship. Probably such had not been his intention.

He stood at the edge of the crowd for some time, listening to one speaker after another, his eyes contemptuous as each struggled to put over an effective message. There were loud-mouthed, bullying types and angry young men who were unable to express themselves. There were also quieter, more thoughtful people, who lacked the personality to stir their shipmates. No one proposed a workable plan of action. For the most part, the speakers were merely repeating what had already been said, and some of the more intelligent turned away to hold their own discussions in small groups, having lost interest in the main meeting.

'You will never get anywhere if you proceed like this,' Parker said on impulse.

He had spoken to those near him, but his words filled a momentary pause in the current diatribe and were heard by most. Parker's accent was rather more genteel than was usual on the lower decks, and he had developed a distinctive manner of speech, as a lawyer's clerk, which he could turn on at will. Then he had used the word 'proceed', whereas most men would have said 'carry on'. The result was immediate attention. Many looked around to see who had spoken. The man who had been holding forth was indignant.

'Who the 'ell are you?' he demanded aggrievedly.

It seemed to those nearest to Parker that he regretted his intervention, but there were many eyes looking his way now. The men were waiting attentively. He had to get on with it.

'Who am I?' He shrugged and gestured his own insignificance. 'I'm just a seaman like you, who has not been paid for six months, and who could earn four times as much serving on one of John o' Company's ships.'

Now men were craning their necks to see him and those in the little groups were turning to look. All were silent and waiting attentively. It was the sort of situation that Parker's ego craved. He started walking forward. A passageway opened before him in the massed ranks.

'Just a seaman who is sick of being treated like a mangy dog by his officers and being robbed of his fair rations by the purser. In short, I'm a sailor with all the grievances

227

that you have, but I won't be content by just talking about it. Talk won't feed my wife or keep a roof over her head. Action is what is needed.'

He had reached the stairway that was being used as a rostrum, conscious that every man was hanging on to his words. He had not looked for leadership in a venture as desperate as this, but the attentive silence of several hundred men, including petty officers, was intoxicating. He allowed himself to be nudged and beckoned onto the gangway steps, grudgingly vacated by the last speaker. Then he deliberately went higher, onto the holy of holies, the quarterdeck itself: the first of the speakers to do so. It created a favourable impression amongst the mutineers because the officers, and the warrant officers who had remained loyal, were clustered at the far end of it.

Parker looked over the sea of faces and felt, as many another demagogue, an exhilarating flush of intense excitement. There were a few sneering, and most were sceptical, but they were his, for the moment. His opening words, he realized, must be more dramatic and potent than any that had so far been spoken.

'Do you really believe that anyone up in London, our Lords of Admiralty, Pitt, or the other fellow, Fox, will lift a finger to improve our conditions if we do nothing more than ask?' he demanded scornfully. 'We've heard of promises given at Spithead, but we still haven't been paid. The purser still issues fourteen ounces to the pound and puts the value of the other two ounces in his pocket. How many of you have had shore leave lately?' He paused and looked around challengingly.

'Dicky Howe said that you were going to get some. The government sent him around the ships at Spithead with a bit of paper in his hand. He climbed the side of every one, an old man turned seventy, because no one would have believed any other admiral. They believed Admiral Howe, and they went to sea. I saw them arrive off Brest. They did what was expected of them, but what has happened to the promises?'

'All right. What are we going to do about it?' someone shouted.

Parker contrived to look astonished that his questioner

228

did not know the answer. He raised his hands in a gesture of appeal.

'There's only one thing to do. We've got to frighten the folk in authority.'

'How?'

Parker smiled sardonically down at the man who had asked the question. 'How will it be,' he paused for effect, 'if we blockade the Thames – for a start?'

The crowd moved restively. He gave them a moment to settle, conscious that he had their undivided attention.

'There are two frigates in from the North Sea Fleet, taking on supplies. We'll send a delegation aboard. And,' he pointed to the north dramatically, 'we'll send another delegation by coach to Yarmouth to bring the rest of the fleet in. I hear that Duncan's got fourteen ships of the line. That should be enough to frighten the government.'

'They'll shit 'emselves,' a little man shouted gleefully.

Parker laughed shortly, without humour. 'If it came to it, we could sail up the Thames and put a broadside amongst the fine fellows sitting in parliament. There's nothing that can stop us.'

There was a rumble of general agreement and a roar of applause from one corner. It had been the most effective speech they had heard.

The officers assembled on the aftermost part of the quarterdeck, were whispering agitatedly, and the elderly captain was demanding to know the name of the speaker. Lieutenant Benson, who had recruited Parker from *Adamant*, wrote his name on a page of his notebook, tore it out and handed it to his captain.

Several courts of enquiry were held in the Admiralty building during the third week in May. The one that Captain Brewster was summoned to attend was to look into the loss of the Russian sloop *Catherine*. On the face of it, it seemed to be a normal straightforward investigation, but Brewster was suspicious. He had discovered that the civil servant McDonald, who had posed as the secretary to the alcoholic Rear Admiral Neilson Clare, was in reality a lawyer. This discovery caused him to examine the antecedents of the seven officers who would be conducting the enquiry. The president of the court was Admiral Quinsey, an uncle of Midshipman Atkins. Three of the captains had served under either Admiral Quinsey or Admiral Seymour. All of them were standard-entry officers, which meant that they had joined the Navy as young gentlemen and not as common seamen, as had Captain Brewster.

As if to emphasize the difference in quality, Brewster was kept waiting for over half an hour in an anteroom. There he could hear the clink of glasses and the buzz of social chatter on the other side of the door. At length, he was bidden to enter and directed to an isolated chair set before a crescent of tables, where sat the captains with Admiral Quinsey in the centre. The glasses had been removed but there was a strong smell of drink about the room.

It must have been obvious to all that the loss of the Russian sloop was the fault of Commander Baratovski. The orders that he had disobeyed were recorded in *Adamant*'s log, signed by Baratovski and witnessed by Lieutenant Prendergast. There was no case to answer so far as Brewster was concerned, but the cold hostility of the captains, which had been evident from the beginning, remained after the president's grudging summary had cleared *Adamant* of all responsibility.

Brewster realized that he had been prejudged on a very different issue. He waited grimly whilst Admiral Quinsey thumbed through the fresh file which McDonald had placed before him.

'There are a few other matters which could conveniently be examined by this assembled court of enquiry,' Admiral Quinsey began. 'You will doubtless be aware, gentlemen, that the leader of the mutiny at the Nore is one Richard Parker. He has gathered about him six ships of the line and divers small craft and declared himself "President of the Floating Republic". We are informed that this man was transferred from *Adamant* to HMS *Sandwich* on the strong recommendation of Captain Brewster. Is that not correct, sir?'

He lowered his spectacles and stared at Brewster.

'His abilities fitted the requirements of the off –'

'Please answer the question, Captain. Is it correct that Parker entered *Sandwich* on your recommendation?' Admiral Quinsey snapped testily.

'It is correct,' Brewster growled.

'Is it not also true that you were aware of the viciousness of this man?'

'Viciousness!'

'You knew him to be a rabble-rouser; the sort of fellow who would gather about him all the undesirables and set himself at their head?'

'No, I didn't know that. He led nobody on *Adamant*.'

'Did he ever challenge authority on *Adamant*?' Quinsey asked in a quieter voice. 'Did he at any time show himself to be antiofficer?'

'I should have dealt with him promptly, had he done so.'

'Would you, Captain? Would you indeed?'

Quinsey's eyes stared balefully into Brewster's for a moment, then his finger prodded the paper before him. His thin lips twisted into a sneer as he looked to left and right.

'Listen carefully to this statement, gentlemen. It was made by one of Captain Brewster's officers and confirmed, albeit very reluctantly, by the second-in-command of HMS *Adamant*, Lieutenant Prendergast.'

He held the note at arm's length, adjusted his spectacles and began to read. '*During a funeral at sea, a man hidden in the crowd of seamen gathered around the waist of the ship, did try to incite those about him to throw a midshipman over the side. When asked by Lieutenant Prendergast if he should try to find the man responsible, Captain Brewster replied. "I recognized the voice. It was that bloody Parker".*'

Quinsey dramatically removed his spectacles, sat back in his chair and looked significantly around the crescent of captains.

'I should like to question the officers concerned over that statement,' Brewster said truculently.

'Perhaps you would like to question the officer who made this statement too, Captain?'

He bent to the file again and took up another paper. '*At eight bells of the midnight watch on April nineteenth/twen-*

tieth I went to the captain's cabin to report a fire at sea, several miles to the south of our position. I found the captain drinking with the master, and I heard him make the following remarks: "God knows, these poor lads have nothing to be patriotic about. They've had no pay for months, no shore leave since they came aboard and, on top of that, they have a bloody admiral who thinks he's God Almighty and can ignore a petition from twenty thousand men".'

He tossed the paper back onto the file and smiled without humour.

'I feel sure that Admiral Howe would be interested in such a statement, Captain Brewster.'

'I feel sure that such a statement, and the one afore it, should not have been read in this court, or anywhere else, except by the witnesses concerned to enable me to challenge the accuracy of the words supposed to have been spoken.'

'You seem to have garnered a fair amount of legal claptrap, Captain Brewster,' the admiral sneered. 'No doubt the result of your tangle with the law over this disgra – this miserable brothel murder in Liverpool.'

I must protest, sir,' Brewster shouted, rising angrily to his feet. 'You've steered this court to your own satisfaction, giving me no chance to reply. And now you've suggested to every man in this room that I am involved in a criminal enquiry. Is that the proper conduct for the president of a naval court?'

'This is outrageous,' Quinsey blustered. 'I would remind you that I am your superior –'

'Is it the proper conduct for a gentleman?' Brewster pursued.

The admiral appeared apoplectic, then controlled himself with an effort.

'I am sure, Captain Brewster, that *you* are not the best judge of a gentleman. As to the rest of it, this enquiry, the latter part of it anyway, is to decide whether or not we should recommend your court martial on the charge of – conduct unworthy of an officer, or even treason, be damned. You will leave this room, but not the building, until we have reached a decision.'

Brewster glared at him and walked out, knowing that

nothing could save him from a court martial. If he were found guilty of the first charge, it would mean dismissal from the Navy and subsequent poverty, unless he could find some merchant willing to trust him with a ship. If they could prove the charge of treason, he would have no worries about future employment. The sentence would be death.

There were several officers in the antechamber, lounging in chairs waiting for appointments with the numerous minions and chiefs in the rooms around. Brewster remained standing aloof from the rest, staring unseeingly at a large painting of some ancient sea battle. He heard someone, in a voice loud enough to dominate all nearby conversation, telling a chance-met, former colleague the latest news of the Nore mutiny. Parker was blockading London and threatening to lead his six ships over to the enemy if Duncan's North Sea Fleet attacked him.

'You're out of date with your news, Mr Preston,' a captain called. 'Yesterday Bligh's ship, the *Director*, went over to the mutineers and they sent Bligh ashore.'

'William Bligh! Late of the *Bounty*, sir?' a younger man exclaimed.

'Aye, the same,' the captain confirmed with a short laugh. 'This time he didn't have so far to row as he did on the previous occasion.'

'There'll be others to follow before long, mark my words,' an elderly officer contributed. 'This fellow Parker seems to have the gift of the gab, and he's forever speechifying from all accounts.'

Mr McDonald came into the anteroom and looked around for Captain Brewster.

'Admiral Quinsey has requested that you return to the court to hear its decision, sir,' he whispered.

Brewster grunted an acknowledgement. If the court had decided upon a charge of treason, this would be his last moment of freedom.

The port admiral at Chatham read through the blue scented paper for the fourth time, then pulled vigorously at the bell-rope. A seaman of medium height in his early fifties, entered from the side office and waited respectfully. Admiral Wren indicated the letter.

'Just heard from London that my nephew still hasn't been near his mother's place, Stringer. What the devil can he be up to?'

Stringer had served Admiral Wren for close on thirty years, at sea and ashore, so he knew better than to offer any suggestions. He pursed his lips and looked concerned but remained silent.

'You say that you saw them off on this hired coach, but you don't know where it came from?'

'Well, sir, a yeller tandem the loikes o' that is not awful common in these parts, so I asks abart a bit when I seed you were worritin' o'er Mr Heward. We-ell, it don't belong to any o' t'locals, neither 'ere nor yet in Rochester.'

'Come on, Stringer. Out with it. Let's have no more games,' the admiral said tolerantly.

He removed his snuff box, took a pinch and sat in the wide window casement. His man pulled a notebook from an inside pocket and thumbed through the pages.

Well, sir, I gets to thinking that the yeller tandem moight ha' come fro' London, 'cause it has a different rig from the craft which plies 'ereabouts. An' if it comes fro' London, it'll loikely ha' been berthed in a local inn-yard o'er-noight, 'cause Mr Heward's party went orf first thing in t'marnin' wi' a pair of fresh 'osses and the pint-work gleaming broight.'

'So you found out where it stayed the night?' the admiral prompted.

'The White Swan, sir. I has a word with the ostler there, an' he remembers the yeller tandem. In fact he 'elped to 'arness the 'osses. The name on t'coach was Williamson, which stuck in his moind on account av it bein' the syme as his mother-in-law. Williamson of Stepney, he told me.'

Admiral Wren walked across to his desk, took out a diary and flicked through the pages.

'I think we might spend a few days in London, Stringer. I'll look up Atkinson at Admiralty and ask him why he doesn't answer letters. You can wander around

Stepney and find the driver of Williamson's yellow tandem.'

'I'll book a passage for tomorrer marnin' on the reg'lar coach, if it pleases you, sir.'

The admiral was pensively drumming his fingers on the desk. Stringer waited.

'You don't think he could have gone off with this young woman, do you, Stringer?'

The man looked thoughtful as he pocketed his note-book and buttoned his coat. 'She's a very foine-looking young woman, sir,' he said noncommittally. 'Very foine indeed! The two o' them did travel alone inside the coach.'

CHAPTER TWENTY-THREE

Heiko Meyer, the captain of the frigate *Monniken-dam*, was not a regular officer in the Batavian Republican Navy. In peacetime his life was fully occupied with the affairs of the family shipping firm of Meyer and Son. This was an enterprise that owed its foundation to an earlier war, in which one of Heiko's ancestors pursued a ship homeward bound from Madras into the Medway, and snatched it from under the guns of Chatham.

In 1797 the last thing the Meyer family wanted was a war with England. Quite apart from being out of sympathy with the spirit of the 'Revolution', they had financial interests in Great Yarmouth and the Lincolnshire port of Boston. In fact, most of their large continental carrying trade passed through the hands of the expanding firm of Watkins and Green. Consequently, Heiko Meyer was delighted to learn that he had a British lieutenant and a midshipman in his net who belonged to the North Sea Fleet, which, as he knew, was based on Yarmouth. He sent for them after *Monnikendam* had dropped anchor in the Zuyder Zee, close by the town of Hoorn.

Captain Meyer, a tall man in his late forties, greeted Lawson and Saunders with a friendly smile and outstretched hand when they were shown into his quarters. He settled them in chairs and gave each a glass of an excellent brandy. Then he enquired about them and their men in fluent English.

'I regret, sir, that I know nothing of Great Yarmouth, being but recently arrived in these waters,' Lawson told him, when the Dutchman asked him.

'It does not matter,' Meyer replied with a dismissive shrug. 'I think that my wife would be happy to make your acquaintance.'

'Your wife, sir?'

'She is English, born in Boston. If you will promise not to run away, or do anything harmful to my people, I shall be pleased to separate you from the rest of my prisoners, who will be going ashore as soon as the soldiers come for them. Then, perhaps you will do me the honour of becoming my guests.'

'That is very kind of you, sir,' Lawson said, 'but I am not at all sure if I am permitted to give my parole.'

'Poo! Think nothing of it. There is quite a community of English officers living in Amsterdam with complete freedom to walk the streets. All have given their parole.'

'Do you think that Mr Saunders and I might have a few minutes to discuss it, sir?'

'By all means. Make yourselves comfortable here. I have a few things to which I must attend. If you use tobacco, you might care to try some of this.'

He pushed over a jar and indicated a number of clay pipes standing in an earthenware elephant's foot. It was a kindness that persuaded them to accept the conditions of parole. They justified their decision with the argument that they would be in a better position to attend to the welfare of their men.

The Meyers lived in a substantial timber-framed, red-brick house with ornamental chimneys. It was strategically placed on the quayside, with a wide, cobbled area before it and a fine view of the anchorage. Of similar construction, but obviously much older, was the warehouse, a three-storied building of timber and brick, with a derrick mounted on the roof for hoisting sacks and bales to the loading door at each level.

'Cannonballs,' Meyer said wryly, having noted Saunders' curiosity about the patches of new brick set in the old warehouse wall. 'It happened two years ago, when the French came to persuade us to get rid of the monarchy. They set fire to our house at the same time.'

'Was that when the French captured the whole of the Dutch Fleet with cavalry?' Lawson asked.

Captain Meyer smiled bitterly and nodded. 'That's right. It is the only time in history that a sea force has suffered such a fate. We had a fool of an admiral who knew that the water was freezing, but he left his ships at anchor. By the time the French arrived with their guns and cavalry, the whole of the Zuyder Zee was frozen solid enough to stand the weight of an army. It was the field guns, firing from the ice, that punched the holes in the warehouse and flattened half the town.'

As they approached the house, a buxom woman in her early forties, with brown hair turning to grey, opened the door and stood beaming on the threshold. She had evidently been warned that English visitors were coming.

'I am very pleased to welcome you,' she said.

She shook each by the hand, but she seemed to be particularly interested in Saunders. After they had entered the house and were sitting at table, she found it hard to share her attention equally between her two visitors. This appeared to amuse Captain Meyer who had been watching his wife's reaction closely. Now he left the room to return a few moments later with a portrait. It was of a youth who could well have been mistaken for Saunders.

'This is whom my wife sees when she speaks to you,' the captain said to Saunders. 'It is our son, Jan. We have not seen him since he went to England two years ago. He is living with his grandparents in Boston, learning the business.'

Thereafter Lawson and Saunders were made very comfortable in the Meyer home. Each had a small room set in the eaves of the house overlooking the harbour. They dined with the family and were allowed to do pretty well as they pleased. They could walk the streets and the harbour. They managed to obtain better accommodation and a degree of freedom for their seamen, who were enabled to earn enough for tobacco and a few delicacies.

In fact, they were all better off than they would have been doing blockade duty off the Texel, or lying at anchor near Yarmouth.

'General Daendels has arrived in Alkmaar,' the lady of the house commented at breakfast, after they had been there for two weeks. 'Apparently there is an Irish gentleman with him, who is a colonel in the French army and newly come from France. I cannot think of his name.'

'I suppose it's not Theobald Wolfe Tone?' Lawson suggested.

'Why yes, I do believe it is. I am told that he and the general are passionately fond of music. They play duets on the flute, and they are very good.'

'I wonder what else they are playing together?' Lawson said later, when he and Saunders had left the house and were walking along the water's edge. 'I shouldn't be surprised if it isn't the invasion game again. Dutch troops for Ireland! I wonder what Mr Atkinson at Admiralty would make of this information?'

'Well, he'll never get it. Not from us anyway. Being on parole makes the prisoner more secure than if he were locked up. That little fishing boat sitting at the far end of the quay would have served to get us to England if we had not given our word that we wouldn't escape.'

Two days later they were fishing from the end of a jetty to the north of Hoorn when a group of officers arrived on foot. They were obviously engaged in some kind of a survey and, since they wore naval and army uniforms, it seemed likely that they might be contemplating a joint exercise: the embarking of troops perhaps.

'Let's get out of their way,' Lawson said, gathering his fishing gear.

They had just reached the end of the jetty with their rods over their shoulders when a small party of horsemen clattered up and dismounted. They walked towards the first group. The central figure was wearing a dark blue jacket with a red breast, which Saunders recognized as the uniform worn by the élite carabineers of the French Army. He had no badges of rank but he was evidently very senior indeed, judging by the brigadier and the two colonels in his train.

'General Daendels, I'll bet,' Saunders said.

Some of the officers were now taking notes of instructions from an elderly major of engineers. The general left them to it and walked along the quay accompanied by an infantry colonel in blue and white with golden epaulettes. The two were about thirty-five years old, of medium height and build. They could have been taken for brothers. The colonel walked with a limp.

'I think that the one with the general could well be the Irishman,' Saunders suggested. 'Mrs Meyer heard that they look very much alike. These two certainly do. What was his name?'

'Theobald Wolfe Tone,' Lawson replied absently.

His attention was on a man hovering in the background. He wore a brown fustian jacket and was the only civilian in the party. His stance seemed familiar. Now he turned and looked at Lawson. As their eyes met, there was instant mutual recognition. It was the Irish spy, Mr Maharg. If he was shaken by the encounter, he didn't show it. He stared at Lawson for two or three seconds, then winked slowly and turned away.

'I don't know what to make of him,' Lawson said when they were alone. 'Is he working for both sides, do you think?'

'We'll probably never know. I must say that I admire his nerve. Are you certain he winked?'

'Yes. I feel sure that we shall see him again before we are much older,' Lawson said thoughtfully. 'More'n likely, General Daendels will stay here overnight. Wolfe Tone is attached to his staff and Maharg seems to have attached himself to our flute-playing Irishman.

'Probably Wolfe Tone's servant, so he'll not be his own man, and independent movement might be difficult. Why would he try to contact us anyway?'

'To make sure that we keep our mouths shut, if nothing else.'

As it turned out, fate made it easy for Maharg to meet them.

Admiral Jan Willem de Winter, commander in chief of the Batavian Navy, flew his flag above the ninety-four-gun *Vrijheid*. She was lying at anchor close by Captain

Meyer's frigate *Monnikendam*. De Winter had been ashore with his family in their house on the island of Texel when he was informed of the unexpected arrival of the general and his staff. He immediately offered the hospitality of the two ships lying close by Hoorn and ordered Captain Meyer and the captain of *Vrijheid* to place themselves at the general's command, pleading sickness as a reason for his own absence.

Captain Meyer invited the senior officers to dine with him ashore, whilst their accommodation was being prepared on the two ships. Lawson and Saunders were offered their dinners either in the privacy of their rooms or in the kitchen. They opted for the kitchen and were astounded to find Maharg and two Dutch non-commissioned officers at the table. It was the natural thing to take a stroll in the garden after the meal.

'I think indade that you'll have to break your parole. 'Tis a sad t'ing for chentlemen, they tell me, an' you'll never be able to lift your heads again in society,' he said mockingly, 'but there's nuthin' else for it, me lads. The information I have must be got away to London, or to Admiral Duncan at least.'

'What information?' Lawson demanded.

'Imminent invasion. Thirty thousand Dutch soldiers are marching towards Hoorn ready to embark. Then there'll be another fifteen thousand from the Dunkirk area. De Winter's ships provide protection for the lot.'

'They'll never get past the North Sea Fleet,' Saunders said. 'Duncan will destroy them.'

'I can see that you've not been using your ears while you've been prisoners here. You'd niver do for my trade.'

'Tell us what we should have heard,' Lawson said testily.

Maharg was determined to make the most out of his advantage. He leered at Lawson.

'I shouldn't wunder if I was told that every man and woman and all the kids in Hoorn know fine that there ain't a British ship anywheres between here and the Norfolk coast. Haven't you noticed the local fishing boats going out? That's 'cause the British are not blockading the Texel any more. They're too busy blockading

London River and looting Yarmouth.'

'What!'

'The North Sea Fleet is in a state of mutiny. They've moved down to the Nore and won't allow any ship to put to sea. What's more, you'll know the leader o' the mutiny. He's a feller called Parker what used to serve on *Adamant*. I niver met the man meself.'

'I know Parker!' Lawson exclaimed.

'Thought you might know 'im. Now as to the mutiny, Captain Brewster is in deep trouble with the Navy about Parker, and if he gets o'er that, there'll be the civil courts after putting a rope around his neck for the murder of some feller in Liverpool.' He shook his head in wonder. 'An' I thought the captain was a respectable, law-abiding –'

'He is,' Lawson interrupted. 'You can take my word for it. Mr Saunders and I will have no difficulty in clearing him of the Liverpool charges. We were there at the time.'

'Were you now? Come to think of it, I heard somethin' about mysteriously disappearing witnesses, just before I left London. I paid little heed. I have enough problems of me own to worry about. So now you've another good reason for breaking your parole, for if you don't get to the captain's assistance soon, it may well be the end of him.'

He gripped Lawson's arm urgently. 'The two sergeants who dined with us are comin' this way now,' he hissed. 'Remember what I told you. Thirty thousand soldiers will be ready to embark in less than a week. The Dutch know for sure that they haven't the British Navy to worry about, so Admiral de Winter is determined to land them in Ireland to support Wolfe Tone and his United Irishmen. Sure, it'll be civil war there, and the unhappy country has enough on its plate wi'out that. Bugger your parole. You'll have to break it.'

'I can think of a better way,' Lawson said quickly. 'You're going to get us arrested and then help us to break out.'

He seized the Irishman by the collar and began to shake him violently.

242

'You damned traitor!' he shouted. 'One of these days, I'll see you pay the penalty for your treachery.'

'Och, you cunnin' darlin', Maharg breathed. 'You're a man after me own heart.'

Suddenly he reached out, gripped Lawson's jacket and butted him with his head. Lawson's nose spurted blood. Then he brought his knee up into Lawson's groin and it became a real fight, which the two sergeants and Saunders had difficulty in stopping. The noise brought the officers out of the house.

'He's broken my bloody nose,' Lawson complained some two hours later, as they lay in the darkness of their new quarters, a prison cell in the middle of town.

Saunders chuckled as he shook up his straw mattress.

'There's nobody in any doubt that you were –' he slipped into a fair imitation of Maharg's speech – 'after killing each other, but bejasus, he got the better of you.'

Lawson was not amused. He got up from the iron bed and walked over to the bars of the cell. They were on the level of the pavement of the street. A nocturnal dog was sniffing around. It cocked its leg up. Lawson jumped back just in time. There was no glass before the bars.

They were under the town hall, and Lawson could see the market square through the bars now that the moon was up.

'I don't know how Maharg is going to get us out of this place,' Saunders yawned, stretching himself more comfortably on his bed.

'Not through these, anyway,' Lawson replied, tapping at the bars. 'Maybe in another ten years, if the dogs keep pissing on 'em.'

'Maybe he'll bribe the guards.'

'Do you know, I don't think there are any. That man they got to open the door with his big bunch of keys, where have you seen him before?'

'Don't know that I have.'

'He was round at the Meyers' this morning delivering wine. He's a wine merchant, and I bet he keeps his wine in the cellars under the town hall. I shouldn't be surprised if we're the only ones in the building at this time of night.'

'We still can't get out, so why don't you go to bed? I'm going to sleep.'

He turned over with a creaking of crisscrossed wrought-iron bands and a rustling of straw. Lawson remained by the bars for another hour before lying down. Even then he couldn't sleep.

'I've been a bloody fool,' he thought savagely. 'An invasion by thirty thousand men planned, and the British Government will likely have no warning of it for the sake of my word of honour. Then there's the captain, the only person who has ever favoured me, and I am letting him down. We could have been well on our way in that fishing boat at the end of the quay. God! If we're too late to help Captain Brewster through my idiotic behaviour, I'll deserve a whipping.'

He tossed on the creaking bed until dawn and then slept soundly until they were awakened by the wine dealer, accompanied by two soldiers, who brought a breakfast of bread and milk.

An hour later they were taken before a fierce little army major whose English accent suggested that he had lived many years in Lincolnshire. The sergeant who had brought them was left in the corridor, but there was a clerk at a desk, a shifty-eyed civilian dressed in black, who was taking notes of the interview. The major seemed to be very conscious of the clerk's presence as he summed up what had been said.

'Captain Meyer was kind to you. He took you into his home and, even after you abused his hospitality, he still asks for you to be allowed to rejoin his family. I cannot permit it. You have attacked and injured the personal servant of a senior officer in the French Army. Your parole is therefore at an end. You will be taken back to the cell that you occupied last night and kept there until an escort can be found to take you to the prisoner-of-war camp at Alkmaar.'

He looked from one to the other, whilst the clerk scribbled busily. Was it the dancing sunlight in the room, or did the major's face really try to convey something to them?

'Do you have anything to say?' he demanded.

244

'No, sir,' they both replied.

'Very well.'

He strode across to the door, opened it dramatically and called to the sergeant.

'You have only yourself to blame,' he told Lawson as they left the room.

Lawson said nothing. He had difficulty in hiding his excitement from the civilian clerk, who watched from his corner. Whilst the irate major had been remonstrating, his fingers had pushed something into Lawson's pocket. It seemed that a vast number of agents had dealings with Mr Atkinson of the Admiralty.

When they had been left in their cell, and the footsteps of the departing wine merchant had receded, Lawson took out the package and opened it on the bed. It contained two pages of fine writing and a cut-down key, freshly worked, with iron filings still clinging to it.

Lawson tried the key on the door of the cell, whilst Saunders kept watch at the barred window. It worked. The second lock would be the one on the door leading to the street, but for that, they should have to wait until dark.

The enclosed letter began with the instruction, 'Read, memorize and burn.' It informed them of the arrangements made for their escape. There followed detailed information of troop movements. Divisions were listed showing their strengths: infantry, cavalry, artillery and engineers: the equipment they had available: the morale of the men and their general fitness. The destination of this force was Londonderry.

'There's too much to learn here,' Saunders said.

'You're right, but we've got to try. We'll manage the essentials between us, then we'll burn the papers. I see that the gaoler has left us a lamp and the means of lighting it. That's strange come to think of it. We had no lamp last night. I wonder if this wine merchant's mixed up with Maharg's crowd?'

'I'm beginning to wonder if all the Dutch people here are opposed to their republican government,' Saunders said. 'I got the impression that the Meyers are. Maybe there's a secret royalist organization in this town.'

'You may well be right,' Lawson said, taking up the paper, 'but the fact remains that the major who slipped me this package was worried about the clerk who was recording our interview. Perhaps he knows he's being watched. We'll not risk his neck by carrying this paper. We've about seven hours of daylight to learn what's written here.'

They bent over the paper and read the items of information to each other over and over again. Then they took a page each and worked on it solidly, except for a short break when they heard the gaolers approaching with food, until it was too dark to see. By then they thought they knew all the facts.

Lawson took up the tinder box. It contained a two-inch length of sharpened steel, a flint inserted in a peg of wood, a scrap of rag, scorched black, and two sulphur dips. He scraped the steel over the flint. After several attempts the tinder caught. He blew it gently until it glowed hot enough to ignite one of the sulphur dips. It burst into flame and he lit the lamp with it. Then they burned their written information and powdered the ash.

CHAPTER TWENTY-FOUR

The moon, which had bathed the market square with light during the early evening, slipped into obscurity before midnight, and a mist, damp and enveloping, began to form. There was no sound from the streets, apart from the wail of a distant cat. It seemed that there could not be a better moment for an escape. Lawson turned from his vigil at the bars and shook Saunders into wakefulness.

'We're going now,' he said.

He inserted the key in the lock and opened the door. The corridor outside was pitch-black, except for a glimmer of light in the distance. They groped their way along the wall, past the doors of several cells, or wine stores, towards the source of light. It came from a barred window over the door that led to the street. The same key served here. They were free.

The square was still and silent. A solitary lantern swung from a rope stretched above the road that led to the harbour. They walked in that direction, wishing that they had thought of tying scraps of blanket around their shoes to muffle the scuff of leather on cobbles. They need not have worried. No faces appeared at the windows. As they drew nearer to the waterfront, the sound of their feet was drowned by the din of revelry from some place ahead.

It came from a tavern at the opposite end of the quay

from where the Meyers lived and quite near the vessel they had been instructed in the paper to steal. Fortunately, the shutters were over the windows, so nobody would have seen them as they walked over to the boat and climbed down from the quay to its deck four feet below. The tide was out.

They removed the gaskets that bound the sails, then checked the steerage. They had often looked at this particular boat, as it had not moved from the quay during the weeks they had been in Hoorn. It was shallow-draughted with a swivelled, pear-shaped leeboard on each side instead of a keel. It was, in fact, a typical Dutch boat, suitable for the shallows of the Zuyder Zee and the coastal waters around the islands.

A sudden increase in the volume of noise warned them that the tavern door had opened. Stretching to his full height, Lawson could see over the edge of the quay. Two men were coming out, silhouetted against the light of the room. Now, it was dark again, and they were invisible, but their drunken voices could be heard approaching. They materialized, one trailing behind the other. The man in the lead was throwing back the front of his unbuttoned long coat and obviously struggling to undo his flies. Lawson joined Saunders behind the mast, where the bundle of sail on the boom would conceal them. The man reached the edge of the quay and stood there swaying. There was the sound of a stream of water falling on the deck and the mud.

Having finished, he turned away to follow the other man. Then he either tripped over his own feet or a mooring rope and fell headlong into the void between the curve of the bow and the shore. His scream was cut off by a dull plump as he hit the mud.

'Dieter! Dieter!' the other fellow shouted from the quayside, peering down into the blackness.

There was no reply. The man gripped the ladder attached to the quay and began to descend. There was no sign that anyone ashore had heard.

'Make sure that he doesn't leave the boat again,' Lawson whispered. 'I'm going to try to find the chap who fell.'

He threw his leg over the bow and was just about to lower himself to the mud, when a thrashing and a flumping close at hand told him that the man had survived the fall. He was up to his waist in mud, retching and struggling ineffectively to reach the side of the boat. Saunders tossed him a line. He clutched at it and tied it around his waist. Then the three of them heaved and plucked him from the mud.

'They'll have to stay with us now,' Lawson said. 'We'll make sure of the dry one first, whilst his mate is recovering.'

An hour later, the incoming tide had floated the boat off the mud bed and set it creaking against the quay. The Dutchmen were both secure in the fish hold and, judging by their snores, they had made themselves comfortable on the heap of nets down there.

At high water, Lawson and Saunders hauled on the mainsail halyard. The gaff slid up the mast, dragging an old patched sail after it. They cast off from the quay and eased the boat into the open river.

Using the various riding lanterns of the anchored fishing boats as a guide, they went out on the ebb, following the line of the channel, which they had committed to memory during their stay in Hoorn. Soon, they were able to identify the two men-of-war, *Vrijheid* and *Monnikendam*, which they knew were lying in the deep water leading to the sea. There would be little chance of going aground now.

The breeze was southerly. Saunders lowered the starboard leeboard deep below the hull. This served better than a keel in shallow water as it could be pivoted up if the boat went aground. Now, they were able to hoist both the jib sail and the triangle of canvas above the gaff. The boat's speed increased. Her bows were pointing towards England. They were sailing away from the gathering dawn and the Hollanders who had treated them so well.

They were not challenged by the guns sited on the south shore of the island of Texel as they slipped between it and the mainland, nor were they questioned by either of the two third-rates at anchor. Many fishing vessels had gone to sea since the departure of the blockading British ships, and this one would seem no different from the others.

About noon, when the coast of Holland and the nearest of the Friesian Islands had merged with the distance, and when it seemed unlikely that they would be pursued, Lawson decided to see if the two men were sober enough to be sent home in the dinghy, which was secured to the deck. They had been banging and shouting for some time.

The prisoners came out with surprising briskness, considering that they had been very drunk only a few hours earlier. Both were excited and voluble but equally unintelligible. Saunders pointed to the dinghy and indicated that they were to take it. They obviously understood his mime, but one of the men still had something urgent to say, until the other one silenced him with a dig in the ribs and a whisper. They hoisted the dinghy over the side, handling the derrick with the ease of experienced seamen, and pushed off without another word.

'They know what they're doing, anyway,' Lawson said, as the men set up the short mast and sail. 'Now that we've got them out of the way, perhaps you will look around to see what sort of rations Maharg has put aboard for us. I hope there's something good. If there's any coffee, I'll have a mug right away. I suppose he'll have remembered fuel for the galley stove.'

Saunders grinned as he looked around.

'As to that, I think I could hack a piece from the bulkhead or even a plank or two out of the deck. This boat's had her day.'

'You're right,' Lawson agreed. 'She steers like a bath tub.'

Saunders went off to search, leaving Lawson to steer by the sun, since there was no compass. Meanwhile, the southerly breeze was equally beneficial to the fishing boat and its departed dinghy. The distance between them increased rapidly.

Saunders looked puzzled when he came aft some time later.

'What's up?'

'I can find neither food nor water. In fact, the boat's been picked clean, as if it had been abandoned. There's not a fork, nor a plate, nor a pan, and even the stove's been taken out. You don't think we made a mistake in the dark and pinched the wrong boat?'

'We made no mistake. This was the one indicated on the paper. I'll have a few things to talk over with Maharg if we ever meet again.'

'I don't suppose we'll suffer any harm if we have to go twenty-four hours without food or water, and it shouldn't take us any longer to make a landfall, if the wind doesn't change.'

'Why not try to catch a fish or two?' Lawson suggested. 'A bit of shirt on a hook will serve as a lure, or maybe you'll find a cod's head that'll do for bait, if you look down in the fish hold.'

Saunders heaved back the hatch cover to look.

'The hold's flooded!' he shouted.

Lawson cursed himself for a fool. If he'd been half a seaman, he would have known from the feel of the tiller that something was wrong.

'Come back here and take the helm. I'll go below.'

Lawson dragged the hatch cover completely clear. The fish hold would be about six feet deep, he estimated. The water swirling around inside occupied about a third of the space. It had been dry when they had locked up the drunks, so the leak had probably been caused by the stresses of sailing. The two shut below would have seen the sea coming in. That was why they had hollered to be let out, and they would have certainly made themselves understood, if he had not given them the only boat.

'I'm not fit to command a canal barge,' he muttered furiously as he lowered himself into the hold.

The mast, which was about ten inches in diameter, passed through the deck to the keel. Lawson waded over to it and looked around. As expected, he could see no indication of a fracture: no turbulence of in-rushing water on the still surface of the flood. The leak would be too small for that, but a leak there was and, since two feet of water had entered in the few hours they had been at sea, they would expect to sink before nightfall, unless they were able to do something about it. The first thing was to find out where the water was getting in, and there was only one way to do that. He took a deep breath and dived under.

He worked his way over the timbers on either side of the keelson, feeling for an inflow of sea. It was not difficult to find. On the leeward side of the mast-step there was a split, not half an inch at its widest, but around three feet long, where the clincher-laid planking had been forced apart by the butt of the mast. Unless they reduced sail to take the pressure off the mast, the split would likely widen.

They lowered the mainsail and set the jib. The boat's speed diminished to almost nothing, If the pump was working, they might eventually reach the coast of England.

All London knew that the Thames was blockaded by mutinous sailors from the Nore and also the North Sea Fleet. If they had not heard, then the price of coal, which had trebled since the start of the mutiny, would surely have suggested that something had happened to the Newcastle coal boats that supplied London's needs. Food had also become more expensive. Add to these facts rumours of looting in Kent and Essex, plus the fear of invasion owing to the absence of the Royal Navy from its duty, and a situation had developed where a scapegoat would have to be found to deflect some of the public anger from Pitt's government.

Admiral Quinsey's court of enquiry had recommended that Captain Brewster should face a court martial on a charge of causing a mutiny. It was a recommendation that would have been rejected out of hand in normal times, but the Admiralty Board was clutching at straws to avoid responsibility. The leader of those blockading the Thames, the self-styled 'President of the Floating Republic', had been Brewster's man, a known troublemaker on HMS *Adamant*.

Captain Brewster had no powerful factions to support him. He was a nobody, who had risen from common seaman. He could be sacrificed without offending anyone of importance. Already the Tory news-sheets were condemning him as a revolutionary, a Jacobite and even Antichrist. However, the publicity brought him an unexpected ally.

Edmund Burke, the member of parliament for Malton, Captain Brewster's home town, was one of the most eloquent Whigs of his day. He wrote several brilliant articles supporting Brewster. The general theme showed the captain as a lion in the defence of his country, now being sacrificed to pay for the Tory government's mistakes.

The result was a flood of cartoons, the most impressive being that of the British lion, looking very like Brewster, with the debris of the Brest barges at its feet, being stabbed in the back by William Pitt. It caught the imagination of the public and turned the mob in Brewster's favour.

Windows were broken at Admiralty. Admiral Quinsey's carriage was stoned. Several senior officers complained bitterly about being jeered at in the streets. The government and their naval puppets began to realize that a reasonably fair court martial would have to be set up, rather than the farce they had intended. They began to look around for a suitably qualified officer, who would not be identified with either political party, to serve as president of the court.

Admiral Wren was in London at this time, staying with his sister and visiting the clubs favoured by naval officers. Stringer, his servant, was trying to trace Midshipman Heward. They had both expected to be back at Chatham within the week, but Stringer was finding his task difficult. The driver of the yellow tandem had died of a fever allegedly caught from a party of sailors.

The members of the Admiralty Board decided unanimously to employ Admiral Wren. The court martial was held on board HMS *Orion*, an old third-rate which was moored alongside the stone quay on the south bank of the river, just opposite the Houses of Parliament. Forty armed marines were placed in readiness along the embankment early in the morning, and a boat-load rowed guard on the river, but there was no need for a show of force. The appointment of Admiral Wren had defused the explosive situation, as expected. When the signal gun was fired at nine o'clock and the flag broken out from the mizzenmasthead to mark the opening of the proceedings, there were no more than a dozen spectators, and they were merely curious bystanders, attracted by the sound of the gun.

It was evident to Captain Brewster from the start that the people present were not hostile, as those at the enquiry conducted by Admiral Quinsey had been. In fact, it seemed as if the president of the court had smiled when he first looked at Brewster. Certainly Admiral Wren was quick to correct the unfortunate officer who was reading out the charges.

'Stop at that point, sir,' he ordered sharply, his eyes fixed on the deck boards above.

The young officer paused with his finger on the page and looked at the admiral apprehensively.

'Sir?' he queried.

The hawk-like nose jerked in his direction. 'You referred to the captain as "Brewster" in that last sentence' Admiral Wren said indignantly.

'It is – er – as written, sir.'

'Is it, indeed? Then you will set to rights the – carelessness, or rudeness, of the author, by reading in the captain's rank, should you find any further omissions.' He turned to the clerk of the court. 'Please record my words exactly.'

This was a severe criticism of Admiral Quinsey, who had signed the summary of evidence from the court of enquiry. The prosecuting officer's eyes met those of the young officer who had been rebuked, with the suspicion of a grimace. He knew that Admiral Wren would have read the charges from his own copy of them, long before the court had assembled, and he could have had the omissions set right, had he so wished. Instead, he had chosen to make it public and, as a result, every man in the court was left with a feeling, nothing more, that the previous enquiry had not been as impartial as naval law demanded.

Admiral Quinsey was not present, nor was any one of the Atkins faction. Inflamed public opinion on the causes of the Nore mutiny suggested that it would be wiser to steer clear of the whole business. Midshipman Atkins would be safe enough anyway. In the circumstances, even if proved not guilty, Captain Brewster could hardly bring a charge of cowardice against Atkins for having deserted Clayton's party at Brest, or one of negligence leading to the deaths of the gunner and Mr Atherton. Any such action would be regarded as a vindictive attempt to even scores.

It was therefore an isolated and bitter Lieutenant Trevelyan who gave evidence. He had looked for advancement from the influential Atkins family. Now, he realized, they had abandoned him, and he was ruined. The contents of his notebook, so assiduously copied by Admiral Seymour at Brest, was in the hands of the prosecution and could not be disowned. He would be branded as a disloyal subordinate, and no captain would willingly employ him. In his attempts to escape the full consequences of his actions, he became an easily confused witness.

Lieutenant Prendergast who, like Trevelyan, had been sent ashore from *Adamant* to give evidence, was clearly finding the experience distasteful. Nevertheless, he was not one to be dominated by a prosecuting officer.

'No sir. I was not surprised that Captain Brewster did not arrest Parker at the time of Mr Atherton's funeral.'

'Why not?'

'In the first place, sir, Captain Brewster was not sure that Parker was indeed the man who had shouted. He said, "I *think* it was Parker". He could not have proved anything against him. However, there is another reason for stating that I was not surprised.'

'Perhaps you will be kind enough to tell us,' the prosecution officer said sarcastically.

'We were in an explosive situation, sir,' Prendergast went on imperturbably. 'Reflect, that we were the *only* naval vessel in the Channel Fleet that was not in a state of mutiny. Our men could easily have taken over the ship and put into the nearest home port. I am of the opinion, sir, that the men remained loyal because they were –'

'Thank you, thank you, Mr Prendergast,' the prosecuting officer interrupted hurriedly with a deprecatory wave of his hand. 'This court is interested only in facts and not in opinions.'

'I am interested in his opinion,' Admiral Wren objected.

'I believe, sir, that the men remained loyal because they had the greatest respect for their captain. After mutiny notices had been circulated around the ship, the men not only maintained station but actually entered a well-fortified enemy harbour and fought a successful action.'

The prosecuting officer capitulated with good grace. Whatever Captain Brewster might be guilty of, no one could doubt that he had done very well to keep his ship at sea. It was inevitable that there would be a verdict of not guilty to the charge of causing a mutiny.

There was still the question of his overheard conversation with Mr Atherton, the master. Several officers took exception to the remarks, freely admitted by Brewster, which clearly demonstrated his sympathy with the mutineers at the time of Spithead. Had he been a standard-entry officer, his sentiments would have been dismissed as a form of eccentricity, but he had risen from common seaman, and so had Atherton.

In fact, the master of a man-of-war was not a gentleman. Even when, a hundred years earlier, he had been senior in rank to a lieutenant, he had always been regarded as a salt-back, traditionally stinking of tar and not accepted in polite circles. Now the rank was vaguely defined as being somewhere just below lieutenant, and it was quite improper for a captain to drink with such a person.

Admiral Wren felt obliged to take note of the opinions voiced by the officers of the court. Brewster was reprimanded. The old admiral went on to praise *Adamant*'s successes against the enemy, to soften the blow of the reprimand, but Brewster's achievements at Brest were not the business of the court martial. If Admiral Wren's kind words were noted at Admiralty, they had no effect upon the Admiralty Board's decision. The Atkins faction had prepared the ground too well. Captain Brewster was relieved of his command.

'I'm sorry it turned out so badly for you, Captain Brewster,' Admiral Wren commiserated some ten days later.

It appeared to be a chance encounter in the large anteroom of the Admiralty building where so many officers waited daily in the hope of being given employment. Admiral Wren took Brewster by the arm and led him away from the others.

'I think that you are wasting your time here, Captain,' he said quietly. 'The truth of the matter is that you've run foul of a certain party, and you'll do no good here whilst their friends are at the helm.' He smiled and winked. 'Oh, it'll not be forever. Meanwhile, the best thing will be for you to draw your reserve pay and take employment elsewhere. I see from your records that you're an old Baltic man.'

'Yes, sir. I spent years there.'

'Well now, it so happens that my family has been involved in the Baltic trade for a long time. Used to be in a big way o' business in my grandfather's day. Matter of fact, we have a three-masted barque held up at Sheerness by the mutineers' blockade. She's still loaded with a cargo of timber and resin to be landed at Dartmouth. Her captain has been sent ashore, very poorly, and it'll be a long job with him according to the doctors. We need a temporary captain. Would you be interested?'

'That's very kind of you, sir. I should be honoured.'

'Right, we'll take it as settled. Perhaps you'll make your way down to Sheerness in the morning.'

'I'll go today, sir. There's nothing to keep me in London.'

'No, I'd like you to dine with me. Fact is, I need your help. I want you to talk some sense into my nephew. He'll maybe listen to you.'

'Your nephew, sir?'

'Midshipman Heward, don't ye know. Took ill with the fever. Nearly died of it from what I've heard. The French filly, Madame whatshername – Lorette – nursed him back to health. Now he wants to marry her. It would ruin his career and, likely as not, his father would cut him off without a penny.'

CHAPTER TWENTY-FIVE

Lawson and Saunders pumped continuously for over thirty hours. In this way they sailed slowly westward over an unusually calm sea, settling ever deeper in the water. They had made buoyancy bundles from bits of fishing net tightly bound in canvas. These, they had lashed to the hatch cover, but they had no real hope that the improvised raft would support their weight for long. Consequently, they were greatly relieved when, just before dawn, they saw a light dead ahead.

It proved to be from a fishing boat that had four lanterns set up with reflectors of burnished metal to attract the herrings into the drift net. It was a technique much practised by English and Scottish drifters in peacetime, but thought to be too dangerous when Dutch privateers were about. Lawson hailed the stationary fishing boat when they were close enough to hear the sounds of activity on her decks. They were clawing their catch over the side.

'Ga' an awa' frae ma nets,' a stentorian voice roared back at them.

'We're sinking,' Lawson shouted. 'Will you take us off?'

There was a long period of silence. Meanwhile, Saunders worked at the pump. The dismal sound must have travelled over the water.

'Hang aboot awhile. I'll send t'boat across to ye, jest as soon as I can git it clear o' the rope and stuff tha's in it.'

An age later, a dilapidated dinghy, propelled by oars of different lengths, appeared alongside. A stout woman in her forties was doing the rowing. Lawson and Saunders thankfully got into it, leaving the Dutch fishing boat to its inevitable end.

'Can ye pay fra yeer vittles and passage?' the skipper demanded by way of a greeting as they landed on his deck. 'I canna feed twa men on nowt.'

'Where are you from?' Lawson asked.

'Tynemouth, an' we're sailing fra hame the day.'

'Set us ashore at the nearest harbour, and I'll give you a bill-of-hand which you can present at your Admiralty Office.'

'A bit o' paper, ye mean?' he hooted indignantly. 'Ach, mon, I've had them things afore. There's only yan bluidy thing yer bits o' paper are guid fer.'

'We've just escaped from Holland and we have urgent information for the government.'

'What ye have tae tell to t'government may weel have 'em bustin' wi' excitement, but it's no likely that they'll gi' us oot fer oor trouble.'

He spat disgustedly on the deck. Lawson leaned closer.

'The Dutchmen may well be in Tynemouth this time next week unless the Navy is warned,' he said quietly.

'That should send the price of fish oop,' the man grinned. 'Nay, dinna fash yerself,' he added hastily when Lawson grabbed him and jerked him closer. 'I spoke in jest.' He patted Lawson's hand soothingly and detached it from his collar. 'We'll manage summat, I've nae doobt. Whitby's no too far off oor course. I'll maybe set ye doon there.'

'Whitby'll do very nicely,' Lawson said and turned away, grinning delightedly at Saunders.

He had not been home for over twelve months. Now he was going to be landed within yards of his own doorstep. They would make their report to the commander of the naval detachment there and request permission to stay for a few days. The prospects were too exciting for him to rest, despite his exhaustion.

Towards noon, with the coast of Yorkshire clearly visible, a vessel, which they had observed approaching from the north, was identified as a naval cutter. It came routinely within hailing distance to check on their nationality. Sick with disappointment, Lawson requested a passage south to deliver urgent messages to the commander in chief of the North Sea Fleet. Before he left the fishing boat, he gave the skipper a sovereign, two single shillings and three pence. It was all the money he had, but he felt guilty for handling the man so roughly.

Two days later they came across HMS *Venerable* and *Adamant* lying at anchor just off Yarmouth. These two ships and a naval pinnace were all that was left of the North Sea Fleet. The flagship had a stairway rigged on the port side. It was lowered to within a few feet of the sea when the cutter signalled that it was carrying dispatches.

'Get ready to go aboard.'

The youthful commander grinned in a devil-may-care manner as he took over the tiller from the helmsman.

He approached the flagship very fast then heaved the tiller hard over. Her bows crossed the wind on the opposite tack, and her beam slid by within inches of the platform at the foot of the stairs. Lawson and Saunders jumped for it, and the thirty-foot cutter went on her way without stopping. She dipped her ensign in salute whilst the commander removed his hat and stood uncovered, in deference to the admiral's flag streaming from the masthead. It had been a foolish display of confidence and daring: one small error of judgement and the cutter could have carried away the stairs and damaged herself in the process.

Lawson and Saunders ascended to the entry port, saluting as they entered the ship. They were met by a familiar figure, Midshipman Atkins, late of *Adamant*, was on duty there. Lawson scowled at him.

'Urgent dispatch for the commander in chief,' he said brusquely.

Atkins studied their dishevelled appearance then turned to the petty officer who shared the watch with him.

'Escort these two – er – gentlemen to Admiral Duncan's clerk,' he ordered.

'Calm down,' Saunders advised, noting Lawson's furious face as they followed the petty officer. 'There's nothing to be done about him. Daddy is looking after his interests, to say nothing of Uncle Oliver and the rest of the clan. Anyone who can get a midshipman's berth on the flagship after being dismissed from *Adamant* has more influence than most.'

Admiral Duncan looked a lot older than at the last interview, but he was as courteous as ever. He made them comfortable and ordered coffee to be brought in.

Prompted occasionally by Saunders, Lawson gave a concise account of their pursuit by the frigates and the timely intervention of the Russians, drawing a 'Damn their impudence!' from the admiral over the appropriation of HMS *Greyhound* by the Imperial Russian Navy. The Dutch resistance movement was of particular interest to him.

'So the Hollanders don't care to wear the hat of revolution. Didn't think it would suit them. They're hardworking, no-nonsense folk.' He rose from the chair. 'You've done very well, very well indeed.'

Lawson and Saunders were on their feet, wondering if he expected them to leave.

'The big question now is, how do we keep their troop transports in the Zuyder Zee? *Adamant* yonder is the only company we have. The rest of the fleet is lying in London River, and this damned mutiny shows no sign of ending. You say they are well aware that the North Sea Fleet is ineffective?'

'According to the spy, Maharg, the mutiny is common knowledge, sir.'

'Then we can expect an invasion attempt just as soon as they can embark their troops. Nothing else for it but to go out there with *Adamant* and *Venerable*. We'll try the same game that your Captain Brewster played so well at Brest, but I don't think it will fool Admiral de Winter in the present circumstances.'

He shrugged off the likely consequences and smiled.

'Rejoin *Adamant*' he said as he shook their hands in turn. 'We shall have to do our duty, come what may, even if it means sailing into their anchorage to do as much damage as possible before they blow us to bits.'

They were at the door when the admiral checked them with a question.

'How well did you know this fellow, Parker?'

'He was in my section, sir,' Lawson replied. 'He joined *Adamant* last October. He's about thirty years old, a good seaman, but lazy.'

'Educated man, I hear.'

'Yes, sir. Reads a lot.'

'Political claptrap, no doubt. His speechifying, from all accounts, might well have come from that rascal Tom Paine. But he is a good orator, and he's leading the men of my fleet by the nose, damn him. He threatens to take them over to join the enemy. Do you think he means it?'

Lawson considered the question. Parker would be enjoying his role as the leader of twenty thousand men, but he was no fool, and he must know that there would be a day of reckoning.

'Parker has a wife, sir, who visited him whilst *Adamant* was at Liverpool. She stayed aboard for a week or more and they seemed to be very attached to each other. He also has family in Exeter. I think it very unlikely that he would willingly cut himself adrift from them. Of course, if the alternative is – er – the death sentence . . .'

Admiral Duncan indicated that they should resume their seats. He stood by the window, with his thumbs hooked in his waistcoat pockets, and looked at them speculatively.

'Gentlemen, I think it possible that the news you have brought me this morning could well provide Parker and his henchmen with an honourable way out. If they heard the story of the impending invasion from your lips, they would not doubt its authenticity, and they could elect to set aside their grievances in the defence of their country. The mutineers would be seen as patriots. If Parker were to play his cards right, I think his cause might be helped.'

He sat at his desk, opened one of the drawers, took out a sheet of embossed paper and a pen and began to write. When he had finished, he signed the letter and impressed a stamp over the signature.

'I think the two of you might serve the King better if

you went to see Parker rather than join *Adamant*. Here's your written authority.' He passed over the paper. 'Go out to HMS *Sandwich*. Talk to Parker and anyone who will listen. Tell them the tale: thirty thousand bayonets just waiting to get busy on British women and children. Lay it on as thick as you like. As to the pardon, I would grant one, under the circumstances, if it were in my power, which, of course, it ain't. However, I shall strongly recommend it, and hopefully Mr Pitt and His Majesty will accept my recommendations.'

He pushed back his chair and stood up. Lawson and Saunders were on their feet immediately.

'Get off with you. See what you can do. If you have anything useful to report, you'll take it to Lord Keith at Sheerness. He's now in command there. I'll write to him directly, explaining matters.'

Sheerness was teaming with militia. There were also two regiments of seasoned troops, newly arrived in Tilbury from India, infantry and artillery. They were all working furiously, setting up their guns and unloading powder barrels. Clearly the government was not in a mood of conciliation, Lawson thought as he viewed the preparations. The prospects of a pardon looked bleak.

There was a scuffle ahead of them. A group of militia at the top of a stone stairway leading to the water were denying sailors access to the quayside from a launch tied up at the foot of the steps. Lawson and Saunders hurried forward. In the launch were sick men, a few on stretchers, others sprawled in the bottom of the boat, some far gone, lying in their own vomit.

'What the devil's going on?' Lawson demanded.

'They're not allowed to come ashore, sir,' the sergeant told him.

'But they're sick men.'

'That's right, sir. They've been sent ashore from the mutinous ships yonder, but his Lordship's sending 'em all back wi'out no treatment. We sent back best part of a 'undred this morning. Every man had his pockets stuffed with handbills for his mates to read.'

'Handbills?'

'Yes, sir. Telling them to arrest their leaders and surrender if they want treatment for their sick, and letting them know that they'll get no more food and water from the victualling yard until they do surrender.'

'I see. Thank you.' Lawson turned away and grimaced at Saunders.

'If Lord Keith is carrying out the orders of the government, I don't think there's much hope of success for our task. Parker and the members of his committee are not going to surrender for a hanging, and that's what it looks like to me.'

'Maybe Pitt will order a different approach when he gets the news about the Hollanders,' Saunders said hopefully.

They examined the anchored vessels that were stopping all traffic on the Thames. There were thirteen big ships, two- and three-deckers, each armed with from fifty to a hundred guns, and another twenty or so smaller naval craft: cutters, sloops, ketches and the like, all pointing their bows towards the ebbing tide and London.

Nothing could get through to supply the hungry capital. Parker was in a position of strength. Short of bringing the entire Channel Fleet from its vital station off the French coast, there was little the government could do.

The regiment of artillery was a threat to the ships. The activity of the gunners had been noted by the mutineers, and orders had evidently been given to a third-rate to leave her moorings and approach. Saunders had his pocket telescope with him. He watched the ship sail against the tide to take station in support of HMS *Nassau*, which lay close by the land.

'It's *Director*!' Saunders exclaimed.

'So it is,' Lawson confirmed.

Their interest was due to the fact that the sixty-four-gun HMS *Director* had been under the command of Captain William Bligh, who with his officers would doubtless be watching the manoeuvres of their ship from the banks of the Thames where they had been set ashore by their own men.

There would be no cause for complaint as to the

seamanship. Whoever was in command of HMS *Director* knew his business. Balancing the wind in the sails to control the speed of this large ship against the thrust of the tide, he stopped her where her port-side battery would cover the positions of the field artillery. As if to demonstrate his superb skill, he held her stationary for twenty minutes or more, maintaining a passage through the water at exactly the same speed as the ebbing tide. Then he dropped anchor and ran out his guns.

'That was bloody marvellous,' Saunders said admiringly. 'If all the mutinous ships are as well-handled as *Director*, there'll be nothing to touch them.'

'You're right there,' Lawson replied. 'It'll be negotiation that'll set things in order. I suppose the sooner we get out to have a few words with Parker, the better it will be. Can you see a boat for hire?'

The wherrymen, who rowed them around the anchored ships to HMS *Sandwich* on the other side of the river, had done the same thing for others, and they knew better than to approach without first obtaining permission. The mutineers had been known to drop a twelve-pounder shot upon any boat that came alongside unannounced.

'Port side,' the man in charge of the watch shouted in reply to Lawson's request.

Lawson and Saunders came aboard, saluting in the usual manner as they entered the ship. The petty officer on duty touched his hat automatically in reply and asked politely what their business was, terminating his question with 'sir'.

He was clean-shaven and neatly dressed, as were the two ordinary seamen with him. It was obvious that he was still in authority over them, and discipline was being maintained.

'Tell Mr Parker there' two gennlemen 'ere from Admiral Duncan to see 'im. They're Mr Lawson and Mr Saunders, who used to serve on *Adamant*.'

'You might add that we're fresh from Holland with the latest news of the war,' Lawson said casually.

As the man went off, Lawson turned away and looked out across the water. He knew that the petty officer and the rating would be wanting to know what was happening in the world beyond the Thames. That was why he had added the information about Holland. It was important that the imminent invasion should become common knowledge throughout the mutinous ships, but the petty officer must ask the questions for his news to be more effective.

'Are they as fed up with the war as we are, sir?' the petty officer asked at last with an embarrassed grin.

'Who?'

'The Dutchmen, sir.'

'They're excited at the moment. At least they were ten days ago when Mr Saunders and I escaped.'

'Excited, sir?'

'Bursting with it – and jubilant about the prospects of coming over here. No doubt you'll see them for yourself soon. Thirty thousand men, with guns and cavalry, were assembling ready for embarkation. They've got the same sort of barges that we destroyed in Brest Harbour.'

'Where, sir?'

'Around the Zuyder Zee. They might even be on board the transports now, waiting for a favourable wind.'

At this point, Saunders looked up at the over-large red flag flying from the masthead. The eyes of the petty officer and the other man automatically did the same. The wind was still blowing towards the continent.

'As soon as it gets away from the west, they'll be sailing out,' Saunders said confidently.

'Do ye ken wheer aboots they'll attack, sir?' the rating asked anxiously.

Lawson raised his shoulders expressively.

'Could be Edinburgh,' Saunders suggested.

The Scotsman looked worried. He would have asked more questions but his fellow seaman had returned to say that Parker would see the visitors. They walked off with the man, confident that all on board *Sandwich* would have heard of the threatening invasion before the day was out.

Parker had aged considerably since they had last seen him. His eyes were sunken and he looked weary, perhaps ill. Unlike Admiral Duncan, he did not rise from his chair when his visitors entered. He indicated that they were to be seated, leaned back and regarded them morosely.

'Now why would Duncan send an acting lieutenant and a midshipman to see me? Does he think that's all I'm worth?'

'I think –' Lawson began, but Parker interrupted him.

'Look out there,' he said dramatically, waving his hand at the view from the stern window. 'I've got Duncan's command there. Just look at them: *Triumph, Bedford, Veteran, Lancaster* and the rest. He's only left with *Venerable* and *Adamant*, and I'll have *Adamant* as soon as those on board learn that Brewster has been relieved of his command. Yet he doesn't know better than try to negotiate with two –'

'We're not here to negotiate,' Lawson said sharply.

'Then you're wasting my time and yours,' Parker said, rising abruptly to his feet.

'Hear me out. It could be to your advantage.'

Parker glared at Lawson belligerently, then nodded and resumed his seat.

'Go on.'

There was a slight twitch in the man's right cheek, Lawson noted. Obviously, he was under tremendous strain. Did he have doubts about maintaining his command of the mutiny? Was he worried that some of the ships were not solidly behind him? He was, at best, in an unenviable situation. If the mutiny were successful and pardons were granted, he would be a marked man and could look for no promotion. If it failed he would be lucky to escape with a hanging. More than likely, he would be flogged around the fleet and hanged at the end of it, dead or alive. The price of his few weeks of glory would be high, and Parker was intelligent enough to know that it must be paid. Did he regret getting involved?

'Admiral Duncan is of the opinion that there is a way out of this business.'

'What do you mean?' Parker said irritably. 'I'm not looking for a way out. I want a settlement. All our demands must be met.'

'If you and your men were seen to be the saviours of your country, ordinary folk would demand justice for you, so you'd achieve what you set out to do. *Adamant* and

Venerable should be off the Texel by now. Admiral Duncan intends to attack the Dutch Fleet should they attempt to come out. If they sacrifice themselves in this way, you and your followers will be reviled by every one from Land's End to John o'Groats. Even those you have led will curse you, the leader, for having been the cause of their alienation from their families and loved ones.'

'If the government settles our claims, we'll settle the Dutch.'

'It'll be too late. They are ready and waiting for this westerly wind to change.'

'*You* tell me this,' Parker scorned.

'*We* tell you. Between us we can recite the regiments, or most of them, that were preparing to take ship for England. Damn it, man, you've known me long enough. I'll take the oath if that'll satisfy you. We were there in Hoorn when General Daendels was inspecting the invasion barges, and the troops were moving into the embarkation area.'

Parker rubbed at his twitching cheek. His eyes revealed his worry. He rose from his seat and walked to the window, standing with his back to them. Lawson went over the details, supplemented by Saunders, of all the information they had gained from the list that had been pushed into his pocket by the Dutch major. Parker remained silent for several minutes after they had finished their recital. Then he turned to face them.

'What exactly do you want me to do, Mr Lawson? I'm not alone in this, you understand. I have a committee to satisfy and every one of us will swing if we surrender without guarantees. We should need the promise of a pardon from King George, nothing less, and it would have to be published in the newspapers.'

'You would end the mutiny if you were pardoned?'

'I should put it to the delegates and recommend it – in the interests of our country.'

Lawson was delighted. He had succeeded in the unlikely task that Admiral Duncan had set for him. Now it needed only the promise of a pardon. The sudden recollection of the sick men lying in the bottom of the boat and the handbills pushed into their pockets demanding the surrender of their ringleaders, reminded him that he was only halfway to success. Lord Keith was an uncompromising man. Parker was quick to notice the flicker of doubt in Lawson's eyes.

'You might have difficulty over the pardon,' he said bitterly. 'Well, it's up to you – and them. Come up with the promise of a King's pardon and I'll see what can be done.'

CHAPTER TWENTY-SIX

In the conference room of Lord Keith's temporary headquarters at Sheerness, seven men, officers and civilians, sat along the length of a massive dining table. Lord Keith presided from the head of the table, with his back to the high window, a dark silhouette against the bright sunlight. He was reading a paper, which Lawson guessed was his report on the visit to HMS *Sandwich*. No one spoke.

Lawson had not been invited to take a seat at the foot of the table, so he remained standing, clutching his hat under his arm. Dazzled by the sun, he could see nothing of Lord Keith's face, so he stared woodenly ahead, well aware that the smartly-dressed gentlemen around the table were weighing him up. He had made it his business to find out who would be sitting on the Council, and he knew none of the officers by reputation except Lord Keith.

Everyone knew Lord Keith. *The Times* had printed a number of articles following the highly successful expedition in South Africa where he had taken Cape Town for the Crown. At fifty-one years, he had become a hard, uncompromising martinet, whose duty to the Navy would not be swayed by any consideration of human frailty. He had been at sea all his life, but his speech was still that of a Scottish gentleman.

'This report of yours', he said, looking up from the

paper and regarding Lawson with piercing eyes, 'suggests that Parker and his friends should escape honourably frae the consequences of their criminal folly.'

'I hope I don't go so far as to make a suggestion, sir. I had intended only to present the facts of the situation.'

'And those are that Parker and his damned committee might condescend tae postpone their mutiny, provided *we* can obtain a pardon frae His Majesty,' he said angrily. 'May the guid Lord give us the light of reason tae resist such folly!'

He slapped the paper down and glared at the faces around the table before continuing in a quieter, incredulous tone.

'They could even become national heroes, gentlemen, if we went oot and thrashed the Dutch. Think on it. Consider what the consequences would be for the Navy. Let 'em get away with this and henceforth no captain will be able tae give an order withoot a by your leave tae the representatives of the People's Committee.' He hammered the table. ''Tis the French disease, I tell ye, gentlemen. We must purrge it oot of the Navy's system. A few hangings are needed. I would rather that the Dutch landed than give the leaders of this disgraceful mutiny an opportunity tae escape their just deserts.'

He thrust out his chin and looked challengingly around. There were no comments, but the older of the two civilians was frowning his disapproval. Lord Keith ignored him and addressed Lawson.

'The information ye have brought with ye aboot the Dutch aspirations will be passed on tae the mutineers by way of a pamphlet which I shall have printed. On the same pamphlet will be my recommendations that all honest men should seize their leaders and return all His Majesty's ships tae their rightful commanders.'

The civilian indicated that he wished to speak. Lord Keith nodded, took out a snuff box and tilted a little on the back of his hand.

'I think it will be advisable to delay your proposed action until the government has been apprised of this new development, my lord.'

The chief of staff completed his snuff-taking before

replying. 'Why, as tae that, Mr Greystone, I have the authority tae take whatever action I consider necessary tae put doon this mutiny. However, I shall make a report immediately and, I feel sure, that your own account of the matter will be in Mr Pitt's hands by this evening. Perhaps other members of the council share your views?'

His eyes passed from face to face. The other civilian stared fixedly at the table top. The officers' faces were impassive. Lord Keith shrugged.

'It would seem, Mr Greystone, that ye are alone in your opinion.'

The man looked as if he would protest, but Lord Keith turned back to Lawson.

'Ye will not see this fellow Parker again, Mr Lawson, unless ye hear from me tae the contrary. Do ye understand?'

'Perfectly, sir.'

'Come tae that, I don't see much point in your staying here. Take yourself and your midshipman back tae –' he glanced at the paper – 'tae *Adamant*. If there's tae be any more negotiating, we shall manage, I dare say.'

'But this officer has a special relationship with Parker,' the civilian protested.

'The Navy canna' afford tae concairn itself with special relationships, Mr Greystone,' Lord Keith said loftily.

He nodded briefly in dismissal. Lawson bowed and left the chamber, taking care to let no expression on his face betray his thoughts on the matter. The commander in chief was a powerful man who could make or break a junior officer, but the civilian, Mr Greystone, must surely be the same gentleman who worked so closely with the under-secretary of the Navy. If so, he could ruin any officer's prospects without having to resort to a court martial. Most appointments passed through his hands.

Saunders was sitting on a bollard with a neglected clay pipe in his hand. As Lawson approached, he stood up and indicated a boat being rowed by two men towards where they were standing. A large man sat at the tiller.

'Do my eyes deceive me?' Saunders asked.

Lawson looked and saw that it was indeed Captain Brewster. He waved. The captain had evidently been looking at them. Now, he raised one hand and put the helm over. Ten minutes later, the three of them were seated in a tavern with pots of ale before them. The oarsmen had been sent back to the three-masted barque, one of the Wren line of Baltic traders, now commanded by Captain Brewster.

There was much to discuss. For Captain Brewster, there was the riddle of their disappearance to be explained. This led on naturally to the encounter with the Russian Fleet and the seizing of HMS *Greyhound* by Admiral Hanikof. At this point, Lawson remembered that he was carrying a letter from Madame Hanikof for Captain Brewster. He handed it over.

'More ale, gentlemen,' Brewster said, raising his hand to the serving girl and miming that he wanted the pots refilling.

He rose from the table and walked over to the deep window casement. They saw him slit open the envelope, then turned to bandy words with the cheerful young woman who had brought a foaming jug to them.

'It seems that Madame Hanikof and her daughters are now expecting to spend the summer in St Petersburg,' Captain Brewster commented as he rejoined them.

'Indeed, sir,' Lawson replied. 'I wonder – would it be possible to write a letter to Miss Victoria?'

'Why, as to that, Mr Lawson, I do believe that I might be in a position to deliver the letter by hand.'

'Are you going there, sir?'

'As soon as the blockade is lifted. First, I shall discharge my cargo at Dartmouth. Then I shall take on another at Woolwich, a rather special consignment for his Imperial Majesty the Tsar, to be delivered to Kronstadt.'

'Kronstadt, sir?'

'The naval base, just a few miles from St Petersburg.'

'I'll see if I can obtain writing materials, sir,' Lawson said, rising to his feet.

'Don't bother, Mr Lawson. It's far too late for you to leave for Yarmouth. You can both stay the night on the barque and first thing in the morning I'll have you set ashore on the Essex coast. That'll put you well on your way. Meanwhile, you'll dine with me here.'

The sun had already disappeared beneath the smoke from distant London as they climbed aboard the barque from the hired wherry. Lawson looked around. There were two merchant ships on their port hand. To starboard lay the sixty-four-gun *Lancaster* with her quarter-deck carronades slewed around threateningly. There would be no attempts by the merchant captains to slip through the blockade under cover of darkness. Nor could they escape into the North Sea. Two frigates lay astern, their topmasts still illuminated against the darkening eastern sky.

Captain Brewster had drunk a lot of wine. Nevertheless, as he led the way aft towards the officers' accommodation under the poop deck, he paused and looked around, noting the positions of the ships near him, and his own bearings previously taken against landmarks. Lawson and Saunders waited, both bemused by the ale and wine they had drunk in an attempt to keep pace with their host. They knew he was looking for changes caused by a dragged anchor. Any experienced seaman would do the same in a crowded tidal river.

'Billy, fetch my glass,' Captain Brewster shouted suddenly.

A small boy, no more than thirteen years, shot out of the door under the poop with a brass telescope in his hands. Brewster took it and focused on a barely visible ship beyond the frigates. Lawson's eyes met those of Saunders. The rig was familiar.

'It seems that you will not need to be landed on the Essex coast after all,' Captain Brewster said, handing the telescope to Lawson. '*Adamant* has come to you.'

Lawson scrutinized the distant vessel briefly. It was sailing slowly up river, struggling against the ebb. He recalled Parker's words, 'I'll have *Adamant* when the ship's company learn that Brewster had been relieved of his command'.

'It looks as if *Adamant* has joined the mutiny, sir.'

'Take her bearings when she drops anchor. Maybe we'll pay them a call later.'

They were not the only ones to have noticed the

arrival of *Adamant*. A signal gun was fired from HMS *Sandwich*, and flags were racing to her masthead. The light was too poor to read them, but Parker's request, to whoever was commanding *Adamant*, was evidently understood. A rocket shot up in acknowledgement. Half an hour later, a launch was seen passing close by on its way to *Sandwich*, with at least a dozen men in her.

'Maybe the entire committee from *Adamant* has gone to parley with Parker,' the captain commented. 'If so, this would be a good time to visit. We'll give it twenty minutes. Should be dark enough then.'

The jolly boat was tied up astern of the barque, dancing in a lively manner and frothing at the bow as the tide passed it by. The two seamen who had been detailed to row them out to *Adamant* hauled it forward until it was level with the ladder rigged amidships, and climbed down. Captain Brewster, Lawson and Saunders followed. They pushed off.

It would be improper for me to enter *Adamant* if Captain Hopton is still aboard,' Brewster said quietly as they were rowed downstream. 'If, however, the officers have been sent ashore, I should consider it my business to try to persuade my former shipmates to return to their duties. You and Mr Saunders will enquire into the situation and I will wait in the boat until I hear from you. They'll think it's a hired boat you came in, so you'll be expected to pay off the boatmen if you're staying on *Adamant*. That'll give you an opportunity to climb down to us again when you know the state of things.'

'Right, sir.'

It was very dark by the time they reached *Adamant*, but there were lights in plenty streaming from gun-ports opened for ventilation, and enough din of music and revelry to guide a blind man. No one challenged them. Lawson and Saunders entered by means of a scrambling net that had been left hanging. As their feet touched the deck, someone who had been leaning over the side further forward from where they were, tapped out his pipe in a flurry of sparks and sauntered over to join them. It was Davies, the gunner's mate.

'Why, it's Mr Lawson,' he said in wonder when he had

approached. 'Saw you coming, sir, but indeed I didn't know who it was, of course.'

'Is the captain aboard, Mr Davies?'

'No, sir. Captain Hopton and all the officers were set ashore at Yarmouth. Most of the warrant officers were packed off with 'em. I was sick at the time, so they left me. Mr Muir's still here, though. He locked himself in the main magazine, and he's threatening to blow up the ship if anyone attempts to break in. I tried to get some food to him today, but the men have set a guard there.'

'You're not with the mutiny then?'

'Not I, sir!'

'I'm pleased to hear that.'

'I'll – er – pay the boatmen, sir,' Saunders volunteered and climbed over the side onto the scrambling net.

'Plenty of women on board, by the sound of it,' Lawson commented as Saunders' head disappeared.

'Aye, sir. Captain Hopton allowed a few "wives" from Chatham and then some more from Yarmouth, maybe twenty-two or -three altogether. After the mutiny started and the officers had been sent ashore, the boats came out to us full of painted whores and jezebels, and there was absolutely nothing that the committee could do about it.'

'The committee?'

'Twelve men, sir: all elected. Apart from giving in about the women, they're keeping a tight ship. Every man gets his ration and no more. That's the wish of the majority, for there are some of the lowest kinds of humanity among us, sir. Worse than the animals indeed. They would make this ship hell if they got the drink into them. The liquor stores and the ale barrels are guarded by armed marines.

At that moment the sound of revelry came closer as a crowd spewed up from below onto the well-deck where Lawson and Davies stood. They had lamps with them and now they were forming a circle: excited men and a few women, obviously ready for some kind of contest. Certainly they had no eyes for the two nonparticipants standing in the shadows, nor did they see Captain Brewster and Saunders climb aboard. All their attention was directed at the two men now entering the ring, each holding a large bird armed with spurs that gleamed in the light of the lamps. The ship's poultry, replenished at Chatham, had evidently included two cocks.

'Let's get away from here,' the captain said. 'Where can we talk, Mr Davies? Can we get into my quarters?'

'Not without being seen, sir,' Davies replied in a voice more Welsh than usual, possibly the result of his shock at finding Captain Brewster on board. 'The committee has given orders that no one is to enter the officers' quarters, and they've set a guard to keep out the thieves.'

'It seems that there are some good men on the committee. Who is in charge?'

'Forster, sir: captain of the foretop. He was elected but he didn't want it from all accounts.'

Brewster nodded. This was one of the men he had predicted would be a leader.

'What about Bainbridge?'

'He did most of the speechifying, sir. Better than a chapel minister from all accounts, but I missed it by being in bed with the fever. He's on the committee.'

'Did he go out to *Sandwich* with the others?'

'To the best of my knowledge, sir, there's not a single committee man left on board. They could not agree who should go to see the – the "Pres-i-dent of the Floating Republic", what was Richard Parker, able seaman,' he said scornfully. 'And so they all went, sir, as if it was to visit roy-al-ty. Indeed, it is difficult to credit that men could be so stupid. I do believe that Forster and Bainbridge are the only intelligent ones among the whole committee, sir.'

Davies went through the rest of the committee men, ticking them off against his fingers. Captain Brewster considered each one.

'I agree that there's no one of much account,' he said when Davies had finished. 'None of them would be a match for the two you've mentioned. Neither Forster nor Bainbridge will have entered into this lightly, so there's nothing I can say to them that'll persuade them to change their minds. We'll speak to the men direct.'

'Shall I rouse them out, sir?'

'No. I have a better idea. Come on.'

He strode off, past the improvised cockpit with its cheering crowd. The others followed, well aware from the nudges and stares of those on the fringe that they had been noticed. This was what the captain had intended, Lawson realized, as they climbed after him to the quarter-deck and walked aft to the captain's quarters.

'Halt!' the sentry shouted as they approached.

'Thank you, sentry. It's Captain Brewster,' he called and walked on.

He had used exactly the same tone of voice and the same acknowledgement that the marine would have heard in normal circumstances. The man sprang to attention. Brewster still had his key. He turned it in the lock and entered the large day cabin. The others followed, with Saunders struggling to keep a straight face as they walked past the astonished sentry.

'Close the door,' Brewster said as he lit the lamp. 'Sit down. We shouldn't have long to wait. The word will already be buzzing around that I'm back, and I expect the marine will be creeping off to tell 'em where we are as soon as he's got over the shock. Then they'll come to see us on their own account. Much better that way, I think. They'll have assembled without being told to do so, and they'll ask me to explain myself. With luck, we'll be able to say quite a lot to them before the leaders get back.'

A short time afterwards the sounds of revelry died away and the ship became very quiet. Then they heard the soft-footed approach of many men and the subdued buzz of a hundred whispers. Finally, there was a tap on the door, respectful but firm.

Lawson opened the door in response to the captain's nod.

A tall thin man with greying hair and pockmarks on his cheeks entered. It was the elderly McGlochlan, a carpenter's mate from Cork: a man with a fine baritone voice and a good repertoire of Irish songs. Lawson knew that he had been with Captain Brewster for years; a chosen man who had followed his captain from ship to ship. That was why his shipmates were using him as spokesman. McGlochlan screwed his cap in his hand and bobbed his head.

'My shipmates have asked me ta say that we're very plaised, sor, ta see yer with the throubles behind yer, so's to speak an' we 'opes that yer'll be cummin' back tay us when this bit o' bother is o'er. Jest now, though, we're not quite right fer yer, as we've joined the mutiny, sor.'

'And what do your shipmates want me to do?'

'Well, there yer 'ave me, sor, for they didn't tell me. I t'ink yer've got us fair pothered, springing up from nowhere's, like yer did. Maybe it 'ud be the right t'ing for yer ta ask the men yerself, sor.'

'I'll do that,' the captain said agreeably, rising to his feet to take McGlochlan by the arm. 'You speak to them first. Tell them that you've asked me to talk to them. I don't want it to seem as if I'm –' he leaned closer and winked – 'pushing myself in where I'm not wanted.'

McGlochlan looked a bit worried, but he went out onto the quarterdeck with the captain. Lawson and the others followed and ranged themselves behind in support. Davies had brought the lamp, which he held high. Before them were over two hundred men whose whispered discussions died as the captain raised his hand. But there were also women in that crowd. The obvious respect of the men was too much for one of them.

"Oo the 'ell does 'e think 'e is?' she jeered.

'Shut your face, you bitch,' a deep growl ordered close by her.

"Ere, I'm not 'aving you –'

There was the sound of a slap, followed by a brief scuffle in the shadows of the middle distance. Then all was quiet again. McGlochlan took a deep breath and indicated Captain Brewster.

'Shipmates, I'd rather be singin' than talkin', as yer knaw, but Captain Brewster is wi' us ternight, an' we all reckon 'im ta be a fair man and t'best o' captains, so I've asked him ta say a few words.'

'You'd no right to ask him wi'out the say-so of t'full committee,' someone at the back shouted.

'Nay, let's hear him,' another called.

There were similar shouts, for and against, back and forth across the ill-lit sea of faces. Brewster waited, making no attempt to speak until a return to silence indicated that the 'fors' had carried the day. Then he took the lamp from Davies, reached up and hooked it onto the overhang of the poop deck above his head. He now removed his hat, letting the light fall on his face, and looked around.

'You'll just about have had your fill of speeches, I'm thinking, so I'll say little. First, I must thank you all for your loyalty to me. I know that you were asked to take *Adamant* into Spithead. Instead, you sailed her into an enemy harbour, past a battery of heavy guns and taught monsoor a lesson that he'll not forget for a long time. Had it not been for you men, setting your country above all things, it is my belief that the French would have landed an invasion force on these shores. I am proud to have served with you on that glorious occasion. The country is proud of you.'

'Aye, sir, but pride won't fill my childers' bellies.'

'It costs the country nowt to be proud. Will t'gov'ment gi' us a pension if we get a leg took off?'

There were several shouts of a similar nature. Brewster held up his hand and silence returned, comparative silence: there were mutterings on all sides. Brewster raised his voice.

'I know how it is, my lads. I know what your complaints are, and I think that they'll be set right before you're much older, provided, of course, that we're not invaded, and that seems likely at the present time. The Hollanders are waiting to come, same as monsoor was waiting in Brest. They've got their invasion barges, just like the ones you burned, and there's an army ready to climb aboard. The difference between Texel and Brest is easily summed up: *Adamant* isn't there to fill the gap.'

'No, sir, and with respect, she'll not be going either.'

It was a clear voice which carried authority and it had come from the back of the crowd. Now there was movement in the ranks as this person came through them. Brewster knew immediately that it was Forster. Obviously those of the committee who had gone over to HMS *Sandwich* had returned. They might have been sent for when it was discovered that officers were aboard.

Forster appeared and took a position on the other side of the suspended lamp.

'Captain Brewster, we have no quarrel with you,' he began in a voice that could be heard by all. 'Probably, if you had stayed in command, we should not have joined the mutiny.'

There was a murmur of agreement from the crowd. Forster turned his head slightly and looked them over. Then he addressed Brewster again in the public speaking manner he had adapted for his present strategy.

'We should probably not have joined, but only because of the affection that we have for you personally, and because we know where your true sympathy lies.'

There was a murmur of approval. Brewster frowned. This suggested that he was a mutineer at heart. He was about to set his position straight, but Forster hurried on.

'Yes, sir. We read the accounts in the newspapers.'

Now a chorus of agreement arose from the crowd and those at the front were smiling and nodding their approval. Clearly, he was a favourite but for reasons that could only cause him more trouble should Admiralty come to hear of it.

'A cheer for Captain Brewster,' a voice from the side shouted.

It sounded like the wretched Jenkins who had been accused of stealing the captain's purse, and everyone knew him for a halfwit, but obviously the men felt committed by him. They cheered self-consciously, much to the astonishment of the officers. It seemed to Lawson, in the background, that Captain Brewster only had to ask and the entire ship's company would have done his bidding. He reckoned without Forster, now joined by the purser's clerk and one-time preacher, Bainbridge.

'You see, Captain, we should have continued to serve *Adamant* if you had been left in command. The fact that they replaced you demonstrates clearly that anyone who is thought to be the seamen's friend is out of favour with those at the top,' Forster told the crowd.

'Perhaps we should thank God for it,' Bainbridge observed in his pulpit voice. 'If we had not supported our comrades here at the Nore, we should not have been worthy of them. These lads are risking everything to improve conditions for us all. Could we have held our heads high if we had not joined them? No. We should have been damned for ever and rightly so.'

'Will you hold your heads high back home among your folks if a foreign army lands on our shores? They're waiting to come,' Brewster said grimly. 'Mr Lawson and Mr Saunders, who you all know, and who are standing just behind me, will tell you of the preparations they saw being made in Holland not many days ago.' He paused and looked around. 'We all want our back pay and we all want better conditions. I wonder how much we'd enjoy these bounties if our mothers and wives and children were murdered by an invading army?'

The captain was obviously enjoying his flight of oratory. He looked as if he were going to expand on the theme, but disputes had broken out among the crowd. many seemed to agree with the captain but, as is often the case, the anti-Establishment body was more vocal. Now they started a chant, obviously well rehearsed and intended to drown rational argument. Foster and Bainbridge, an unlikely combination in any other circumstances, smiled at each other and waited confidently.

'Fire! Fire below!'

The cry, bordering on panic, instantly stopped the chant and the few scuffles that had broken out. Nothing in a wooden ship liberally coated with pitch could be more terrifying than fire, particularly when there was enough gunpowder on board to blow them all to bits. Prompt action and good leadership were needed. Forster was good enough to have risen to the occasion, but he was conditioned by years of obeying orders given by the man standing opposite him. He hesitated and lost his opportunity. Captain Brewster was in command.

'Whereabouts below?'

'For'ard of the bread store, sir, on the sta'board side. Someone's got at the liquor. They've bin drinking and smoking down there.'

'Bastards!' a voice shouted.

'Right, my lads, we'll see what the firemen can do. They've had plenty of training. Rouse out your hose, couple up and run it down the for'ard stairway. It took you six minutes on the last drill. See if you can manage it in five this time. Mr Lawson, take command below.'

Lawson and the ship's fire party doubled away. The rest of the men waited tensely for orders. They were waiting for Captain Brewster, and not one of the elected committee members disputed his authority.

CHAPTER TWENTY-SEVEN

A full-scale fire drill was a monthly affair on HM Ships, but some captains, including Brewster, held them more often. Each man in the fire party had a specific task, which, through constant practice, he could perform at speed. Lawson had never been the officer in charge, but he knew what he had to do.

The fire was amongst bales of clothing from the purser's store in the hold, and the bales had set fire to the frame of the ship. Flames were licking at the timber knees that supported the deck beams above. They were lazy, smoky flames, which needed a through draught to turn them into white heat. They would get plenty if they burned a hole through to the orlop deck above, Lawson realized.

'You see where the danger is?' he said, grabbing the arm of the nearest man and pointing. 'Get up on the orlop deck. Gather the fire buckets there and empty them at that spot.'

The man ran off, glad to escape from the smoke-filled hold. Lawson's eyes were streaming. He took his knife and slashed open one of the bales of clothing. It contained jerseys. He pulled several out and passed them to the men with him.

'Wet them and wrap them around your faces.'

'No water yet, sir.'

The captain had asked the fire party to beat their

previous record of six minutes. They had not done so. But that had only been a drill. Today there were no warrant officers to drive them, and this was the real thing. Those were hot sparks that were flying, and the magazine was dangerously close.

A section of pipe came snaking down to them, closely followed by a second and a third. Saunders' voice could be heard from the gun-deck, ordering his party to work the pumps.

The hoses writhed as they filled with sea water. Now, under pressure, they were casting up mist-like sprays from many pinprick holes in the canvas, glistening as colourful as rainbows in the light of the lamps. One of the pipes bulged like a football.

'See to that,' Lawson ordered.

He left the man to bind the weak section with rope and went to direct the men with the nozzles.

Acrid smoke and steam soon made breathing difficult in the hold. One of the men was carried out unconscious. Another stood gasping at the foot of the ladder. Lawson took a hose and crawled over to the scene of the fire, keeping low to avoid the smoke. There he lay on his back and directed the powerful jet at the flames above. Shortly afterwards someone stood on his left arm. He wrenched it free with an oath, but whoever it was wore boots. The men were all barefooted. Captain Brewster knelt at his side.

'I've given orders back there for one of the hoses to be directed at the magazine every few minutes to wet the walls. I've spoken to Mr Muir. He'll stand by ready to flood the place if need be, but I doubt if it will come to that, as long as you keep your hoses going.'

'We'll do that, sir.'

'I'm going back to the quarterdeck. Send for me if you think the fire's out of control. You'll maybe feel the ship getting under way shortly. It's our duty to stand clear of the other shipping, if there's a danger of blowing up. That's laid down in the regulations.'

He squeezed Lawson's shoulder, an unprecedented gesture, which was probably in lieu of the unseen wink that would certainly have accompanied that last sentence.

Lawson smiled as the captain went off. Once *Adamant* was clear of the guns and the certain intervention of the men in the mutinous frigates, Brewster would be in a good position to take over permanently. Meanwhile there was the fire to put out.

Tongues of flame were running along the timbers, seeking exit through the deck boards above, and burning pitch was dripping from the seams. Carefully Lawson swept the danger area with the jet. His clothes steamed and his forelock of hair shrivelled to ash. Terrified rats ran over him. Hot pitch burned him, but he stayed in his dangerous position dousing the flames. Eventually others crawled over to join him until there were four hoses in use, and between them they seemed to be winning. So long as Saunders kept the pumps going, they should soon be out of danger.

Was it Lawson's fancy, or wishful thinking that he had detected the sound of the capstan in between the crackling and hissing of the fire? If so, they might expect some trouble any minute, because the clanking of the capstan pawls and the pounding of so many feet on deck boards would certainly be heard and recognized by the watches on the nearby ships. *Adamant* was being hauled up to her anchor. Would she be fired upon?

The ship heeled slightly over to port. Her anchor was free of the mud and she was turning onto a starboard tack. As the breeze caught the broad side of the ship, her decks heaved to a twenty-degree list, and she dipped her bows. The movement sent a solid wall of water over the forward deck of the hold, rolling Lawson, and the other men who had been lying on the boards, over to leeward. The water was from the bilges together with the tons that the hoses had poured into her, warm from its contact with the fire. As it passed on its way, the distinct sound of gunfire was heard by all. Then there was a crash overhead.

'Some bugger's shooting at us,' an indignant voice shouted.

Lawson got to his feet and reclaimed the hose that had twisted out of his hands as he was being buffeted by the flood.

'Never mind the shooting. Concentrate your hoses on the flames above you.'

The water had swilled first to starboard, dousing the flames on the floor of the hold, and then to port, where it stayed, swirling with the movement of the ship and belching escaping air from the submerged bales of clothing. The only flames surviving seemed to be from the huge timber knees supporting the deck over their heads.

Mr Davies came forward holding a lamp high, looking for Lawson.

'I've come from Mr Muir, sir. He's asked me to tell you that he is ready to flood the magazine, should you require it.'

'Tell him the danger's just about over now, Mr Davies. What do you make of the gunfire?'

'The mutineers have orders to shoot at anyone who weighs anchor without permission, sir. They warned us most particular when we arrived. Maybe some ships have had enough of this mutiny and want to be out of it.'

There was another crash on one of the decks above, followed by a second and third.

'What are the silly bastards up to?' one man demanded.

'Oh it's some stupid sod who doesn't know what he's doing. One gun would start another off. You know how it happens.'

There were two more crashes in quick succession. The man who had been up against the butt of the foremast where it joined the keel leapt away from it.

'Some one knaws what he's a-doing. They's tryin' to disable us, that's what. They 'it the foremast then. I felt the shock right down 'ere.'

'To hell wi' Parker and his bloody Floatin' Republic. If this is t'way he treat his mates, I'll stick wi' King George,' a Yorkshire voice declared.

'There's no water in my hose,' one of the men warned.

Lawson's had also stopped. Now the others were complaining that they had no pressure.

'I'll bet one of those last shots hit the pump, sir!'

'Maybe you're right, but we've more than one pump,'

Lawson said reassuringly. 'They'll soon have it connected. One of you go up top and make sure that Mr Saunders knows.'

Suddenly the ship yawed. It was as if the helmsmen had released the wheel, or the steerage was damaged. The movement disturbed the stacked bales of clothing and bedding, with their lashings and retaining canvas blackened and charred in the early stages of the fire. Several from the top fell and burst open, spewing smouldering contents over the deck boards of the hold. They burst into flame immediately.

'God help us! We'll never put that out now,' someone cried as the fire flared up.

The men were now backing away from the heat. One turned and ran for the stairway. Lawson looked at the blaze helplessly, then hurried to the magazine. Mr Muir and Mr Davies were standing by the valve that would send sea water into the pipes above the magazine, to drench the gunpowder barrels and filled cartridges.

Lawson hesitated. Was there time to ask Captain Brewster's permission to flood the place?

There was a crash close by on the starboard bow. They had the briefest glimpse of flying splinters against the flames of the fire, engulfed in an instant by a torrent of sea, like a jet from a massive hose pipe. Then the water stopped just as suddenly as it had started, but it was only a brief respite. A few seconds later, *Adamant* dipped her bows again and a second powerful jet drenched everyone and everything in the forward part of the ship. They had been holed by a cannonball on the water line, and *Adamant* was sailing fast.

There was no longer any anxiety about the fire, it seemed. They went forward to inspect the damage. Mr Muir looked around him.

'In the absence of the carpenter, who went ashore with Captain Hopton, I think I'll do somethin' aboot the hole yonder, Mr Lawson. I ken weel where the plugs are kept and 'tis a thing I've done before today. So if ye'd care tae go and join the captain, and let two or three men bide by me, ye can be sure that all will be well doon here. We'll need the pumps, o' course, tae take the water oot fra the hold, so perhaps ye'll look intae what has happened tae them as ye go by, sir.'

Another great arc of water was hurled into the hold as *Adamant* pitched. Everything loose was flopping about in the flood that was twelve inches deep on the shallow side. Certainly, there was no chance that the fire would be rekindled.

'Right, I'll leave you to it, Mr Muir, and I'll have the pumps working as soon as possible. What shall I tell the captain about the magazine?'

'Tell him that the powder will be dry enough, except for that in the bottom kegs where the flood caught them.'

Lawson hurried away. Saunders would have been at the pump, and Lawson was convinced that the pump's failure had been caused by the shots fired into the ship. Suddenly he realized how much his cheerful shipmate meant to him. He climbed rapidly to the orlop deck and on to the gun deck above, where the main pump was situated.

There were two bodies lying side by side under a canvas cover, and a gory mess on the deck boards. A pair of feet wearing shoes with buckles just like those worn by Saunders were sticking out. Lawson bent, sick at heart, took the corner of the cover, hesitated, then lifted it. Part of the man's head was missing, but it was not Saunders.

'Who is it?' he gasped, controlling with difficulty an urge to vomit.

'Mr Bainbridge, pusser's clerk, sir. Don't know what hit him. Might ha' bin a lump of iron from t'bulkhead there.' The man indicated the jagged hole in the side of the ship close by a gun-port. 'Might ha' bin t'shot itself. What I do know is, it were his own mates, t'fellers from t'bloody "Floating Republic", what blowed his face off. An' he thought they was so wunnerful. I wonder what 'is wife'll think about 'em, when she's tellt?'

The other men close by, two of them being bandaged, seemed to share his poor opinion of the mutineers. Lawson wondered how many more regretted having listened to Bainbridge's persuasive tongue.

'Where's Mr Saunders?'

'Rigging number two pump, sir.'

Lawson went to find him. It was important that they should start pumping the water out of the hold now that the fire was extinguished. Every spare man would have to be employed on the task. *Adamant* had been a leaky old ship before the pounding she had received.

Having given Saunders his orders, Lawson climbed to the open deck to report to Captain Brewster. There he saw that *Adamant* had moved quite a distance downstream, and the swiftly ebbing tide was taking her farther away from Parker's frigates. Captain Brewster was standing near to the helmsman. Close by was Forster, the leader of the mutiny, looking angry. Lawson understood the warning look that came his way from the captain. Now was not the time to report that the fire was out and the magazine safe from sparks.

Forster said, 'It seems to me that we are far enough from the other ships. We'd do them no harm at this distance if we blew up.'

His words were polite, but there was steel in his voice.

'Do you think that we are safe from the guns of your friends?' Brewster asked.

'I think, sir, that there would have been no shooting at all if you had informed the neighbouring frigates about the fire,' Forster said coldly. 'We must anchor now. Then our comrades will know that we are not deserting the cause. At dawn, we shall rejoin them.'

'Very good. Drop anchor, Mr Lawson.'

The ship was brought to the wind and the anchor sent plunging away into the depths. By the time the sails were furled onto the yards, a glimmer in the eastern sky announced that dawn was not far off. Brewster went below to inspect the damage, leaving Lawson on watch.

Distant gunfire brought everybody onto the open decks half an hour later.

'Seems like a repeat of last night, sir, except that there are two ships breaking out this time,' Lawson told the captain when he appeared.

'Unlike *Adamant* they appear to be firing back, sir,' Saunders supplemented.

'Do you think we started a new fashion, Mr Saunders?' Brewster asked jocularly, taking his small telescope from

291

his coat-tails and focusing it.

Mr Davies approached the captain and whispered, 'I've brought a brace of loaded pistols, sir. Do you want them?'

'No, thank you, Mr Davies. Words are going to win or lose the day,' Brewster replied, trying to recognize the distant ships in the half-light of early dawn. 'Here, what do you make of them, Mr Lawson? Your eyes are younger than mine.'

'Can't say for sure, sir,' Lawson replied after a brief examination, 'but it looks as if two ships are trying to leave and the rest are doing their damnedest to stop them.'

Fifty or more men had drawn close but nothing was said as the captain climbed a few feet above the deck and turned his telescope upon the distant battle for several minutes. There were anxious faces in that group as they waited. If the mutiny were breaking up, the leaders would have no chance of insisting upon pardons from the Admiralty. The penalty for mutiny could be death. Brewster lowered his telescope and looked down.

'*Leopard* is one of the ships making a run for it,' he said in a voice that could be heard by everyone nearby. 'I think the other is *Repulse*, and she seems to be fighting her way out.'

'Looks as if the mutiny is coming to an end, sir,' Lawson called back, correctly interpreting the captain's intentions and making sure that his words would be heard by all.

'It does, indeed. I pray that my poor lads will have the good sense to keep clear of it at this stage.'

Brewster climbed stiffly down to the deck. A passage opened through the crowd. All eyes were on him, but no one spoke. He joined the two midshipmen and Davies. At that moment the ship's bell began to ring urgently.

Men were assembling around the forward end of the quarterdeck. Those near to Brewster began to move in that direction. Forster and his committee had called a meeting. The captain, Lawson and Saunders went with the crowd. Forster was the first speaker and he was angry.

'I didn't look for the position which you gave me. You

demanded that I should be your leader. I agreed but imposed just one condition, which you readily accepted. You promised to abide by the ruling of your committee in all things. Well, this is the test. Your committee has ruled that we rejoin the other ships at the Nore immediately. Certain men among you, including some who had a lot to say about the rights of seamen, but who were afraid to serve on the committee when it came to mutiny, are now ready to run like curs back to Admiral Duncan to crave his forgiveness.'

'Treacherous, yellow-bellied bastards,' one of the cluster of committee men behind Forster shouted.

A big man, who was wearing a leather apron, gesticulated with a clenched fist.

'There's no bluidy mon wi' sense that'll want ta join a crowd what's just murdered oor shipmates. They kilt Billy Crompton last neet, one o' t'best blacksmiths that e'er cum oot to sea. There's a wife an' three bairns'll go hungry on Tyneside because o' your friend Parker.'

'They even killed the purser's clerk, one of your committee members,' another supported.

'That was entirely the fault of Captain Brewster,' Forster shouted, pointing at the officers. 'If he had informed the frigate next to us of his intentions and the reason for them, there would have been no shots fired and no one hurt. They knew nothing of the fire in the hold.'

'Maybe you're right. But it's a fine thing when the only way they can keep the mutiny together is to shoot at their own mates.'

There was a rumble of gunfire from the distant fleet. All heads turned to look over the water. A few had telescopes. The man who had called them yellow-bellied bastards continued to harangue them, but not many were listening.

'It looks like the *Repulse* has gone aground and they're all having a go at her,' one man with a telescope said.

'Bloody glad I'm not on *Repulse*,' another commented. 'It's bad enough getting your head shot off by the French. It's a bugger when your own mates are doing it.'

The committee men were now bandying words with

the crowd. They were on the defensive. Forster silenced them all by ringing the bell again. He looked around the faces before him, his eyes glinting challengingly, his head held high.

'Those on *Repulse* deserve all they're getting. The men who survive will go back to the same conditions that drove us to this mutiny. No, it will be worse, for who is going to take heed of cowardly curs?'

Someone interrupted. He was quickly silenced by those near him. Forster ignored the man. His eyes told the depths of his feelings as he looked around. The men were hanging on to his words.

'I am glad they went aground. They've got their just deserts, and it will serve them right if they're all killed. The other ship that's running away has managed to keep clear of the mudbanks. I'm told it is *Leopard*. Its present course will bring it well within range of *our* guns. We're going to drive her back, or sink her. That'll stop any others from deserting the cause. We'll set the main courses and t'gallants. Slip the anchor cable and load our guns. *Adamant* will strike a blow for freedom that will be remembered in the Navy forever.' His voice rose excitedly. 'Fight for the rights of seamen. As you load your guns, remember that you are doing it for your wives and families. Go to. Go to. Clear for action!'

The marine drummer had been standing close by Forster from the beginning with his drum hooked onto his belt and his drumsticks held in his gloved hands. Forster had obviously arranged that he should be there, and his last words were the boy's cue to beat them to action stations. It was a clever move. As his sticks crashed onto the drumskin, most of the men, conditioned by years of responding to such a stimulus, turned to go about their duties, although there was doubt in many eyes. Clearly it was a critical moment. The roll of the drum was driving them, as Forster had intended that it should.

'Hold it, my lads,' Brewster shouted.

The drummer continued, faster and louder, his eyes fixed on Forster's face, as if hypnotized by the man. Those nearest to Brewster halted. The others were dispersing to their stations, when the drum stopped suddenly.

'Beat it, lad,' Forster ordered sharply.

The boy gestured to him helplessly and pointed to his drum. Someone had slashed through the skin with a knife.

'Perhaps you can hear me now,' Brewster shouted from the fringe of the crowd as they steadied. 'Hear me out before you make a mistake that can never be set right.' He raised his hand to quieten the few dissident voices around him. 'Whatever the rights and wrongs of your cause, you must see that you'll gain nothing by joining a mutiny that's falling apart. It's now become a case of a great number of men being held together by a few. There are rocks ahead that'll be the ruin of them all. Those who can see where they're heading, the men of *Repulse* and *Leopard*, are being shot at because the leaders, the few, know that their example will be followed by the rest. *You* shouldn't get involved at this stage, lads. Trust me, you're better out of it.'

'Aye, the captain's right.'

'Shut your bloody mouth!'

There was the sound of a fist striking flesh, then a dozen men were fighting. Forster watched for a moment, defeat in his face, before reaching for the clapper of the bell and jerking it to left and right until the two factions were pulled apart. He looked them over with contempt and bitterness in his eyes.

'Well, you've shown what you think of the committee you elected and vowed to support,' he said, his voice dripping with scorn. 'Now you'd better have a vote on what you intend to do.'

'We've already voted. We're going to stand by the committee,' someone on the fringe of the crowd shouted.

'We're for the mutiny. Them as isn't can join the women ashore,' another supported.

'Aye, and let the bastards swim there.'

'Use your brain, if you've got one, you crackpot,' the big blacksmith scorned.

'All right!' Forster called sharply, when it seemed as if another fight was about to develop. 'We'll get nowhere like this. A vote it has to be.' He paused and looked around. 'All those who want to call off the mutiny, and take this ship back to Admiral Duncan, raise a hand.'

There was no need for a count. Some who had voted were obviously ashamed of themselves. Others chose to hide their shame in aggression, but the majority were just despondent and beaten. Together, they accounted for two-thirds of the ship's company. Forster turned to Captain Brewster. He was grey with fatigue. He removed his hat and bowed his head slightly.

'*Adamant* is yours, sir.'

'Thank you, Mr Forster.'

Brewster's face showed no elation. His expression was one of great sadness, and he looked old. To his left was Lawson. There were tears in his eyes.

EPILOGUE

After *Leopard* and *Repulse* deserted the mutinous fleet, ship after ship lowered the red flag and made for the open sea. Four days later, on Friday, 13 June 1797, Richard Parker surrendered on board HMS *Sandwich*, and the Nore mutiny was at an end.

Hundreds of seamen were court-martialled and many sentenced to death but, owing to the representations made by most captains, including the notorious William Bligh, on behalf of their own men, only twenty-nine were executed, a remarkable example of humanity for the period.

Richard Parker was hanged from the yardarm of the ship that had provided the spark for the mutiny. His last recorded declaration was: 'Remember never to make yourself the busybody of the lower classes, for they are cowardly, selfish and ungrateful; the least trifle will intimidate them, and him whom they have exalted one moment as their demagogue, the next day they will not scruple to exalt upon the gallows.'

The North Sea Fleet, commanded by Admiral Duncan, met Admiral de Winter's Dutch Fleet on 9 October off Camperdown. The Dutch used the shallows to good advantage, but Duncan won the day and so ended the threat of invasion from Holland.

Admiral Duncan was rewarded with the title of

viscount. Some time later he was astonished to receive a demand from the Imperial Russian Fleet, which had been in the Baltic during the battle of Camperdown, for a share of the prize money.